I0817838

Praise for

LIEUTENANT TRUFANT

Shaw's tormented characters in *Lieutenant Trufant* leap right off the pages right into your gut, in a plot that doesn't let go till the last word. What a movie this engrossing, well-detailed detective story would make.

—Ed Gruber, Author, former U.S. Navy Combat Correspondent and Advertising Creative Director

The author's gripping crime mystery is a riveting journey with twists and turns that grabs one by the throat and never lets go! The author, a former cop and the author of a memoir, *Who I Am: The Man Behind the Badge,* weaves a fascinating tale in his first novel. The writing is crisp, descriptive and captivating. He draws the reader in to this engrossing thriller. I was hooked from the first page and you'll be too."

—Charles Gomez, former CBS, NBC news correspondent. Emmy Award winner. Author of *Cuban Son Rising*

This novel has a jagged heart, sympathetic and furious at the same time. A thrilling police procedural set upon a landscape of grief and loneliness and haunted by the shadows of war. Jeff Shaw writes with authority, bringing readers into an immersive and startling story. A great accomplishment!

—Steven Cooper, author of *Desert Remains* and the rest of the *Gus Parker and Alex Mills mysteries*

Jeff Shaw writes a fast-paced, violent story involving the murders of seemingly unrelated military veterans. Shaw's background in law enforcement lends a stark reality to this novel.

—Sandy Flutie, retired homicide sergeant

LIEUTENANT TRUFANT

Other Books by
Jeff Shaw

Who I Am: The Man Behind the Badge, 2020

The Bloodline Series

Lieutenant Trufant, 2022
LeAnn and the Clean Man, 2023

THE BLOODLINE SERIES

LIEUTENANT TRUFANT

Jeff Shaw

AUTHOR OF
WHO I AM: THE MAN BEHIND THE BADGE

Alpharetta, GA

This is a work of fiction. Names, characters, businesses, places, and events are either the products of the author's imagination or are used in a fictitious manner. Any resemblance to actual persons, living or dead, or actual events is purely coincidental.

ISBN: 978-1-6653-0315-6 – Paperback
ISBN: 978-1-6653-0314-9 – Hardcover
eISBN: 978-1-6653-0316-3 – ePub

Library of Congress Control Number: 2022900497

10 9 8 7 6 5 4 3 2 121622

♾This paper meets the requirements of ANSI/NISO Z39.48-1992 (Permanence of Paper)

For Sarah and Stephen, I did my best.

CHAPTER 1

ARMSTRONG

David Armstrong and Travis huddled under the awning of an abandoned bakery on Mason Street. Both were trying to stay warm and dry, and this time David feared he would die first.

For the third day in a row a cold drizzle was blowing in from the Pacific, and he heard the next few days would be more of the same. The black sheet of Visqueen he had stolen from the construction site next door wasn't wide enough to protect them both from the rain, but with the building's overhang only his good leg was exposed, and it was soaked.

He had been wet and miserable for so long that he could no longer feel his fingers, and his left leg was numb. His body had burned through his last hit of black tar heroin hours ago, and he was feeling the first effects of withdrawal. His bones ached and his teeth chattered and not just from the cold. Travis shivered constantly too and neither of them had slept more than a few hours. Now the icy wind was cutting through the thin plastic sheeting like a knife.

Across the street six of the thousands of unsheltered men and women on this side of San Francisco had already staked out the sewer grate. He had tried to sleep close enough to it last night to feel the warm air currents coming up from the cable car tunnels, but the big man with the acne scars and the yellow and black plaid coat threatened Travis with a knife, so they had moved back across the street.

The cold concrete and unrelenting chill made it difficult to get comfortable and David pulled the dog closer, hoping its body heat would help. But it wasn't the cold, or the rain. He was dopesick now and it was only going to get worse. He stretched out as far as he could, closed his eyes, and finally the exhaustion and lack of sleep caught up to him. For the next two hours he was back in Afghanistan, where it was warm and dry, and he felt safe—safe and Travis was alive again.

***

Standing behind Travis in the chow line, they worked their way toward the front when the first rocket landed outside. The blast was on the far side of the base, but they both felt the concussion, and the lights swayed on their chains, casting moving shadows on the floor. The next one was closer but still too far away to do any damage.

This was the third attack by the Taliban this week, and like the rest, this 107 mm unguided rocket fell short, landing outside the forward fire base's perimeter wall, but each round was closer than the last, and it seemed the insurgents had an unlimited supply of both men and rockets.

After each attack, photos of the destroyed Type 63 launchers and the dead Taliban were passed around. They were gruesome scenes, pictures of men blown apart by either Hellfire missiles or 30 mm shells from a chain gun. Some officer must have thought the images would bolster morale, and for some, it probably did. "Fuck those towelheads!" they said, but to David, they were just dead men.

Loaded up with slabs of meatloaf, lima beans, and mashed potatoes, the two of them sat across from each other eating in silence, thinking more about the afternoon's mission than the tasteless food.

"I think it will be hot again," Travis said.

"It's always hot, Travis," David said, stabbing another chunk of meatloaf.

The familiar *brrrp* of an Apache's gun interrupted their meal, and they looked at the far wall, picturing the dust and debris rising from the mountain beyond it.

"That fucked them up," Travis said in a thick Brooklyn accent that always made everything sound funny.

***

There were no more rockets in this dream and all too soon the cold returned.

He listened to the steady popping of the rain hitting the aluminum awning, mixed with the buzzing of a streetlamp, and tried to remember if it had ever rained while he was overseas.

The thought of his best friend's death always left him numb. It had been eight years since the real Travis died on a dirt road in Afghanistan. But some memories never lose their sharpness, or the pain that follows them.

He felt Travis lift his head and a deep growl came from the dog's chest. In the dim light, he saw Travis looking across the street at the dark, ghostly shapes of the men sleeping next to the grate. Then one of the shapes moved, and a glint of steel reflected in the light.

He pulled Travis closer and cupped his hand over the dog's snout, and the growling stopped, but his eyes remained on the moving shape across the street. The dog was trembling.

From sixty feet away and in the dim light, David felt the shape was staring at him, but it was hard to be sure as the steady drizzle began mixing with the first wisps of fog. The tiny droplets illuminated by the yellow streetlight floated on a breeze from left to right, helping to obscure the man's silhouetted face. He couldn't see anything but the form of someone crouched next to the others—but there was a feeling of dread he couldn't shake. He sensed death.

Death is watching me!

He held Travis still for several more minutes, his hand still cupped over the dog's snout. The figure of the man never moved. Hallucinations weren't new to David, and so much time passed that he began to doubt what he had seen. Still, he felt this wasn't his drug-addled brain playing tricks on him.

The dark shape began to move, slowly at first, rising until it stood next to one of the sleeping men. It looked like a man, but was it? Could a woman exude such a feeling of dread as he felt right now? It had to be a man, a short man covered in a dark rain jacket with a hood that hid his face.

The shape stepped away from the sleeping men and into the street toward him. Again, and for what seemed like an eternity, David felt the stare as Travis continued to tremble.

It was closer now, close enough that he could see vapor rising from under the hood each time it took a slow, steady, silent breath, and he hoped his own breathing wasn't as visible.

Eight years ago, in another lifetime, he would have stood and faced this man. Knife or no knife, he had never cowered from a threat. But he wasn't that man anymore. The shrapnel that had killed his best friend had torn into him as well.

"The lack of testosterone will have an adverse effect on you, Sergeant," the doctor had said.

Travis began to whine, the sound mixing with the rattling sound of rain on the awning, and David hoped it was loud enough to drown Travis out.

"Shh," he whispered. Finally, the man turned and moved silently down the street toward Shepard Place and disappeared into the thickening fog, leaving a wake of swirling mist.

He eased his hand away from Travis, and the dog turned and looked at him, the low whine intensifying, and again he could feel a vibration in the dog's chest. Then they both shivered, and he pulled the dog in tight, trying to fight the chill and the fear.

"He's gone now, Travis."

Travis quit whining but stared silently across the street.

David could see all the sleeping shapes. Some of them were snoring, and he hoped what he had seen was just another part of the dream. He looked down Shepard Place, now just fog and shadows, any of which could conceal a man.

He waited for thirty minutes. The fog had thickened, and the rain was nothing more than a drizzle now. Two surveillance cameras were pointed at the front door of the shop behind the men. He knew there were more hidden in the fog, but he had to move. He had to know for sure what he had seen wasn't just another nightmare.

His knee popped like a firecracker, and his bones ached as fear and withdrawal left him weak. He looked one final time toward Shepard Place, hoping the man had moved on. Pain in both knees almost made him cry out, and only the fear of what could be in the darkness kept him silent. Tying Travis to the wrought iron security gate behind him, he wrapped the plastic over his head and limped across the street. His good leg was still numb from the cold, and it took all his concentration to keep his head down and away from the cameras. The uneven steel cable car rails embedded in the street and the patchwork of concrete tripped him twice, but he made it across without falling or making enough noise to wake the sleeping men.

There were six of them under the awning and around the grate. Two of them were older men with patchy gray beards, in their sixties at least, but it was hard to tell. They were the ones snoring. Two others were younger and breathing deeply. The light reflecting off the plastic they were using for protection flickered with each man's breath.

It was hard for him to focus and harder to think clearly, but even so, he knew the other two men would never breathe again. Their throats were slashed, and a vast torrent of each man's blood mixed with the rainwater and ran down the sidewalk, disappearing into the grate. In the yellow tint of the sodium vapor streetlight, the pool of blood looked like black ink as it made a jagged path along the whiter concrete.

He knelt over the big man with the yellow and black plaid jacket and felt his pockets. He found the knife—a cheap imitation of a Swiss Army knife, a blood-stained syringe, two small bags of brown powder, a ball of crumpled aluminum foil, and thirty-five cents.

He held the bags to his nose and inhaled a slight chemical smell, not the acrid odor of vinegar common with cheap heroin. They were probably China White, a powerful synthetic rarer than the Black Tar heroin common on the streets of the city. Knowing what it was helped him focus on his next move, to get away from these dead men and find a safe place to smoke the first bag.

Across the street Travis barked as he stuffed the two bags, the coins, and the knife in his pocket. Then he looked at the syringe and thought of keeping it for himself, but needles were one of the few things that he still feared, too easy to OD, and too much work. Chasing the dragon, or inhaling heroin, was simpler, requiring just a Bic lighter, some foil, and a straw. Still, the needle was hard to throw away.

It was hours before sunrise, and he wanted to be long gone before the sleeping men woke. Hopefully, the fog and the rain would make most of the surveillance cameras useless, but he kept his head down as he untied Travis and began shuffling north toward the Broadway Tunnel.

CHAPTER 2

TRUFANT

Lieutenant Marcus Trufant sat in his overstuffed recliner studying the dregs swirling in the bottom of his wine bottle.

"What the hell are they?" he said aloud.

One year ago tonight, he was standing over the body of a dead US soldier at Pier 35 next to Fisherman's Wharf, but tonight he was home alone wondering when the phone would ring. Sleep was impossible, hence the wine.

One year ago, he was also a happily married man. But like that April night so long ago, tonight he was living a different life.

On the end table, a half-eaten frozen dinner sat cold. The smell of it cooking in the microwave wasn't bad, but it had tasted like powdered cheese and old macaroni and looking at it now made him sick.

The tiny fragments in the last drops of merlot were more appetizing, and reminded him of Adelaide, his wife of thirty-two years, that is, until she walked out of his life. This was a bottle of her favorite wine. *You should try a glass, Marcus. It will calm your nerves.*

"Fuck it," he said, lifting the bottle and swallowing the gritty dregs.

The silent phone sat on the end table like a ball and chain. He was helpless knowing that somewhere in the city a man was dying, and there was nothing he could do to save him.

He closed his eyes just after 1 a.m. Seconds later, the bottle fell to the floor and rolled across the carpet.

In his brief dream, Adelaide said, *I told you not to bring your anger into my house. Look at you,* and he did. What he saw was his father, once again lying on the bathroom floor, stinking of gin and covered in his own puke. And what seemed like seconds later, the phone did ring.

"Trufant," he said, knowing what was waiting on the other end of the line.

He listened, and then said, "Call in the rest of my squad. I'll be there in forty minutes."

***

Lieutenant Trufant and Inspector Carlos Amato stood over the two bodies as the medical examiner began peeling away the layers of plastic and blankets the men had been using for warmth. Thankfully, the rain had stopped, but the next storm was due in less than an hour and they had to work fast.

"Jesus, Lieutenant, this one's almost decapitated," Amato said.

Trufant's head ached, and he could feel the hollow pit in his stomach rumbling. He hoped the rancid taste of wine in his mouth wasn't also on his breath. Adelaide was right about one thing—he was drinking too much.

"Looks too familiar, doesn't it, Carlos?"

As the medical examiner studied the two dead men, Trufant looked down the street. Yellow crime scene tape stretched across the outer perimeter flapped in the morning breeze coming off the bay. Small barricades made from white plastic panels made up the inner perimeter and shielded the scene from the onlookers and media trucks. Dozens of uniformed officers redirected cars and pedestrians to the adjacent streets, creating mayhem in the morning rush hour.

Inside the perimeter, Trufant watched a crime scene technician set the laser mapping system on its tripod while two others began photographing everything from the victim's clothing to the storefronts on both sides of the street.

He counted seven surveillance cameras that he hoped worked and were pointed at either the perpetrator or the victims as they came and went from the scene. He would need all the help he could get just identifying who these two men were.

Satisfied everything was moving smoothly, he looked up at the darkening sky and thought of having someone set up the big tent.

As a Black man who grew up in rural Louisiana, San Francisco's weather still felt alien, but even he knew a storm was coming, and rain was the worst thing that could happen to a crime scene.

"How much longer, Emma?"

"Almost done," she said.

The petite, Vietnamese medical examiner was on her knees adjusting an L-shaped micro-scale next to a victim's neck for the photographer. Her jet-black hair was covered by a see-through hairnet made of the same material as her protective gown.

He knelt next to her, careful not to allow his knee to touch the damp concrete. At fifty-two and six-foot-three, kneeling was not as simple as it used to be. The pavement beneath him looked clean, but the suit was expensive, and he had ruined too many of them over the years. His shoes were another story. He would have to leave them on the balcony again tonight.

The first victim was nude now, and Trufant saw burn scars all along the left side of his abdomen and thigh. Mixed in with the burns were smaller scars that looked like shrapnel wounds and skin grafts that had healed years before. Wounds of war. What horrors had this man witnessed and what memories had died with him?

He studied the gash across the man's neck. At first blush the wound seemed simple, one deep, long horizontal slash exposing his larynx and the thyroid cartilage—the laceration severing the carotid artery, the jugular vein, and the man's trachea in one movement. No easy feat for anyone, especially considering the weather and the fact the killer had to crouch next to the victims, who could have woken up and confronted him.

"There are no signs of defensive wounds," the doctor said. "I would say the time of death would be just after midnight, hard to be sure though with all the rain and the low temperatures, but I would say midnight at the earliest. There was a lot more blood mixed in with the rainwater that has drained off into the sewer. Both men died quickly, which is odd if it was one perpetrator. There are no signs of a struggle, and I would think the sounds of a man dying would have woken up the second victim."

"Is it like the others?" Trufant asked.

Dr. Lew glanced up at him and looked back at the heavy man in the plaid coat.

"I think so. I wasn't on the scene of the last one, but I saw the results, and of course the dates match up. The only difference I see so far is we have multiple victims this time."

Trufant kneeled again and looked at the crude tattoo on the man's calf, a five-pointed star and ARMY spelled out in capital letters. The tattoo was done by an amateur, probably a fellow soldier in boot camp. It was old and faded, much like the man himself. But as bad a shape as the man was in, he would still have made a formidable adversary. It had to take some balls to kill these two men with a knife, some big balls or a lot of confidence. And why two this time?

Today was April 11th, six victims now in two years, eight if he counted the two in Chicago. All eight killed on either April 11th or December 1st. The big guy was an Army veteran and probably served in Iraq like the previous victims. Trufant looked at the smaller man, still dressed in clothes too large for his thin frame. The gaping wound was identical, and he nodded to himself knowing he was right. Some big balls maybe, but a lot of skill too.

The last two victims had served in different units in Fallujah between 2005 and 2008. What was this second guy's story—Army, Marine? His age looked to be right, but there were no tattoos, no wounds. Physically, he looked more like an accountant, but even the Army needed accountants. Trufant would know soon enough.

The first six victims had one thing linking them together, one common denominator. They had all served in the US military. He looked at the dead men and hoped one of them might provide something, a single clue that would define motive.

"No ID on either guy, Emma. We'll have to ID them from prints like the last two," he said as he took off the latex gloves and threw them in a red biohazard bag. "Call me when you're ready to autopsy them."

His phone rang as he walked back to his car, and he saw it was the chief. Trufant knew what the man was going to say, but he answered anyway.

"Chief Lozano?"

"Trufant, how is it I hear about these two homicides from a television reporter and not my own homicide lieutenant?"

"I was just about to call you, Chief, but I had blood on my hands and didn't want to contaminate my phone—you know how it is, right, Chief?"

"Don't be sarcastic, Trufant, I did my time on the road. The media is already camped outside my office. I want you here in thirty minutes to tell them what you know—thirty minutes, Trufant!"

Trufant looked at his watch, just after ten in the morning and he was pissed off already. Lozano had a knack for finding his weak spots. Maybe Adelaide was right, about his anger issues at least.

She had always been there when he needed to talk, especially after a rough call. But something changed when he transferred to homicide and began bringing death into their home.

***

An hour later he walked past several television news vans, ignoring the reporters standing next to them, and into city hall. The department's public information officer met him at the front door, and Trufant handed the man some handwritten notes on the back of a paper napkin.

"You talk to the media and tell the chief while the two of you were enjoying your late breakfast, I was eating a muffin out of a McDonald's bag."

In the comfort of the homicide office, Trufant and two of his inspectors watched the first video on the big screen. The rest of his squad were still out on the street, knocking on doors trying to find more footage, but this was a good one and was pointed right at the sleeping men.

"There are six of them, Jesus!" he said.

Five bodies—all men, wrapped in plastic and raincoats. The sixth man arrived at 11:05, if the time stamp was accurate, and covered himself in a large piece of stiff cardboard. By midnight they all appeared to be asleep.

Twenty minutes later, a seventh person came into view, wrapped in a raincoat or possibly the same black plastic the sleeping men were using.

Trufant's phone rang. He paused the video, and this time the call was from the station's front lobby.

"Trufant," he said.

"Lieutenant, there's a woman to see you in the lobby."

"My wife?"

"No, sir."

"I'll be right down."

Whoever it was could wait another few minutes, and he returned to the video.

The seventh man knelt between the two victims, facing the big guy, as they were now calling the man in the plaid coat. There was no movement except for an occasional wisp of fog drifting past the camera. Then Trufant saw a glint of steel and the big guy's leg jerked, touching the second victim and waking him up. As the second man lifted his head, the new arrival's arm slashed out like lightning, and they saw the black gash appear on the man's throat.

"Damn, he's fast!" Amato said.

The man's head bounced once on the sidewalk, and again there was no movement except for the dark pool forming between the two victims. Trufant watched the motionless seventh man as gravity began pulling the pool of blood toward the drain.

"He's waiting to see if anyone else wakes up," Amato said. "Or he's deciding if he wants to kill another one."

Trufant didn't think so. "I think victim number two wasn't planned. I think he heard or felt something, looked up and saw our subject's face and was just collateral damage."

The subject finally stood and looked across the street, then took several steps away from the sleeping men. The shifting fog acted like a veil at times, leaving an odd, ghostly image on the screen. The far side of the street, the focus of the man's stare, was entirely grayed out by the fog.

"Now what's he looking at?"

"Hard to say, Carlos."

Then the man turned and walked southbound, disappearing into the fog.

"Notice how he kept his face away from the camera?" Carlos said.

Trufant fast-forwarded, wanting to see the sleeping men wake up and find their friends murdered. He watched the wisps of fog and mist race past the men, and the stiff cardboard covering one of the men drooped as it soaked up the rain and slowly fell completely apart.

Then the man in black walked back into view from the far side of the street.

"He's back," Amato said.

The man knelt in the same spot and searched one of the victims. This was not the same man, Trufant realized, too tall and not as thin, and from this view, he saw the shaft of a prosthetic leg. An eighth man now. "This is a different guy," Trufant said.

The man put something in his pocket and walked back across the street and out of view.

"Damn it! Who the hell was that?" Carlos asked.

"Let's hope we get a few more videos as clear as this one and maybe we'll find out."

His phone rang again, one of the junior inspectors. "Lt. Trufant, I got an ID on one of your guys, Gerome Callaway, forty-one years old, last known address was in Murfreesboro, Tennessee. The National Crime Information Center shows a few misdemeanor arrests, mostly drunk and disorderly. His last arrest was three months ago here in SF, urinating in public. He used his Tennessee address and was released with time served. No warrants, no current driver's license either, but there was a DUI arrest in Tennessee five years ago."

"The big guy?"

"Yes, the one with the tattoo."

"Any mention of military history?"

"No sir. I can check on it too and so far, nothing on your other guy."

"Okay, thanks."

His phone buzzed again. Chief Lozano. He let it ring until voice mail took it.

Trufant watched the rest of the video, and just as the sun rose, so did the first survivor. The blood stains were changing from black to crimson now as the sunlight brought out the colors. The older man that had been using the cardboard stared at the gaping wound on his friend's throat.

He shook the man next to him, and one by one the four men grabbed their belongings and walked out of the camera's view.

Why hadn't any of them called the police?

"How does this guy know which of them were veterans?" Amato asked.

"There's an answer somewhere, but I'll be damned if I can see it," Trufant said.

Passing pedestrians stepped around the dead men without ever looking at them. It was the store owner who finally called the police, and although the rain had washed most of the blood away, it didn't hide the gaping wounds on the men's necks.

"Thanks for the call, folks!" Amato said.

Trufant probably had thirty minutes before the chief knocked on his door.

"Carlos, call the guys on the street and have them go two

blocks north and south on Mason Street, and let's see if we can track the subject and the new guy with the prosthetic. We can expand it out as far as we need to later."

Ten minutes later the medical examiner called.

"Carlos, want to go to an autopsy?"

***

On the way downstairs they stopped in the lobby, and Trufant looked through the glass door.

Sitting in the waiting room was an attractive Asian woman in her early thirties, well-dressed in a maroon skirt and matching jacket. He opened the door, and the woman stood.

"Lt. Trufant, nice to see you."

"Have we met?" He offered her his hand, and she placed an envelope in it.

"I'm afraid not. But you've been served."

The woman turned to leave, and Trufant saw his neighbor's name and business address on the envelope. The neighbor was a divorce attorney, and after thirty-two years of marriage, Adelaide had finally decided to end it.

"Bad news, Lieutenant?" Amato asked.

"Not really, give me a second." He stepped back through the door and put the envelope through the shredder, watching the tiny strips fall into the basket.

His marriage had begun to fail last summer, but it had turned bitter in the last few months before Adelaide finally moved out.

Marcus, you are letting this job eat you alive. I want the old Marcus back, the one I married. I don't know if it's this grudge with your chief, or these damned homicides, but you're not the man I married. When you can put all that aside and be my husband again, call me.

How long ago had that last conversation been? Six months or was it seven now?

"Okay, Carlos, let's go."

***

Twenty-nine hundred miles away, Leilah Aquino sat in the library of King's College in Manhattan. Wearing latex gloves, she logged on to her new Gmail account. There was one new message, and she read each word carefully, took notes, and deleted the account.

She looked around, making sure she still had this section of the room to herself. With her new Monteverde fountain pen, she began writing using the slow and deliberate strokes her mother had taught her so many years ago. Once she was satisfied, she carefully folded the paper and put it in an envelope, wiped down the keyboard, and walked out. An hour later, the letter was in a public mailbox in Grand Central Station.

***

Dr. Lew and two other examiners stood over the body of Gerome Callaway. She pointed out the burns and the scars on his left thigh and abdomen. In several areas on his back, small squares of skin had been removed and used as grafts on the worst of the burns.

"My guess is most of this damage occurred at least ten years ago," she said. "Some of the contracture—the tightening of the skin—has been treated more recently with the grafts. No doubt he was in constant pain ever since."

Callaway's body had been x-rayed, and Lew pointed to dozens of small fragments in the areas matching the wounds. Most were small, no bigger than BBs, but one wedged up next to his spine was the size and shape of a bottle cap.

"He was also a heavy drug user. There are cutaneous stigmata in all the normal injections sites. Look here," she said, pointing to the inside of his elbows and the veins in his feet.

Trufant could see the vertical scarring following a vein just below the man's skin.

"This wound," she said, touching the victim's neck with a gloved finger, "was probably done from left to right using something sharper than an ordinary knife. Usually, you can see evidence of elasticity as the skin shrinks slightly on withdrawal of a regular knife, even a sharp one. This blade was thin, non-serrated, almost like a scalpel, and entered the skin at a right angle across the throat. You can see the slit started and ended almost identically."

"Like he was a professional?" Amato asked.

"I don't know about a professional, Inspector, but he knew what he was doing. Let me show you the difference with the second man's wound."

John Doe was lying on his own stainless steel tray across the aisle.

"You can see the difference as this wound is not as perpendicular, more of a diagonal to the throat. The entry and exit of the knife's blade is not as even, not as calculated, and as you told me, this was probably done as the victim was lifting his head. Other than that, the wound was just as thorough, deep enough that it scored the C4 vertebrae."

John Doe looked closer to fifty, and thinner, almost gaunt compared with Callaway. There were no tattoos or significant marks other than a small scar on his abdomen that Dr. Lew thought was probably the result of hernia surgery.

The body had been washed, but there was still dirt under the nails of his hands and feet, feet calloused by years of walking in shoes that were probably worn-out or the wrong size.

"Lieutenant, if you're ready I'll go ahead and get started," Lew said through her mask, holding the tiny scalpel in her hand.

"We're going to pass, Emma, I've seen enough and there is still too much to do."

***

Before heading back to the station, they ate lunch at The Codmother on Beach Street. Trufant enjoyed the distraction lunch provided. For those brief minutes he could distance himself from the emotions of the job, the pain and suffering of others, and he enjoyed Carlos's company. But he couldn't stop thinking about those damned divorce papers. He had never given up hope that the two of them could work it out, that once these homicides had been solved, things would be different. Adelaide had always shared his emotions, his empathy for the victims. Had he changed, or had she?

"Come on, L.T., I can see you're pissed off about something. What is it?"

"Adelaide has filed for divorce, at least I think she did. Those papers earlier were from my neighbor. He lives on my floor, two doors down, and he specializes in divorce. I probably should have read them. Too late now."

"Sorry, that's gotta be painful. I was hoping you two would patch things up."

"Thanks, Carlos, it may still happen."

Carlos was hired after spending six years in the Navy. Trufant had read one of the man's first reports as a patrol officer and noticed how well it had been written. He had recommended Carlos's transfer to the investigations bureau and eventually moved him over to homicide. "How's your mother doing, Carlos, she still in Mexico?"

"She's doing okay, still in Ensenada with her sister, the woman just won't leave. We've tried everything to get her to move up here. The immigration paperwork is all done, but she's stubborn, says she wants to die in her homeland."

"I can understand. Leaving your homeland is a hard thing for a strong woman to deal with and she doesn't speak English. Christ, my mother still curses in Creole."

Trufant finished the last bite of fish and dabbed a fry in malt vinegar. Lunch was over, and once again the weight of the two dead men rested square between his shoulder blades.

With Carlos behind the wheel, they pulled into the station in time to see the chief and his aide driving out. Through the passenger window, the chief mouthed *asshole* as they passed by. Trufant gave the chief a quick salute as they parked.

"He's going to be pissed, L.T."

"Don't I know it," he said, taking two steps at a time up the back stairwell.

A patrol officer was waiting for them in the homicide office.

"Lt. Trufant, these videos just came in."

Carlos and Trufant watched another color video, one of four taken from cameras along Mason Street. He fast-forwarded until 10 p.m. when the first of the six homeless men walked past the camera.

"It's the old guy, the first one to wake up," Carlos said. "He shouldn't be too hard to find."

Minutes later Gerome Callaway walked across the screen. He was easy to pick out with the yellow and black coat showing through a clear plastic poncho, and he appeared to be angry, shouting and pointing his finger at the older man.

On the far side of the street, someone walked through the camera's view with a dog on a leash. The angle wouldn't allow them to see any more than just the sidewalk, and all they saw of the man was from the knees down. Trufant dismissed this guy, too early and on the wrong side of the street.

A lot of people went past the camera in the next hour, and any one of them could have been the killer or a witness. Most of them were bundled up against the rain and cold, and by midnight the fog had thickened so much even the sidewalk was hard to see.

The next video was useless, too much moisture on the lens to see anything.

In the last video, which pointed away from the victims, Trufant saw the shape of a man and a dog sleeping under the eaves of an old bakery. It was the dog he had seen in the first video, a black Labrador, and just past midnight, the dog lifted its head and looked across the street. The man moved his arm and pulled the dog closer, and for the next thirty minutes, the two of them remained motionless.

Then the man rose, tied the dog to the old iron bars, and walked away and out of the video.

"He saw it happen and took something from the big guy," Amato said. "We need to find him."

"A homeless man with a black dog and a prosthetic leg. Let's get the word out and see if we can find him and the old guy too." Trufant took a screenshot of the old man and emailed it as a department-wide "be on the lookout." The BOLO image would be on everyone's computer, including the patrol officers' laptops, instantly, and he sat back and waited—for three days.

CHAPTER 3

ARMSTRONG

Dawn was just breaking, but it would be noon before the fog burned away enough to cast any shadows. This morning, like most every morning, Armstrong was behind a dozen men and women waiting for the baker to open the back door and begin passing out yesterday's unsold bread.

He thanked the man and sat on a bench in front of Pier 39, facing Beach Street.

The sourdough loaf tasted like it had just come out of the oven, and he tossed some of the small bits to the seagulls and pigeons at his feet, watching as the birds fought over every crumb. There were hundreds of them in the small plaza, and the sidewalk and the bench he was sitting on were covered in bird shit.

He felt good. The China White was a mix of heroin and fentanyl, and it had been clean, but it wasn't always. Any street drug was a gamble, even buying from the same dealer. Three times in two different cities he had woken up only to find himself in an emergency room handcuffed to a gurney.

"Mr. Armstrong," the doctor said on one of those nights, "If it weren't for the EMTs, you would be dead. Your heroin was laced with fentanyl, a lethal dose, and it was cut with talcum powder and baking soda. You need to count your blessings, sir, and get your life together."

Hours after leaving that hospital he was in a vacant alley

snorting a bag of Mexican Brown. How many times had he been close to death in those early days and gotten lucky?

Today, though, he was good to go. In a few hours he would cook another bag of dope, and the routine would start all over. Get high, walk a few miles, try and make a buck here and there, score a few bags, and make it through another day.

"That's it, Travis, that's all there is." He was content at the moment. Tomorrow, though, was always another story.

Travis seemed content too, watching the gulls swooping down and fighting over the crumbs with indifference. The dog had already eaten his share of the loaf and was happy to sit after the long walk from the tunnel.

Around noon another homeless man, pulling an old luggage carrier, sat next to him and looked at his leg, then at Travis.

"The cops are looking for you," he said.

David looked at the toothless man but said nothing.

"Looking for a man with a big black dog and a fake leg, I hear."

"You heard that?"

"I just heard it when I was at Union Square. I'm just saying it must be you is all. What happened to your leg?"

He didn't want to tell the old guy, he never wanted to talk about what had happened over there, but the man had gone out of his way to warn him.

"Afghanistan."

"Lots of bad shit over there, I hear. I was in Germany in the nineties, never saw any combat, though." He turned to David and whispered, "You have any dope?"

"No."

"Well, that's okay. I had to ask," the man said.

"I know."

The man stood, began shuffling off and turned again, "Be careful, someone killed a grunt a few days ago. Killed him and another guy in their sleep, I heard."

David had seen the big man in the black and yellow coat several times over the last few months but had never spoken to him until the day before the man was murdered. The man was a veteran—Army, if this old guy knew what he was talking about. The thin guy was never in any branch of the service. He'd seen the guy on the street near this same bakery many times. A civilian, probably an office worker, but not a soldier.

Still, the big guy was an ass, and maybe he had finally pissed off the wrong person. He had threatened Travis with a knife. *If he had tried to use it, I might have been killed too.* The man who did kill the big guy could have been another homeless man with a grudge. It made no difference to David. *But why are the cops looking for me?*

There was a light pole in front of him and he saw the camera perched on top, pointing directly at him. They were everywhere, and the ones on Mason Street must have recorded him and Travis. *They think I killed that man.*

The killer had been wearing something black too, black and shiny like David's sheet of Visqueen.

He had two choices, find out why they wanted him or leave San Francisco. He had been in San Francisco for more than a year now, and it felt like home. He knew where to sleep and where not to, where the cops would run him off, and where they would leave him alone. He knew where he could eat, and the people at the VA treated him decently, not like those in Detroit or Phoenix.

***

It had all started in a dirt alley in Helmand Province when the medic jammed morphine into his vein, and it continued all the way to Landstuhl in Germany. Not that he could remember much during those first few days, except screaming and a surge of warmth as the medical staff pumped more and more pain killers into his IV.

The months of physical therapy in Bethesda always included pain medication. Fentanyl, Dilaudid, and morphine were a daily routine. Once he learned to walk again, oxycodone was prescribed, and he was discharged, although kicked out would be a better term. The local VA in Baltimore attempted to wean him off the opioids, but it was too little and too late.

It wasn't his addiction that killed his marriage, though—or the loss of his leg. It was the humiliation. Caitlin had been with him every day since he arrived in Landstuhl, days where he languished in a pain-free, drug-induced fog. She volunteered at the hospital to be close to him during the months of physical therapy and the brief rehab in Baltimore. It was the other injuries, coupled with the addiction, that ruined his marriage.

"Look at me, Cait. Look what it did to me!"

It was the only time he had stood nude in front of her. The shrapnel had damaged his testicles, and the surgeon was forced to remove them. That and the damage and scarring to his penis was too much for him to bear.

"David, I know what you're thinking, but I love you! We can work this out."

The physical wounds had also destroyed him mentally. The psychologist recommended testosterone supplements, but they had their own side effects and coupled with his worsening addiction to opioids, he soon gave up. He could never be the husband she deserved, and so he walked away.

When he moved to Detroit, the VA put him on a wait list, four to six months for basic addiction treatment and longer for any physical therapy. He moved to Phoenix, where he tried living with his mother. The VA was better in Arizona, but he was soon living on the street. The shame was more than he could take. He could see the pain in his mother's eyes every time she looked at him, so he walked out, not wanting her to see what was left of her son.

San Francisco was a different story. It was home now, or close to it. He was accepted here, and the VA treated him with respect. It was the closest thing to home since that forward firebase, Fiddler's Green, in Afghanistan.

David had been in San Francisco for only a short time when he dreamed of that last day in Afghanistan when he and his fellow

Marines were gearing up for the big push into one of the Taliban's strongholds.

In the dream, Master Sergeant Travis McClanahan stood and said, "Semper fi, motherfuckers!"

"Oorah!" David had responded. In this dream as it was that day, it was the last word they said to each other.

As the dream faded that morning, he woke and found the strange dog sleeping next to him.

"I'm going to call you Travis, Oorah!"

***

All he wanted in life now was to be left alone. He didn't need or want friends. Friends were baggage he could not afford to carry, and he had Travis.

"C'mon boy, time to move on."

Travis had found a dry spot under the bench and was slow to get up. David wondered how old the Lab was. Last year he had taken him to a veterinarian, who thought Travis was three or four years old, but today David noticed a few white hairs on the dog's muzzle.

"You okay?" he asked.

***

The next morning, they walked along the side streets to St Vincent, and after waiting outside for an hour he was able to shower and wash his two sets of clothes. Melissa, his favorite volunteer there, had also given him a small sample bottle of Rid for the lice which had been driving him crazy. He was clean, at least outwardly, for the first time in weeks. He left Travis with Melissa, who loved the dog like he was her own, and headed west along the crowded sidewalks toward the VA center.

It had been ten hours since his last hit of the dead man's China White, and the withdrawal was making the walk difficult. His good leg hurt and the tremors made walking painful. Depression and anxiety were just a few hours away.

St. Vincent had fed him lunch each day and paid him sixty dollars a week for cleaning the church each Tuesday. Some weeks he was able to get a second day of work, and every dollar he earned he spent on heroin. The money never went for food. Paying good money for food was a luxury he couldn't afford. Even now he was hungry, but his fingers caressed the two twenties in his pocket, and he thought of his next score.

He was daydreaming as he walked. The woman in front of him reminded him of Cait—her reddish blonde hair, the shape of her waist, and her long stride, and he realized that he was weeping.

The first stages of withdrawal were always an emotional roller coaster. The depression and loss of self-esteem were crippling. He could feel them creeping into his every thought. How many of his fellow junkies had taken the easy way out and shot that lethal dose?

"Jug me," he'd heard one say.

The man's friend shot a dose straight into the guy's jugular, and he was dead seconds later.

The idea of checking out permanently was an appealing one at times. One bad night he had three bags lined up, ready to go, one-two-three, and it would be lights out, a moment of peace and his suffering would be over. But he passed out after injecting the first round, and when he came to hours later, someone had stolen his last two bags, the syringe, and his backpack. That was the last time he tried to kill himself.

Today, though, he wasn't thinking about death—he wanted to live. Some part of him clung to the idea that he could still recover and get back into living, and like a wakeup call, withdrawal hit him like a brick and he couldn't go any further.

In an alley behind a seafood restaurant, he cooked the brown powder, watching the crystals melt in the aluminum foil and inhaled the vapors through a piece of plastic straw. The relief he craved took five minutes because this bag was shit heroin.

"Bastard!"

Creepy Joe, as they called the dealer in Lafayette Park, had sold him decent dope in the past, but this time the heroin was cut with so much baking soda it had looked like China White. Still, it had enough real dope in it that he felt the aches in his joints and the nausea let up enough that he thought he could make it through the VA visit and maybe even into the afternoon. Once he was out of the hospital he would head back downtown to find Joe, and this time get another two days' worth of the best black tar heroin he could afford.

As he walked the last mile, the sun made its first appearance of the day. The sunshine and the muted opioid high made him forget how cold and miserable he'd been only days ago.

Just blocks to go, he told himself, feeling the ache in his knee. It was even worse now and the free Tylenol was no longer making it bearable. Maybe he could talk the VA doc into giving him something stronger, oxycodone would be better than great. But he knew it was a long shot. No one gives oxycodone to a junkie.

CHAPTER 4

TRUFANT

Three days after the homicides on Mason Street, Trufant held the single sheet of paper, wearing an identical pair of gloves to the ones that had last held it in New York City.

"Though Death be poor, it ends a mortal woe."

Trufant could feel his blood boil just looking at the letter. It was a taunt, and like the last two notes, he was taking it personally—the man was fucking with him.

"Beautiful handwriting," Carlos said, "just like the others. What do you think, Lieutenant?"

"I think it's BS. Another quote by Shakespeare, from *King Richard* this time, and it's postmarked from Manhattan, the same day our victims were killed."

"The man does get around," Amado said.

Trufant wondered if it would be possible to have a plane ticket ready to go and be in New York in time. Yes, but it felt wrong, too much trouble, and too much of a risk.

"Why would he use the US mail, Carlos? Why not just send an email? Why pretend you're in New York? I think this is something else. I think the letters are a game to him. He's studied serial killers. They all want to toy with the police, and he's copying them—and I think someone is helping him."

"I'm no expert, Lieutenant, but this handwriting looks feminine."

"You're right, but I thought the same of John Hancock's signature on the Constitution when I first saw it, so I don't know if it matters with script like this." Trufant held it up to the light, hoping doing so would help him decide. Male or female?

"You're probably right, Carlos. Not many men practice cursive nowadays, or anyone, really."

"It's a dead art, L.T."

"Carlos, we need to ask ourselves again—how is our subject identifying veterans? How does he pick them out of a crowd of vagrants in a city this big?"

One of his junior inspectors knocked twice and stepped in. "Lieutenant, I got three possible hits back from ViCAP." ViCAP was the FBI's database on violent crime, the go-to place for communications between law enforcement agencies.

Trufant looked up. "Where?"

"Two were in Florida, Miami and Melbourne, and another one from the GBI in Atlanta. All were veterans with knife wounds to the throat, no arrests, no suspects, and none of these agencies seem to be aware of each other.

"Any details on the victims or when they occurred?"

"No, you want me to ask?"

"Yes, I want everything they'll send us, and ask if they received any quotes too."

"Yes, sir, and one of the patrol officers got a tip on our guy with the dog. His name may be David and he hangs out near St. Vincent."

"Okay, great, finally some good news. Get that name out to the guys on the street. I want everyone looking for him and I want him to know it. Maybe he'll come to us."

***

A week later Trufant looked again at a photocopy of the latest quote. "Though Death be poor, it ends a mortal woe."

Still taunting me, he thought, but in doing so, it was a clear link tying these homicides to the ones in Chicago. So far, revenge seemed to be the motivator, but revenge for what? Or was it some compulsive need—a statement to satisfy his anger?

So many questions and not a single answer and just like the others, this case was going cold fast. Maybe this David guy could fill in some of the missing pieces.

ViCap was designed to alert agencies to similar crimes, like a clearinghouse, but in this case, it had failed. He called the FBI's San Francisco office and was told an agent was already on his way to speak with him. They had ignored his previous calls after the last homicide—this double homicide must have gotten their attention.

He gathered up the files on the previous four victims and headed for the conference room. Amato came in a minute later with a severe-looking woman dressed in a charcoal-gray pantsuit. He recognized her, Agent Sheffield. Everything about the woman, including her ID hanging from a lanyard around her neck, screamed federal agent.

"Special Agent Sheffield, nice to see you again."

They sat at the conference table, and Amato filled her in on the latest information on the new homicides, the crime scene photos, and the photocopy of the most recent quote.

"If you remember, this was the first one that occurred in Chicago," Trufant said, handing the copy to Sheffield. "Postmarked from Cincinnati the same day as the murder. No one connected the quote to the homicide until the next one in December. Now we have a total of eight victims, two in Chicago and six here in San Francisco and there might be more."

"How all occasions do inform against me and spur my dull revenge," Sheffield read aloud. "Any theories, Marcus?"

"I don't have a clue. It could be anything from terrorism to a crazed wanna-be soldier kicked out of boot camp now seeking revenge. I don't know how many hours I've wasted trying to find a connection to these dates, something that would set some lunatic off. He or she is so meticulous we can't find even a single hair, and yet we get these damned quotes taunting us. Everything points to revenge. To the killer, it's really important that we know that, but revenge for what?"

"Marcus, I'm no profiler, but I've been to enough classes to know these seem to be more than simple revenge killings. Revenge requires gratification, and that's where the killing comes in, but there *is* a message in these quotes, a different type of gratification, something to do with our military," Sheffield said.

"How is it none of these murders have been linked with the ones in Florida and Atlanta? ViCAP should have picked them up."

"It depends on how they were entered, Marcus. Not the right keywords and it could miss them. You know the old saying, 'Garbage in, garbage out.'"

"You're right," Trufant said. "It makes me wonder how many more are out there. This guy is making us look like fools, and he's enjoying it."

Chapter 5

Armstrong

The last block was the hardest. He had the nods now, sitting in the shade of a banyan tree just outside the VA's main entrance. It wasn't just the nods, though, it was anxiety. Sitting indoors with strangers was uncomfortable. It was so much easier being outside. What he wanted to do was close his eyes and catch a few z's, and he almost did until the itch below his knee reminded him of why he had walked so far.

The last few yards of sidewalk in front of the hospital felt strange. The sound of the dog padding next to him was missing. He was alone now, and his social anxiety was thrumming like a taut string in the breeze. But the police were looking for a man with a black dog, and he wasn't ready or willing to be confronted by the cops.

A CCTV camera was mounted directly above the automatic doors, and he kept his head down as he made his way up the half dozen concrete steps. The doors opened with a whoosh of warm air, and several people inside turned and looked at him. Out of habit he avoided eye contact with them. He hated the look in their eyes, and the way they stepped aside, fearing he might brush into them. He understood the reason, but he hated it even so.

Of the forty or so people in the waiting room, only a few were women, and they sat apart from the men. They were all ages. Some looked to be in their eighties and others as young as eighteen. The women here were cleaner, their clothes newer, and none of them looked like they were living on the street.

He envied the women. By the look on their faces, their military service had had no lasting effects. But maybe there were things he couldn't see. Things hidden either by their new clothes or things in their minds, things that haunted them the way Afghanistan haunted him.

And as he thought of Afghanistan, the people in the room vanished, and for a brief fragment in time, he was lying on a filthy dirt road looking at his severed leg and smelling the mix of cordite and blood.

A name was called, not his, but it brought him back from that hot summer day, where his first life ended, and this new one began.

An old television mounted on the wall showed a black man in a dark suit behind a podium as "Serial Killer at Large" scrolled across the screen. Standing next to the black man was a white man in a police uniform, the stars on his epaulets identifying him as the chief of police.

"Another veteran," the old man next to him said. A worn-out blue ball cap with USS Okinawa stitched in gold across the front covered what few hairs the man had left. "That's five now. It's a damn shame."

The old man looked away, and David saw the shakes in the man's bony hands and wondered if they were just due to age. The man had to be in his eighties, his skin paper-thin and his long arms nothing but bone and sinew but otherwise healthy. But David had lived long enough with junkies to know this man was just old. A minute later they called the old guy's name. He stood, using a cane to steady himself and shuffled across the room.

One by one, men and women stood and disappeared behind closed doors. Two hours later they called his name. A young woman in green scrubs led him into a six-foot square exam room that smelled like Lysol.

There was no clock in this room, but his perception of time told him he had been waiting there for at least half an hour. The room was cold and the exam table, covered in thin paper, was uncomfortable. He paced back and forth, checking his fingers every few minutes afraid of the shakes he might see. Fifteen minutes later, someone knocked softly and the door opened.

"Good afternoon Mr. Armstrong, I'm sorry for the wait. I'm Dr. Williams," the woman said.

He looked at her and was glad he had showered and changed into clean clothes before he came in. She was young, maybe a few years younger than he was, and she was wearing the whitest scrubs he had ever seen. It was a simple V-neck shirt and pants, but she had ironed creases into her sleeves and pant legs. She was pretty, and he felt ashamed and unworthy of her attention.

"Mr. Armstrong, I understand you're having problems with your prosthetic. Can I see it?"

She sat in a chair next to the exam table and lifted his carbon fiber and titanium calf. She was sitting close enough that he could smell her perfume, the fragrance of a flower he couldn't name.

She touched the redness where the skin graft met the stainless steel. "I see the inflammation, how painful is it?"

"It's not too bad, but I know it's going to get worse. They warned me it might happen."

She looked at a computer screen, scrolled through a few pages, and said, "You got this prosthetic in 2012, ten years ago. Have you had any other problems since then?"

"With the leg?" he asked.

"With anything."

"No, just pain around the joint. I've tried Tylenol but it's not helping. I was hoping for something stronger."

"I see," she said, looking back at the monitor.

"Maybe some oxycodone," he said, trying to sound casual.

"Your chart shows you were treated for opioid addiction twice, once in 2012 during your recovery and again in 2013. I don't think oxy is a good idea, Mr. Armstrong."

She turned back to him, looked him in the eye, and said, "But you know that, don't you?"

"I guess I'm good then, Doctor." He stood and wanted to leave, embarrassed about what he knew was coming next.

"I only ask because I'm going to give you some heavy antibiotics that should clear up this infection and some prednisone that should help with the pain. I have a few samples of extra strength Tylenol that should help if you want them."

"Thank you, but I'll be okay."

"You know, Mr. Armstrong, our addiction treatment has come a long way since 2013, that and PTSD counseling, you should keep it in mind. If you're interested, I lead a therapy group every other Thursday."

"I'll remember that."

"The American Legion building across the street, 7 p.m.," she said, handing him her card.

"Get dressed and one of our assistants will be in soon to give you a couple of injections. Take care of yourself, sir."

***

As promised, he got two injections, ceftriaxone for the infection and a steroid, and a dozen samples of Tylenol. On the way out the door, he handed the Tylenol to one of the men waiting in the lobby and stepped out into the afternoon sun.

The warmth felt good on his face. He took his ragged fatigue jacket off and wrapped it around his waist. As he walked away, he looked one more time at his hands and saw the first quiver, so slight, but it was there. *Two hours max, and I'll need another bag.*

Out on the street, he saw the detective from the newscast get out of a dark blue Chevrolet Impala and walk toward the hospital's front door. The man gave him a quick glance and nodded as he walked by. A glance he had seen a few times, a simple look of acknowledgment, not the one of dismissal he had expected, but he wished the man hadn't seen him at all. Hopefully the detective would see him as just another homeless man among the thousands of others, and he thanked God he had left Travis at the church.

The cops are looking for you. Looking for a man with a dog and a fake leg, I hear.

He walked eastbound, back toward Lafayette Park, wondering what the detective was looking for at the hospital. Someone was killing veterans, and he had seen the last two die. But was the detective looking for a link or was he looking for me? The Veterans Affairs Medical Center was just an obvious place to search for a homeless veteran's records, he hoped.

***

On an average day, he would avoid confrontations, especially ones that could lead to a fight. He had never backed away from violence before Fiddlers Green, but over the years he had lost his aggression and the will to fight.

Creepy Joe was in his usual spot next to a dying oak tree in the back of the park. He started to leave when he saw Armstrong but wasn't fast enough.

"Joe!"

"Hey Army man, how's things? I was just thinking about you."

"First, I'm a Marine, asshole. That was some shit you sold me this morning."

"Yeah, I heard it wasn't the best, man, but that was all I had. I have some better stuff now. How much do you need?"

"Let me see it."

"You have the cash, man? Show me the money first, Army man."

"How about I kick your ass for selling me shit dope!"

"I got some real good stuff right after you left. Don't get up in my face!"

The two walked down a path of dead grass to an orange, one-man tent. Joe went inside and came out with a blue plastic coffee container.

"This is really good stuff, man. I want to try some myself but . . . you know, I can't. These guys don't cut me no slack. I got no cash of my own."

Armstrong saw Joe's eyes darting from the street to one of the other tents nearby, as if he were being watched.

"I don't give a shit, Joe. Give me eight bags and one for that shit you sold me this morning, and I won't tell anyone you're ripping us off."

Joe fished nine bags out of his stash, and Armstrong glimpsed what looked like another thirty or forty bags of the dark brown Black Tar inside. He opened one and holding the sticky chunk to his nose, took a deep breath. The rich vinegar smell was enough to satisfy him for now, and he put all nine bags in his pocket.

"Here's forty. This better be good this time, Joe, or I'll be back."

"I don't like threats, Army man, just take your stuff and go."

"Marine, Joe, Marine!"

He knew it was good. It had the right smell and he couldn't wait to smoke the first bag. But the fading light told him he needed to get back to the church if he was going to eat tonight.

As he walked back to the church, he felt his anger fading and was surprised that he had been able to confront the man at all. The feeling was eerie, and he knew he could have fought Joe, and maybe even beaten him. He walked a little faster now, no longer feeling the itch in his knee.

***

The lights were on inside St. Vincent, and the smell of something cooking and Travis met him at the door. They ate in silence as others all around him talked in hushed tones. Beef stew served from a massive stainless steel kettle, fresh bread, and apple crumb cake left him full. Even Travis left a few boiled potatoes in the bottom of his bowl.

He would miss this place. He would miss San Francisco too, but he couldn't stay. If the police found him, he had no doubt they would take him to the station, and Travis would be lucky if they only took him to the pound. Stray men in San Francisco had an easy life—stray dogs did not.

He felt the quiver in his fingers as he washed the last of the dishes, and he knew it was time to leave.

As the last of the day turned black, he stretched out on a section of concrete easement outside the Mission District along Thirteenth Street. With Travis leashed to his right wrist, he used the dead man's knife to cut the chunk of black tar in half, and with a spoon and a lighter, he began cooking the heroin, inhaling the vapors with the straw.

The effects of chasing the dragon were slow at first, just a feeling of warmth spreading to his arms and legs, and as the last of the tar boiled away, he laid back and closed his eyes. He was now thoroughly relaxed, the pain in his knee and the argument with Joe were just memories and everything was right in his life, but Travis began to whine. The dog knew better.

"I'm good to go, Travis."

This was the best part, the first few minutes where everything was better than good. He was whole again, and there was no fear of being dopesick, no ache in his heart for his wife, no pain as he watched his best friend die in the dirt and dust of Afghanistan. The warmth alone was enough, if only it lasted a few minutes longer.

The sound of Travis whining and the image of Dr. William's face were the last things he remembered.

Chapter 6

Trufant

Marcus Trufant sat and waited in the lobby of the VA almost as long as David Armstrong had. He had been told twice he would have to wait until someone with authority was free to speak with him.

"You can leave your card and maybe they will call you," the woman had said. As he looked around the office, he had the feeling that call would never happen.

"Lt. Trufant?" a woman in scrubs finally asked.

"Yes."

"I'm Dr. Williams."

She was young, and he was surprised to learn that she was more than just someone's assistant.

"I'm sorry you had to wait so long, Lieutenant, but most of the people out there have been waiting months for their appointment. I didn't feel it was right to have them wait any longer. How can I help you?"

"Dr. Williams, I'm investigating the most recent homicide of a veteran, and I'm hoping you have some record of him. We're at a dead end trying to locate next of kin, and maybe he has been here for treatment. His name was Gerome Callaway, date of birth, January 16, 1970."

"I can't tell you much. The HIPAA privacy rule protects all our patients."

"The man is dead."

"Yes, I heard you, but there are still protections," she said. "I can't give you someone's file without a court order, but if you could be more specific, I might be able to answer some questions."

"Can you tell me the last time he was here and is there anyone listed as next of kin or any contact information?"

He watched the glow from the computer screen flicker on her face as she logged on. She nodded to herself a few times, apparently satisfied she had the right patient.

"His first visit here was in 2015, and his last visit was three weeks ago. I see no next of kin and no contact information. He used the hospital's address when he registered.

"Here?"

"Yes, it's a common practice with unsheltered veterans."

He was here two days before he was killed. The hospital has to be the connection between the victims and the killer.

"Can you tell me why he was here?"

"He needed a prescription refill, Xanax. It's frequently given to PTSD victims. That's all I can tell you, though. Perhaps the military can give you more information."

"Thank you, Doctor. One more thing, we're also looking for another homeless man, he has an artificial left leg, an expensive looking one, and we think he may be a veteran also. He might have a black Labrador Retriever with him, any chance he sounds familiar?"

"Is he a suspect?"

"No, we don't think he had anything to do with the man's death but may have witnessed it."

He watched her eyes and saw a moment of hesitation, there was something she thought of just before she answered.

"I'm sorry, no."

Hoping she would add whatever it was she had thought of, he waited a second before getting up, then thanked her and gave her his card. "Call me if you think of anything."

As he walked down the lobby, he bumped into a man pushing

a mop bucket, and soapy water sloshed out, soaking the man's pants.

"Jesus, I'm sorry," Trufant said.

"It's my fault, sir, no problem."

Trufant saw the word "volunteer" in red letters on the man's name tag, and he walked back to Dr. William's office.

"Doctor, how many volunteers work at the hospital?"

"I'm not sure, maybe you can ask someone in resource management."

Resource management was not an easy place to find. It was across the street, and the man at the desk was far from helpful, but he said at any one time there were as many as sixty volunteers on the roster, but the number varied. Today, there were just sixteen scheduled and only nine showed up.

"What can I say?" he said. "We need all the help we can get, and they work for free."

***

Another dead end, possibly, he thought as he headed back to the station.

At his desk, he checked for messages and saw none. More than just a few homicides had been cleared with just a simple message or an anonymous tip and the pin map on the wall held no clues, either.

"Shit!"

"Problem, L.T.?" Amato asked from across the room.

"No, just thinking out loud."

The phone on his desk rang. It was Agent Sheffield.

"I've been scouring NCIC, Lieutenant, and I'm coming up blank," the agent said. "So I sent a request to Chicago for a copy of their homicide files. It seems there is more to it than you might think. Nothing big but you should check it out."

"What do you mean nothing big?"

"Just a few more clues left behind, a possible witness, and some of the detective's theories. Shall I send you a copy?"

"Yes, please do."

He hung up and thought back about what he knew of the Chicago murders. Chicago detectives had thought it was just a random murder until the second one in December of 2019.

"Carlos, I'm thinking of going to Chicago to see what they have. I want to look at all of it and talk to these detectives face-to-face."

"The Chief will shit if you ask to go to Chicago."

"He will shit when he knows you're coming with me. Sometimes you need to stand in the middle of the crime scene to see and feel what the victims were seeing—to get the vibes of the place."

"Vibes?"

"Yeah—vibes, premonitions, feelings, call it whatever you like. I also want to hear it from their detectives. There is nothing better than a face-to-face conversation. Better go home and pack a bag, Carlos."

Chapter 7

Armstrong

South Carolina was hot as hell in July, and Paris Island was right in the middle of a heat wave. David Armstrong was in the last mile of a five-mile run in full gear when he blacked out.

He knew it was coming, he had stopped sweating fifteen minutes ago, and the moisture in his soaked shirt had evaporated. He felt cold and his vision had begun to tunnel and all he saw in the last few seconds was the green rucksack of the recruit in front of him. Then Private Travis McClanahan was pouring water on his face from a canteen.

Now it was McKnight, the drill instructor, staring down at him, his face scarlet. "You need to hydrate, recruit, are you stupid?" As the man screamed his spit flew everywhere, but most of it rained down on Armstrong's face. "Hydration is life!" the instructor screamed at the platoon as Armstrong was carried off the field.

Six hours later, his entire squad was forced to run to make up for the mile Armstrong couldn't finish, this time with their rucksacks over their heads. It was dark now, and at least it was a few degrees cooler. The guys were pissed, all of them except Travis.

Running had always been hard for him. As a kid, he suffered from asthma and had never been able to run more than half a mile, but as he grew older, the symptoms eased. There was never enough money for college, so the summer after high school, he ran week after week, until he was able to complete his first ten-kilometer race, and like his father and brother before him, he joined the Marine Corps.

"Your ass is mine, Armstrong," someone behind him whispered.

"Don't listen to those bastards," Travis said. It'll pass as soon as the next guy drops."

But it didn't pass, and McKnight harassed them both the entire thirteen weeks. He assigned them as "battle buddies," a less-than-flattering term.

One night Travis had had enough. They had just sat in the mess hall when their squad leader passed close to them, muttering something under his breath. All Travis heard the man say was the word queer or queen, and in an instant, Travis body-slammed him, knocking the leader to the ground.

Armstrong saw Travis was about to drive his massive fist into the guy's face, and he tackled him, holding him in a bear hug until he felt him relax.

The squad leader, an equally big guy from Texas, got to his feet, looked at Travis and walked away.

"Leave it, Travis, it's not a big deal."

Travis was a big man, and when he was pissed, he was hard to control. The Texan was one thing, but he was afraid McKnight would soon be Travis's next target.

Travis looked at his tray. The chicken and gravy now cold, and he pushed it away.

"Armstrong, it is a big deal," he whispered. "I am gay."

"Don't screw around, man. Let's eat and get the hell out of here."

"I *am* gay. Do I look like I'm fucking joking? I've been harassed my whole life. There were times when I was beaten up every day in school because kids knew I was different." Travis looked around the mess hall and whispered, "How many of these guys would sit next to me if they knew—none. I'm telling you this Armstrong because I know you aren't one of them."

"I've never known a gay man, Travis, not really. A classmate once and a kid that lived down the street."

"You do now, Armstrong. So, are you going to move to another table, or just ignore me now like some of the others?"

"Travis, I'm not going anywhere. Semper Fi to the end, right?"

The Texan never looked at either of them again during the final six weeks.

A month after basic training ended, the two of them were accepted into Forced Recon training at Camp Pendleton, where he met and married Caitlin.

It was a small wedding, and Travis stood next to him at the altar as best man. His parents and Cait's parents sat on the same pew, with Travis's mother beaming between them.

***

Twelve months later they were standing on the tarmac at the Kabul International Airport.

"I don't like the smell here, Armstrong."

"I don't smell anything."

"Exactly."

They fell in line with the rest of his squad and walked past a C-17 whose crew was loading five flag-draped coffins on the aircraft's ramp. The squad stopped, and on an unspoken command, each gave a slow hand salute.

"Armstrong, when I die over here, take me home and tell my momma I died like a man. I don't want her to know how. She's not a strong woman, so spare her the details."

"We're not dying over here, Travis."

"I'm not so sure about that. Sometimes I can feel my future, sense what's next in my life. I can't feel anything after this place. Just do it for me, you know, if it happens."

"Will do, but we ain't dying over here, Travis. We're going home, and we're going to grow old. Caitlin and I are going to have six kids and move to the mountains."

"I'll never get married, Armstrong."

"Damn, I was hoping to be your best man one day."

"Never gonna happen."

Those were the best years of my life.

But Travis was gone now, and once Armstrong had healed enough to make the trip, he fulfilled his promise.

Travis's mother was grateful knowing that Armstrong was with her son at the end and that he didn't die alone. Armstrong followed Travis's wishes and spared her the gruesome details of her son's death—a vision she didn't need, and one he could never forget.

***

Thunder echoed off in the distance and he opened his eyes. He sat up under the bridge off Thirteenth Street, and Travis was gone.

"Travis!"

His backpack was also gone. He still had his VA card, the dead man's knife, and a twenty-dollar bill stuffed in his pocket.

"Travis!" The sound reverberated in his skull, leaving him weak and queasy, the aftereffects of cheap black tar heroin. Judging from the shadows it was midmorning and he had been out for twelve hours.

"Travis!" His voice hurt his throat this time.

It was quiet, just the sound of heavy traffic on the bridge above him and then he heard another crack of thunder. Thunder was rare, but rain was not and as he stood feeling the pain in the right stump of his leg, it began to pour.

He walked out into the rain and called the dog again.

"Larry took your dog."

He turned and saw the old woman under a tent made of cardboard.

"The dog was howling, and Larry took it," she said. "You were talking in your sleep, and the dog was howling. We thought you were dying."

"Where?"

The woman pointed south with a single gnarled finger and said, "He goes to the liquor store on Page Street."

He turned and stepped back out into the rain again, and the toothless woman yelled, "Ain't you gonna give me sompthin?"

He ignored her and hurried out down Van Ness, ignoring the pain in his leg and those cursing at him under their umbrellas.

"Travis!" The ache in his head was clearing, the nausea was bearable, and the cold rain was leaching away the last of the fog in his brain.

Somewhere up ahead he heard a dog bark. Running and limping he zeroed in on where he thought the bark had come from. Was it even Travis?

"Travis," he yelled again, but there was no reply. For the rest of the afternoon and well into the night he looked for the dog, calling his name until his throat was raw and withdrawal left him too weak to walk. Travis meant everything to him, but the fear of having lost his dog was losing out to his need for a fix.

In one of the city parks, he found a man in a fatigue jacket selling China White. All he had was the crumpled twenty, enough for a single waxed bag of the powerful synthetic. He walked deeper into the shadows of the park, and twenty minutes later he lost consciousness.

Bright sunshine and someone shaking him roused him from a nightmare. It was the man in the fatigue jacket leaning over him.

"Man, you gave me a good scare. I thought you were a goner."

He sat up, felt his stomach cramp, and looked around for Travis.

"Have you seen my dog? He's a black Lab."

"No, I didn't. You came in here last night alone, no dog."

Armstrong looked up at the sun and the shadows and figured it was early afternoon.

"So how was it?" the man asked.

"It almost killed me," he said, wondering how close he really came to overdosing.

He tried to remember where he was and how to find Page Street. He needed to find Larry, and maybe someone near the liquor store would remember seeing Travis.

***

The K&G Package Store was on the corner, and he looked up and down the street hoping he would see either the dog or recognize Larry. Larry had to be one of the men he saw with the woman under the bridge, but there were too many people on the sidewalk to pick him out.

"Travis!" he yelled, ignoring the looks from the people around him.

Not hearing the dog, he walked inside the run-down liquor store and asked the woman behind the register if she had seen a man named Larry with a dog.

"I know Larry. He comes in two or three times a week usually just before lunch. He was here an hour ago. I think he did have a dog today."

She came from behind the counter, opened the door, and looked down the street.

"He went west, toward the park, I think."

***

Buena Vista Park covered several square blocks, and there were hundreds of colorful pop-up tents. Destitute vagrants were mixed in with men, women, and children with nowhere to go. The lucky ones had the tents, most of which would allow a single person a respite from the city's notoriously damp and cold weather.

"Travis," he yelled, feeling the soreness of his throat again. Silence. He walked to the far side of the park, scanning left to right, looking ahead and behind him.

"Travis," he yelled again, and this time he heard a dog bark, and then several more dogs barking, but that first one sounded like Travis.

Walking eastbound, he called again, and this time he knew it was Travis, an urgent, but welcome bark. Another hundred yards straight ahead and he saw the dog tied to an old red tent and the legs of a sleeping man sticking out from the zippered flap.

Travis was happy to see him and looked like he was in good shape after spending almost two days with "Larry." He untied Travis and kicked the man's feet several times until he finally woke.

Armstrong was relieved and angry and the anger gave him confidence. He couldn't remember ever being as pissed off as he was right then, and he kicked the man's feet again.

Travis began growling as the man inched his way out of the tent.

"Hey, watcha doing with my dog," Larry yelled as he stood.

Larry was old but wiry and looked like he was not used to anyone arguing with him. "Damn it, you can't take my dog!"

Holding a wine bottle in a brown paper bag like a weapon, Larry stepped one foot too close, and Armstrong kneed him in the groin with his good leg. The man doubled over, making a whooshing sound and collapsed, dropping the bottle on a strip of concrete. Breaking glass and red wine flew everywhere. The wine splashed on a woman who had stopped to watch the two men arguing.

Another, younger man began cursing at Armstrong, and he thought he was going to have to fight this guy too, but Travis got between them and snarled. The man stared down at him, deciding whether he wanted to fight the dog, thought better of it, and walked away.

"Where's my backpack?" Armstrong screamed down at Larry, who was still trying to catch his breath.

A crowd began gathering behind Larry, who now looked like a victim, having been knocked down by a much younger man.

Two women knelt sympathetically and Armstrong knew it was time to go.

There was still no sign of his backpack.

"If you ever touch my dog again, I will kill you!"

Armstrong and Travis walked north as a light rain began. Armstrong looked back a few times, making sure the old drunk didn't follow them.

At the first intersection, he knelt and held Travis, holding his face close to his.

"I'm sorry, Travis, it's okay, I'm here now," he said stroking his damp fur.

Tears welled up as he thought of losing the dog, vowing he wouldn't let it happen again and knowing it might.

Travis led the way but looked back at him every few minutes anyway, making sure he was still behind him, and it wasn't until they neared the church that the dog relaxed.

St. Vincent was just another block farther down the street, and he hoped he hadn't missed the chance for a sandwich and some scraps for Travis. Armstrong had been losing weight. He could feel the looseness in his jeans, and he looked down at Travis and saw the dog's ribcage. He had to do better, for the dog at least.

He remembered something the priest said as he was cleaning the church last week, "When you hit rock bottom son, you will know it, and you will know when you're ready to recover."

He felt the first twinge of being there, like he could touch the empty pit in his stomach, and desperation, a feeling that he would be better off dead. Only the fear of dope sickness was stronger. Once that started, there was no other thought than scoring another bag of dope. It was an endless cycle: get high, depression, and another desperate search for dope. Yes, rock bottom was closer now.

They turned the corner and saw a few of his fellow homeless, or "unsheltered persons" as the politicians liked to call them, still lined up behind the church.

"Hello, Travis," Melissa said, and set a sandwich down where the dog could reach it. "I have these too," she said, giving him two boxes of Milk-Bone dog biscuits. "Someone dropped off a case this morning."

"Thank you, Melissa."

He sat under the awning and saw the sun was finally out. He stripped off his wet jacket, hoping it would dry out some. His head was aching, but his appetite was excellent, and thankfully he kept the sandwich down.

He looked down at the Lab and thought of the real Travis, a Black man with an Irish name. Travis took a lot of shit in boot camp for his name, but once out of Basic and into Special Ops, nobody ever messed with him.

Chapter 8

Trufant

Standing in the parking lot of an old neighborhood bar across the street from the Illinois State Police headquarters, Trufant and Carlos listened as Detective Reece explained how the body was found.

"I found the victim, Felipe Martinez across the street in our parking lot as I was leaving the station. The blood trail led here next to a dumpster that was right where you're standing. A lot has changed though since 2019, but this was the crime scene. I interviewed the bar manager who said the victim was drinking with another man and had left about two a.m."

"Who was the other man?" Carlos asked.

"The manager wasn't the best witness. He had never seen the suspect before and described the man as average—average height, average weight, brown hair, between twenty and thirty years old, possibly Hispanic. He did a composite sketch with our artist, and we ran it on the news for a week. We did get a few tips, but they all checked out, except one that we couldn't eliminate."

"Tell us about that one."

"We got a call from an elderly woman who thought she saw someone similar to the sketch enter the vacant house next door. A forensic team went through it but found nothing of value, still we surveilled it for weeks but never saw any traffic. The woman was pretty old, but I got the impression she was credible, so for months I used to stop by it and shake the door. It belongs to an investment company in Mississauga, Canada. We had the locals in Canada check on it but it was a boarded-up storefront. I don't think they looked any further.

"Detective, what can you tell me about this victim?" Trufant said.

"The bartender said he was a regular customer, an Army vet who worked at a welding shop down the street. The shop is closed now. It went out of business a few months after the homicide. He was a white male, forty, and in good shape. He was having marital issues, and his wife said he was drinking too much, which added to their problems. Clean military record, did a total of six years. Pretty typical guy, no enemies that didn't check out, we went back and re-interviewed everybody once we linked this murder with the one in December, still nothing."

"Did the manager think the two guys were friends?" Trufant said.

"I don't remember him saying so, but he said the victim often ranted about the war in Iraq, hated the "towelheads" as he called them, but he also said the man never saw combat."

"Tell me about the letter," Trufant said.

"We didn't know about the letter at the time. It came in a few days later with no reference to the victim. The mail clerk thought it was weird enough to save it, though. They keep everything that seems threatening. She logged it in to the property room, and it wasn't until the second guy was killed and another letter came in that someone remembered the first one."

"So, no suspects or leads on either guy?" Amato said.

"None. There was no DNA, no fingerprints, and no witnesses. As you can see here, there are no cameras, either. Both crime scenes were in isolated parking lots. Our cameras don't cover the exit where we found the first guy."

"Anything on the autopsies?" Trufant said.

"The wounds on both men were incised, almost surgical. The ME said the weapon might have been a scalpel except for the depth, so it might have been a straight edge razor. Victim number one's wound was different, though, like the suspect had started and stopped and then finished the cut. The ME said both wounds were from left to right, probably a right-hander. The subject could have been in front of the victims or standing behind them. There were no defensive wounds, but the victims had some abrasions from falling, and arterial spray showed they were both standing when attacked. I have copies of everything for you, including a taped statement from the bartender."

Trufant looked back across the street and imagined the scene at night—the dead of night in an old, almost-deserted neighborhood with the state police headquarters right across the street. Someone was waiting out here for the victim to come outside. The victim was probably drunk, there was a quick conversation and, like the video from Mason Street, a flick of the wrist and a spray of blood. But the man wasn't dying fast enough. Maybe he missed the carotid, so he cut deeper the second time. It made sense, in a way. Or he could be totally wrong, and the killer was sitting next to the man buying him drinks, listening to his war stories until he got up the nerve to slash the man's throat.

Trufant stepped back, envisioning the dead man at his feet, the pool of blood spreading out around him, his adrenaline pumping, but something was wrong—killing the man wasn't enough, killing was just a small part of something he needed to satisfy.

"He was afraid the man wouldn't be found here quick enough," Trufant said, "so he dragged him over to your headquarters so he would be. I'll bet he was nearby watching."

"We thought so too. We watched all our videos, for twenty-four hours before and after, and never saw anyone suspicious," Reece said. "There was the one camera right there aiming toward the street," the detective said pointing to a light pole, "but the only cars we saw were identified and eliminated."

"Took a lot of guts to haul him across the street to a police station," Carlos said.

"Yeah, it reinforces my idea that killing them is just part of it," Trufant said. "Putting their deaths in our face is another."

"Tell us about the December case."

"The scene is right down the street, I'll show you."

Minutes later they were in the parking lot of the Northern Food Bank.

"This is a church-run food bank now, open only on Wednesday and Saturday. It was a vacant grocery store in December 2019, and it had been vacant for years. The victim, Robert Godfrey was found on Sunday, December 1st, just after dawn. The coroner said he had been dead about six hours, no cameras, no witnesses, and no evidence of any kind. He was a Marine, did one tour in Iraq, and dishonorably discharged in 2007 for insubordination when he refused to go on a mission.

"He was later diagnosed with an acute case of PTSD, and the Corps was reviewing his discharge in light of the PTSD when he was killed. He lived around the corner with his mother, had a problem with his temper, she said. He was arrested twice for simple battery, once in 2008 and again in June of 2009."

"So, he died about midnight," Amato said.

"Close enough to it, it was pretty cold that night. I remember the blood was frozen in the asphalt."

"Your report mentioned meth," Trufant said.

"Lots of drug activity along this street. He had traces of methamphetamine in him, so it's possible he had just scored and was with his dealer, but we canvassed everything and everybody for a two-block radius and came up with zilch."

"Well, I can't think of anything else, Detective Reece, thanks again for your help."

The detective drove off, leaving them alone in the empty lot.

"You getting any of those vibes you were looking for, Lieutenant?"

"A few, Carlos. Notice anything different about this place?"

"It's colder," Carlos said, laughing, "and it's out in the open."

"That's right. All our victims were killed in heavily populated sections of downtown. Even though the streets were deserted, it's still downtown—tall buildings with thousands of windows and a potential witness behind each one of them, and they were all killed while they slept. The tallest building here is an abandoned two-story office building across the street. The scenes couldn't be more different."

"Maybe he's changing, he's becoming more confident," Carlos said.

"I'm not sure, Carlos. These two victims were awake and standing, probably talking to their killer. I think the MOs couldn't be more different. Let's go look at that vacant house."

***

Thirty minutes later, Carlos parked the rented Honda Accord in the driveway of a dilapidated one-story wood-frame house in an old section of East Chicago. A partially burned-out house stood in the lot next door. Its roof had collapsed inward, leaving charred trusses sticking straight up into the gray sky like burnt fingers.

The fire must have happened long ago as there was no odor of burned wood, even standing downwind. There was a smell, though, and not a pleasant one, the smell of decay, all too common in neighborhoods like this one. These were old houses, lived in by old people, and the trash strewn in the street looked like it had been there for years. A rusted-out Chevrolet pickup truck on blocks sat like a sentinel in a driveway next door. The house standing in front of them was in better shape, at least its roof was intact.

Trufant stepped onto the old wooden porch, testing the wood with each step, and knocked on the door, not expecting a reply. The house had been pale yellow once. Now the paint was peeling away in big sections, and gray mold was taking root on the bare wood.

He knocked again and tried the knob and found it turned. It turned too easily, like it had been used a lot recently. The door swung inward silently, and the hair on the back of his neck and arms rose.

"Someone's been in here," he whispered.

"Should we get a warrant, L.T.?"

"That would take hours. This is probably nothing but stay sharp. If we see anything of value, we'll back out and call the locals. They can get the warrant."

He knocked again on the doorjamb and waited, listening to the silence inside.

"Police officers! Anyone inside?"

Still nothing. With his Sig Sauer in his hand, Trufant stepped over the threshold and into a small foyer, causing a squeal in the old floorboards. He paused and Carlos eased in next to him. The two of them waited, listening for anything, but the house was still eerily quiet.

The only furniture visible from the foyer was an old folding table. There were no chairs around it, but right on top was a Domino's pizza box. He pointed to it, and both men moved into the main room.

The box was empty. Trufant had hoped to find something in it that would give him a clue how long the box had been sitting there—was it hours or was it months, there was no way to tell. They moved into the kitchenette, and Carlos opened a refrigerator, which must have been made in the early sixties. It was dark and empty and stank like sour milk.

Trufant turned toward a bedroom in time to see a nude man lunge through the doorway and swing at his throat. He felt a searing pain, and at the same instant heard his gun fire. He flinched when he heard the gun fire a second time and clutched at his throat, feeling warm blood flowing between his fingers. He began to fall, first to his knees, and finally forward, landing on top of the naked man already on the floor.

He rolled off the now-motionless body and waited to die. *I'm not supposed to die like this*. His death was supposed to be different, somehow dramatic, not in an old run-down, abandoned house taken out by surprise.

What would be the first signs of his own death? Probably

tunnel vision, then blackness. He waited for the symptoms, but he was breathing, and if he could breathe, he wasn't dying, at least not yet. He looked at the naked man lying face down next to him. The man was dead or dying. He wasn't sure and didn't care.

"Marcus! Can you hear me?"

He was afraid to let go of his throat, fearing he would see his blood spray across the room as his carotid artery burst.

"Lieutenant!"

It was Carlos, his face inches away from his own, screaming down at him. The young inspector looked sick. His skin was usually darker but was pale now, ashen, and there was a sheen of sweat on his face. *How surreal, seeing those tiny beads of sweat on the man's face as I lay dying.*

"Lieutenant, let go, let me see it."

The sound of the gunfire must have done something to his hearing. Carlos's voice sounded muffled and far away, or else deafness must be another precursor of death.

"Jesus, goddamn it!" Carlos said into his cell phone. "I need someone here right now!"

Trufant looked back at the body next to him and saw the man twitch and noticed the thick pool of deep red blood forming under the man's side. If he didn't move soon, the pool would engulf him too. He turned to Carlos and sat up.

"Calm down, Carlos, I don't think this is as bad as it looks."

"Let me see," Carlos said again.

He watched Carlos's eyes, trying to read what the man was seeing.

"How bad is it, Carlos?"

"You're a lucky bastard, Lieutenant. It's a good gash, but it looks like it missed everything. Christ, I can see your fucking trachea, though, there's a tiny nick in the cartilage. Another eighth of an inch and you'd be breathing through your neck hole. Just keep the pressure on it, rescue is on the way—I hope."

"Don't worry, I don't want to see any more of my own blood, but I do want to see what else is here before the shitstorm starts.

Get a few pictures of this guy's tattoos. Use your phone, later we can send them to Greggs in the Gang Unit and see if he knows what they are. Get a picture of that weird knife too."

Every inch of the man's back was covered in elaborate tattoos, some of it artistic, some of it done by an amateur. A green-scaled dragon's head was the tattoos' focal point. Smaller, meaningless words and symbols covered what the dragon's head didn't. Above the dragon, encircling what they could see of the man's neck, were the wings of an Egyptian bird, like a necklace of blue and red feathers.

The tattoos stopped just above the man's elbows, reminding Trufant of the Japanese mobsters seen in Hollywood movies, the Yakuza, their tattoos hidden by dress shirts and suits. In the man's hand was an ornate knife, a butterfly knife. Tiny symbols were etched or carved into the blade and handles. Blood covered most of the symbols—my blood.

"That's no doubt our murder weapon," Carlos said, looking at the thin blade.

Trufant couldn't care less at the moment.

Bastard! He wanted to kick the man in the ribs, stomp on his face, and hear his skull crush under his shoe. Instead, he knelt and looked closely at the dragon.

Everyone was getting into tattoos these days, Trufant thought, but these tattoos were different. It seemed these were personal, not to be seen by strangers, but by close family, or maybe just a reminder to the man when he looked in the mirror.

The man's one visible eye was already glazing over, looking into the gates of hell, Trufant hoped. The man looked young, maybe still in his teens, thin but muscular with close-cropped black hair, a hint of sideburns, but no other facial hair. He may have been young, but he was damned fast.

The two exit wounds were almost hidden in the tattoos. One bullet had destroyed the dragon's left eye, and it oozed the last bit of blood still in the man's lungs. The blood looked like pink foam. Several tiny bubbles popped as more surfaced and took their place.

Still clutching his throat, Trufant followed Carlos through the door into the only other room in the house.

The bedroom was as bare as the main room. The man's clothes were neatly folded on one side of the room. There was a gym bag next to the rug, and Carlos put on a pair of latex gloves and opened it. Inside the bag, he found a US passport, a Visa card, a large roll of hundred dollar bills held by a rubber band, and two photographs.

Both pictures were five by sevens on standard inkjet paper. The first one was a color copy of a United States Uniformed Service card that expired in 2008. A woman in her early thirties smiled at the camera. She would be in her early or mid-forties now.

"This is an ID card issued to spouses," Carlos said. "My wife had one too, lets you shop on the base commissary. Stephanie Marshall, and her husband is Timothy Marshall, a USMC corporal."

The second picture was of a man in his thirties walking a dog next to the Cable Car Museum in San Francisco. "David Armstrong" was printed in bold letters underneath. "Special Forces Afghanistan" was written in smaller letters on the back.

"Get a picture of those," Trufant said.

David Armstrong, Trufant said to himself. They had been searching for a man named David with a dog like that for weeks and here, this man in Chicago had his full name and a picture.

"This is fucking weird, L.T."

"What?"

"This is a US passport made out to a white female, Zoe Cruz, but the picture looks like our guy."

They heard the first siren as they turned the body over and into the pool of his own blood. Only it wasn't a man at all, it was a woman. Her dead, lifeless eyes were looking at Trufant and he moved away to avoid the stare.

"Weird enough?" Carlos asked. "Unless he cut off his own junk, this is a woman, and look at her chest."

Trufant saw a two-inch scar where each breast should have

been. The dragon's tail wrapped itself around the two scars and pointed down toward her vagina.

"This girl is young, and her face is . . . ?"

"Is what? Trufant asked.

"Androgynous?"

"Yeah, that's the word. I couldn't put my finger on it—I just assumed she was a man, maybe it was the tattoos. Damn, she was fast."

"You okay? We can sit outside and wait." Carlos said.

"No, I'm good. I've never had to fire this thing except during qualifications. It wasn't what I expected at all and it happened so damn fast."

"Come on, L.T., let's go outside and get some fresh air."

They left the body where it was and walked outside as the first patrol car skidded to a stop in the grass and weeds of the front yard.

A young officer jumped out, and Trufant was afraid the rookie was going to draw his weapon. Trufant looked down at his white dress shirt where blood had stained and seeped all the way down onto his belt. He probably would have thought of pulling his gun too if the situation was reversed.

Chapter 9

Armstrong

"C'mon boy, we're almost there."

One block ahead he saw the Legion of Honor building and knew it was now or never. He had walked six miles trying to make the decision, hoping something along the way would help him make up his mind.

It was almost seven, and he had twenty minutes to decide if he was going inside or keep walking.

Travis pulled on the leash, and he let the dog choose. It was a soft, shady spot Travis wanted, a simple green patch of grass next to a park bench.

He sat while Travis sniffed around, and from this angle, he could see the rear of the VA building. As he watched, an old white ambulance backed up to a shipping door, and two men opened the rear of the ambulance. A few seconds later they rolled a sheet-covered corpse up the ramp and through the open doors.

It was an unmarked entrance, and he knew what it was—it was the VA's morgue. Another dead soldier coming home. That was the cue he needed.

"Let's go, boy."

Travis was reluctant, but stood and followed him inside.

He found a seat in the last row. The entire front row was empty, and the next had a few women sitting near the aisles. The last three rows were almost full, and he took one of the few remaining chairs as Dr. Williams was introducing herself. Travis sat beside him and tried to camouflage himself on the black tile floor.

Tonight the doctor was wearing old Levi's and an olive green fatigue shirt with "Williams" stenciled across the left pocket. She was also thinner than he remembered.

As she spoke, he looked at each man and woman in the room. Each probably had different stories and different reasons for being here, but they each had a similar look in their eyes. Like they needed to latch on to something the doctor was saying, as if she would speak a word or sentence that would save them.

He saw another man look his way, and he nodded like men do when they pass each other in the street or in the chow line on a military base. He turned back and listened as the doctor spoke.

"No one knows what you have seen, not even the people sitting next to you," she said. "But you have all seen something that has shaken you, shaken you so hard, even you might not know what it is, or maybe you're here in support of a loved one."

Dr. Williams paused looking down at her notes, but David could see her eyes watering and her bottom lip twitching. She has a few memories of her own.

"You walk down the street and pass people every day," she said. "And you wonder what their lives would be like. You want to walk in their shoes and see what it's like to be free," she said. "Part of you wants them to know what you've seen, what you've experienced."

It was like a church sermon, and she was the preacher, and they were her flock. He listened, and he saw some of the crowd nodding as if she was speaking to them, reading their minds, and hoping she could help them. He would not have been surprised if someone stood and shouted, "Amen, sister!"

He had seen some of the horrible things she was talking about. He had plenty of those nightmares, and maybe that was the reason he had to leave everything and everybody he knew behind.

No, he didn't want anyone to know what he had seen.

He started to leave and slip out the back when the doctor announced she was taking a break. Everyone stood up and half of them headed to the exit. He had just gotten outside when he heard her voice.

"Mr. Armstrong."

She was right behind him.

"Yes, ma'am?"

"I was hoping you'd come by. Right after you left, a detective came in, and I think he was looking for you. Well . . . now that I see your dog, I know he was looking for you."

"I heard. Something about those guys getting killed a few weeks ago. I had nothing to do with it."

"I think he knows that. Your dog is beautiful. Can I pet him?"

"I'm sure he would enjoy it. His name is Travis." He winced saying the name, and she looked up.

"Travis is a handsome name, Mr. Armstrong."

"Call me David."

"I'm Brook. So, what do you think of the meeting so far?"

"Okay, I guess."

"Just okay?"

"I'm sorry, I didn't mean it like that. I see how the others are listening. They need to hear your words. It's helping them somehow."

"But not you?"

"I'm not sure I'm ready. I was just in the area and thought I would stop in."

"Does anybody know when they're ready, David?"

"I thought that was how it worked. When you're ready you'll know it."

"Well, I would love it if you would stay to the end, it's only another forty-five minutes. If I went on any longer, most everyone would leave." She laughed and he liked the sound of it.

"I'll stay, no promises though."

"Fair enough."

***

Forty-five minutes later as the crowd was shuffling outside, she turned off the lights and locked the door behind her.

Until David met Brook Williams, he hadn't noticed a woman's looks in more than a year, maybe two. She was attractive. He'd learned in his first years on the street to be wary of women. Most men would give away everything they had for a chance at sex, and the women on the road used sex as if it were a tool.

"Walk with me, David. There's an open-air coffee shop one block up, and I'll treat Travis to a scone.

"A double French dark roast and a lemon scone, please," she said to the barista. "David, do you want anything?"

"Just a regular coffee, black, please."

They sat next to a wall away from the wind as the sun set. Soon the cold wind would be blowing in from the bay, followed by thick fog, and he waited for the questions to start.

"So, tell me about your leg, any more pain?"

"It's good, thanks. I walk a lot, you know." He looked away, out toward Angel Island, afraid of what he might see in her face.

"I bet you do."

She was silent now, all he heard was Travis eating the scone from her hand.

"My father died homeless when I was in high school," she said.

He turned and looked at her as she fed his dog. That was the last thing he expected to hear. "I'm sorry."

"Yeah, me too, I was hoping he would at least make it to my graduation. It was leukemia. He left mom and me soon after the diagnosis. He was a lifer in the Air Force and made lieutenant colonel before they grounded him. It hit him pretty hard, then it was the chemo, that actually worked by the way, but it fried his brain—he was losing his short term memory . . . and one day he left us. Then we got a phone call, and he was really gone, as in deceased. That's the way my mom likes to tell it."

They sipped the last of their coffee as Travis licked the crumbs from her fingers.

"Tonight, I felt like I needed someone to talk to," she said. "I was glad when I saw you come in."

"I'm glad I could help, but I want you to know I'm addicted to heroin. It's my life now. It's all I do, trying to score the next hit. I want it to be over, I really do, but I know I'm not ready, not yet anyway."

"Dying of an overdose would scare the hell out of me," she said.

"I'm more afraid of the withdrawal than I am of death. Have you ever had the flu? After the first few days, you begin to wonder if you're dying and sometimes it feels like death would be a relief. That's what dopesick feels like."

"I'm sorry," she said.

"Me too."

Chapter 10

Trufant

The University of Illinois Hospital's emergency room smelled like every other hospital. There was no single word to describe all the smells and all the sounds, but organized chaos came close.

No one seemed happy to be there, and Doctor Deidra Wight, was no exception.

"You are one lucky man, officer," she said.

"I know. I keep hearing that," Trufant said.

The doctor stepped back and gave him the evil eye, leaving a long black suture hanging from his neck.

"What are you talking about—I'm talking about me!" she said. "You are lucky I am here today to sew up your neck. I should be at the beach, or working my abs in Zumba class, not reattaching your head."

Trufant looked at the woman in her clean scrubs, scrubs that were one size too small, and said, "Woman, you have never done abs in your life."

She held the needle and her stare a moment longer, then laughed so loud he was afraid she would pull out the last stitch.

"Come on, woman, the Novocain is wearing off."

"Serves you right!"

"Doctor, you keep jabbing with that needle and that Novocain stings like hell, can't you give me a real pain killer, morphine or something?"

"You cops are supposed to be tough guys. A woman probably wouldn't need anything for a few tiny stitches."

As the morphine worked its way up his arm, the coldness he had felt since lying on the floor of the old house was replaced by warmth. He felt the tension in his neck and back release and felt like he could finally breathe.

"That's the ticket," he said.

The door opened behind him, and a big round, redheaded man walked in.

"Lieutenant, how are you doing?" the man said.

"Much better now."

"I'm Homicide Sgt. Cameron. I see my old friend Dr. Wight is taking good care of you."

The sergeant gave the doctor a look, and Trufant couldn't tell if he was being humorous or not.

"I spoke to your partner, Lieutenant, and he gave us his statement. I'll need one from you in the next day or two, whenever you can. Maybe I can get the PD to fly me out to San Francisco." He laughed and said, "As if that would happen."

"Can't this statement stuff wait? I've got delicate work to do."

"Dee, you can't make him look any worse," Cameron said. "Oh, and Lieutenant, sorry I had to impound your gun. Ballistics needs it for a day or two, and you can have it back after your statement."

"You're leaving me in Chicago without a gun?"

"I'm way ahead of you, Lieutenant," he said, handing him an old gym bag. "It's my spare, Glock 17. Not as fancy as your Sig, of course, but it's better than nothing. I'll swap with you again when you come back. Good luck with the scar." He winked at the doctor and walked out.

"I'm sorry, but you're not going anywhere tonight, no sir," Dr. Wight said. We're keeping you here for observation."

***

One hundred and sixty stitches later, they put him in his own room with an Illinois state trooper at the door.

"Did you piss off the doctor? Those are the nastiest-looking stitches I've ever seen. It looks like she used old shoelaces," Carlos said, admiring Trufant's neck.

"Maybe. Anything new?"

"I sent Greggs the pictures of the tats. He says he needs some time to study them, but he has this so far." Amato read from his notepad, "He says it's an Eastern dragon and probably done by a master tattoo artist. He says a shrink could have a field day with it and probably get half of it wrong. One thing he does know—" he turned the iPhone so Trufant could see what he was pointing at and zoomed in.

"Hidden in the dragon's talons are the letters BNG. Greggs says it was a Filipino prison gang, the Bahala Na Gang, now more of a street gang. The fact it's obscured by the dragon probably means she was thrown out of the gang or quit and doesn't want to show their sign. He says they are known for their violence and street fighting skills."

"That makes sense," Trufant said.

"There's more, some of these other tattoos suggest she was into martial arts. See the FMA initials in the dragon's talons? They are probably meant to hide her old gang sign. FMA stands for Filipino Martial Arts. It's a style, not a gang, and its focus is knife fighting."

"I guess the good doctor was right. I was lucky."

"Greggs thinks these other symbols show she held the rank of a master. The weapon of choice for the FMA is the Balisong, or butterfly knife."

"She's dead now, and I'm alive. So fuck her and her dragon and fuck the FMA. I want to get out of here, Carlos, sitting in this bed is driving me insane."

The truth was he needed a drink. He had never fired his gun in anger and now he had killed a woman, and the feeling was not what he expected. Who was she, could he have somehow handled things differently, in a way that he could at least ask her why? Now, he would never know.

"I booked a room across the street," Carlos said, "but I'll stay here for a while. I want to talk. I'm still trying to remember how the whole thing happened. I about shit myself, LT, no lie."

"Yeah, me too. All I remember was the blur of her coming out of the doorway and swinging at me. I fell back, and I think I just flinched or something—and the gun went off. I can't remember pulling the trigger. The next thing I knew I was on the floor bleeding. She almost fucking killed me. I was a fraction of an inch from being a corpse."

"Well, at least you fired. I froze, Lieutenant, that's what bothers me. I saw her come out and I watched you fire, twice. I think I just stood there, like a spectator. The thought of pulling my gun out never occurred to me, and before I even realized the threat, she was on the ground."

"Don't be too hard on yourself, Carlos. I don't feel much better. I feel like I was just damn lucky and she wasn't."

CHAPTER 11

MOTHER

"Your sister is dead," she said, sitting in the dark.

She waited, listening to the silence and watched as the puffs of smoke escaped her mouth with each word, then dissipated in the dim light of the phone.

She wondered if he could still understand her. Her voice, always deep, was deeper now, and the cigarettes were determined to finish off what little voice she had left.

"Did you hear what I said?"

"How?"

"The cop, Trufant, the one from San Francisco, shot her."

"Madinah was here?"

"No, he was at the house in Chicago."

Another painful silence but she knew better than to rush him. He had always been slow to speak what was on his mind, and it was hard to picture the boy running through the backyard laughing so many years ago.

"Then I will kill Trufant, also."

"The woman must be first. I want her to suffer in front of her husband the way I suffered, then the policeman, and I want pictures, Ramzi!"

"David Armstrong will be first, Mother!"

"Why him when this other man killed your sister?"

"You know why, Mother. He saw me kill those men. He

shamed me and you know it. Now I cannot eat or sleep. I cannot let him live."

"Your shame is more important than your sister's life?"

There was a long pause again but she could hear his breathing.

"It's different, Mother."

"Madinah is in a county morgue, alone." She hoped that would motivate him to kill the detective first, but he ignored her. "I have made arrangements to retrieve her body."

"Where are you taking her?"

"She's coming here. She deserves a Christian burial."

"She despised religion, Mother," her son said.

A coughing fit stopped her from cursing him. Spitting the bloody phlegm into the ash tray sent a cloud of ashes into the air, causing another fit.

"She was born a Christian and she will be buried as one," she said, her voice just a hoarse whisper now. "So, are you coming here or not?"

No answer.

"I left a message for Leilah. She may come, she may not, and I expect Madinah's body to arrive Friday. I would not be surprised to find the Chicago police too far behind, but I have made arrangements."

The police would resist giving up the body. They would want to question anyone showing an interest in her—a Jane Doe with a forged passport, a woman who had tried to kill one of their own. As much as she hated the lawyer, he was willing to get a court order and arrange the transportation. Money was always the key to solving her problems in that wretched country.

She heard a change in the noise level and knew he had ended the call.

"Damn him!"

God had forsaken her, made her and her family suffer needlessly, and she refused to speak to Him even now, but she would bury her child in a Christian ceremony whether Jesus approved of it or not.

Snuffing out the glowing stub of the Gold Flake King between her finger and thumb, she pulled another out of the box, ripped off the filter, and lit the ragged end.

CHAPTER 12

TRUFANT

The itching on his neck started two days later over Iowa. Trufant stuck his finger under the gauze bandage and felt the still-tacky blood around the stitches, but he removed the gauze anyway and stuffed it inside a puke bag in the seatback. He felt instant relief.

"Seriously, L.T.?" Carlos said. "Every germ on this plane is going to land right on your neck."

"Screw it. It itches, and no germ is going to do more damage than the knife did."

The flight attendant made her way toward their row, and he asked her for a Jack Daniels.

"Oh my God!" She recoiled and almost dropped her tray on the man in front of them, then he noticed the entire cabin section was staring at him.

"Jeez, you look like Frankenstein," Carlos said.

The whiskey went down smooth, so Trufant asked the attendant for another.

Through Carlos's window, Trufant saw the last of the daylight wink out, replaced by the single green navigation light at the end of the wing.

"Hell of a week, Carlos, hell of a week."

"Yes, sir, it was. So the million-dollar question is, do you think it's over? Do you think she was our killer?"

"I'm hoping she was, Carlos, I'm sure hoping. You have people searching for Armstrong and the Marshall woman on the military ID card, right?"

"Yes, a couple of local hits came up on Armstrong before we left, no warrants, just a few misdemeanors. Nothing on the woman, though, she's probably moved a few times since that card was issued."

"I worry about them, Carlos. I have the feeling they were her next targets."

"Well, she's dead, she's not going to kill anybody now."

"I hope you're right."

"December 1st is still five months away, L.T."

"Then that gives us five months to prove it."

The Jack Daniels was satisfying that insatiable need. His entire nervous system had been on fire since he walked out of the hospital, and he could feel the whiskey working on his nerves the same way the morphine had killed his pain.

Easing his seat back, he ignored the complaint behind him and closed his eyes . . . and he was back in the dilapidated house again, he could smell the old wood and mold, he heard the floor creak and the woman was in front of him, the knife swinging up toward his throat in a slow arc. Daylight from an open window reflected off the blade as it passed by his throat and a tiny drop of crimson flew in slow motion across his vision.

He opened his eyes, and Carlos was staring at him, a look of concern etched on his face.

"I'm good," Trufant said.

He looked up and turned the cabin light on, afraid to close his eyes again.

He brought his seat back upright and wondered if Adelaide had heard the news yet. There were times she would have felt it, like ESP. She always knew when something bad had happened, and she would be at the door, waiting. They were that close once, but the bond had disintegrated, and now he was alone.

Although he'd shredded the first set of divorce papers, there would be more, and he decided he would sign the next set and move on with his life. Six more years and he would have his thirty and retire, the last goal in his life, but that life was supposed to include Adelaide.

I'm going to put an end to this case, I'm going to forget about Lozano, and I'm going to quit drinking. I am not my father, it's just this damned case.

***

Walter Trufant had been a hard worker, and a hard drinker. As a kid in primary school, Trufant remembered his father coming home late at night, listening to the arguments with his mother, and finding him sleeping in the living room the next day. Trufant was thirteen when he found his father on the bathroom floor, lying in a puddle of his own vomit. That image stayed with him into his adult life, and he swore to his mother and himself he would never drink alcohol.

Trufant tried to recall when he broke his vow and started drinking. It was sometime after the third veteran's homicide went cold. It was his case to investigate, and to solve, and like the two previous deaths, he didn't have a single clue. Three victims slaughtered on his watch, and his marriage began to fall apart.

***

The hydraulic pumps whined beneath his feet, and he felt the plane decelerating, then start a turn to the left and the lights of San Francisco were in the window. As the wheels touched down, he felt his tension ease. He was home now, on familiar ground, and the feeling of being a victim was replaced by something feral–-he was the predator now.

The plane was still taxiing to the gate when his phone vibrated.

"Asshole," he whispered, looking at the message on the phone. "What now?"

"The chief wants me in Internal Affairs tomorrow morning."

"You're good, L.T, no one can fault you. It was a good shoot, and it was in Chicago."

"You don't know the chief like I do, Carlos. I called him out on something years ago when we were both patrol officers, and he's made me suffer for it ever since."

"Tell me," Carlos said.

"Fifteen years ago, maybe sixteen, he arrested some kid for burglary. It was a shaky arrest, and he falsified some of what he put on the arrest form and wanted me to cosign and I refused. Later he charged the kid with a half dozen open burglary cases. He was up for promotion, and we all knew he was padding his stats. The kid spent two years in prison. A year later I was in Burglary, and I arrested someone who admitted breaking into the homes the kid had been charged with. I proved it, and he's had a hard-on for me ever since."

"Shit," Carlos said. "He's in tight with the mayor too, but how are they going to put a negative spin on this? You shot a possible serial killer."

"The mayor was the one who promoted him. Just watch and see what happens."

***

Silence greeted Trufant and not even the hum of his refrigerator welcomed him home.

Dead tired, he poured a full glass from the last bottle of Adelaide's favorite merlot and sat in the recliner listening to Stan Getz playing sax. The wine was smooth and warmed his chest as it made its way down. Swirling the wine in his glass reminded him of his father, who had done the same thing forty-five years ago.

Never! He had promised his mother.

But some promises weren't meant to be kept. At first, it was Adelaide's idea. "Try it Marcus, it will relieve the tension." Then he developed a taste for the sweet red wine. Something about that simple glass of wine did ease his anxiety, as if his nervous system had a volume knob and the wine could mute it slightly, bringing the level down to a comfortable setting, but he seldom drank more than a glass, and never alone, that is, until things began to go south.

He closed his eyes, listening to the smooth saxophone on his vintage stereo, and was snoring twenty minutes later, an empty glass on his lap.

A text message on his phone woke him six hours later.

Weak sunlight coming through the curtains hurt his eyes. Still in the recliner, he tried to remember what he had done last night when the wine glass rolled off his lap and shattered.

Sweeping up the crystal shards, he was relieved to see the wine bottle was still half-full. *It's just been a rough couple of days.*

***

Three days' worth of reports sat waiting on his desk the next morning, reports that would have to wait another day or two.

He swept them all into a pile and walked out of the office. He found Inspector John Greggs alone on the third floor. Internal Affairs would have to wait.

"Damn, when are you going to get those stitches out, Lieutenant?"

"Soon, but I kind of like them—they keep people out of my office. John, look at these photos again and tell me everything you see."

Greggs spread out the high resolution eight by tens and started with the woman's back.

"Okay, this is your basic Chinese Dragon. It has five toes, which means royalty, or sometimes purity. On a woman, it also signifies strength and protection. On a man, it can include power and violence. I bring up masculinity because the fact she had her breasts removed tells me she may have been transgender."

Both men stared at the photo of the dead woman. "In reality," Greggs continued, "the dragon signifies whatever the artist and the customer want it to. All too often a customer comes in having no idea what they want. They open a catalog and pick out whatever looks cool to them at the time. Not so with this girl, though, these are messages. The tail pointing to her crotch is either a warning or a threat, like go there and you'll die.

"The BNG we talked about on the phone. When you cover up a gang sign, it's a sign of either disgrace or contempt. This FMA, however, is obviously important to her. It's bold," he said pointing to the letters," and the dragon is wielding it like a weapon."

"What about these feathers around her neck?" Trufant said.

"They are the wings of Isis. Isis had many roles in mythology. In some, she helped restore the souls of the dead and help them pass into the afterlife. This last one I had to look up. Sky-Ba was also known as Petbe, he's the god of revenge."

"Revenge, that's the key. But revenge for what?" Trufant said.

"Lieutenant, you see all these diagonal slashes, like hash marks? In gang tats they usually mean kills. There are twelve of them here, and the redness around this last one tells me it's fresh."

"Nice woman."

The big Irishman looked back at the photos and said, "This girl was fucked up, for sure."

"She's killing US soldiers," Trufant said. "Do you see anything to make you think she may have been a religious fanatic, or a terrorist?"

"Not really, I think we would see something obvious to indicate those. But this girl was making a bold statement. If anything, I see sex and revenge," Greggs said. "I can't put it all together for you, to her it all probably makes sense. I would go up to Psych and talk to Kira Pinchon, she's young, but she knows what she's doing."

"Okay thanks, Greggs, call me if you think of anything else."

"Will do L.T., keep your head down, that was a close one."

"Don't I know it."

***

He took the stairs two at a time, knowing there was a good chance the chief would be in the elevator. At eleven-fifteen every day, he and his compadres left for lunch and by two-thirty they would be on their way back up.

Several times he had recommended the chief send Kira to Quantico's Behavioral Research and Instruction Unit to become a certified profiler, and each time the man rejected it. It would add another line to the psychologist résumé and the term criminal profiler always impressed a jury.

The department needed its own profiler, a fact he had spelled out in great detail, but the chief ignored it. He knew it was important to frustrate his senior homicide lieutenant whenever he could. Trufant decided that next time, he'd have Lt. Gracia make the request.

Kira's door was open and Trufant helped himself to a seat.

"That wound looks horrible, Lieutenant," the young woman said.

"Thank you, you're not the first person to point that out. Kira, do you have anything for a headache?"

His head ached, a deep throb in the middle of his brain. How much sleep had he gotten in the last week? Not enough, probably.

"Tylenol okay? I heard most of what happened, but I want to hear all about it from you one day. I'm sure it's fascinating. But truthfully, I can't wait to hear about this woman. What have you got?"

He spread the photos on her desk like a giant colorful deck of cards, but there were no jokers in this hand. Instead, there were photos of all the homicide victims and those of the girl in Chicago.

"My God, how awful, I heard some of the background on these homicides. I want to hear what the FBI profiler says. I want her take on it after I've made mine."

Kira was silent as she studied the photos of the girl. "A lot of symbolism here, Marcus."

"The tattoos?"

"Yes, and the mutilation. I would talk to the ME in Chicago and get her opinion on the mastectomy. How recent was it and just how surgical. This is not something you can do with a paring knife in your garage."

"I'll be honest, I was in no shape to examine her at the time."

"It must have been horrifying, Marcus."

"It was so quick I didn't have time to be horrified. But *now* I'm horrified. I can't sleep more than a few hours at a time. I had often pictured what it would be like to shoot someone, to intend to kill another human being, but Kira, it was nothing like I expected."

"Come see me when you're ready to talk about it, Marcus, maybe I can help you with that."

She picked up the picture of the girl lying on the stainless table in a Chicago morgue.

"I wonder if she thought she was denying men the opportunity to admire her, cutting off her breasts to spite them. And I think the tattoos themselves are another form of mutilation. Any one of them could be beautiful, but put them together with her history and she's a walking billboard for chaos and revenge."

"It's interesting you said that, Kira. Greggs said he saw sex and revenge."

"Well, I would add anger in there too," she said.

***

The drive home seemed longer than normal, the traffic heavier, and it was tough to stay focused on the cars all around him. Bits and pieces of the scene in the old house kept creeping back from wherever he wanted them locked away.

The blade slashed out in front of him again for the hundredth time, and he was almost rear-ended when he slammed on the brakes. One passing driver flashed him the finger and raced off before he could do the same.

"Bastard!"

He made it to his building, parked, and waited for the elevator. As the door opened, his neighbor, who was also his wife's new lawyer, stepped out, startling him and he started to reach for his Sig Sauer.

"Hey, Marcus, how are you feeling? I heard what happened in Chicago. Tell me all about it one day, I gotta run. See you."

And then the man was gone.

Adelaide had heard about it after all.

"No, I don't think I will tell you about it at all," he said to himself.

***

His frozen dinner tasted like warm paste and garlic, but the wine was delicious. He switched on the television, muted the volume, and turned on the stereo, carefully setting the needle down on the first track of an old vinyl LP.

Pouring a second glass, he closed his eyes and tried to listen to Stan Getz, but the image of the tattooed girl kept forcing its way into his consciousness. He poured a third glass and walked over to the window and stared out at the city lights.

Somewhere out there, people were leading normal lives, sitting at their dinner tables with their families, making small talk and never seeing the things he had.

***

Once again the buzzing of his phone woke him just after dawn. He had slept in the recliner again, two days in a row, but this time, the wine bottle was empty and another was open on the table next to him. He was into the cheap wine now, and his headache was worse than ever.

The lasagna tray next to the recliner was only half-eaten and the smell of garlic and cheese nauseated him.

Jesus, his eyes burned and his throat felt like he had been

eating sand, but what scared him was, he couldn't remember opening the second bottle.

Shit, Marcus, it was just a rough day, Adelaide whispered.

***

Another bad night and another migraine and only a single Advil in the medicine cabinet, the bottle of oxycodone Dr. Wight had prescribed was still full, though. He took one and remembered the message on his phone.

The text was thirty minutes old, demanding he be in the chief's office at 8 a.m. It was already ten past eight, and twenty minutes later he was fighting rush hour traffic and cursing that first glass of wine.

***

At 9:15, he was sitting next to a window on the sixth floor in the chief's office watching a big blue freighter ease away from the pier below. His head was clear now, and he felt relaxed and confident, a by-product of the pain killer perhaps, but he was still thankful. He wanted to be sharp sitting with the chief, and a hangover would have made the meeting unbearable.

Twenty-five minutes later he was still waiting, and the ship was now making its turn to the north, probably bound for some foreign port. Anxiety was beginning to inch its way back into his consciousness and he struggled to sit still. He shifted his weight in the chair but still felt uncomfortable, stood, and looked out the window at the horizon again.

Damn this man!

He knew the chief well enough to know this was a game to him, payback for ignoring him the last couple of days. He checked the time on his phone and was ready to leave when Lozano's clerk-typist came through the door.

"The chief will see you now, Lieutenant."

He saw the smugness on the clerk's face, had something humorous just happened behind the closed door? Did it involve him? Of course, it did.

"Trufant, have a seat," the chief said, sitting in his high-backed, opulent desk chair.

Trufant noticed the regular chair, the nice one that was usually placed opposite the chief, had been moved to the far side of the room. The one in front of the desk now was a simple office chair made of chrome tubes and plastic, probably brought up from the mailroom minutes before he walked in.

He walked over to the better chair and dragged it back across the carpet until he could sit face-to-face with the man. The chief's already red face flushed, highlighting the spidery veins around his nose that spread out onto his cheeks.

"What the fuck are you doing, Trufant? You think you can come into my office and move shit around?"

"I wanted to be comfortable, Chief. You should ease up, you know. All this anger is bad for your blood pressure."

"Trufant, I'm thinking of replacing you on this investigation. I don't think you're up to the task anymore, and to be honest, I don't like the way you have handled things. Look at yourself, you look like shit. Christ, some little girl almost killed you. Maybe you're getting a little too old to be out on the street."

"Who's going to find these killers, Chief—you?"

"Anyone would be an improvement, and why didn't you report to Internal Affairs? That was an order, Lieutenant. Maybe a demotion back to sergeant will improve your attitude. I am the chief of police, in case you've forgotten."

"Chief, you would have been fired years ago if not for your cozy relationship with the mayor, and are you aware of what happened in Chicago? Do you know how big this case is? And it's not just in San Francisco, it's Chicago, Florida, and who knows where else? There could be others out there, this girl didn't work alone, and now the FBI is involved. This wasn't some local burglar you can pin false charges on."

"There's the Trufant I remember, champion of the destitute! You're an asshole, Trufant, I arrested that fucking wetback, and you freed him—big fucking deal. You think that makes you a hero?"

Trufant pulled out his iPhone and held it up for the man to see.

"Hero? No, but I hear you may be running for mayor next year, Chief. I'll bet you're hoping right now I didn't record you referring to a third of your voters as wetbacks."

Lozano jerked himself up from the chair, looking at the phone, and his false bravado vanished.

"You know, Chief, if you and that Mexican kid were drowning in a car, and I could only save one of you, which one do you think I would save? Which one of you is the better man?"

"You will report to Internal Affairs right now, you hear me? If I find you were recording our conversation, I'll demote you today, and if you don't give IA a statement, I will demote you then too. You will be lucky to have a job next week, Trufant, now get out of my office."

***

Internal Affairs was waiting for him, two sergeants and a captain, all friends of the chief, or compadres, as he liked to call them. They sat at a long table, and he took a seat across from them.

"Lt. Trufant," Captain Brown said, smiling, "I want to see your phone."

"Which one?" Trufant answered.

The captain's smile faded, "How many do you have?"

"Two, my personal phone and the one issued to me by the department."

Trufant saw the hesitation on the captain's face, and he handed him the city's phone.

"Did you record a conversation with the chief just now or at any other time?"

"No, I did not. The lock code on that phone is my ID number."

"Can I see your personal phone?"

"No, you cannot."

"Lieutenant, city policy states you cannot have personal electronics on your person while on duty."

"Captain, you have one on you right now. I can see it in your pocket, and I know it's not a department-issued phone."

One of the sergeants smiled, and the captain changed the subject.

"Lieutenant Trufant, you were ordered by the chief to come in and give a statement regarding your shooting in Chicago and you failed to appear."

"I've been busy and I almost died. It's all related to the homicides I'm working on. I can understand being up here on the fourth floor you don't get out much, you haven't had to confront real criminals in years, but a serial killer was working in San Francisco. Hopefully, the dead woman in Chicago was our killer, but it's still a dangerous world out there, Captain." He loosened his tie, pulling the collar down to expose the length and thickness of the scar. "I'm more afraid of people like her than missing an internal affairs appointment with you."

"Let's talk about that shooting in Chicago," Brown said.

"I can probably have my union representative here day after tomorrow morning, if that's convenient for you."

"I want to talk about it now."

"Captain, you know I'm not going to give you a statement without a rep. I tried to set one up with you as soon as we landed, and you wouldn't return my emails."

"So you're refusing to give a statement?"

"No, I am not. I'll be here day after tomorrow with my union representative as per our contract, and I'll be glad to give you a statement."

"Why not tomorrow?"

"I'll be in Chicago giving their homicide detectives my statement, remember?" he said, tapping the scars under his collar.

"Lieutenant, I am making a permanent note in your personnel

file stating that you failed to show for a previously scheduled statement regarding a-use-of-force, and that you carry an unauthorized cell phone. You can leave now, and I will see you at nine o'clock day after tomorrow."

***

That went well, he thought, as he waited for the elevator to take him back down to his floor. When the doors opened, the chief and his clerk-typist were inside staring at him. Trufant looked at his watch—eleven-fifteen on the dot.

He stepped in and enjoyed the awkwardness of the moment as the car descended to the Investigation Division. He could feel both men staring at his back as he watched their reflection in the stainless steel doors. The car seemed to be moving slower than usual, and the chime announcing each floor was louder than he remembered.

Finally, the doors slid open on his floor.

"Have a nice lunch!" he said, before the doors closed.

***

The flight was boring and cramped in coach, and after a three-hour statement with Chicago's state attorney and a room full of detectives, he found himself on a similarly cramped flight back to San Francisco.

The return flight was a rough one. Turbulence over the Rockies was so bad the flight attendants canceled the beverage service, and after relating the death of a woman and how she had cut his throat, he needed a drink.

Flying west was like time travel, and by midafternoon he was sitting in his office with the door closed, a pile of morbid photos and reports from the scene in Chicago spread out across his desk. He stared at them, wanting something to jump off the pages and give him a hint, another lead to follow, anything!

His phone chirped, a call from Carlos. "Lieutenant, I got a lead on the wife in the photo, her last known address is just outside of Oakland. I called their sheriff, and he's sending a car by. I'm heading there now to talk to her."

"Okay, Carlos, I'm running down a few leads at the station, let me know what you find."

Reading the crime scene report from Chicago again left him with more questions than answers.

The big question was, is it over? Was she working alone or is there another one out there?

Everything he saw in the photos told him she had been there only a few hours, maybe a day at most. So where did she come from? Where did she live?

So far, she was a Jane Doe. Her passport was forged, a good one, but still a forgery. The stamps were real, though. Chicago detectives had found out that six months ago the woman had traveled by bus from Buffalo to Toronto, then by air to Singapore and back to Chicago, arriving the day before the two men were killed on Mason Street. She would have been hard-pressed to backtrack to San Francisco and kill them. Why not just land at SFO and do it?

The pictures and the reports were like a half-completed jigsaw puzzle, and none of his pieces were matching up.

His phone chirped, Carlos again. "Lieutenant, she and her husband are dead. You need to come out here now. I'm texting you the address. Come quick."

Trufant looked at his watch and called his psychologist. "Kira, grab your things, you're coming with me."

He tore through the afternoon rush hour traffic and looked over at the terrified psychologist sitting next to him. The fingers on her right hand had a death grip on the door handle, and her left was braced against the dashboard.

"Relax, Kira, I took a course in pursuit driving twenty-four years ago." His humor fell flat, as Kira pressed her feet into the floorboards and stared wide-eyed at the traffic through the windshield.

Trufant stood on the gas pedal and raced onto the first section of the Bay Bridge, ignoring the horns and screeching tires behind him until traffic came to a complete stop. He considered sticking the blue strobe light on the roof, but cars and trucks were bottlenecked, and the blue light would just add confusion to the already frustrated drivers.

"What did he say?" she asked as they waited. "I've never been on a crime scene, you know. I'm already feeling nauseous, and I'm not sure it's just your driving."

"Carlos said we were too late . . . and that it was bad. You wanted to be the department's profiler, and this is what it's all about, Kira, today will be your first day of training. Just look around, put yourself in the killer's shoes, and try to feel what it must take to do what he did. Put yourself in the victim's shoes too—try to understand what they were feeling. I'm not an expert. I tried thinking along those lines once, and it slowed me down, it distracted me. I don't have the time to get emotional."

As he drove, he prayed that the crime scene was old, and that the victims had been killed last week by the woman in Chicago. He needed this to be over, but somehow, he knew it was just beginning.

The traffic was moving again, and fifteen minutes later they pulled into a rural lot with a dozen marked and unmarked police cars and TV trucks lined up and down the street. A crowd of reporters milled behind yellow crime scene tape, watching him, and one shouted out to him.

"Lieutenant Trufant!"

He ignored the reporter and led Kira by the arm. "This is what we call a shitstorm, Kira."

A uniformed officer met them at the sidewalk, handing them a pair of disposable booties and nitrile gloves.

"Please sign in, sir. You're both cleared to enter the living room only. Stay there until you're authorized by the crime scene detective."

As they stepped in, Trufant could smell it already: the blood, the urine, and the fecal odors all mixing together—a typical homicide scene, but not one that was a week old, this one was fresh. He looked over at the psychologist and tried to read the emotions on her face.

"You get used to it after a while. It's never pleasant, but it gets bearable."

Carlos and another woman came up from the basement, and Carlos introduced her to Trufant as Oakland's Homicide Lieutenant, Jessica Nelson.

"And your name, ma'am?" Lt. Nelson asked.

"Kira Pinchon. I'm our department's psychologist."

"Nice to meet you," Nelson smiled but looked uneasy. "Carlos told me about Chicago, great job, and I like your souvenir, sir," Nelson said, looking at Trufant's still-healing scar.

Trufant felt the stitches in his neck and decided he had played with them long enough.

"Before we go down there, Lt. Trufant," she spoke to him but her eyes were on Kira. "I want to warn you, this is bad, and it's personal."

"To me?" he asked.

"I'm afraid so. I'll need you both to put on a full suit, not for your protection, it's for the scene. Everything's been laser scanned and mapped down there as well as up here, but we're still lifting prints and fluid samples, so please don't step in or touch anything. The FBI is on the way too, and I have a feeling the Feeb's are going to kick us out as soon as they arrive."

Dressed in white Tyvek suits and masks, the four of them walked down the wooden staircase and into the basement.

Trufant took in the entire scene and looked over at his psychologist. She was pale and frozen on the last step of the staircase, staring at the nude body slumped across a heavy chair.

"Take a second and analyze what you see. Don't think of her as a person, she is now just part of your scene, so when you're ready, move forward."

Trufant saw the chalk marks indicating the safe route to both bodies. They had probably already used an alternate light source to pick out bodily fluids and had determined where they could walk.

The woman's face was not visible. Her blonde hair hung forward like a golden curtain, resting in the crimson pool of her own blood. Trufant saw each strand of her hair had wicked up the red fluid like a burning candle feeds on liquid wax.

There were different shades of blood, on her and on the floor. Some was brown, already dried, while most was still red and fresh, no more than an hour old. She had been tortured for hours.

The man's body was close by, curled in a fetal position. He was dressed as if he had been jogging, but his shoes were off to one side, and one of his white socks was stuffed into his mouth. The blood around his throat was thick and coagulated but still looked fresh. He had died last.

Next to his hands, a bloody butterfly knife rested on a sheet of paper.

"What's this?" Trufant said.

"This is the personal part," Lt. Nelson said. "We took a photo of the note before we knew the FBI was on the way." She showed him the image on her phone. Written in block letters were three words: "You're next, Trufant." At the bottom of the page was a picture of him standing at the crime scene on Mason Street, taken weeks before.

"That knife is an exact copy of the one that sliced open my throat," Trufant said.

Now, he looked around the room as a bystander and saw the horror for what it was. Gruesome. Maybe the worst scene he could recall.

"Carlos, I guess our woman in Chicago wasn't the end we'd hoped for. We need to find Armstrong fast. Can you take care of that? Get as many people as you can, check St. Vincent and go to the VA again. Get with the doctor I spoke with, I think she has an idea who he is. Dr. Williams is her name. Tell her Armstrong is in grave danger."

"You're in danger too, Lieutenant," Carlos said. Maybe we all are now."

Trufant couldn't think about that right now. There were clues here—the note was hand written, now they had another weapon, possibly fingerprints, and hopefully, some DNA.

He looked back at the woman once again, but this time as an investigator. He knew what happened here. At first, it appeared the woman was the target. She was meant to suffer, but Trufant suspected that the husband may have been the actual target, made to watch as his wife was tortured and defiled. At some point, the killer felt he had reached his objective and finished them both off.

"You have positive IDs on them yet?" he asked.

"Nothing positive yet, we haven't touched them, but we're pretty sure it's Marshall and his wife."

He thought of the smiling woman in the photograph and wanted to hold on to that image, not the one in front of him.

Kira had stepped off the landing and was a few feet closer to the woman now.

"What do you see now, Kira?"

"She was supposed to suffer as long as possible, I would say. I can't see it, but she's probably gagged, and her screaming would have been intense. She could have blacked out several times and come to only for him to start again. There are many long lacerations along her back, just deep enough to bleed. No obvious sign of sexual battery, but the way she's positioned over the chair tells me the killer wanted to humiliate her, or her husband."

"I agree," Nelson said. "The FBI guys said not to touch anything else, and my captain promised him we wouldn't."

At that moment, the FBI's deputy director, Lee Merriweather, came down the stairs and ordered everyone out.

Nelson looked at Trufant and winked. "Let's go outside and compare notes while these Feeb guys dick around."

Trufant noticed the color was coming back into Kira's cheeks as they stepped outside and into fresh air.

"Remember how I described the woman in Chicago," she said,

"the tattoos, the self-mutilation, what she may have been capable of and the things that may have driven her? I have that same feeling here. Some very strange, ritualistic need, but that woman is dead, so there is another one out there—just like her."

He agreed, and he knew things had changed.

"The dates are no longer critical to whoever killed these two victims. He or they are going to be killing at random now," he said. "They all do, eventually. He's off the leash now."

CHAPTER 13

ARMSTRONG

Armstrong sat on a bench in brilliant sunlight, a Styrofoam cup of hot coffee in one hand, watching the steam blow downwind toward the bay. He had spent a dollar on cheap coffee hoping the caffeine would kill the jitters.

It had been twelve hours since his last bag of China White. The powerful synthetic was killing addicts throughout San Francisco, but it was all he had been able to find. His fear of dying still controlled his addiction to a point, but eventually he would need to do it all again. Even now he knew he would use the last ten dollars in his pocket to buy another bag.

The aches always seemed worse after China White. The fentanyl that was mixed in with the heroin left him with dry mouth, chills, and paranoia, and they were running rampant now. He had hoped the caffeine might help.

Dr. Williams was right about some things: "You want to walk in their shoes and see what it's like to be free of addiction."

He needed to be free all right, but he wasn't free, wandering the streets tied to a drug he had no control of was anything but freedom. What he needed was to reengage with his old life, to be who he was long ago.

But Williams was wrong about other things: "Part of you wants them to know what you've seen and what you've experienced."

He wasn't going to share anything with anybody. His experiences then and now were private, and to speak of them would dishonor his memory of Travis, and who in their right mind would want to know something so painful? And there was Caitlin—when he left her, he had betrayed her and broken her heart, one of the most sacred of wedding vows.

"We can work this out, David, there is nothing we can't handle together," she'd said.

The first time he saw her, he knew he was going to marry her. It was during the summer at Camp Pendleton, and she was waitressing at her mother's restaurant just off the base. She was a beautiful woman, dressed in a red checkered uniform and white apron. But it wasn't just her beauty, he felt like he had known her his whole life, and he just knew.

"Hey, Armstrong," Travis had said that afternoon. "Are we here to eat or what?"

"I'm going to ask that woman to marry me, Travis, and she will say yes."

Travis had laughed his loud guffaw as if that was the craziest thing he had ever heard, loud enough that she turned and smiled.

"Can I help you?" she asked.

"I would like to propose to you if you don't mind."

"Well, Mr. Armstrong," she said, looking at the name on his fatigue shirt, "you are the third soldier to ask me today."

Travis laughed again.

"Well, I am a Marine, and I am the one you are going to marry, maybe not today, but soon."

It took her two months to say yes, but they were married in the First Baptist Church of Oceanside that October.

Sitting in the sun, he felt the hot tears run down his face and that beautiful image of Cait in her gown vanished.

I'm a coward.

The thought of seeing Caitlin in real life terrified him now. Those memories, those experiences, they were going to drive him insane. He wanted to lock them away forever, but there were days that they were all he had and he knew that part of him wanted that life back.

But he had to beat heroin before that could happen, and it seemed these memories were fueling his addiction.

"It's like I'm stuck on the merry-go-round from hell, Travis."

The dog looked up and whined. *Maybe he can sense what's happening to me.*

He threw the cup in the trash just as Travis pulled hard on the leash, then just as quickly, backed up and hid under his leg. The dog was shaking uncontrollably.

He had seen Travis afraid just once, weeks ago on Mason Street.

"What is it, boy?"

The dog was watching a man walking toward them, probably a kid in college. He made eye contact and in that instant Armstrong felt a chill. The guy looked like every other person in the throng around him, but there was something in his eyes, something cold, something that made his skin crawl.

The kid looked away just as quickly but kept coming toward him. The dog's whine turned into a growl, and Travis stood up, baring his teeth.

He had never seen the dog act this way. Travis wasn't afraid now, he was ready to fight. The fur along the dog's back bristled, and his white fangs repeatedly snapped as he pulled hard on the leash. The kid saw it too, turned away and vanished just as quickly as he had appeared.

Armstrong stood up and looked for him, a young guy with a bright yellow sweatshirt, but he was gone, swallowed up by a sea of pedestrians.

"Who was it, Travis, was it him?"

He didn't have to ask, he felt it. That same creepy sensation he had that night on Mason Street.

The kid was gone, but now another man stood in front of him. This man was Hispanic, a little older, in his late twenties, and dressed in a gray suit. Travis relaxed and sat but kept watching the crowd, his brown eyes darting back and forth and sniffing upwind trying to catch a scent of the man. The dog had no interest in this new man.

"Mr. Armstrong? David Armstrong?"

For a half-second he thought of running, but he was sitting on a bus bench, the man was right on top of him, and he had Travis. Where would he go?

"Yes."

"I'm Inspector Amato, SFPD. We need to talk."

"Have a seat."

"I don't think it's safe to talk here. I'd rather go somewhere else, even if it's sitting in my car. I have a story to tell you, and I think you have one to tell me."

"Travis will have to come with me."

"No problem."

***

The white, unmarked Ford Taurus pulled into city hall, and the three of them sat on a concrete bench in the building's tree-lined atrium.

"Mr. Armstrong, three weeks ago two men were murdered, and you were there. Tell me what you saw."

He looked down at Travis and thought, was it three weeks ago?

"You saw me on the camera, right?" Armstrong said. "You know I didn't kill them."

"We know, but you saw the man who did. Can you tell me anything about him? Could you recognize him if you saw him again?"

"Well," he said, thinking of the man he just saw in the park, "I'm not even sure it was a man. I never saw his face, but I knew he killed them and Travis knew too."

"We think whoever killed them saw you, and we think you're in danger."

"How would he know who I am?"

"We don't know," Carlos said. "We've been beating the bushes looking for you for three weeks, and it's possible he heard about our search. He killed two more people just a few hours ago, and I think you may be next."

Carlos told him about the veterans who were killed in Miami, Chicago, San Francisco, and that there might be others. Then he told him about the tattooed woman in Chicago. "She had your picture, Mr. Armstrong," Carlos said. "It was taken within days of those first two homicides on Mason Street. There was a second picture of a woman, a Marine's wife. She and her husband were the ones slaughtered in Oakland today."

"I don't understand, why me?"

"I don't know. I do know the guy is a fucking maniac, you're a veteran, and maybe that is all it takes, who knows, but he's targeted you, and now you and my lieutenant are on his list."

"I think I just saw him at the park, just before you walked up. I think it was him—the way he moved, so smooth like he glides when he walks, and his eyes."

"What about his eyes, tell me what you saw."

"He was looking at me, staring, but like I was his target. I know the look. It's like tunnel vision, you see your target and nothing else. Like a soldier on a mission."

"Tell me what he looked like."

"Just an average looking kid. I think Travis recognized him, the smell maybe."

"You said he was a kid?"

"Not a kid, twenty or so. I think he was a student, dressed all preppy with a backpack, and I think he was wearing a yellow college sweatshirt. He was thin, and I thought nothing of it . . . except for the brief second we made eye contact. It was creepy, but it was so quick, then Travis reacted."

"Would you recognize him again?"

"I'm really not sure. His face was strange, so . . . "

"What do you mean?"

"I'm not even sure it was a guy, Inspector."

"You think it could have been a woman?"

"It could have been. I thought it was a guy at first, but now I'm not sure. His face was . . . "

"Androgynous?"

"Yes, something like that."

Amato pulled out another photo. "Something like this woman?"

It was a hard picture to look at, and at first, he thought no, the guy didn't look anything like this tattooed person, but as he studied her face and blocked out everything else, he thought she could look similar.

"To be honest, I'm not sure, yes, maybe, same hairstyle, same age."

"Well, that's more than we knew earlier, Mr. Armstrong."

"What do you want me to do?"

"Is there a different place you can stay, someplace new?"

Armstrong laughed. "Look at me, Inspector, last night I slept under a bridge, and I was going to sleep in that park tonight. I can stay at the Presidio. Travis and I will be safe there. I . . . I'm struggling right now with—shit, I'll just tell you. I'm a heroin addict, and I'm on the verge of withdrawal. I've wanted to see if I could . . . could quit, but I can't, not yet."

"Let's go, Mr. Armstrong. I'll take you there, but I need you to stay in touch with me or my partner. You may be our only lead on this guy, and something has changed, he's changed, and we think things are going to get worse."

CHAPTER 14

TRUFANT

The sun had set and now the dark of night ruled the Pacific. Fog horns bleated, a dog barked somewhere down the street, and John Lee Hooker's "Chill Out," played through Trufant's stereo.

He stared at the living room's far wall, the only wall without a window or decorations, barren of all distractions. His eyes were focused far beyond the wall though, miles away . . . in the Marshall's basement. The knife, the note, the new clues, the changing modus operandi, more pieces for his slowly expanding puzzle. All he had to do was rotate them a few more times until they fit perfectly with the others.

The husband was a veteran, now a part-time professor at Berkeley. His wife was a nobody. She didn't fit, at least as far as her profile compared with the other victims, and she was tortured, another new twist for this psycho.

The man should have a nickname. Every serial killer had a nickname—BTK, the Green River Killer, Son of Sam, Jack the Ripper—it was a tradition dating back to ancient times.

Nothing fit this guy, or this woman.

It's a man. I know it. It must be.

Pacing in the living room helped him think, calmed the frayed nerves that were interfering with his thought process. Images of the Marshall's basement kept popping up like a slideshow, and he couldn't think. He stopped in front of Adelaide's china cabinet and pulled out a bottle of red wine and stared at the label, remembering the image of his father bathed in his own vomit.

Recalling the morning's hangover and the anxiety it had caused him in the chief's office, Trufant put the bottle back in the cabinet. Wine was not the answer, at least not tonight. Making some progress in the case, any progress, was the answer, and more importantly, it was the cure.

He thought of what Carlos had told him earlier. "Armstrong saw a young college kid that could have been the guy."

Marshall taught at Berkeley.

Coincidence? Maybe, but a possible puzzle piece.

"Next to useless," he whispered to the wall. But, still, it was better than nothing.

The images of Stephanie Marshall continued as John Lee Hooker's guitar reverberated in the living room. But the wall remained silent.

Stripping off his suit and shirt and tossing them into the dry-cleaning pile, he then took a hot shower. The heat felt good, stinging his back and gradually cooling as it reached his legs. He watched it swirl at his feet and tried to visualize his stress in the water, cooling, then disappearing as it sped toward the sewer.

Leaving the stereo on, he went to bed feeling he could sleep for two days. The ceiling was bathed in red from the neon sign across the street, pulsing on and off slightly faster than his breath. On-off-on-off until his breathing caught up with the sign's tempo and he was wide-awake.

He tossed and turned until midnight, then gave up.

With a glass of wine, he listened to a rerun of an old black-and-white western with his eyes closed. He followed the dialogue for a few minutes, then drifted off to sleep and into the Marshall's basement.

In this dream, the killer stood behind him, narrating how he had killed the woman. Trufant tried to turn around and look at the man, but each time the killer slipped away, remaining just beyond his field of vision.

"I did this for you, Marcus," the killer said. The voice though, was Adelaide's.

***

Morning came, he opened his eyes and closed them again. The bright light coming through the curtain felt like a cattle prod deep in his skull.

The bottle next to him was nearly full and the glass was almost empty. Not a hangover. He had slept only three hours and lack of sleep had always been a trigger for his migraines.

By the time his coffee finished brewing, the headache was pounding.

Then he remembered the dream, and Adelaide's voice repeated, "I did this for you, Marcus."

Dreams are supposed to mean something, but what? *What am I trying to tell myself?*

He swallowed an oxycodone with his first sip of coffee and put another one next to his keys, grateful that Dr. Wight in Chicago had prescribed something more potent than Tylenol, then sat on the balcony as the sun tried to burn through the mist. Slowly the drug kicked in, the throb in his head eased, the remnants of the dream faded, and that feeling of bliss waged war with the last of the pain.

The morning rush hour traffic was smooth, and he eased in and out of the lanes without effort. An hour ago, he was in agony and now he was enjoying his commute. Was this a side effect of the oxycodone, was this the euphoria junkies live for? If so, it was a pleasant one.

He coasted past the front of the station, which was lined with news trucks and reporters surrounded the department's public information officer. Trufant eased down in the seat, hoping none of them saw him.

Yeah, better you than me!

After parking in the back lot, he took the service elevator up to his floor and found his young inspector already hard at work.

"Anything new, Carlos?"

"Nah, but you look like shit, Lieutenant."

"Like a man that didn't sleep?"

"Well, I managed to get a few hours," Carlos said. "There was an email from Sgt. Cameron in Chicago. Still no ID on our Jane Doe and the body is still unclaimed at the morgue, but he said someone did call asking about her. No other info on the caller. He says he's trying to get hold of the investment company that owns the house but no contact yet, and he wants to know if you're still milking the Frankenstein look."

"Scars are like tattoos, my friend, only with better stories."

"That's a story you can live to tell L.T."

"Carlos, how does our guy pick his victims, not the Marshalls, I think that was something else, something new. The previous guys, it's not like they were wearing uniforms. None of them have anything recent in common except being out on the streets. Do you think the VA hospital could be a link?"

"Could be, a member of the staff, a fellow veteran with a grudge. Most of the homeless vets would go there first. It's their only option for health care."

"I thought so too. I asked their administration for a list of their volunteers a week ago. It's a start. I'll have one of the guys go by again and ask for it. Also, Timothy Marshall taught at Berkeley. Armstrong thought the guy he saw was a student, did you ask him why?"

"Yeah, he said the guy was preppy and wore a bright yellow college sweatshirt," Carlos said.

"Berkeley's colors are yellow and blue, that may be a link. I'm going to call Lt. Nelson, maybe she can look into Marshall's students for the last two years, see if she can get names and picture IDs on all of them."

"Just two years?"

"I think so, most of these guys are obsessive, once they lock on to a victim, they can't sit back and wait long. Torturing the woman was probably a side effect of his frustration. We'll start with two years for now. What about Armstrong, where is he?" Trufant asked.

"I dropped him off near the Presidio. He mentioned heading north to get out of the city and promised to call once he settled somewhere."

"Good, I don't want to find him butchered like the Marshalls. Anything from the FBI yet?"

"No, I hear they're keeping it all in-house. Pricks!"

"Don't be too hard on them, they know what they're doing."

"You should take a few hours off, LT, nothing new happening around here. I'll get with Nelson and take care of Berkeley. Go home and get some sleep, you do look a little rough."

"I'm okay, Carlos. I felt like shit this morning but I'm okay now. I kept seeing the Marshall woman. I finally stopped seeing Jane Doe in my dreams and now I have this one."

"You and me both. That was a bad one, Lieutenant, worst I've seen yet. I want to get this guy—us—not the Feds, you know what I mean?"

"I do, Carlos, I do."

"L.T., do you . . . never mind."

"What?"

"You don't think our wives are in danger do you?"

"I want to say no, Carlos, but this guy is an enigma. I don't think we should take anything for granted."

"I'm going to call my wife, maybe she and the kids can spend some time with my mother."

"Not a bad idea, Mexico should be safe."

"What about Adelaide, you hear from her?"

"No, but I expect a new set of divorce papers soon. I should have just signed them and been done with it. I'll call her now."

Chapter 15

Armstrong

It was dark by the time Armstrong reached the old bridge, he could feel the vibrations as the last of the tourist's cars left the park. The smell here wasn't too bad, urine and old dirt mostly. Fine motes of pulverized concrete, rat shit, and who knew what else drifted in front of the headlights each time a big truck rumbled across. *I'm breathing that dust.*

Fortunately, the breeze was blowing most of the fetid dust to the other side of the bridge, and the view was peaceful. Farther out, the lights of Fort Point lit up the empty cannon turrets that once guarded the bay from the Confederate States Navy that never arrived.

An old woman carrying a flashlight and a folded section of a cardboard box sat opposite him and lit a fire in front of herself using the broken slats of an old pallet. Two men soon joined her and sat around the fire sharing a bottle of cheap wine.

"Join us," the woman said, but one of the men gave him a look that said stay away.

Travis curled next to him, his head on his knee and his eyes looking up at him, somehow the dog knew what was coming next.

Today, forty dollars had gotten him three bags of cheap brown heroin, but it was all he could find on this side of the city.

Watching the heat from the butane lighter melt the brown powder, he inhaled as the vapors began rising.

Travis whined, and he said, "I'm sorry boy," and closed his eyes. Over the years, each high was less satisfying than the last, no euphoric high but still, the gratification was instantaneous. The chill of the night air vanished, replaced by warmth like no other, and for a few hours, the fear of withdrawal was replaced with peace.

"I'm sorry, Travis, I can never quit," he said, and sighed.

***

Caitlin was propped up on one elbow with her small breasts half-hidden in the bedsheets.

"I want three, but at least one of them has to be a girl," she said.

David stroked her strawberry blonde hair, strands of spun gold, as she laughed. She was so beautiful.

In the next moment, he was following Travis through a market, down a dirty street in Afghanistan, and God it was hot. Travis flipped an empty water bottle over his shoulder, and he ducked.

"Hydration, Armstrong! Hydration is life, never forget that!" Travis said, mimicking their old drill sergeant. Travis was built like an NFL lineman, and Armstrong had to keep moving left or right to see around the man's wide back.

The two of them walked behind the armored personnel carrier with the rest of the squad. Cases of water bottles and spare diesel fuel were strapped to the APC's rear, and the smell of the exhaust was right in their faces as there was no breeze. Travis moved to the right of the personnel carrier to get out of the stench and under a patch of shade from the side of an empty vegetable market.

Up ahead two small boys ran from the Stryker and disappeared into an alley. Armstrong tensed, a chill creeping up his arms. The market was empty, and the kids usually ran toward them, begging for candy or chewing gum.

"Travis, something is wrong, get back behind the truck."

"I'm tired of smelling that stink, Armstrong!"

"You're a crazy motherfucker, Travis, get behind the truck. Now!"

"Oorah!" was Travis's last word.

The impact from the 105 mm IED lifted the rear of the Stryker three feet off the ground, sending most of the shockwave toward them and Travis caught it full force. His body was torn in half and when Armstrong came to, most of his friend was lying on top of him.

He screamed until a medic jammed morphine into his thigh. The drug swept through him and blackness replaced the searing pain. He had been addicted ever since.

***

The desert warmth ended, and the San Francisco cold returned. The sun was out and Travis was asleep beside him.

It was Travis's body that had shielded him from the blast that day in the Helmand Province. Seeing Travis's mutilated body, Armstrong knew he would have been killed as well. When he saw the stump of his leg for the first time, the stump wasn't the worst part. The look on Caitlin's face was far worse.

"Let's go, boy," he said, waking the dog.

Their homeless neighbors were still sleeping on different pieces of cardboard. The old woman farted and rolled over into the dirt, snorted, then was motionless. The breeze had changed during the night, and the smells of old urine and shit were now blowing in his direction.

***

They walked the short walk on El Camino to the VA and looked for Dr. Williams. He was relieved when they said she was with a patient.

He wrote a note on a pad and gave it to the receptionist.

"Tell her I stopped by."

He wasn't afraid of her, but he feared disappointing the woman, seeing the look on her face, and her knowing that he wasn't coming back. He had seen the same look on his wife's face and his mother's and the few friends he made on the street in Maryland, and in every city, all the way to California.

All he wanted was to say goodbye, just leaving would have been wrong. She had tried, and he owed her that much.

Several vets watched Travis as the two of them walked through the lobby of the waiting room, most nodded, others just stared at the floor.

Halfway across the Golden Gate Bridge, he looked back at Fort Point and saw the beauty of the city. It was a shame he had to get this far away to not see the misery in the streets. Somewhere in that beauty was a madman who wanted to kill him, and there was a cop and a doctor who wanted to save him. Leaving was the easier choice.

He looked north toward Sausalito, and it too was beautiful. With any luck, someone on the other side of the bridge would offer them a ride, and they would be in Seattle by morning.

Chapter 16

Trufant

Trufant parked in one of the last available spots at the FBI's San Francisco headquarters.

Deputy Director Merriweather had summoned him to a conference to share what the FBI knew so far on the Marshall homicides and to connect them with those in San Francisco, a brainstorming share-fest. Trufant feared he would be the one sharing and not the other way around.

He looked across the room at his Oakland PD counterpart Jessica Nelson and rolled his eyes. Chicago's Sergeant Cameron was also there. The detective made a slicing gesture across his throat and smiled.

Trufant took a seat and watched Merriweather write on a dry-erase board.

Taped above the whiteboard were several dozen color photographs of the still-unidentified woman in Chicago and the slashed throats of seven men. The worst of the photos were from Stephanie Marshall's basement.

"We have homicides now linked in one way or another to this woman," Merriweather said, pointing to Jane Doe, "and at least one accomplice still at large. The Marshalls are linked through photographs and the others by quotes mailed to both the Chicago PD and San Francisco."

"I have agents looking into several more along the East Coast with similar circumstances. Special Agent Nouri has worked up a profile on the latest homicides in Oakland. Agent Nouri, what can you tell us?"

Trufant guessed the tall, thin woman was in her mid to late fifties, older than him by a few years. Her gray-streaked, raven black hair was pulled tight in a bun, and her glasses were old-fashioned, reminding him of his high school English teacher or maybe a librarian, purposeful and intelligent, and Trufant wondered if it was an aura she was trying to cultivate. He wished Kira was in the room, but the chief had denied his request to bring her along.

"As we can see from all these photos on the right side of the board, these men suffered quick, painless deaths. Probably painless anyway, most of them were killed in their sleep. For the others, they may have had a few seconds of confusion before they died. I think that's important because most psychopaths get pleasure from inflicting pain, sometimes even sexual gratification. So something else was driving this killer."

The woman spoke well, and Trufant found he liked her voice. She was a no-nonsense type of speaker, unlike her boss.

"As Director Merriweather said, most, but not all, of these deaths were followed with lines from Shakespeare's tragedies, laced with hints about death and revenge."

She pointed to a photo of a man lying prone in front of a bus bench wearing an old faded T-shirt with the Vietnam service ribbon across his back.

"We think this is the earliest victim. Toronto, December 1st, 2017, four months before yours in Chicago, Detective Cameron. There was no note, and this victim was sitting on a bus bench and stabbed in the back, a totally different MO, but witnesses described a young teen running from the scene. A surveillance camera caught this single image."

It was a grainy black-and-white photo of a teenager running straight at the camera. Trufant thought it looked like the dead woman in Chicago, although much younger.

"I've spent the last few days going over everything I can find, trying to put together some type of picture of what's happening with these deaths."

"From these earliest homicides, I see a killer learning through experience. I see organization between at least two people, one of which is probably dead now," she said, glancing at Trufant.

"At first it appears the deaths occur on only two dates, December 1st and April 11th. Those dates were all followed by the quotes, but there are others. I think those deaths started with revenge as a primary motivator. Everything we see on this woman's body tells me that," she said, pointing to the tattooed woman from Chicago. "But I also see something that tells me at least one of them is enjoying killing and may have moved on from pure revenge."

"This last victim, the veteran's wife, was the only victim that was tortured—the first and only victim showing any possible sexual motive. At first blush, it's easy to think this killer was motivated by sex, but not the act of sex—his or her gratification may come from simple dominance, stripping his victim of dignity.

"As far as we know, Lt. Trufant is the only man who has met one of them and lived. Lt. Trufant, I believe, is probably on this killer's short list, you and David Armstrong," she said, looking at him again.

The rest of the room turned and looked at him also, and he was glad he'd decided to have the stitches removed.

"Anything to add, Lieutenant?"

"Two things," Trufant said. "I can't help but wonder why David Armstrong is a target. San Francisco Police have already checked him out, and until we identified him, no one knew he was a veteran. Second, I want to point out how different the homicides in Chicago are to ours in San Francisco."

"How so?" Jessica Nelson asked.

"In Chicago, the victims were upright and awake, face-to-face with the killer when their throats were cut, indicating the killer was fearless. In San Francisco, all the victims were killed in their sleep. My first thought was our killer is a coward, afraid of a confrontation and taking the easy kills. But I'm not so sure now after seeing the Marshalls, unless someone else killed them."

"They are linked though, Lieutenant," Merriweather said. "The woman in Chicago had a connection to both the Marshalls and your victims or a cult perhaps, like the Manson family."

"Possibly, or a street gang maybe, she did have gang tats. I don't think we can rule out anything yet. The woman in Chicago was in the planning stages to kill the Marshalls. Finding out why she wanted them dead may be the key," Agent Nouri said.

"What do you know about this woman's husband?" Cameron asked.

Merriweather answered. "He was in the Army, did four years stateside, most recently a part-time professor at San Francisco State University and Berkeley."

Trufant interrupted him. "Two days ago David Armstrong was approached by someone he thought may have been a student at Berkeley, a white male wearing a yellow sweatshirt. We're not sure what scared him off, either Armstrong's dog or my inspector. Armstrong said the male looked similar to the Jane Doe in Chicago, so perhaps a family member."

"That's excellent, and a significant link. Marshall was in the military, and his students would probably know that. I'd like one of our agents to interview Armstrong. Is he available?"

"I'll see if we can locate him," Trufant said. "For his own safety he was going to leave the city."

The session droned on with one agent after another detailing the Marshall's crime scene, nothing new. Trufant's thoughts turned to his immediate problem, Adelaide, and he looked at his watch.

***

Two hours later he was sitting in the back of Capurro's Italian Restaurant watching the door. On any other day, he would relax and breathe in the aroma of fresh-baked garlic bread and wood-roasted crab, but now each time the door opened all he thought of was someone coming in to kill him, or his wife storming in.

Which one did he fear the most?

Anxiety pulsed through him like electricity and the Smirnoff in his second Moscow Mule was beginning to cloud his vision.

Fuck it, he thought, and ordered a third.

Capurro's had been one of their favorite places to meet after work. Their Dungeness crab was the best in town, and he and Adelaide had sat at this same table twice a week in better times.

He walked over to the bar, pretending to read captions under the old photographs, a black-and-white image of the Golden Gate Bridge half-completed, another of the downtown area burning after the big quake in 1906.

The door opened, and he caught a flash of red fabric. For an instant, it was the tattooed woman. He froze, unable to move, then found himself reaching for his gun—but this time it was Adelaide.

***

Adelaide Laveau Trufant stormed in like she was ready to do battle. Wearing her dark red gym outfit, her straight black hair was pulled tight in a ponytail with a gold-colored French clip. Because it was Thursday, he knew she had just finished her twice-weekly Pilates workout.

Several strands of her dark hair escaped the ponytail and clung to her neck in a sheen of sweat, and he thought she had never looked more beautiful.

He stood to greet her, and she allowed him to kiss her cheek, then sat down across from him.

"Marcus, I can't believe what I'm hearing! Why didn't you call me? Oh my God, that scar is hideous."

This is what he had feared as much as standing toe-to-toe with a psychopath . . . still, it was good to see her.

"I'm fine, and what would I have told you?" he said. "I was

almost killed, but I wasn't. I had my hands full for a few days, believe me. I'm sorry, and I'm sorry I didn't sign the papers."

"Marcus, you're slurring your words. You never drank a sip on duty before. Why don't you retire now, get out, you don't need this."

It was the same conversation they had months and years ago. This is where the marriage had begun to turn. She had understood and loved his passion for the job for so many years. She relished hearing about the things he had seen and done. Then he was transferred to Homicide, and he brought death into the house. Hearing him talk about his day, hearing of the suffering and the dying was bad enough, but hearing how they had died was too much and somewhere along that last year, she stopped listening.

"Retire and do what, Adelaide, teach at the academy? I'm fine. Did you bring the papers?"

"I did," she said, taking them out of her purse.

He signed each page and handed them back. The door opened, and an older couple came in. Just two more early birds coming in for dinner, but it triggered the Marshalls and how the man had been forced to watch his wife die.

"Adelaide, can you stay with your sister for a week or two?"

"What?"

"This case has taken a serious turn, and I worry about you."

"I'm not going back to Louisiana, especially at this time of year. Tell me what happened, Marcus."

This was exactly the type of information that had driven her away. He'd been hoping to avoid telling her about the Marshalls and the threatening note left in their basement. He left out some of the worst details and watched her eyes as he described the scene and how the note was left behind.

"Marcus, I wasn't going to tell you because I thought you would overreact, but two days ago, I couldn't get my key in the dead bolt of my apartment. The locksmith said someone had tried to pick the lock. There was a piece of metal broken off inside. I thought it was just a random burglary attempt. What do you think?"

"Adelaide, I think you should leave this afternoon. As soon as you get back, pack a bag and stay at a hotel, or even with me until you can get a flight to New Orleans."

She looked at him with those prying eyes and he knew she was thinking the worst.

"Adelaide, I'm not bullshitting you. This is serious."

"All right, Marcus, but I'm staying in my apartment tonight. I'll tell security and I'll book a flight in the morning."

***

Several miles away, Andrew Gellar watched his rod tip bend and felt the tug on the line. The seventy-year-old Israeli pulled hard, hoping to set the treble hook deep, and watched the rod bend toward the bay. At first, he suspected he had snagged a rock on the bottom, but slowly, inch by inch, he was gaining, and something big was coming up.

He was fighting the tide as well, the outgoing current was sweeping everything out of the bay and toward the Pacific.

All along Baker Beach, spectators made their way down to the sand and watched, then cheered as the brass swivel and the first few feet of stainless steel leader wire broke the surface.

Someone behind him screamed and he stopped reeling. At the end of the six-foot leader was a body. The hook was sunk deep into its elbow and the index finger of a dead hand pointed right at him.

***

Sober now and driving home on US 280, Trufant motored through the beginnings of the afternoon rush hour.

That went well, at least I got the damned papers signed.

Not long ago he felt his marriage was bulletproof, and now it would be soon over. At least she had agreed to stay with her sister in Shreveport and would be safe.

The killer's game had changed with Stephanie Marshall, and as long as he was out there, Adelaide was at risk. Her staying in Louisiana would be one less thing to worry about.

Traffic came to a stop, and he found himself staring absent-mindedly at the sea of brake lights in front of him. His right hand ached as he gripped the steering wheel. His knuckles were white, and he let go of the wheel, flexing his fingers. He wanted another drink, a drink and a few minutes in the recliner with some soft blues. Just the thought of a glass in his hand and Ella Fitzgerald's sweet voice eased the tension and anxiety. Was it Adelaide or spending a day with the FBI that had him so stressed?

"Lieutenant Trufant, are you on this channel?"

The radio killed the thought. "Trufant here," he said into the Motorola's microphone.

"Lieutenant, it's Suarez in Robbery, I'm down at Baker Beach, and I have a body on shore here. I was driving through and some fisherman flagged me down. I spoke to Amato, and he's on his way. He wants you here too. He said it was important."

"Tell him I'm on my way."

The drive to the beach seemed to take hours. He was deep into rush hour traffic now, and as the miles clicked past, dread washed over him like a heavy blanket. Was it David Armstrong, veteran, junkie, a homeless man cast aside by all those he had once fought for?

Or was it Adelaide? He had just left her and hour ago. Of course it was. That's why Carlos hadn't called him himself. Trufant patted his pants pocket and felt the last pill, pulled it out and swallowed it dry without thinking twice about the side effects.

***

He parked the Impala as close as he could near the crowd of bystanders and heard someone call his name.

"Trufant, wait!" The Chief Medical Examiner tripped and

caught herself as she stepped over the yellow crime scene tape sagging between two patrol cars.

"Dr. Lew!"

"What is it, do you know?"

"All I know is I was almost home. Let's go see."

Carlos Amato was crouched in the sand next to a woman's body. She was slender with blonde hair, and there were two deep lacerations crisscrossing her throat. The salt water had washed the wounds clean, exposing both ends of her carotid artery and the jugular vein.

Trufant bent down next to Amato and looked closely at the woman's face. She was unrecognizable, too much damage, but he knew who she was. He had just spoken with her two weeks ago, and Dr. Williams was stitched in bold pink letters on her white uniform.

"She's the doctor from the VA." Trufant said. He turned, and saw the hospital's roofline from the beach. "I was just there a few weeks ago, asking her about David Armstrong."

Trufant scanned the beach, wondering where she could have been killed. Somewhere there was a crime scene with a lot of blood and maybe something important they could use.

"Emma, how long do you think she's been in the water?"

"A day or two, maybe even a week. The water is cold, and she might never have come up. But the abrasions from the current dragging her on the bottom, and the damage from sea-life say less. I say two to three days max."

"The crime scene could be miles away," Trufant said. "Let the techs take their photos and get her out of here."

He looked west at the old rust-colored bridge and doubted she had been thrown off. Even a dead body would have suffered noticeable damage from the fall.

"I'll get with the shift commanders and see how many units they can spare to start looking for the scene. Carlos, we need to speak to Armstrong again, ASAP."

***

It was eleven o'clock before he was able to finally take his shoes off and sit on the bed. He looked at the enormous four-poster, thinking of Adelaide asleep under the comforter.

He sat in his boxers, thinking about the doctor, her young face, her mind full of dreams and ambitions. He remembered the image of the soldier and his wife dying on the concrete floor of their basement, then his phone rang.

"Carlos, what is it?"

"Lieutenant, we found the doctor's crime scene. Not much to it and we're wrapping it up now. It's not why I called."

"What is it, Carlos?"

"Lieutenant, I've been in Homicide for two years. I've seen some horrible things, you know it, you've seen them all too. But this is fucking me up, LT, and I'm having a hard time dealing with this, especially since the Marshalls. I can't sleep. I keep finding myself back in that basement, and it's more than just the image. I feel for her loss, I feel what her husband probably felt, and I'm worried about my wife. I'm driving home across the bridge and I'm soaked in my own sweat and I know I won't sleep again tonight."

"Me either, Carlos, you and I both have the Marshall woman and now the doctor and tattooed woman. I killed that woman and I'm still trying to process that.

"I want this case to be over. I want to get that bastard," Carlos said.

"We will, but don't let it get to you, don't let it change you. These memories will fade only when you get new ones to replace them. You will never forget, but you will learn to deal with it, and don't worry about sleep—you will find a way because someone has to do what we do."

"Okay LT, I'm almost home. Sorry to call so late, we'll talk more in the morning."

He ended the call wishing he could take his own advice. At least Carlos had someone to talk to. Maybe he would take Kira up on her offer to talk about killing the woman in Chicago and the stress of this investigation.

He was dead tired now, beyond simple exhaustion, but his mind was racing with visions of the doctor's pasty white body, the shrapnel burns and scars on the big guy, and the dragon with a bullet hole for an eye staring at him. The images played like a slide show each time he closed his eyes.

What was his name, the big guy?

He never forgot a victim's name but it wouldn't come to him.

He stared at the wall until he remembered.

Gerome Callaway!

He felt relief as the man's name resurfaced.

The wine cabinet was empty, and a half-empty bottle of Jack Daniels was above the sink. He free-poured a shot and swallowed it, poured a second, and went back to the bedroom.

Staring at the ceiling above his bed, he thought of Adelaide alone in her apartment, probably sound asleep, oblivious to the danger that might be right outside her door.

"Shit!" he said, wishing he hadn't thought of her. "I'll never sleep now."

He dressed, grabbed his gun, and drove the six miles to her apartment, then parked across the street and called her.

"Marcus?" she said.

"Just checking to see if you're okay."

"I'm fine. I was just turning off the lights. I told the security guard to keep an eye out for anything unusual. I didn't want to tell him everything, but now I think maybe I should have."

"You'll be fine, Adelaide, get some sleep and catch that first flight to your sister's in the morning and tell her I said hello."

"I will, Marcus. Good night."

As she ended the call, he watched the uniformed guard walking through the parking lot. The man used an entry card to open the lobby door and disappeared inside. There would be at least one more, and maybe two more exit doors in the back of the building with similar electronic locks. He stretched out as far as he could behind the wheel and waited. Sunrise was still seven hours away.

Thirty minutes later, the guard came back through the lot and into the lobby again. The man probably had to punch a key clock on a time schedule in different parts of the building to prove he wasn't sleeping on duty. Trufant watched him for two hours, then just after two, the man was late. Five minutes, then ten, and at fifteen Trufant grabbed his flashlight and radio and ran into the parking lot. No one had come out or gone through the front lobby, so he ran south to check the rear door.

Out of breath now, he turned the corner and two feet from the door, the guard lay crumpled in a heap next to a hedge. With his gun in his right hand, Trufant checked the man for a pulse and found none.

"3101," he shouted on the radio, "I have a homicide at 856 Green Street, one man down, looks like a knife wound, subject may be on the third floor."

He waited until the dispatcher acknowledged that she had heard it correctly, then charged in through the rear door, which had been propped open with the guard's nightstick.

Taking two stairs at a time and breathing hard, he reached the third floor just in time to see a man in a long black coat standing next to Adelaide's door. The man turned and ran down the hall toward the far staircase. Trufant yelled, "Stop!" and fired two rounds at the man, knowing he was late. Both .45 caliber bullets hit the now-closing steel door and went no farther.

He ran to Adelaide's door and saw the steel lockpick still in the new deadbolt's keyhole.

"Adelaide," he yelled.

Doors were opening now up and down the hallway as tenants looked out to see Trufant standing with his gun in his hand and just as quickly, they slammed their doors.

"I'm a police officer," he yelled down the now-empty hall.

Adelaide opened her door with a terrified look on her face. She was such a strong woman, and it hurt him to see her like this, like a child, helpless and alone. She reached out and pulled him close, trembling in his arms.

"It's okay, he's gone."

She saw the pick sticking out of the deadbolt and collapsed, dragging them both to the threshold of her doorway. He held her tight, feeling her heart pounding against him.

How close had he come to losing her, seconds, probably. The man killed the guard effortlessly, how easy a target would his own wife have been? The thought angered him. A year ago, he wouldn't have been so careless, *and a year ago, I wasn't drinking.*

Chief Lozano and Carlos arrived at the same time, and shortly, even Captain Brown was on the scene with several crime scene technicians.

"What happened here, Trufant?" the chief asked.

He considered not giving the chief and the internal affairs captain a statement, not without a union representative, but decided against it.

"I was worried about my wife and came by to check on her. I found the guard dead, ran up here, and saw the man trying to pick her lock."

Brown stepped closer and asked, "Lieutenant, have you been drinking?"

"Yes, I had a glass of wine earlier, Captain."

Lozano looked at the dead guard, then at Brown. "We will discuss this in the morning, Trufant. I want Lt. Gracia in charge of this scene."

The chief turned to leave and stopped, looked back, and asked, "Is your wife okay?"

"She is, Chief. Thank you for asking."

"You going to be okay, boss?" Carlos asked.

"I'm not sure, Carlos. I did have a drink earlier, and Brown could really try and fuck me for it, but hell, I was off duty."

"Well, you were right about one thing."

"What's that, Carlos?"

"It's us against him now."

***

Trufant helped Adelaide pack and drove her to the airport just before sunrise, then watched her board. As the plane pushed back from the gate, he felt a sense of relief knowing she would be safe, or at least safer, in Louisiana.

Pine Grove, Louisiana, was a speck on the map, a rural, unincorporated community miles from any real town, and her sister lived on farmland twenty-five miles from the community center. Trufant hoped the killer's focus would remain in San Francisco.

His eyes were on fire, he hadn't slept in thirty-six hours, and he felt drained, but he was also so wound up that he knew trying to sleep would be a waste of time.

Sitting at the dining table, he stared at the small brown pill bottle in front of him. When he'd left Chicago, it had been full, sixty pills prescribed by Dr. Wight. "Two a day, tough guy," she had said. Now the bottle was nearly empty, and there were no refills.

As he held the bottle, his hands shook hard enough that he could hear the four remaining oxycodone rattling inside.

"I'm in trouble," he whispered to his wife as her plane sped across the great state of Texas.

My drinking is out of control, and now I'm just as afraid of these pills as I am a glass of wine!

He threw the bottle across the room where it hit his thinking wall, a wall that was still silent. He pictured the new puzzle pieces slowly spinning but going nowhere. Too many missing pieces.

He stank like old sweat, fear, and nervous tension, but he didn't want to move. If he moved at all, he was afraid he would grab the pill bottle, and he knew he would take two of the last four.

How can I quit when all I can think about is refilling the bottle?

Every nerve in his body felt like a live wire, crackling with electricity.

The man tried to kill my wife, to butcher her, just to make me suffer!

Well, it was working. He leaned over and picked the bottle up off the floor.

Chapter 17

Armstrong

Armstrong stopped at three different churches as he walked through the city of San Rafael. Two were locked tight, and one of the two had a rusty chain and padlock looped through the door handles. Weeds and trash littered the abandoned church's dying grass.

The third church looked promising. Its tall white steeple had fresh paint, and someone had recently mowed the lawn, the scent of fresh-cut grass still in the air. An old woman greeted him at the door with a broom in her hand. She was polite, but all she had to offer was a suggestion.

"There's a homeless shelter in the old downtown area, four miles back, but they only serve a sandwich at noon, and I'm afraid you're too late."

He was regretting his decision to leave San Francisco. Six hours since his last hit, and eight hours since his last meal.

This was how it had been in Detroit and Denver, churches with locked doors—or worse, ones that were open but wouldn't let you inside. The police would be different here too.

Travis whined. The dog was hungry, and Armstrong felt the gnawing in his own stomach as well.

"I know, Travis, we need to eat."

Travis looked up and wagged his tail and pulled on the leash.

The sun was low on the horizon now, and it would be dark in

an hour. He stood at the edge of US 101 looking north and saw little in front of him, a few small storefronts, a residential neighborhood, an elementary school, and a Denny's Restaurant. This was where San Rafael ended, and he knew there would be nothing else for the next several miles.

To the west, storm clouds were moving in from the coast and lightning flashed. It was too far off to hear the thunder, but he hoped it would drift east and wash away the dust in the streets.

What a difference a few miles made. The buildings here were clean and beautiful, but dying grass and wilting shrubs were everywhere.

Travis pulled hard on the leash again.

"What is it, boy?"

The dog looked back at him and pulled again, leading him down an alley toward the rear of a restaurant.

On top of a full dumpster, several dozen well-done hamburger patties sat on a paper take-out plate. They were cold and dry and had more than a few flies on them, but they smelled safe, and he let Travis try one first.

"Is it okay?"

Travis wolfed the burger in two bites and wanted more, so Armstrong took a chance and tried one. Not bad. He took the entire plate as the back door of the restaurant opened.

"Hey! You can't be back here. Get lost before I call the cops."

Travis growled, and Armstrong pulled the dog back toward the highway, ignoring the still-grumbling man.

As the sun set, the rain started, and the two of them finished off the burgers under a covered pedestrian bridge.

As they ate, he surveyed the graffiti on the concrete supports. Most of the art was done by amateurs, kids with a can of their father's spray paint probably. One was different, beautifully sculptured three-dimensional letters spelled out "No Future" in shades of black and gray. The "o" in "No" was a balloon, the string held by an African American child. He wasn't sure if it was a boy or a girl and maybe that was the artist's intent. There was a lonely, distant look in the child's eyes.

Lightning flashed, making it seem like the child had come to life, and the thunder was immediate, startling them both.

"Jesus, that was close!"

If the rain bothered the dog, it didn't show. Travis simply stared out into the dim light as the rainwater rushed down the bridge's embankments and into a concrete culvert where it disappeared into a storm drain.

The streetlight on the walkway above them clicked on, then flickered twice with an eerie humming noise. The bright light illuminated everything around the bridge but left them in dark shadows underneath.

He had hoped to be farther north by now, at least as far as Eureka where he had the name of a shelter allowing dogs, tomorrow maybe. He was too tired to think of anything else, but being tired was easy. Dopesick was worse. His fingers began twitching, the chills and sweats would be next. He tried ignoring the signs and listened to the sound of the rain. He was broke now, and by morning he knew he was going to be in withdrawal.

Ten dollars for a bag of dope would get him through until tomorrow, but where was he going to get ten dollars and where would he find a dealer in this city who would sell it to him? He should have saved a few dollars for the dope, at least, dope and food for Travis.

His gut cramped as a wave of nausea swept through him. He looked at Travis and wondered how he was going to make it to sunrise.

"I'm in trouble, Travis, I should have stayed in the city. First thing in the morning we'll start back." The dog cocked his head as if he was confused.

"I know it's a long way back. But it's home, we should never have left."

Closing his eyes, he pictured Travis in the chow line cracking jokes with anyone who would listen. The sound of the rain hissed all around him like white noise, and he . . . was back on Mason Street watching the strange man wearing a black plastic poncho. He saw the blue flash of steel again, like an electrical spark and the cold eyes underneath the hood. The man rose and walked into the street and kicked him hard in the ribs. Travis howled, and the man kicked him again and said . . .

"Get up, mister, I'm not going to say it again."

It was still dark and a blinding beam of light hovered above him. Travis howled again, and he heard the dog yelp. He jumped up and an explosion of pain hit him in the chest.

***

He was tossed from side to side, handcuffed to a steel eyebolt welded to the floor of a paddy wagon, listening to the crackling sound of a police radio.

"One to the stockade," he heard a woman say from the front seat. He couldn't see the driver. Sheet metal separated them.

The sun was up now and sounds of heavy traffic surrounded him.

"How does it feel to be tased?" the female voice asked.

"Where is my dog?"

"I'm not sure where your dog is now. Animal Control took it. He bit one of the officers and will probably be in quarantine unless they put him down."

Unless they put him down!!

He was wrong to leave San Francisco. He should have moved to the Haight-Ashbury district until the police caught the man. Now Travis was in a cage somewhere, scared and in pain. What had they done to him?

"Why did you tase me, did you tase my dog too?"

"I didn't Taser anyone, I'm just transporting you."

The van smelled like he was back under the bridge near the Presidio, but it was cleaner than most places he had slept recently. The prison van made a few sharp turns, and he fell off the bench once and felt something pop in his shoulder.

"You're going to kill me back here."

"Sorry, we're late. I wanted to get you in on the morning docket, but we're not going to make it. It means you're staying in lockup tonight unless you can make bail."

"What am I charged with? I was just sleeping."

"You were charged with vagrancy in a school zone, Mr. Armstrong. Parents don't like their kids walking by homeless men sleeping under a bridge on their way to school. You'll probably have a bail hearing tomorrow morning, or maybe the next. It's usually a five hundred dollar bail."

"Are they going to kill my dog?"

"Probably not."

The van stopped. The back doors opened and the sunlight blinded him. She used a key on her gun belt to unlock the shackles and led him inside a fenced sally port and into the city jail, which looked just like others he had seen over the years.

The chevrons on the woman's sleeves and her name tag told him she was Corporal M. Jenson. She was as tall as he was and in better shape. Her red hair looked like fine strands of copper wire, braided and tied off with a gray band that matched her uniform. She had a firm grip on his forearm as she led him down a stark hallway, and the few doors he passed had small windows embedded with wire mesh and industrial-sized electric locks. The one in front of her buzzed and opened.

Jenson led him through the booking procedures, and a young guy, probably fresh out of high school, took his fingerprints and two photos, then she pointed to a shower stall.

"Use this. It's for lice," she said, handing him a bottle of shampoo.

"I don't have lice."

"Use it anyway.

"Can I get some privacy or are you going to watch me shower?"

"Someone has to. You want one of the guys to come down here?"

He stripped and threw his clothes in a plastic bag.

She observed him as he undressed, studying all the scarring from the shrapnel and the burns and finally his groin.

"What happened to you, a car crash?"

"War."

She looked up at him. "Put these on when you're finished," handing him a folded orange jumpsuit and a pair of rubber flip-flops.

"I'll check on your dog. I know someone over there."

There was a different tone in her voice now. It had been cold and condescending in the van, simple answers that sounded rehearsed. Now, she looked him in the eye when she spoke, and he hoped it meant Travis would be okay. She did watch him shower, though.

Jenson left, and two hours later he was eating a cold ham and cheese sandwich on stale bread. The old hamburgers had tasted better.

"Unless they put him down," the corporal had said. She said she would check on Travis, but that was two hours ago. He pounded on the steel door until a uniformed guard looked through the window.

"Officer, I need to make a phone call."

"Not until lunch is over, another hour and I can get you to the phone."

"Inspector Carlos Amato's business card is in my pants pocket. Can you call him? I think he's looking for me."

The officer didn't answer and walked away. Armstrong heard the man's footsteps and heard a door bang shut. The sound reverberated, causing even the walls to shake.

He was alone in a ten by ten cell with a stainless steel bench and matching toilet and sink. The cell looked new. The whole jail looked new, and he could smell fresh paint. Scratched into the wall, he saw John 3:16.

"Jesus, help me," he whispered.

He had no sense of time, but shifts changed, the next day came and went, and no word on Travis or Inspector Amato. It was hard to stand upright this deep into withdrawal, so he sat in a fetal position in one corner of the room.

Hunger pains and nausea flip-flopped for hours, each time a little worse than the last. There were no clocks visible and no signs of daylight, but his stomach told him it had to be at least four in the afternoon.

Slamming prison doors announced another shift change, then dinner was served on paper trays, something that looked like meatloaf and lukewarm mashed potatoes.

Is this my second dinner, or third?

Dope sickness always had a way of playing tricks with his sense of time.

Sound waves from his door shook his metal bench, and he saw a new face in the window, a tall man who looked familiar, like Morgan Freeman except for the vivid pink scar above the collar of his shirt.

"Who are you?"

"I'm your new best friend, Mr. Armstrong."

CHAPTER 18

TRUFANT

Lt. Gracia was waiting for him at the station. "Marcus, you look like shit, my friend."

"I feel like shit, Ralph, not enough hours in the day to get enough sleep."

"I just wanted to let you know how things are working out at your wife's scene."

"Let me guess," Trufant said. "You got nothing."

"That's pretty much it. No surveillance cameras, no prints, and no DNA anywhere. The ME said the victim suffered a single stab wound to the heart from a knife with a blade similar to the one left at the Marshalls. Death was instant. Too bad you missed him at the staircase."

"I hesitated, just a fraction of a second. I was off duty, and I wasn't sure if he was the guy at first. I had to add it all up before I could pull the trigger—dead guard, black coat like the guy on Mason Street, and standing at my wife's door."

"Marcus, just to let you know, Brown is really wanting to go after you about your drinking that night, but the chief is reining him in."

"The chief? I'm surprised he hasn't suspended me already. I did have a drink that night, though."

"Well, just watch out for Brown, Marcus."

"Will do."

***

Traffic on the 101 was light as he crossed into Sausalito and by midmorning, he was walking through the holding cells with a Marin County corrections officer.

Armstrong was thinner than he had imagined, gaunt, like so many others on the street.

The first interview was always the most telling. First impressions revealed the true personality.

Armstrong's eyes betrayed his persona. At first glance the man seemed weak, humbled by his environment, but his eyes said different. This was not a weak man.

They were moved to an interview room. The metal table between them was bolted to the concrete floor, and Armstrong's hands and feet were shackled to the table's frame. His own stark white dress shirt and tie contrasted with Armstrong's orange Marin County Corrections jumpsuit.

"We were just sleeping. We weren't bothering anyone."

"I'm sorry you were arrested, Mr. Armstrong, but I have some questions—"

"They're going to kill my dog, Lieutenant. They said Travis bit someone, but it wasn't his fault."

Conflict contorted Armstrong's face. He was trying not to look weak, but he was weak when it came to his dog. He was also angry, and Trufant realized this man could be dangerous. Just as he'd come to that conclusion, he discerned that the ex-special forces Marine had been profiling him too.

What does he see in me? He's a junkie, but I have my problems too!

Armstrong pounded his fists on the table, straining against the shackles until his wrists bled, and tears ran down his face until his shoulders slumped and the tension in his neck eased.

"I'm sorry," he said, his voice quivering. It's been two days. I'm dopesick. I feel like I'm dying, and my dog is probably already dead."

"I've already checked on your dog, he's fine, and I'll make sure someone picks him up tomorrow if you like. You'll have to spend at least another night in here, and you may see the magistrate as early as tomorrow morning. There's nothing I can do about that. Your bond, it's five hundred dollars cash, and I have forty-three dollars and some change in my pocket. They'll ask you to plead no contest and give you time served. That's what the desk sergeant told me."

"So why are you here, Lieutenant, where is Amato?"

"He's been busy with something new and I wanted to see you. I want you to tell me what you told Amato. I want to hear it from you, word for word, Mr. Armstrong, then I have a few things to tell you."

"I told him I didn't see the man's face the night he killed those men. But I saw him later, a few days ago." Then Armstrong told him everything he could remember about the man in the park. "I want to be honest with you, Lieutenant," he said. "I'm a heroin addict, so I have hallucinations sometimes, and nightmares every time I close my eyes, so even when they're open, I don't know if what I've seen is real anymore."

His shackles began to rattle under the table.

"Do you know what it's like to have nightmares every time you close your eyes, Lieutenant?"

"Nightmares? Let me show you what I dream about every night."

Armstrong's eyes locked onto the thick scar. He sat back in the chair, took a deep breath, and nodded.

"Yes, I have a few nightmares of my own, Mr. Armstrong."

Trufant watched the ex-Marine soften and felt the tension in the room evaporate. Armstrong's shackled hands and his feet twitching in the blue flip-flops were still now, he stretched his legs out as far as the chains would allow. Yes, he was suffering from opioid withdrawal. Trufant had seen it often enough to recognize it, but it was something he couldn't help him with—at least not yet.

He showed Armstrong copies of the two pictures, Stephanie Marshall's military ID and the one of him walking his dog next to the cable car museum, and he nodded.

"Inspector Amato showed them to me."

"The woman who cut my throat had these pictures taken probably just a week after you saw those two men murdered, and Inspector Amato told you about the Marshalls. This is a picture of what the killer did to her." He watched as Armstrong took in all the details, saw his red eyes watering as he pushed the photos back across the table.

"Amato told me I should leave or I could be next—so I left. I did exactly as he said, now here I am, sitting in a cell.

"Dr. Brook Williams, do you remember her?"

Armstrong looked up, confused by the question, "Yes, from the VA?"

"She was killed a few days ago—murdered and thrown into the bay like trash. She had your name written on a pad in her car, written next to it was the word 'promising,' any idea what she meant?"

"Oh my God," Armstrong whispered, and slammed his forehead into the table. Trufant saw a smear of blood across his eyebrow and was afraid he was going to do it a second time, but he collapsed, sobbing, facedown on the table.

He watched Armstrong's finger tracing a groove in the tabletop, he could see his eyes darting back and forth, red and watery, as he searched for something to say. He leaned forward, resting his head on the table. When he finally looked up, he wiped the tears onto the sleeve of the jumpsuit and leaned back.

"She was a good woman. I attended a recovery session at the VA she hosted, and we had coffee after. She probably thought she could save me."

"Maybe she thought you were worth saving."

"She was a good woman," he repeated. "I've tried rehab so many times, in so many different cities, I've lost count. I may have gone back to see her eventually, but after what Amato said, I knew I should leave. How could I have known?" he asked. "Do you think she died because of me, was her death my fault?"

"I don't know if you could have made any difference. He may have killed her out of frustration when he couldn't get to you, or maybe he hoped her death would make you suffer—only he knows why. He tried to kill my wife two nights ago because he wanted me to suffer, so I sent her to another state. He's a psychopath, Mr. Armstrong, and psychopaths are usually extremely intelligent and very obsessive. Ted Bundy, do you know the name?"

"No."

"Bundy confessed to killing thirty women, but some people think it may have been twice as many. He preyed on college girls. Bundy could be standing next to you at a bar, and you would want to buy him a beer. That was a statement from someone he met hours after killing two women in Florida. He was evil incarnate, Mr. Armstrong. There was no motive of revenge, no reason to hate them, he just loved to kill women."

Armstrong nodded as if he finally understood.

"I'm not here to pity you, Mr. Armstrong. If that's what you need, I can't help you. I came to see if you could help me, and now that I'm here, maybe I can help you. I read your file, I read what you went through, and I won't pretend to say I understand what you're going through right now."

"All those things in my file are just words. I'm not that man anymore."

"Maybe, maybe not, I do think that Dr. Williams would disagree, though."

Armstrong looked at him, his eyes still red and watery, but he didn't speak.

"Mr. Armstrong, I need to get going. I'll try and pick up your dog tomorrow morning, Travis, right? I hope he doesn't bite. Inspector Amato said he will be at your bond hearing and drive you back into the city."

***

The sun was setting by the time he got back in the city and traffic was already thinning.

He went right for the wine cabinet and pulled out a bottle at random, some type of red he'd picked up the day before.

With the bay window open, he listened to the same nightly sounds he found comforting. The nagging feeling that he was missing something bothered him. He always felt it, even with the easy cases.

He looked at his thinking wall and pictured a thousand jigsaw puzzle pieces spread out in front of him. Some fit, making bits and pieces of a bigger picture. But most of them lay haphazardly with no obvious connection.

This was the biggest, most complex, case he had ever worked. With so many threads going out in different directions, it was impossible to stay on top of them all, probably a good thing the FBI was involved. But damn it, he wanted to be the one to nail this bastard.

The wine bottle was empty now. He threw it in the trash, on top of two others.

Tomorrow may be the day—the big break I want so I can finally quit drinking. Lord knows I need to.

***

But the next morning started just like the last. The alarm clock too loud, too early, a pounding hangover and a touch of nausea.

He had always enjoyed the early hours of a new day, coffee, reading the morning paper, an occasional romantic moment with Adelaide. Now he dreaded every sunrise. He knew alcohol was the problem—and chasing hangovers with pain killers—but it was the alcohol that kept the nightmares at bay, a vicious whirlpool trying to drag him under.

He had dealt with rough cases before, dealt with a nightmare now and then too, but then he had his wife who would listen to him, and somehow that was enough. Telling her of the grief he witnessed every day was what drove her away.

After a hot shower, hotter coffee, and his last oxycodone, the ache in his head began to fade. He was in traffic making his way north to San Rafael to pick up Armstrong's dog. With the police dispatcher talking in the background, he began running the case in his head, his to-do list. He wanted to recheck the VA's list of volunteers. It was one possible link to the dead men. None of them served together, different branches of the service, different theaters of conflict, and two had never left the states. Berkeley was another clue and maybe comparing the two lists would give him another link. He made a note to contact Oakland to see if Lieutenant Nelson had worked on that.

First things first, though, he wanted to pick up the dog. If he wanted any credibility with Armstrong, he had to keep his promise.

"What am I going to do with a dog?" he asked the image of his wife in the seat next to him.

Adelaide had always wanted a dog, someone she could talk to while she was home alone. He had argued that it was a bigger responsibility than just feeding it. "Adelaide, it's like a child, are you sure you want to take that on? You can't leave it here in the apartment all day."

As he drove past the town of Alto, he decided to keep the dog in the apartment until Armstrong was back on the street, hopefully tomorrow morning. The dog was going to have to listen to his stories to earn its keep.

***

Travis sat in the passenger seat, staring out the window intently at the drivers in each car they passed.

"You looking for your buddy? Are you looking for David?"

The dog would make brief eye contact, then turn away when he spoke.

"I know, you don't like me."

They rode in silence all the way back into San Francisco, Travis looking frantically for his owner. It was depressing trying to reason with the dog.

Chapter 19

Mother

As she had expected, the American's FBI and Canada's RCMP agents were at the graveyard waiting. Three dark-gray vans and several other new rental cars were scattered throughout the forty acres of grassy hills. The two dozen mourners were probably being photographed, their license plates recorded, and the federal agents would spend weeks trying to figure out who they were.

She never saw any of this sitting in her home in Mississauga. She sat on her porch watching the deep blue water of the river flowing east toward Lake Ontario, where it would eventually find its way into the Atlantic Ocean.

She thought of the old passage in the book of Matthew, do unto others, words spoken by Jesus himself, and somewhere in a room above her, a crucifix hung from a bedroom wall.

"You did this to us," she said aloud.

She had been raised as a Catholic since birth. Even after she married her Muslim husband, she raised her children as Christians—and Jesus had made them all suffer.

After that fateful day in Al-Masafer, she had vowed never to speak to God again. He had turned his back on her and her family in their time of need, and she would never forgive him for it.

"Why?" she asked, looking at the ceiling.

It had been a difficult marriage. Her Christian values often clashed with the Koran, and she and Nasim would argue deep into the night. But they always found common ground.

"Chanda, my cigarettes, please!"

"Can you see me up there, Nasim? Look what I've become."

She had become too weak to light her own cigarette now. She heard the door open behind her, and expected her niece, but it was her son that lit the match. Dressed in a black suit and tie, he looked younger than his twenty-three years.

"Black, how fitting Ramzi, and I see you've cut yourself."

Her son looked at the nick in his thumb, and she saw his face flush. Was he embarrassed at such a simple thing?

"You play with your knives for hours every day. A little blood is not a sign of weakness, Ramzi."

She knew that was precisely what he was thinking. His obsession with those damn Balisongs was her fault anyway.

"You look excellent, Mother," he said, deflecting her comment.

She tried to laugh, but it sounded more like someone crushing newspaper. "I don't feel excellent, Ramzi, I feel like shit! I had my last chemo treatment two days ago, and I'm still vomiting everything I swallow. The doctor says that will pass soon enough, but I think he's bullshitting me. I'll be lucky enough to see Trufant's death before I die.

I want to see the picture of his lifeless body, Ramzi, I think you owe me that much! I believe I will be ready to pass on and join Madinah, Halima, and your father, then you can stick my ashes in the crypt yourself."

"I owe you?" he asked.

She watched his face, trying to read his emotions, hoping the mention of her death might trigger something, but saw only a vacant stare. Maybe he is just grieving for his twin sister in his own way. They had remained close these last few years.

"You don't owe me anything, Ramzi," she finally said.

"I drove past the cemetery on the way here, Mother, who are those people?"

"Who knows?" she said. "Chanda and her brother posted

flyers on his campus and a few students showed up. The police are there too. She said there were more cops than mourners. I would like to go just to see them sitting around like fools."

"Trufant is not there. He is still in San Francisco."

"How do you know?"

"I track him."

She looked at him and decided not to ask.

"Leilah will be here soon, and after dark, we will all ride to the cemetery as a family and see Madinah. She would understand and approve."

"Madinah hated her life, Mother. She looked forward to dying, did you know that? She told me every time we spoke. She didn't want to die as much as she didn't want to live. When was the last time you heard her laugh or even smile? I remember—she was twelve years old and she had just stabbed a man in the back. We ran away through the park, and she laughed. That was the last time, Mother."

"Ramzi, I sit and live in this house, a house paid for by American money—blood money. They think paying us made things right, like throwing millions of dollars at us will erase the memory of my dead husband, my dead Halima, and my broken family. I cannot even use my own name here! You lecture me on death and misery, but I am the one dying now and I have just as much reason to hate them as you do. All I can do now is live my life vicariously through your revenge, yours, and Madinah's, and now she is dead too!"

She looked at a small boat drifting in the majestic Credit River and saw a young family enjoying the last hours of sunlight. She felt her rage richen, her hands trembling so violently the freshly lit cigarette fell to the old weathered deck and Ramzi started to reach for it.

"Leave it, Ramzi. Take me inside please."

***

The sun finally set and she knew Leilah was not coming. Her youngest child had drifted further away from the family until the only contact they had was an occasional email and a text on her birthday.

But she was twenty-one, an adult now and studying some useless course in another college, New York City this time. She had her own money, and she made it clear she wanted no interference from her mother.

You smother me, Mother, I am not a child!

She thinks she knows it all.

She thought of all the money, as if the atrocities could be assigned a dollar amount. With enough money, though, anything can happen.

***

"It's time to go, Chanda."

The van crept through the dark cemetery and stopped next to the mausoleum. She waited for her niece to lower the ramp, but it was Ramzi who pushed her chair through the crypt's open door.

"Mother, how do you know we aren't being watched right now?" Ramzi asked.

"Chanda's brother has been here all night, no one is watching."

Inside the crypt, a woman dressed in a red two-piece suit turned. Her youngest daughter had come after all. Her hair had grown longer than she remembered and she had two thinly braided strands on each side of her face. Dark eyeshadow made it difficult to see who Leilah was looking at, and the lighting was too dim to see her face in any detail.

"Leilah, you couldn't come to the house? Was it too much to bear—to eat with your family?"

"I prefer the name LeAnn, Mother, and I am here, but I came to see my sister's ashes, not to break bread with you."

"Why do you hate me so much, Leilah," she said, ignoring this new name, "what have I done?"

She watched the girl turn toward her father and sister's crypts, and the new hole in the wall where Madinah's urn was now resting.

"I don't hate you, Mother. Hate is too strong of an emotion. My classmates think I'm cold, they ridicule me, and I'm going to kill a few of them soon. But I don't hate them, either, I find them insignificant in my life—as I do you."

"Insignificant?"

"Yes, Mother, but don't take it personally. I'm a sociopath. My psychiatrist said I suffer from an antisocial personality disorder. Just being here reaffirms what she said. I came just to experience my sister's burial, to see how it affects me."

"And does it?" Ramzi asked.

"No, it doesn't, my brother, and I'm leaving now. I've seen enough for one day."

She watched her walk out through the mausoleum and into the night. The moonlight stole the red from her dress, turning it dull gray. As her daughter strolled between the headstones of the dead and disappeared into the darkness, she knew she would never see her again.

"Ramzi?" She waited, listening to her son's breathing and knowing that he was right behind her. "Take me home."

***

The old woman sat alone on her second-story deck, watching the dawn's light reflect off the Credit River, and the image reminded her of a sunrise in another life.

That had been such a beautiful morning. The same pinks and reds brightened the sky as the sun lifted itself above the horizon.

The woman had been sitting in a rocker, sipping the black coffee her husband had brewed before he left for the market. As a devout Christian missionary living in an Arab world, she savored these few minutes of sunrise, when she could smoke her first cigarette of the day, free from the watchful eyes of her neighbors.

As the last bit of coffee cooled, she flicked the stub of her cigarette onto the dirt pathway and carried her empty cup back into the house.

She had just set breakfast on the table when the front door exploded in a shower of wooden splinters, and Halima, her fourteen-year-old daughter, was the first to scream. The woman turned and saw four men wearing desert camouflage uniforms storm the kitchen. One turned toward her and hit her head with the butt of his rifle.

How long she was strapped to the chair she didn't know, but when she came to, she saw Halima on the floor, covered in her own blood. Then her husband, Nasim, rushed in, screaming, and one of the other soldiers slammed a huge knife into his chest. As he fell to the floor, the soldier cut Nasim's throat, and mercifully, she blacked out and was spared what followed.

CHAPTER 20

RAMZI

Sleep on the flight from Toronto to San Francisco was impossible. Turbulence wasn't the problem. It was claustrophobia. Six people were sitting within one foot of him, anyone of which could reach out and touch him. He was breathing everything they were exhaling, and the woman next to him kept bumping his arm on the armrest, her skin touching his. The feeling was nauseating, and he closed his eyes, wishing they were all dead.

He was at war with his emotions now, seeing his mother, Madinah's death, and the need to kill either Armstrong or Trufant. Killing the doctor had offered little relief, she was a nobody, but Armstrong had to pay some price. Ramzi had failed to kill Armstrong in the park, and now he had failed to kill Trufant's wife. Two failures in one week. It was all he could do to sit still at thirty thousand feet.

Sweat dripping down his shirt made him fear the inevitable confrontation with a US customs officer. He had always traveled during peak hours just to catch the agents at their busiest times, when they would be fatigued by the sheer numbers of international passengers. But this plane would arrive just before dawn, the airport would be empty, and the customs agents would be fresh and alert.

His fears never materialized. Two flights, one from Tokyo and another from Seoul, had landed just in front of his, and he stopped and studied the arrivals monitor until most of the passengers of all three flights lined up ahead of him. It was all he could hope for. Providence would determine his fate now.

Stay calm and speak the names: Smith, Gonzalez, Washington, Curry.

Silently he repeated the names of the men who had destroyed his family. He never knew which of them had raped him, so he memorized each name. He had two new names now, Trufant and Armstrong, and soon, hopefully today, he would eliminate one of them—Trufant.

He stepped up to the counter, making eye contact with the woman at the desk.

"Good morning, ma'am."

"Good morning, Mr. Ocampo," she said, studying the photo on his passport. I see you live here in San Francisco, were you traveling on business or pleasure?"

"Neither, I was attending my sister's funeral."

"Oh, I'm sorry."

The woman typed furiously at a keyboard, and he wished he could see what she was typing. More sweat ran down his spine, and his armpits felt soaked. Hopefully, his face was dry.

The woman looked up and smiled, handed him his passport, and said, "Welcome back, Mr. Ocampo."

***

He stood nude in front of the mirrored wall in his apartment and whispered, "Have I no room for grief?"

His sister's ashes were sealed in a cold concrete vault now, thousands of miles away. Her service had been a waste of his time, still, he had to see it through, she was his twin, after all. They had shared their mother's womb, and yet he felt no grief.

It was not the first time he had felt the lack of emotion, especially grief. All those years in the Philippines, seeing one doctor after another, left him doubting which of his emotions were real and which were just coping mechanisms.

Rage was the only emotion he was sure of, that and the frustration of not being able to satisfy it.

Yes, his sister was dead, and another man's name was on his list, another man and another tattoo. He enjoyed the aftermath, watching the needles puncture and color his skin, almost as much as killing the men each of them represented.

"Why do you want such an unremarkable tattoo?" the Chinese tattoo master had asked him years ago.

"It may be a simple mark to you," he had said, "but I will cherish it."

He turned in front of the mirror, studying his back, still feeling the pride from the first black slash. It was almost lost now among all the others, but it was the one held by the dragon's talons, and tomorrow he would add two more.

He had followed Armstrong and his dog for four days, learning what he could of the man. Armstrong had seen his face twice now and showed no sign of recognition—but the dog knew.

Armstrong had seen him kill—the man had watched him fulfill his vow, like a voyeur watching someone masturbate. He had been so careful and yet—the man had seen him!

He had prepared himself to kill Armstrong right on the bus bench in broad daylight—no more sneaking around at night murdering defenseless men as they slept. His hand had been on the blade when the dog turned. It had recognized him, and he prepared to kill them both. Then the cop appeared.

He had failed again, and there would be great suffering now.

Lifting the jeweled lid off the old box, he picked up two of the dozen ancient Balisongs, crafted long before even his mother was born. He opened them and studied the blades, repeating the sacred words he was taught by the Tagalog masters in Manila, then began flipping each one open and closed, open and closed, and then both in unison, synchronizing the sounds until they became one and his rage left him.

The knives rotated around him in a blur as his lips continued to move. Beads of sweat soon covered the mirror and floor, then the sixty-minute timer chimed.

As he cooled down, he studied his body again. "The body is the vessel that wields the blade," the old master often said. "You must cherish it because without it, you are nothing."

His dragon was an exact opposite of Madinah's. The dragon stared back at him, the eyes dark red, always piercing him with its own rage. The tattoo master was dead now, but his work was done. The dragon was magnificent. His sweat glistened on its bloodred scales as if the dragon was alive and breathing, ready to strike out at his command.

After cleaning the knives with an oil-soaked rag, he placed them back in the old teak box, then knelt in front of them and prayed. He had memorized the names of each life he had taken, and he cursed them all every night, and blessed them too, blessed them because they had each moved him closer to his goal.

He mopped the floor several times, then wiped the mirror with a soap brush and squeegee. In the reflection, he saw his now-dead twin sister, and she was ten years old again.

He pulled out the knives and reset the timer.

CHAPTER 21

TRUFANT

Travis stank worse than any dog he had ever known. Two days locked up in the county's animal control kennel probably had a lot to do with it.

At least he didn't bite, but he could tell the dog didn't trust him, wouldn't even look at him, and whined all the way back to the city.

"You sleep here tonight, Travis."

The dog sat by the front door and refused to move, eat, or drink. Trufant tried stretching out on the floor and talking to him, but nothing worked. Finally, Travis curled up on the mat and stopped whining, but never closed his eyes.

"Have it your way."

Hours later, Trufant stripped off his clothes, leaving them piled on the floor with yesterday's and lay on the big four-poster.

Sleep was impossible, even without the dog he would have been wide-awake. He was afraid this night would be like the last, and the night before that—dreams so real, so realistic, and so vengeful.

Each time he closed his eyes, the woman's knife slashed out of the darkness, and each time the knife cut deeper. The dreams were so real he could feel the sting of the blade and smell the cordite as his gun fired. Waking, soaked in sweat, and reaching for his gun on the nightstand night after night. Now, Stephanie Marshall and Dr. Williams were competing for air time.

He spent the next few hours with his eyes wide open, watching the familiar red glow from the neon sign across the street pulse on his ceiling.

It's simple anxiety, Marcus!

Adelaide thought she had a cure for everything.

Anxiety!

He stumbled into the bathroom and found Adelaide's old bottle of Xanax and swallowed two of the cream-colored pills, thought about the dosage, and took another.

Maybe she was right this time.

As he began to drift off, he heard the dog pad into the bedroom and felt Travis jump onto the bed and curl up as his feet. Soon after, he slept too, and when he opened his eyes, it was 9 a.m.

"Damn it!" he said, nudging the sleeping dog. "We're late."

The Xanax left him drowsy, an aftereffect, but at least he had a few good hours of sleep, and sleep was something he was beginning to cherish.

He called Carlos and told him what was going on with Armstrong and his dog. Carlos said he could be at the Marin County Courthouse for the arraignment and bring Armstrong back to the station.

"I'm going to drop his dog off at the pet groomer on Fillmore Street. Can you pick him up on the way back?"

Kira had recommended The Dog Palace, and she had called ahead to make an appointment. By ten he was in the waiting area watching as a Doberman pinscher eyed Travis. The Doberman's muscles rippled every time it pulled on its leash, a leash that was short enough, but would the woman holding it have the strength to hold it if the dog wanted to get a piece of him or Travis?

The big red Doberman walked over as far as the leash would allow and wagged its stubby tail. Trufant stretched across the gap and scratched it behind the ears.

"Her name is Annie," the woman said.

Travis watched, sitting unconcerned next to him.

Dogs must have some secret code of communication.

"Mr. Trufant?" a woman behind the counter asked. "Is this Travis?"

"Yes, it is, I'm watching him for a friend. He stinks and needs a bath and probably something to eat. I'm really late, but I'll have him picked up in a few hours."

As the woman led him away, Travis looked back with sad eyes, leaving him feeling guilty. How many strangers has this poor dog been with in the last forty-eight hours?

Armstrong said he thought an officer had tased the dog, which was probably true if it had bitten one of them, but at the moment, it looked anything but threatening.

If I had been tased by a stranger, I wouldn't be so friendly.

Back out on Fillmore Street, he drove toward the station. He had missed the worst of rush hour, but now it was raining and he was competing with the tourists and the Big Red bus tours. Driving behind one of the big double-decker buses was frustrating. The back of the bus blocked his view of everything and he couldn't get around it.

What a week. Now I have to deal with a fricking dog.

Two small kids on the back of the sightseeing bus were looking down at him and laughing. They waved, oblivious to the rain, their yellow ponchos flapping uselessly in the wind, their clothes soaked, and their wet hair matted and tangled. He smiled and waved back.

***

A strange woman was sitting outside his office. She stood once he got close, obviously waiting for him.

Christ, I can't get a break!

He had hoped he could close his door and grab thirty minutes of shut-eye while things in the station were still quiet.

Who was she? Mid-thirties, too attractive, too confident, and dressed in a dark-gray pin-striped suit—another civilian attorney, shit!

She started to speak and he cut her off.

"I signed the papers last week," he said, opening his office door. "My wife has them already."

"I'm Caitlin Armstrong, Lt. Trufant. You left a message on my phone asking about my husband."

Caught off guard, he turned and tried to speak. "Yes," was all he could get out of his mouth. "I'm sorry. I wasn't expecting you. I didn't know you were in San Francisco."

"I wasn't. I was in Denver, but I haven't heard from David in almost a year, and my curiosity got the best of me. Do you know where he is?"

"I do. But come into my office. It's complicated, and this will take a few minutes."

"Is he in trouble, Lt. Trufant?"

"Well . . . he's in danger. He's involved in a case we're working, the homicides I mentioned on the phone. Your husband witnessed one of them, and the man we're looking for may be after him now."

"I've seen the news on CNN, the serial killer, is that the man you're talking about?"

"Yes, it is. Mrs. Armstrong, I had a long conversation with your husband two days ago, are you still married? I ask because I assumed the two of you have long been divorced."

"We are still technically married. I began divorce proceedings twice, but I couldn't go through with it. We've been separated for eight years now."

"I can imagine how difficult it was for you. People change. My wife left me recently, and I can't blame her." He hoped the last part sounded humorous, but knew it didn't.

"Lt. Trufant, I didn't leave David, he left me. Did he tell you what happened to him?"

"I know he was wounded. Afghanistan, I think he said, and I saw his leg."

"Yes, the leg," she said, looking away. "I flew to Germany right after I got the phone call. I helped him recover from his wounds, the physical ones anyway. I helped him in rehab where they taught him to walk again and where they also made him a drug addict. I helped him through the physical part, but he shut me out, thanks to the mental wounds."

Caitlin looked out his window as if deciding whether or not she wanted to continue, then looked back at Trufant.

"You see, it wasn't just the leg, Lt. Trufant, although he hates that thing—always trying to keep it covered, but the leg was the least of it. The doctor came in to see me right after I got to the hospital. He said a fragment the size of a baseball hit David in the groin. It . . . it did a lot of damage. Please don't ever tell him I told you this, but as the doctor told me, 'I was only able to leave him just enough to pee with.'"

"I'm sorry, Mrs. Armstrong. I can't imagine how much you've both suffered," Trufant said. "I won't share this information with anyone."

"Before his last deployment, all we talked about was starting a family. I think being a father was more important to him than being a husband."

She stopped and looked at a picture of Adelaide on his desk, her blue eyes staring through the photo at something only she could see, then just as quickly looked back at him.

"You said your wife left you, and yet you have her picture on your desk. Maybe you understand a little of how I feel."

He looked at the picture, and he couldn't think of a reason he hadn't put it away.

"Maybe I do," he said.

"I woke up one morning, and David was gone. I knew it was going to happen. He couldn't bear the thought of us as a couple anymore. He felt unworthy. He said I deserved a real man, 'a whole man,' were his actual words."

Trufant nodded, waiting for her to continue.

"The doctors said it was probably the loss of testosterone that changed him, that made him feel that way. Intercourse was definitely out of the question, and I could live with that. God, I told him that so many times, but I could see it in his face. He just couldn't live with it. He lost the fire in his eyes. The first time I met him, I saw that fire. It was the look of a man who loved life, and he did."

He studied her as she spoke, saw the different emotions flashing across her face, watched her eyes look up at the ceiling as she remembered painful events and crossed her legs when she feared she may have said too much.

"The drugs and living on the street are his coping mechanisms," Cait said. "They keep him from forming relationships. When he was injured—when the explosion happened—his best friend, Travis, was killed. Travis and David were a team, they complemented each other, like . . . I don't know how to say it. They each made up for the other guy's deficiencies—they fed off each other and became better people, better Marines. Had Travis lived that day, things might be different."

"Well, that explains the dog's name."

"He named the dog Travis?"

He nodded, and thought she was finished talking. There were no tears, but she masked the pain, her lips stretched taut in a grimace, her eyes staring out the window behind him. *What does she see out there?*

"He has money, you know," she said, still looking outside. "He gets a disability check every month, direct deposit. But he won't touch it. The only time he's asked for money was to pay a veterinarian. That was eight months ago. I think that was the last time we spoke."

"Well . . . ," he paused, not knowing how she would take his next few words. "He should be on his way here now, from San Rafael."

"David is on his way here now?"

Chapter 22

Armstrong

"David Armstrong," the magistrate said.

He stood, fighting nausea and the shaking of his good leg. The man in the black robe said, "You're charged with sleeping on posted county property—how do you plead?"

Inspector Amato in the second row, along with two other spectators, looked at David and nodded as the prosecutor announced an agreement had been reached. He would plead guilty and receive a sentence of time served, and he would be free to go once the magistrate's trial calendar was complete.

He sat with two other prisoners for an hour as each case was read. Some of the people were released and walked out the front door with their attorneys, while others were led out another door, still in handcuffs. Eventually, he was escorted back to his cell where they gave him his old clothes, four crumpled dollars, two quarters, and his wallet, everything he had owned except the pocket knife he had taken off the dead man.

Dressed in his old jeans and fatigue jacket and still shaking from withdrawal, he met Amato in the lobby.

"Not so bad, right?" Amato asked.

"Humiliating, maybe, but it comes with the lifestyle, and I've dealt with worse over the years. I had my own cell this time, that doesn't happen often."

"I'm sorry about Dr. Williams," Amato said as they walked outside. "Trufant told me how you knew her."

"I barely knew her at all. We had a cup of coffee. I think she had a few demons of her own and just wanted to talk about them. She was a nice woman—I liked her, and I think I would have gone back to another meeting. Sitting alone in a freezing cell all night, dopesick, and puking everything I tried to eat gave me some time to think, Inspector. I might try it again—rehab. I think I owe Dr. Williams that much. Did she suffer?"

"I doubt it. I went to the crime scene. She was getting in or out of her car near the VA. She was a jogger, a friend said. She would run several miles every other night alone near Crissy Field in the Presidio. She did it like clockwork, so it was an easy schedule for this guy to see. I think her death was quick, like the homeless guys on Mason Street. A few seconds of confusion, probably, and she lost consciousness."

David watched the scenery along Route 101 as the inspector talked. He would have been okay with silence too, but he liked listening to the man. There was no feeling of being judged, no condescension, and no unsolicited advice that everyone else felt obligated to offer.

"Are you hungry now? Amato asked.

"Yes, but I don't think I can hold it down. Maybe later, thanks."

The images of the doctor came and went like the billboards along the side of the highway. He could see her standing on the old plywood podium at the Legion of Honor, sitting on the bench in the park feeding Travis, and her face up close as she talked about her father. Soon, just like Master Sergeant Travis McClanahan, he would have trouble remembering her face—except in his dreams. In dreams, he remembered them too well.

"We're stopping to get your dog," Amato said several miles later. "The lieutenant took him home last night and said the dog kept him up all night whining, and he smelled like shit. He's at a pet grooming place getting spruced up."

"I've smelled worse," Armstrong said. "I had a cold shower yesterday, but my clothes still stink. I didn't realize how bad they were until I wore the prison jumpsuit."

***

They stopped in the town of Waldo for lunch, Amato ate while Armstrong nursed black coffee, then drove across the Golden Gate Bridge in the early afternoon. The sky had cleared, and the ferry boats were heading to Alcatraz and Angel Island. The white-capped water in the bay was a deep blue, darker than the sky above it.

Amato's phone rang.

"Yes, Lieutenant?"

David recognized Trufant's voice but couldn't hear what he was saying.

"Okay, I'll tell him."

"What now?" David said.

"Your wife is in the lieutenant's office."

Caitlin was in San Francisco!

David stared at Alcatraz, at the cold rocks and the decaying buildings and tried to imagine life inside the old prison, tough probably, but facing Caitlin was terrifying. He looked at the stains on his jeans and imagined how he would smell to her. He would have preferred the solitude of prison over the humility of facing her now.

"I haven't seen her in more than a year. I didn't think we were still married."

***

They pulled into a strip mall off Fillmore Street and parked in front of The Dog Palace.

The big Labrador retriever looked confused as he came out from behind the counter, but jumped into David's arms, almost knocking him over.

He buried his face in the dog's fur. "I missed you too, Travis. God, you smell good."

With Travis on an old leather leash, the three of them stepped outside. The air was fresh, and he smelled something pleasant blooming nearby, jasmine maybe.

Then Travis growled and yanked hard on the leash, ripping it out of his hands.

Chapter 23

Ramzi

Northbound traffic on 101 was beginning to build as commuters made their way into the city and as Ramzi passed through Brisbane. The sky was clear, and the high-rises in downtown San Francisco were bathed in sunlight. It was a good omen.

Killing a man was always a high and this morning was no different. Adrenaline rushes surged through him like lightning, one after another, each one taking a physical toll on him—excited one minute and fatigued the next.

With the laptop open he watched the two icons moving on the map, one showing Trufant's car still parked at the police station, the other, Inspector Amato's vehicle near the Golden Gate Bridge.

Ramzi wanted Trufant today—to kill him right now, but it was not going to be possible, storming into the police station would be suicide. Trufant would have to wait. He would have to draw him out into the open, and he would wait until the moment was perfect.

None of his contacts on the street had seen Armstrong in days. He couldn't get to that man either, but Trufant's partner was on the move. Amato's car was moving slowly southbound across the bridge and was probably headed to the police station five miles away.

He hit the gas, passing slower traffic and heard a few protesting horns as he swerved between lanes.

Traffic slowed in the southbound lanes, and he needed to get off the 101 and follow the cop until he could confront him. With any luck, he could take him out right in their station's parking lot.

As he drove, he visualized Trufant's partner lying at his feet, blood pooling around the body, and wiping the blade clean on the man's clothing. His heart began pumping more adrenaline into his system, and he felt the fog of fatigue clear—he heard every sound around him, colors were sharper, and he knew that right now he was invincible, and like the doctor, the cop would soon be another tattoo.

Ramzi parked in a lot off Fillmore Street and waited, watching the icon inching eastward along Lombard. Then the cop's symbol merged with his own, and the white Ford Taurus was right in front of him. Two men were in the car, and the passenger looked like Armstrong.

I can kill them both!

He checked the laptop to make sure it was the same car, then accelerated onto the roadway.

A white furniture truck swerved into his lane and stopped in front of him. He watched helplessly as the Taurus disappeared around a turn and was gone.

He hit his horn, pressing as hard as he could, as if pushing harder would move the big truck. The driver of the *Father and Two Sons* truck got out and walked back to confront him, and he picked one of the knives off the front seat.

Killing this man would be easy. But I must stay focused. I want Armstrong.

He put the Honda in reverse, backed up and rear-ended the car behind him, pushing it backward until he had enough room to get around the truck and accelerated into the middle lane.

He was moving again, but now the Taurus was too far ahead to see. He mouthed his oaths and the names aloud as he swerved in and out of the southbound lanes, ignoring the horns sounding all around him.

"Smith, Gonzalez, Washington, Curry, Trufant, Armstrong!"

The shame of losing Armstrong again was going to be great, and he remembered his mother's warning.

Your obsession with Armstrong has become an expensive distraction, Ramzi!

She knew nothing of how deep his obsessions were. He swerved into the left lane and heard brakes squeal and crumpling metal somewhere behind him and then he was in the clear. The traffic had thinned out, but the Taurus was gone.

The tracker showed the car was still southbound, but slowing, then stopped somewhere just ahead of him.

The Taurus was parked in a strip mall on the right side of the road. He cruised past the last entrance, and parked across the street.

If he could kill both men here, Trufant would arrive in minutes. In the chaos, Ramzi may have a chance to get him too. The sensation of killing all three would be euphoric.

He was as ready as he could be. He would kill them both, a single slash for each of them, and be back in his car as their blood ran across the asphalt. That image of them lying together excited him, and he was surprised to feel his erection.

Squeezing the steering wheel with both hands drained away the anxiety and helped him think, helped him focus. His hatred for Armstrong was irrational, and he knew it, more so than it had been for any of the people he had killed. Their deaths had relieved him no differently than reaching the peak of a mountain after a long hike. It was merely a goal, a destiny that had to be fulfilled.

There was no great pleasure in killing them, either, they were strangers, men he and Madinah had identified as soldiers, had they been any one of the men on his list, it would be different. Now a man he did hate was somewhere in that shopping center—one of the new names on his list was within his reach.

He walked across the street, keeping his head down and away from any cameras, the cold stainless steel of his knives warming as he held them in the pockets of his sweatshirt.

For all the shame he had endured the last several weeks, he was about to kill again, and his shame would be forgotten.

He forced all thought and emotion from his mind and approached the cop's car. It was empty. He stopped, looked at the stores around him, and saw Armstrong coming out of a pet shop with Amato behind him. He pulled the knives from his pockets, hearing the metallic snap as each of them opened in unison.

He repeated the names and his oaths silently.

Smith, Gonzalez, Washington, Curry, Trufant, Armstrong. For my father, for my sisters!

Dopamine and adrenaline rushed through his veins, and he knew he could kill everyone in the parking lot if he had to. But Armstrong would be the first to die—he was the closer of the two men. Ramzi focused on the pink flesh of the man's neck. Every detail was sharp, the week-old stubble of a beard, the open collar of his faded fatigue jacket. But the neck—he could almost see the man's carotid artery pulsing—that was his target.

He would start with the knife in his right hand, swinging left to right, and as the man fell, Amato would be next. One step forward, then he could slash the other knife across the man's throat right to left. Two movements—two seconds—and it would be over. He would walk across the street to his car, and if things went well, he would wait for Trufant.

With the knives in his hands, he saw the recognition in Armstrong's face as the Balisong began its upward arc—then he heard a sound—and everything changed.

Chapter 24

Armstrong

Travis was making that noise again, a combination of a sharp snarl and a deep, guttural growl. He looked down at the dog. Its hackles were raised, exposing the pale flesh along its spine.

In front of him, moving a little faster than everything else, was the preppy kid with the cold, empty eyes. He came out from between two parked cars and those strange eyes zeroed in on him.

Time slowed to a crawl. He'd had one moment in his life like this—when the two small boys ran away from the Stryker and the IED exploded—showering him in shreds of clear plastic water bottles mixed with the flesh and bone of his best friend.

Now, the air around him thickened, and he felt like he was moving through molasses, but this young college student seemed immune. The man looked like he could have been as young as sixteen, or as old as twenty-five, there was an agelessness in his face. He was dressed again in a yellow Berkeley University sweatshirt and dark blue pants, and his lips were moving as if he were talking to someone. Then Armstrong saw the two strange knives, one in each of the man's hands.

The man took another step forward, and one of the knives began to rise, gripped by bone-white knuckles.

Sunlight reflected off the blade, a flash so intense that Armstrong wanted to close his eyes—to surrender and let it happen. He could feel each beat of his heart, each one causing an ache somewhere deep in his head and in his bowels, and he feared he was going to fall or shit himself.

But he didn't. Instead, he tried to recall the hours of training in hand-to-hand combat, to focus on the greatest threat, and deal with it first. His mind seemed sharp but his reflexes were too slow. He watched the blade as it arced toward his face, then somewhere in front of him, he heard a terrifying new noise. He wanted to look down to see what was making the horrible sound, but he couldn't take his eyes off the shining blade.

Something black—the source of the noise that now sounded like a child screaming—flew out in front of him, blocking his view of the knife. Travis!

The dog sank his white teeth into the yellow sweatshirt and shook his head back and forth, ripping off shreds of yellow fabric drenched in bright red blood, then pink bits of loose flesh, tearing through the man's forearm and crunching against bone.

In those last few seconds—seconds that stretched into eternity—Armstrong felt like a spectator watching a horror movie, detached from all his emotions—until the knife slammed into his shoulder. The knife was lodged deep into the joint and the assailant yanked on the knife, trying to free it. It felt like a pry bar was pulling his shoulder apart, and the blade snapped. Searing pain radiated along his arm and neck, and he fell to his knees as his own blood sprayed out in front of him.

A small black piece of fur fell on the asphalt, followed by drops of bright red blood. He realized it was one of the dog's ears, then Travis collapsed, and he reached out with his good arm and pulled him closer. Helpless and still on the ground, he saw the assailant slam the remaining few inches of the broken knife into Amato's ribcage.

Amato's eyes stayed focused, even as the blade sank into his chest. The inspector's gun was out, and he fired once, the bullet slamming into the assailant's left shoulder and the second knife flew uselessly through the air.

The gunfire was deafening, and Armstrong's ears rang as he watched Amato fall, his gun dropping between his knees.

Amato's head bounced against the asphalt as if it was rubber. Amato looked at him and tried to speak, but Armstrong's ears were still ringing and if the inspector had said anything, he couldn't hear him.

Then Amato's eyes moved to the gun next to him. *Pick it up, kill him!*

The man's once bright yellow sweatshirt was stained red now, and fresh blood blossomed from a jagged hole covering the *y* in Berkeley. Armstrong watched thick blood, like red string, drip off the fingers of the man's right hand and onto his linen-colored shoes. *Why won't he just die?*

Amato's gun was four feet away. Armstrong would have to let go of Travis to reach it and the man was too close, only a step away. He would kill Travis.

Armed only with a broken knife, the man stared down at him. His eyes were as black as the river rocks at the tourist shops in town. His lips were no longer speaking those silent words, now they were locked in a grimace that was either hatred or pain. Travis broke free from his grasp and stood snarling, inching forward, his white teeth stained with red blood.

Watching Travis, he hesitated and took a step back, and then another, still gripping the broken knife. Another few feet and he could reach the gun.

Just another few inches!

The man turned and looked across the street, took another step backward and walked away, out into the street.

Armstrong stood up and reached for the gun, feeling his rubber-soled shoes slipping in the growing pool of blood. The gun's plastic grips were slick, making it hard to hold.

The pain in his right shoulder made lifting and aiming impossible, but he fired anyway and saw a piece of cloth and blood fly from the man's right thigh. Then he fired a second time, and the gun kicked hard and slipped from his hands. He picked it up again but had no strength to aim it—and the man was gone.

Armstrong crawled over to Amato and turned him over. He could hear now, and what he heard was a rattling sound each time the man took a breath.

"I've got you, Inspector, you're going to be okay."

Amato smiled. "Tell Trufant . . . "

"Tell him what?"

"Tell him I didn't freeze."

Chapter 25

Ramzi

Have I failed again?

This is all wrong—this is not how it was supposed to end!

He looked down at the cop. The man was clearly dying. Blood poured from his white dress shirt and flowed downhill toward Armstrong. Armstrong was down too, but his eyes were open, and he was cradling the dog in his left arm, the dog still snarling and trying to pull free from the man's grasp. Blood had soaked the man's old jacket, and he could see the broken edge of the Balisong's blade protruding through its fabric. Hopefully, he had severed an artery. If so, it could be a fatal wound.

His good knife was nowhere in sight, and he looked at the broken blade of the knife still in his hand. He could use it to finish Armstrong, but people were already coming out of the shops having heard the gunfire. Some stood in the doorways staring at him while others held their phones up recording him. A moment ago, he could have killed them all without effort, like sheep.

But the damned dog! It was a threat now. It had pulled free from Armstrong's grasp and stood in front of him, its bared teeth and that snarling terrified him.

Leave, or die here, or worse, be captured and face Trufant?

He turned and walked toward his car and was halfway across the street when a .40 caliber bullet tore a chunk of flesh from his thigh. Another shot echoed off the building in front of him, and he slipped and fell face-first on the asphalt, cracking one of his front teeth.

He spit out a piece of the tooth, tasting blood. Intense pain was now coursing through his arm and leg. He pushed himself up and saw his index finger was missing. Instead, it was right in front of him, and he stepped on it, not realizing what it was at first.

He glanced back and saw Armstrong with the cop's gun in his hand.

Running was not an option, so he limped the final twenty yards to his Honda, expecting to hear another shot, but it never happened.

His keys were in his left pocket, and that arm was ruined. He threw the broken knife into the gutter next to the car and dug the keys out with his right hand.

It was the damn dog!

He had been so consumed with killing Armstrong that he had never seen the animal.

I should have killed it!

It might still die. He had felt his knife go deep across the dog's skull.

He eased the silver Honda out into traffic and looked back at the pet shop. A crowd had already gathered outside around Armstrong and Amato. Some were kneeling to help while others were pointing at him as he drove away.

They will be looking for this car soon.

He had leased the Civic knowing it was a popular car and would be one of thousands of similar vehicles roaming the streets of San Francisco. Like camouflage, he hoped the car would blend in unnoticed as he drove to his apartment.

***

Fifteen minutes. That's how much time it would take for the police to get the call, run his tag number in their computer and send officers to his address. Fifteen minutes!

Will I live that long?

The street in front of his building was deserted, no cars and no one walking, and he pulled into the underground garage. Getting to the third floor was not going to be easy, every step caused fresh crippling pain.

His yellow sweatshirt was covered with blood from the gunshot wound and the dog bite. His rain jacket would hide the worst of the blood but getting it on was agonizing. His left arm hung useless, and the other screamed in pain. The dog had torn away big pieces of muscle, and the wounds burned like acid had been poured into the raw flesh. Looking at the wounds made him weak and sick to his stomach, only adrenaline kept him moving.

He looked back and even in the dim lighting of the garage, the trail of blood would still be hard to miss.

It didn't matter now. In fifteen minutes he would be gone, and he would never need to come back.

The cops and Trufant would be looking for Hector Bolivar for weeks and months, maybe even years, because Hector's trail would end right here. He would have to destroy the Bolivar passport and ID cards soon. They had been expensive to obtain, and he had been comfortable with the alias. His Ocampo identification was solid, though, he had tested it just days earlier, which now seemed like months ago.

He pressed the third-floor button in the elevator, leaving a red smear that glowed crimson as the tiny lightbulb activated. The car lurched and started its climb and stopped on the first floor and the doors opened.

A woman and a small child stepped in, and the girl started to press the second-floor button, her finger just an inch from the blood-smeared button above it.

"Mama!"

The girl looked at the blood, then looked at the blood dripping from his fingertips and pooling on the elevator's tile floor.

"Not now," the woman said, never looking down.

The girl looked at him, her big blue eyes wanting to ask a question.

"I cut myself."

The doors opened, and the woman pulled her out into the hallway. The woman never looked back, but the girl watched him until the doors closed.

Alone again, he felt weak and wanted to slide down the car's wall and sit on the floor.

I will not die on the floor of this dirty elevator! I have seen my death, and this is not how it ends!

At his feet were large drops of blood, and he smeared them into the tile floor with his shoe as the doors opened.

Ten more minutes!

Suffering another fresh jab of pain, he brought the keys up to the lock.

He looked back toward the elevator, and if there was a blood trail, it was hidden, absorbed or camouflaged, in the rust-colored carpet. His door opened and he locked it from the inside, stripped off his ruined clothes and threw them in a pile on the bedroom floor.

His shoulder wound was the worst. In the mirror, he saw the entry hole was small and round. It puckered around the edges and was smaller than he had expected. It was the exit wound that scared him. It was a gaping, jagged wound with flesh torn away like the petals of a dying flower. The bullet had passed through his shoulder blade, and he could see tiny bits of cream-colored bone and gray fragments of the bullet around the edges of the exposed muscle.

The sight made him sick, and he heaved over the toilet twice before the sensation ended. Without someone's help, he was going to certainly die.

The dog bites and the gunshot to his thigh he could deal with himself. The thigh wound was ugly, the entry hole was small but inflamed, and a thin stream of dried blood was already crusting on his calf. The exit hole, like the one in his shoulder, had peeled outward, and fresh blood flowed freely down his calf and into his sock. Using duct tape and Ace bandages, he bound all the wounds as tight as the pain would allow and sponged off the remaining blood on his chest. He was fighting to stay conscious.

Five minutes!

The bare mattress on the floor called for him. He wanted to lie down and close his eyes and let sleep start the healing process, but the first police officer could be coming through the door at any time.

They would be looking for someone in a yellow sweatshirt, so he put on his only other shirt, the black dress shirt he had worn to Madinah's funeral.

He looked into each room, picturing how Trufant and his friends would see them. The wall in the second bedroom was all they would find interesting. There was nothing in here he needed, so he grabbed the duffel bag from the walk-in closet, stuffed his bloody clothes inside, and headed back to the car. The bag was heavy in his right hand. It was hard to carry, but he needed everything in it.

He was now several blocks away from his apartment when the first of several SFPD police cars passed him in the opposite direction, sirens quiet but blue lights flashing.

Driving with one hand, he pressed the phone button on the steering wheel, and said, "Call Mother."

He waited for the connection as each pothole and cable car rail sent new waves of pain through his shoulder.

"Yes, Ramzi?" he heard her rasp.

CHAPTER 26

MOTHER

Diwata studied the black-and-white picture on her phone, a young woman with blonde hair lying near the open door of a car, her throat cut in a way only Ramzi was capable of doing. Some doctor, a nobody, a wasted death. Did he think this woman's murder would quench her insatiable thirst for revenge? No, but he was driven like a moth to a lamp once he set his course.

Alone on her second-story deck, she wept, remembering the morning she had forced her son to watch her kill the soldier as he drank coffee in a market near Bagdad.

"That's how you will forget, Ramzi, that's what will keep the monsters from your room at night. You are a warrior now, never forget that."

She moved her surviving family back to her hometown of Manila and lived with her aunt's family, hoping distance would cure them all. But her pain and hatred followed her and weeks later, her aunt asked her to move out when Ramzi and Madinah had killed the family's dog.

"Your son has schizophrenia, among other things, including an obsessive-compulsive disorder," the doctors in Manila had said. She had allowed them to medicate him to the point he had become so dysfunctional, he couldn't even leave the hospital.

It was a Tagalog blade master who brought Ramzi back to reality by focusing his obsessive behavior on something he could understand. The discipline allowed him to control his delusions to such a degree that he flourished and returned to school—until the fire.

The fire changed everything.

The screams that night still haunted her. The victims were relatives, and most of them were children, and she hated herself for it. But she had oaths to keep. Oaths to her husband, whose last vision on earth was of his daughter being brutalized and slaughtered like a lamb, oaths to her murdered daughter and son, and even to Araya, who had been miles away. Keeping those oaths meant she and her family needed to start a new life, a life with no threads to the past. and no loose ends.

Ramzi tossed the match through an open window as she watched from across the street It was a dry, hot night and the hundred-year-old building was engulfed in seconds.

***

The afternoon shadows crept across the lawn, the days were getting shorter as the last of the summer breezes blew across the lake. Soon the green leaves would turn to red, then brown and die. Winter was coming, and she knew she would never live to see snow again.

Her phone vibrated in her lap, disturbing one of the few peaceful moments she cherished at the end of each day. It was her son, and she prayed he had finally avenged her daughter's death.

"Yes, Ramzi."

"Mother, I . . . "

She heard the pain and terror in his voice, and images of every nightmare she had ever had flashed in front of her, screaming a silent scream, picturing her son, covered in blood, again.

"Where are you? What happened?"

"I went after Armstrong and Trufant's partner. The cop is probably dead, maybe Armstrong is too, but . . . I'm shot and I can't stop the bleeding."

She sat in her wheelchair, helpless, more than helpless—he was twenty-two hundred miles away. She could hear the fear and desperation in his voice, a voice that for years had been so self-assured, so arrogant, and now each word trembled like the child he used to be.

"Where are you going? I hear traffic, are you driving?"

"I . . . I'm crossing the Bay Bridge into Oakland now. I know a medical student there who might help me, but I don't know if I'm going to make it. I've lost so much blood, Mother."

His voice trailed off, and all she heard was him breathing.

"Ramzi!"

"I've failed you, Mother. I may be dying. I'm sorry."

"You have not failed me, Ramzi, not yet. You must stay alive a few more hours. Call me when you reach your friend. I will try to find someone who will help you."

She ended the call and called the attorney in Chicago.

***

"What can I do for you, Ms. Aquino?"

"My son is seriously injured in Oakland, California. I need your assistance again, Mr. Silva. I want him brought here for medical treatment."

"Seriously injured? I'll need to charter a plane and a flight crew with medical experience. They will have many questions. How badly is he injured?"

"He has been shot."

"I see. It will be an expensive problem, Ms. Aquino. Gunshot wounds must be reported to the police."

"Can you do it or not, Mr. Silva?"

"Of course I can. I will call you the moment I have made the arrangements."

***

Twenty minutes later she redialed Ramzi and listened to him breathing hard.

"Stop moving," she heard a woman say.

"Ramzi!"

"I'm here, Mother."

"Are you okay?"

"Yes—no, Mother, my friend is doing what she can. The bleeding has slowed, but the pain is unbearable. I can't drive, and I'm sure they are looking for my car."

"Forget about the car. You must go to Buchanan Field Airport, an airplane will be there in one hour to bring you here. Do you understand?"

"Buchanan Field, do you know where it is?" she heard him ask the woman.

"I will be there," he said.

"Get this woman to drive you to the airport and listen for the pilot's call. He has your number but do not say a word to him Ramzi, not a word. One hour—don't be late."

***

Ramzi, her only son, may be dying. She loved him beyond measure, even as damaged as he was. She knew it was a different love than it had been, remembering him as he played soccer with Madinah and Leilah in the dirt yard behind the house—so bright and full of life. He was different now, but who wouldn't be?

She flicked her cigarette butt into the ceramic ashtray with the others and contemplated the cost.

Twenty-five thousand dollars, plus expenses. The plane alone could be another twenty thousand. Ramzi had made another expensive mistake, and this one might have lasting consequences—if he lived.

Now they would have everything they needed to link Ramzi to Madinah. Soon a search would be on for the rest of the family. Now the FBI was involved as well. If he had killed a police officer, the end was near. They would not rest until they had turned over every stone she had spent years burying.

She lit another Gold Flake and thought about her final days.

She had hoped to die in this majestic house with its magnificent views of the river that never seemed to bring her any joy. Built in 1892, the seven-bedroom home, paid for with American blood money, was supposed to house her children for years, but they had all fled to distant parts of the country she hated the most. How ironic.

She must warn her surviving children.

She called Leilah's number and listened as it rang a dozen times, not even allowing her to leave a message. Had the girl finally blocked her?

She tried Araya, knowing the girl would never answer but listened to the automated voice and waited for the cue.

Careful not to name anyone, Diwata said, "Your brother has been gravely injured. I know you care for him. His sister is dead and now he may die as well. You may also be in danger—please call me."

The last photo she had of Araya stared back at her on the phone. Her eldest daughter was standing in front of the house in Chicago with a blanket of snow covering the yard. The house she had never seen in person, and the one Araya lived in less than a year before abandoning it and moving back to Manila.

The twenty-year-old girl smiled awkwardly in the picture, posing for some unknown person behind the camera, a smile which was probably expected, but not felt.

Would Araya even hear her message? Was the number still hers? Diwata had not spoken with her or heard from her since she left Chicago, ever since she learned Ramzi and Madinah had killed a man in Singapore—that man, and many others, and Araya blamed her for the murders.

Araya was still a devout Christian. Diwata had underestimated her daughter's faith, and that mistake had ended their relationship.

"Mother, I forgave those men—but you? You, I cannot forgive. You have turned what is left of my family into monsters."

The image on her phone switched to the photo of her dead husband taken at their wedding. Happier times. He had been a decent man and a good husband and father—the only man she had ever loved.

"Oh, Nasim, I have failed us all, I'm afraid."

***

The old, weathered oak floor creaked as she rolled her wheelchair down the hallway, passing each child's old room and into the parlor.

Two hours, plus a five-hour flight to Downsview Airport outside Toronto. Silva said it was the only way to get him into Canada without risking everything. Seven hours—add an hour for traffic and he would arrive soon after midnight. Then she would have to keep him alive.

"Chanda!" she screamed down the hall.

"Yes, Diwata?"

"Call your friend, tell her to be here before midnight and to bring everything we discussed. I have calls of my own to make."

Chanda's friend worked as a cashier at North American Medical Supplies and had helped Diwata several times before with simple items she needed during her cancer treatment. She hoped those would be enough to save him.

Chapter 27

Trufant

Carlos's body was in room number three, not a room really, just one of twelve curtained-off areas inside the emergency room.

They had stripped off his bloody clothing, which was now underneath the gurney in a clear plastic bag. They'd left him some dignity, he thought, he still wore his plaid boxers. The IV port still in his arm and the ventilator tube still in his throat made Trufant angry. They had left Carlos lying on the table like a cadaver, and he deserved better.

Part of him knew Carlos was now just that, a body void of life, meat that would soon rot in a coffin underground. Rage rose like bile, and he had trouble breathing.

Carlos looked so peaceful, and if not for the small, puckered laceration between his ribs, he might open his eyes, sit up and ask, "What's the big deal, L.T.?"

The thought reminded him of the phone call just a few nights ago.

Lieutenant, I'm driving home across the bridge and I'm soaked in my own sweat and I know I won't sleep tonight.

"I'm sorry, Carlos."

"He was dead on the scene," said a voice behind him.

Trufant spun around with his hand on the grips of his gun and almost pulled it from the holster.

It was the fire rescue captain. "But we worked him anyway,

pumping his chest and starting IVs. We didn't want to leave him lying in the parking lot with a crowd of his fellow officers and spectators watching."

Trufant was grateful for that. The captain had fresh blood stains on his white shirt—he had done all he could.

"Thank you, Captain."

"Lieutenant," he heard. It was Rachel Adams, an ER nurse he'd met years ago on his first visit to the San Francisco General Hospital as a rookie.

"Come in, Rachel."

"I'm sorry to intrude, Lieutenant. I've known Carlos for a few years, and I know he was a good man," she said. "His wife will be here soon, though, and I don't know if she should see him like this."

"She's a strong woman, but the ME will need to see him just the way he is. Emma is still at the crime scene and won't be free for hours. Just cover him and hide the bag with his bloody shirt."

They heard a commotion from behind the curtain.

"This way, Chief," someone said, and the curtain opened. Lozano and Captain Brown stood, slack-jawed, staring at Carlos.

"Chief," he said respectfully, ignoring the other man.

"Marcus, I'm sorry for your loss. Carlos was a good man, and we will all miss him."

Lozano took a quick look at the body and stepped back outside, but Captain Brown stayed in the room.

"I need a moment alone with Lt. Trufant, please."

Bile began rising in his throat again.

He looked at Brown's dull, flat face, trying to anticipate what was coming next. Nothing good, that was for sure.

Brown's eyes were perpetually squinting, and he had a habit of looking down when he spoke. The only hint of emotion Trufant had ever noticed in the man was when he felt threatened—his cheeks flushed, and they were crimson now.

"Lieutenant, the chief is placing you on paid administrative leave. As you know, you are to remain at home during your normal duty hours. Should you need to leave your home during those hours, you will notify me at Internal Affairs. The cases you are working now will be reassigned to Lt. Gracia. Do you understand everything I've said?"

"You're suspending me?"

"The Chief wants you on paid leave pending a review, Lieutenant, so yes, I am suspending you. Is that clear enough?"

"Yes, Captain."

"Good, I'll walk you to your car."

They passed the chief on the way outside, and Lozano looked away.

"Didn't have the balls to tell me yourself, Chief?"

Lozano ignored him, and Trufant walked out into the parking lot. As he did, Carlos's wife arrived.

He stopped to meet her, but Brown stepped in front of him. "You're to leave the scene immediately, Lieutenant. I'll take care of Mrs. Amato."

"You're an ass, Brown, not as bad as Lozano, but still an ass."

He turned and walked to his car. At least they hadn't taken that away, yet. He ignored the chief's orders and drove to the shooting scene, knowing Brown and the chief would be busy holding a press conference at the hospital.

He found Emma Lew on her hands and knees next to a bullet fragment.

"Lieutenant," she said.

"Emma, I have been placed on leave."

She looked up at him, her eyes questioning him.

"He took me off the damn case, Emma!"

He saw her recoil and was sorry he had yelled, but emotionally he was spent, and physically he was wound too tight.

"Sorry, I needed to vent, but I should tell you I'm not here officially."

"So are they blaming you for Carlos's death?"

"No, the chief just wants to fuck me, Emma. Sorry for the French."

"I've heard worse." She stood and pointed to the shell casings with the yellow plastic markers over them.

"It looks like three shots were fired. Three was the number most of the witnesses heard too. Some have said as many as six, but I've only found three empty cases. All are Speer 40 caliber."

"This bullet," she said, pointing to a marker with the number three on it," hit soft tissue and neither Armstrong nor Inspector Amato suffered from a gunshot wound. The different blood patterns and pieces of flesh on two nearby cars indicate the subject was hit more than once and underneath marker number four is part of the subject's finger."

"So Carlos got a piece of him at least. Gracia's working the case now, has he been here?"

"He was and just left in a hurry. He was visibly shaken.

"I can imagine," he said, looking at one of Gracia's inspectors interviewing a pet shop employee.

"The subject ran across the street, and a witness said he was bleeding heavily from a shoulder wound. They have a tag number and an address. I think Gracia was headed there. I called in two more examiners to help me, and one is on his way to the hospital to begin examining Inspector Amato."

"Emma, I need to know if this guy's DNA matches the woman in Chicago."

The sound of several big V-8s racing to the scene made them both pause. A black Chevrolet Suburban pulled onto the curb just outside the perimeter, and Deputy Director Merriweather stepped out with a man in an Army uniform, a major, judging by the oak leaf on his shirt. The major nodded and both men slipped under the crime scene tape of the inner perimeter.

"Never mind, Emma, I think the FBI will be taking care of the DNA."

"What the fuck happened here, Marcus?" Merriweather asked.

"Our perp went after Armstrong or Amato, or both, I don't know. But I'm off the case now as you probably already know. I just had to come by and see the scene for myself."

"Emma Lew, this is Director Merriweather. She will fill you in, Director, but I want to go now."

***

Months ago, he would have opened the door and Etta Baker or B.B. King's vocals would be drifting from his wife's new stereo. He looked at the shelf where her Sony had been, but today, all he heard was the refrigerator humming.

He put a vinyl LP on his old turntable, a relic from his days at Tulane, and filled the room with a Cajun tune from J.J. Cale. He'd bought a six-pack of Corona, and several bottles of good wine on the way home. Popping the cap off a Corona, his last conversation with Carlos, just hours earlier, floated through his mind.

We're on our way to pick up the dog, L.T.

The dog! He had forgotten about Armstrong's dog. Shit! He dug the phone out of his back pocket and called Kira.

"Kira, I know you're probably busy, but I need a favor."

"Anything, Marcus. I'm so sorry, I . . . I don't know what to do here. Everyone is running around in a panic, but I have nothing to do. How can I help?"

"Kira, I left Armstrong's wife at the station. I need you to check on her and his dog if you can. I heard she was on the way to the hospital, but I don't know about his dog. I know the dog was injured too. Can you make sure someone is taking care of it?"

"I will, Marcus, no problem."

"I guess you heard the chief placed me on leave, so I'll be at home. Call me if you hear anything."

Chapter 28

Armstrong

Consciousness returned one fragment at a time. First, floating in a void, completely numb, a feeling that both frightened and calmed him. He relished the comfort, but he was aware that he should be screaming in terror.

Then his peaceful void was shattered. A high-pitched wailing screamed all around him. His eyes refused to focus as he was jostled back and forth, each movement causing searing pain in his chest. He was disoriented and his brain convinced him he was back in Afghanistan.

"Travis," he screamed.

He is not going to die this time. I'm going to save him!

He tried to sit up, and the familiar warmth of morphine flowed up his left arm. All the pain and sounds dissolved back into the familiar void.

I'm dead again.

***

If he was dead, how could this incessant beeping permeate the bliss of death?

Still free of pain, he recognized the sound of a heart monitor, and that told him he was indeed still alive.

A shape sitting next to him moved, his eyes blurred uselessly, but he knew someone was there. Then a woman called his name, but it was too hard to concentrate and so much easier to close his eyes and sleep. Twice more he woke, confused, feeling the woman's presence, then closing his eyes again, but this time the void eluded him and the nightmare returned.

"Travis! Get behind the truck, Goddamn it!"

"I'm tired of that stink, Armstrong!"

"You're a crazy motherfucker, Travis!"

"Oorah!"

"David?"

The woman's voice, and this time it sounded familiar. The dream of walking along the dirt road faded, and the stink of the armored personnel carriers' exhaust became a smell only a hospital could produce.

There was a strange metallic taste in his mouth, warmth when he should be cold, the absence of pain but knowing he had been stabbed, but most obvious, he should still be deep in withdrawal. He knew he was on morphine again—or some other opioid just as bad—*and the feeling was glorious.*

"David, can you hear me?"

He couldn't see her yet, but he tried to answer, "Yes."

It sounded more like a croak than a word, but it was enough.

"It's Caitlin, I'm here."

Just like in the hospital in Germany, Caitlin was somehow next to him.

Those few minutes in the pet groomer's parking lot flooded back into memory. He had been stabbed, his dog was probably dead, and Carlos Amato, a man he had just begun to trust, was definitely dead. And now his wife was sitting next to him.

"How bad is it?" he asked.

"You were in surgery for five hours, but the surgeon thinks it went well. You've been out since yesterday afternoon."

"Is my dog okay?"

"He was cut with a knife, and he lost an ear, but he's okay. He's at a veterinarian now."

"Inspector Amato is dead, isn't he? I saw him die right next to me."

"Yes, I'm afraid he is."

Afghanistan—all over again.

"I was right there, and I couldn't help him. Why can't I ever help them?"

He tried opening his eyes again and maybe it was the tears that helped but he still couldn't focus on her, at least not yet, she was just a colorful shape in a chair. He remembered how bad he had smelled in Amato's car and he hoped they had cleaned him up.

I've been fucking stabbed. Why do I care how I smell?

"He was a good man. I just met him, but I liked him. That's what happens to people I like, Caitlin. I told you to stay away from me."

He could hear his words slurring and his throat burned like he had swallowed battery acid.

"Don't try and talk David, you were intubated when I first got here, and you're doped up pretty good."

Her words trailed off, and he slept for an hour or maybe just minutes because when he opened his eyes, she was still in the chair next to him.

"Do I smell bad? Where is my dog? Where is Lt. Trufant? We were on our way to see him when all this happened. I need to tell him something. Did they catch the guy? How is my dog?"

If she answered any of his questions, he couldn't hear, he was rambling and trying to stay awake and focused, but he needed to know. "Don't let them give me any more morphine, Cait, no more pain killers. I have to get off this shit, and I would rather feel the pain."

"I'll tell them, David, but the knife did a lot of damage."

"Did you meet Trufant?"

Yes, I met the lieutenant, but he ran out when he heard the news on the radio. I haven't seen him since yesterday, and there are two armed police officers outside the door. I haven't heard anything about the man, but I know he got away."

"I think I shot him. I hope he burns in hell."

"Just rest, David, let the police worry about him."

"I saw his eyes, Cait, something is wrong with him. He was chanting people's names as he was attacking us, he . . . ," he closed his eyes picturing the man's moving lips. "No more morphine . . . I . . . Travis . . . "

Caitlin waited for him to finish, but he nodded off again. She watched him dream of the horrors of the dead and the dying—just like he had ten years ago.

Chapter 29

Trufant

At four in the morning, he gave up any attempt at sleep. He was too angry to relax, and in his head, he was fighting numerous losing battles with Brown and Lozano.

Fucking bastards, he said to himself, trying to rinse the burn out of his eyes with cold water. In the mirror, he looked twenty years older than he had just a month ago. *Bastards.*

He turned the TV on several times, watching the news reporters describing the scene at The Dog Palace, and each time they switched to Lozano's briefing at the hospital, he turned it off again. By noon he was on his third beer for the day when someone knocked on the door. He grabbed his gun and looked through the peephole, expecting either the IA captain or the man that had killed Carlos coming to kill him too, but it was the Army major he has seen with Merriweather.

"Major! Sorry, I was expecting someone else," he said when the man looked down at the gun, still pointing at him.

"Call me Tristan, Lieutenant, but most people just call me Flórez. I hope you don't mind me stopping by uninvited, especially now, but I have some information and I thought you might want some company."

"Come in, Tristan, I was sitting here wallowing in depression and frustration. It's like I'm on house arrest. I'm so pissed off, and there's nothing I can do about it. Have a seat. Can I get you a beer?"

"Certainly, but before I start, what's the story with you and your chief?"

"It's a long story, let's just say he's an asshole."

"Well, I've worked for a few myself. Let me get right to it."

The major had a well-worn case file under his arm and began pulling out photos that looked old and yellowed.

"I'm with the 110th Special Investigation Unit. My staff sergeant came across the news of your homicides a few days ago and remembered an incident I was involved in that we think is related. I was briefing Director Merriweather at the FBI building when your partner was shot. Merriweather asked me to get with you and tell you all I know."

"I appreciate that, Major."

"In 2009, as an MP, I was involved in a homicide case. A colonel in Baghdad was murdered, and there are some obvious similarities."

"Iraq is a long way from San Francisco, Major."

"Yes, it is, and a long time ago. But it was a terrible tragedy for everyone. What I'm going to tell you now is still classified but has been leaked so many times it might as well be public knowledge. On December 1, 2009, Colonel Greg Stenson was killed outside a coffee shop in Baghdad. His throat had been slashed, ear to ear. Stenson was the unit commander of an infantry regiment near Al-Masafer."

"December 1st," Trufant repeated.

"Yes, December 1, 2009, but there is more. Eight months earlier, on April 11, 2009, four members of a private contracting firm raped and killed a fourteen-year-old girl in the village of Al-Masafer. They killed her father, who was trying to defend her, and raped her ten-year-old twin sister and brother—all while her mother was tied to a chair and forced to watch."

Trufant jumped out of his chair, startling the major.

"You know the significance of those two dates?"

"Yes, I do, now. It was that link that caught our attention. I wish we could have caught it sooner, but my unit had been reassigned, and until now, we never heard a peep."

"So, who killed this colonel?"

"We don't know. We weren't even aware of the incident at Al-Masafer for weeks and by then the contractors had been rotated out. The Iraqi Army handled the initial investigation, and the mother was so distraught, she was hospitalized and sedated for days. Once she was able to speak, we tracked down the entire unit. Two of them were ex-US Army soldiers, discharged in 2005. They are serving life sentences at Leavenworth. The other two, a French national and a Brit, are serving time at Fort Lewis in Washington.

"Their arrest brought some peace to Al-Masafer—or so we thought until the colonel was killed. Ironically, it was the colonel who initiated the investigation and testified for the prosecution."

"By contractors, you mean hired mercenaries?"

"Yes, hired by the US government to provide security and other functions the politicians don't want anyone to know about. It's a very lucrative business, lots of cash for anyone who is awarded the contracts. In this case it was a senator from Virginia, who has since left office and died a few years ago of natural causes.

"So why would someone retaliate against US soldiers?"

"First, you need to understand these contractors looked and acted like uniformed American soldiers. Most of them had been soldiers serving in Iraq, and to the Iraqi civilians, especially in the smaller villages like Al-Masafer, they *were* American soldiers."

The major leafed through several pages and found a photocopy encased in plastic and handed it to him.

"Colonel Stenson had this note stapled to his chest. Look familiar?"

I will have such revenges on you both,
That all the world shall—I will do such things—
What they are yet I know not but they shall be
the terrors of the Earth.

He saw the gray stains, blood stains probably, made grayscale by an inkjet printer, and the imprint of the staple holes. The quote was handwritten, in beautiful flowing cursive, and he knew now the quotes were more than just bullshit.

"Shakespeare, from 'King Lear,'" the major said.

"Goddamn it!" Trufant exhaled, and sat back in his chair. "Do you have suspects in the colonel's murder?"

"Everyone in the village was a suspect, including the dead girl's family. We ruled out the family though, none of them would have been capable of overpowering the colonel on their own. It's technically still an open investigation, by us and the Iraqis, although I doubt they are putting any effort into it."

"Well, that explains the dates. Damn, this is fucked up!" He could feel the buzz of his third beer affecting his speech, and probably his anger. "Where is this family now?"

Flórez opened his file, spread out several photos, and passed him the black-and-white picture of a young woman. The date stamped underneath said March 1997. Her dark, straight hair looked Asian, but her eyes were piercing, round, and light-colored, possibly pale blue. He'd never seen anyone like her. She was extraordinary.

"Diwata Haddad, the mother. She was a Christian missionary born and raised in Manila and taught English in a small school outside of Al-Masafer, where she met and married an Iraqi named Nasim Haddad. They had five children. She, and the surviving four, immigrated back to Manila in early 2010. Coincidentally, she studied literature in college—she did a thesis on the English Renaissance, including Shakespeare."

Trufant looked at the major. "I want to go to Manila and talk to her."

"She's dead," Flórez said, "killed in an apartment fire in 2011. Sixteen bodies were recovered, three separate families, including all but one of the Haddads. The eldest daughter was several miles away in a Christian academy. I spoke with them all just one month before the fire."

"Jesus, they're young," he said, looking at glossy photos of the children. "What were your impressions when you spoke to the mother? Did she offer anything new?" Trufant asked. Impressions were everything during an interview and reading a transcribed statement left so many variables. "Any chance you recorded it?"

"She wouldn't allow it. She was cold—like ice. I guess I can't blame her, but if looks could kill, I wouldn't be here today."

"And the kids?"

"They stood behind her and never said a word."

"Do we know where the oldest one is now?"

Flórez picked up the eight by ten picture of a girl Trufant thought was in her late teens. She was an exact copy of her mother, the same pale blue eyes, eyes you had trouble looking away from.

"Araya," he said. "Fortunately for her, she was in school the day her family was attacked, last I heard she was still in the Philippines. But with the fire, the brass closed the case and I returned to the States. That is, until we heard of these killings. The Army is now fully involved. A dozen investigators are on their way back to Iraq and Manila, and the FBI, as you know, is poring over everything in the States."

"She would be what," Trufant asked, looking at the young girl's picture, doing the math in his head, "twenty-eight now? Are you trying to find her?"

"We have people looking for her, but nothing yet."

Trufant closed his eyes, wishing he had stopped at one beer. Then he thought of Carlos, and wished he had something stronger.

"Merriweather isn't happy your chief took you off the case. You must have made an impression on him. He wants to bring you in. Apparently, someone in Washington doesn't take the killing of its veterans lightly."

"I don't take any homicide lightly, but it's personal now. This guy couldn't get to me, so he tried to kill my wife, and he killed Carlos, and I want him to pay."

"I'll be honest with you, Trufant, something about that fire in Manila seemed hokey, just a gut feeling, but I've learned to trust my instincts. That's one of the things I asked my people to check on. If my theory is correct and this is the Haddad family, you killed the man's sister. Age wise, the dead girl in Chicago was

Madinah Haddad, and her only brother was her twin, Ramzi. You're lucky you're alive."

"I know, when you knocked, I was sure it would be him. I was hoping it was, actually. Dr. Lew thinks Carlos may have shot him at least twice, pretty decent blood spray and part of a finger at the scene. Maybe we'll get lucky and find him in an ER somewhere—or dead."

"Witnesses are saying Armstrong fired two of the rounds," Flórez said. "But he's still in surgery, and it will be a while before he's ready to talk. Merriweather's crew called all the hospitals in a hundred-mile radius and gave them a description of the guy, but no word yet."

"It sucks, Tristan. My partner is dead, I'm here in an empty apartment, and my chief wants my ass in a sling. I'm wondering who will get to me first, Lozano or this Haddad kid."

"I think your situation with your chief might change soon. Your mayor should be getting a call from Washington right about now. Let's take a ride, I want to show you something."

***

Patrol cars with their lights flashing blocked both ends of Fulton Street but let them pass after checking their IDs. In front of a four-story condominium, two black Chevrolet SUVs and a white panel truck were double-parked outside the main entrance.

"It's been almost twenty-four hours and you're still working this crime scene?"

"Wait until you see what's inside," Flórez said.

"You know my chief lives in this building."

"Yes, but we're not here to see the chief, follow me."

Crime scene tape and an FBI agent blocked the doors to both elevators, so they took the stairwell to the third floor where they met Deputy Director Merriweather in the hallway.

"Afternoon, Lt. Trufant, my condolences on the loss of your partner, I know firsthand how devastating that can be. Hopefully you and I can work together to end this. I spoke with your mayor, and he reinstated you and was more than happy to detach you temporarily. You work for me now, if that's okay with you."

"Yes, sir, and I'm grateful. Just to let you know, I was home and drinking a beer when the Major came by, so I've had a bit to drink."

"Well, let's not make that a habit, Marcus, because I know this is personal for you. You'll have to put that aside if you want back in," Merriweather said.

"I won't be a liability. You have my word."

"Very good, let's get started. First, your patrol officers traced the subject's license plate to this condo within minutes of the shooting. They missed the man by just seconds, according to a woman in the parking lot. There is a significant blood trail leading to this condo and back to the garage. Our crime scene investigators have gone over most of it, and we're preserving the scene for further examination. Let me show you what we found inside."

The door was ajar, the knob smeared with dried blood. Below it, three drops of blood inches apart were marked with a plastic evidence marker.

He took a deep breath, knowing that just inside this door lived the man he had been hunting for years, the man that had shot and killed Carlos, the man that had probably ruined his marriage.

Seeing the man's blood, though, brought some relief, and knowing he was probably in pain was gratifying, but it wasn't enough. That hollow feeling in his gut told him so.

"There's blood everywhere, Marcus, it's all been sampled and documented but watch what you touch."

"You have a warrant, I presume?"

"Yes, with all the blood, we entered on exigent circumstances and got the warrant once we knew he wasn't inside."

"I have specialists flying in from Washington to detail the scene, psychological profilers who want to witness this firsthand. What's inside is something rare, something few people in law enforcement will ever see. I know what I saw in there,

Lieutenant, but tell me everything you see, and then we can compare notes."

Trufant stepped into what should have been the living room. Two of the three walls were floor-to-ceiling glass mirrors, and the flooring was a black rubberized mat found in gymnasiums. On the floor was a white plastic egg timer, similar to the one his mother used in Pine Grove, Louisiana. She would wind it up and set it for sixty minutes, the maximum duration, and he had to practice his saxophone until the timer chimed. *What was this man timing?*

He looked again at the glass and the flooring. "He does some type of timed workout here, probably every day, like a ritual."

"Yes, martial arts of some kind, we think. You will see why in one of the bedrooms."

The third wall and the ceiling were painted dark red, there was no furniture and no decorations, only a simple light fixture and the timer.

Small drops of blood speckled the mat and led into the hallway, where the rubber mat was replaced by cream-colored travertine. The larger drops were still crimson in their centers, while the outer areas were dry and rusty brown.

He stepped carefully across the drops and walked into the first of two bedrooms. The walls of the hallway and this bedroom were bare like the living room, but were painted stark white. A low profile twin mattress, covered in a plain white fitted sheet, was centered on the floor. The simplicity and shape of the bed reminded him of his dorm at Tulane. There were no pillows or blankets in the room, but the bed appeared to have been slept on.

"He lives like a monk, and not in a good way."

"He's obsessive-compulsive, Lieutenant, among other psychological disorders, we think."

The single window in this bedroom would have provided a spectacular view of the bay and downtown San Francisco, but it was covered in aluminum foil. Like the living room, a cheap fixture provided the only light in the room, unusual for a high-end condo in this section of the city. He looked closer and saw the indentations where someone had removed the original light and replaced it with the cheap, single-bulb fixture.

"He changed the light," Trufant said, "must have been too much for him, too distracting, too much decor could be chaotic for him."

The trail of blood led to the primary bedroom's walk-in closet. The door was open and inside were three identical yellow sweatshirts with the University of California Berkeley logo, and on the rod below them, three pairs of dark blue Dockers slacks. There were two empty hangers on each rod, and Trufant knew they had probably held matching sweatshirts and pants.

The blood drops, each smaller than the ones in the hallway, now collected in the back of the closet in a tight grouping.

"He stood here for a minute, and the bleeding has slowed."

Merriweather nodded.

In the corner, a light layer of dust surrounded a clean spot the size of a small suitcase or gym bag.

"Something he needed was right here, and he took it with him. Probably had a bag ready to go. He's not planning on coming back."

"I agree," Merriweather said. "He's been shot, and there's nothing he needs here. He's on the move now, probably trying to find a hospital or clinic that won't report a gunshot wound."

"That's if he's not dead already," Trufant said.

"Lieutenant, you need to see the other room."

The second bedroom was nothing like the rest of the condo. Where the other rooms were austere, void of any sign of personality, this room was a jumble of random images. Photos and newspaper clippings covered one entire wall. An amateurishly painted dragon covered the second wall. Red, yellow, and green shades of paint dripped randomly, as if the artist was working in a frenzy, not caring about the quality of his work.

The window to this room was also covered in aluminum foil, but a small round hole had been cut out of the center, and a beam of late afternoon sunlight created a spot on the east wall. December 1st was scrawled in black, handwritten block letters with an arrow pointing to a circle on the floor. Closer to one of the other walls and in the same handwriting was April 11th, next to another circle.

"It's a solar calendar," Trufant said.

He looked back at the photo collage and saw his own picture near the bottom of the group. It was a duplicate of the picture he'd found in the dead woman's house in Chicago, and next to it were pictures of Timothy and Stephanie Marshall, dead on their basement floor. Several, but not all, of the images were of living people. Most had names, some had addresses and birthdates, and a few had social security numbers. The last picture in the bottom row was one of Dr. Williams with the date July 22, probably written with the Sharpie on the floor underneath it.

"How many?"

"There are at least sixty different people on this wall," Merriweather said, "and sixteen of them are apparently dead. Two we recognize as your first homicide victims from 2020. I have dozens of analysts in Washington going over each photo now, hopefully, we'll be able to identify them all."

"I recognize this scene," Trufant said, pointing to a man in a fetal position. The man's back was facing the camera, his body partially obscured by tall weeds in a trash-strewn field.

"This is still an open case. His name was Haupt and we never developed any leads or suspects. He was stabbed in the back about two years ago. Nothing on his case is similar to the others. He was an unemployed insurance agent from Seattle and never in the military."

Trufant pointed to a second photo. "This is familiar too, but it wasn't my case, another stabbing, I think. Gracia handled it. This one," he said, "that's San Jose's city hall in the background. I'd recognize that dome anywhere."

"We'll get them all sorted out," Merriweather said. "He'll pay for these."

"He won't pin Carlos's picture up here—not if I can help it."

"I don't see either of the Chicago victims," Flórez said.

"I think the woman killed them. Carlos and I were just talking about the dissimilar MOs. It's possible she has her own photo collage somewhere. You're sure this guy and the girl are the Haddad twins?" Trufant said.

"I am." Merriweather reached into his jacket and unfolded a sheet of paper. "This is a copy of the lease agreement signed in 2016 by Hector Bolivar with a picture of his driver's license. Ramzi Haddad's birthday is the same date as the one on this license. Maybe he found it easier to remember."

Trufant looked at the picture and saw the blade flash at his neck again. The man's face was unremarkable, but holding the photo in his hand gave him chills. After so many years, the killer had a face and a name now, but it had cost Carlos his life. "Identical twins. It's them."

"Yes, I thought you would say that. It won't be hard now to match their DNA. Homeland Security is also looking into the possibility the whole Haddad family entered the US using that same last name."

The room had the same cheap light on the ceiling, an empty walk-in closet, and a small chest of drawers. Inside was a half-full opened box of disposable coveralls, a sealed box of medium latex gloves, and an open but full box of condoms. The three boxes were exactly one inch apart.

"The bottom drawer contains twelve by twelve-foot sheets of plastic drop cloths," Merriweather said. "He wanted to protect himself at crime scenes, but if you notice, very little of it has been used. For some reason, he changed his mind."

"Most of his victims died in the street," Trufant said. He wouldn't need all this there, maybe the suits to keep the blood off his clothing. But maybe some we don't know about were killed in their homes. It would make cleaning those scenes a lot easier."

"Marcus, what's your take on these condoms? None of the victims we know about were sexually assaulted."

"None of the men were, are you sure about the Marshall woman?"

"No, but there was no semen, no pubic hair, and no evidence of a condom," Merriweather said.

"Probably not sexual in the way we think," Trufant said. "Domination of his victims seems to get him off. As far as the condoms, I think he's extremely meticulous—he contemplates every possible scenario. With his OCD, I think he bought all of this expecting he may need to use them."

"Let's look at what's *not* in here. There are almost no electronics except for the alarm clock on the floor next to his bed. There's no Wi-Fi, no computers or laptops, no phones or even phone chargers. But if you look at what's on this wall, he has access to the internet, he, or someone, does some serious advanced research on his victims prior to their murders.

"Maybe he was pirating a neighbor's Wi-Fi, that shouldn't be too hard to figure out," Merriweather said.

"I think he has a network of people helping him, more than just the sister in Chicago. Look at this picture of me," Trufant said. "Someone was close to me. It's a portrait photo, notice how everything in front and behind me is out of focus? This was taken by someone intent on perfection. Someone who does this a lot."

"What about social media—Facebook, Twitter, Instagram—he has to communicate with them somehow.?" Trufant asked.

"He has no digital footprint we can find," Merriweather said. "Quantico is searching but so far nothing. Most likely he uses burner phones, maybe keeps a laptop in his car and uses Gmail or Hotmail. They are more difficult to track and even harder to get a search warrant, even if we had his user name."

"What do the neighbors say? Have you canvassed each floor?"

"Most of the ones living on this floor tell the same story. He was quiet, eccentric, always wore the same outfit, never spoke, but was also never rude. Most of them said they were happy to leave him alone. Few people on the other floors knew him at all."

"Well, if there's nothing else, I need to get some sleep," Trufant said, trying to cover a yawn. "I haven't slept much in the last three days."

As he walked out into the hallway, he envisioned Carlos's killer limping toward the elevators, bleeding and in pain. *If I'm going to dream tonight, this is what I want to dream about.*

***

Flórez drove him home and the few short blocks to his apartment drifted past his window unnoticed until he was unlocking his front door.

He threw the half-empty Corona in the trash and poured a glass of 19 Crimes Hard Chard into last night's dirty glass.

The Australian wine went down smoothly. He considered turning on the stereo but decided silence was a better choice. He stared at his thinking wall, where a few more of the puzzle pieces now connected, and others moved around at random. He let them. What he needed was to let the case go, let himself concentrate on the loss of his friend and the dread of his funeral.

He poured a second glass promising himself it would be the last. Sitting in the recliner, he closed his eyes, listening to the foghorn in the bay. Something felt different, better, in a way. He set the full glass on the end table and thought of Adelaide. She was probably sitting with her sister on the front porch, telling stories about him. It was a pleasant thought. *How I wish I was with you right now, Adelaide.*

Soon there would be a grand funeral, probably on Saturday. The mayor would plan most of it, with or without the widow's approval. Saturday would guarantee the politicians a huge crowd of mourning strangers, the curious and the gawkers.

The media coverage would probably be live also, unless the Giants were playing. Funerals were great photo ops for politicians, a chance to see and be seen, an opportunity to press the flesh, as they liked to call it. No smiling, though, no kissing of the babies in this crowd, just a few handshakes and some solemn words at an interview, and off to a late lunch.

Those truly grieving, his family, friends, coworkers, and even those who had never met Carlos but wanted to honor his sacrifice, would be there no matter what day it was held. They would stand in the rain, the cold, or the heat for hours. He knew this because he had done it himself more times than he wanted to count.

***

Ten hours later, his phone woke him and it was eight in the morning.

"Lieutenant, it's Kira Pinchon. I'm sorry it's so early, but I just left the veterinarian."

"It's fine, Kira, I was just about to start a pot of coffee, how is he?"

"Travis will live, but he has sixty stitches. They have him in a kennel, doped up, but when he's awake, he won't stop whining. I tried to talk to him myself, but nothing helped, I felt bad leaving him there like that."

"I'll stop by and pick him up in a few minutes, Kira. Don't worry about him."

"Great," she said. "Also, I just got a text message from my supervisor. Carlos's funeral will be this Saturday at Calvary Presbyterian Church. I'd like to ride with you if that's okay."

"Of course, Kira, I don't want to go alone either."

His Class A uniform hung in the foyer closet, protected by a clear plastic dry-cleaning bag. He took the long-sleeved dress shirt out of the bag and tried it on. It was a little tighter in the waist, but it would do. He looked at the date on the receipt stapled to the bag. November 6th of last year—a funeral for an Oakland firefighter.

He opened a window facing the bay, where the foghorns were still groaning like old toads in a Louisiana swamp, and from somewhere, a ship's horn answered. The cool breeze refreshed him, and he wondered how long it had been since he felt this good so early in the morning.

On the end table, he noticed the half-empty glass of wine and poured it down the kitchen sink. He washed Adelaide's cherished glass and put it back inside the china cabinet.

Honking cars stuck in morning traffic reminded him of the dog, and he rushed through his morning routine.

***

An hour later he pulled into the vet's office and heard a blood-curdling howl coming from one of the back rooms.

"How much do I owe you?" he asked the young receptionist.

"Dr. Sitahal said no charge, sir."

Then the big, bearded veterinarian walked up behind her.

"I am sorry for the loss of your friend, Lieutenant, it seems every day another officer is killed somewhere. Kira told me you were his partner, how terrible," the man said.

"I understand Travis is a hero, and I heard it could have been much worse. He seems such a gentle dog, especially now after having been through something so traumatic. Animals don't have the coping mechanisms we are blessed with—but still, he is going to be okay."

"He's a good dog. I just wish he could have saved Carlos too. Can I see him?"

"Yes. Physically Travis is doing well, but emotionally it is a different story. I think he is grieving."

"When will he be able to leave?"

"I would say he can leave now. I would like to keep him longer, of course, for his injuries, but he needs companionship now more than anything. Just keep in mind he does need to rest at home. Let's go see him."

They passed several other dogs in individual kennels, some standing near the chain-link gates, others curled on sleeping mats, but they all seemed to have the same sad look in their eyes. The same look he had seen in Armstrong's eyes when he was shackled to a table.

The howling stopped as they turned the corner. Travis was curled up on one of the same padded mats, and he watched Trufant and the doctor through the wire gate, his head bobbing like a drunk trying to appear sober. His right ear was missing. Six inches of raw flesh and black sutures started where the ear had been and circled over the top of his head and back toward his neck.

"I know exactly how that feels, old boy."

Travis put his head down as if it were too heavy. He looked much different now than the night he had taken him home. The missing ear and the wound were different, but his black coat now had a deep shine, making it almost blue in the light.

"That's a fentanyl patch behind his good ear," the doctor whispered. "It will keep him pain-free for up to three days. He's also on a broad spectrum antibiotic to stop any infection. Just keep an eye on him and I think he'll be fine. How is his owner? I understand he was gravely wounded as well?"

"Yes—David Armstrong. He'll be in the hospital for a week or two at least, and I'm heading there now. Can I take Travis with me?"

"I don't see why not, just keep the wound clean, but let's see how he feels about leaving with you."

"Travis?" he said.

The dog lifted his head and studied him, then stood.

"Travis, do you remember me?"

Travis took a step forward wobbling on shaky legs and sniffed his hand and slowly laid down at his feet.

"That's the fentanyl making him drowsy."

"Come on, boy, let's get out of here."

The dog didn't move for a good minute, looking up at him and the vet, and Trufant wondered if he was deciding if he wanted to go with him or stay in his cage. Finally, he rose, took a shaky step and then another, and ambled toward the door.

"I guess he's ready to go."

Trufant walked behind him, matching the dog's pace back into the lobby, and Travis wanted to keep going, staring out through the glass door.

"You'll need his leash—we cleaned all the blood off. Also, his collar may pull at the stitches so don't put that on him yet, but we have a vest he can wear that will keep the pressure away from the wound."

He knelt next to Travis, wondering what his reaction might be. Witnesses had described how Travis had torn into the killer's arm. It was hard to compare that scene to the gentle creature sitting at the door, waiting to go home. Travis leaned against him, resting his wounded head on his shoulder. Travis had protected his human, had saved Armstrong's life, with no thought of himself. Trufant eased the vest on, then adjusted the Velcro straps and attached the leather leash.

"Let's go, boy. I guess we're both ready."

***

Rachel Adams was on a bench outside the emergency room's front door, taking her last drag from a cigarette in one hand, holding a steaming cup of black coffee in the other.

"That will kill you one day, Rachel."

The nurse crushed the butt into the dirt. "The coffee or the cigarette?"

"The cigarette of course, coffee fuels the soul."

Travis rested his head on her leg, panting as if he had just run a marathon.

"Is this the dog I heard about on the news?" she asked, rubbing under his neck. "I thought he would look scarier for some reason."

"He's pretty doped up and disoriented right now."

"He's going to a have a scar just like yours, Marcus."

"It looks better on him, I'm sure. Rachel, I need a favor. I need to get him into David Armstrong's room."

"You want to bring a dog into the ICU?"

"Yes."

She gazed at the ER's entrance without answering, then nodded as if she had been arguing with herself, and lost. "Okay, I've seen worse. Stay here and I'll be right back."

Moments later she came back outside pushing an oversized wheelchair. Between the two of them, they lifted Travis into the seat and covered everything but his head with a blanket. If he was in any pain, the fentanyl was working. Before they reached the elevator, the dog was sound asleep.

"Thanks, Rachel, I owe you again."

"It's on me, Marcus."

The two patrol officers guarding Armstrong's door looked down at the Lab as they approached and nodded in approval.

"I hope he got in a few good bites, Lieutenant."

"I heard he did."

Trufant tapped on the door and Caitlin Armstrong opened it. Her eyes were red and swollen, and he wondered if he had woken her or if she had been crying.

"Good morning," she said, wiping her eyes with a tissue. "So, this is his dog?" she asked.

"Yes, this is Travis."

Trufant looked at all the wires and tubes running under the sheets of Armstrong's bed, reminding him of his short stay at the hospital in Chicago.

"How is he?"

"He cries out in his sleep once in a while and curses at Travis occasionally, but I think it's his friend Travis he's yelling at. The doctor said he will probably lose some use of his arm. The knife cut through a nerve, an artery too, and she said he should have bled to death, but someone from the pet shop saved his life. He's medicated now but the pain blocker they used during surgery should be wearing off soon. I promised him I wouldn't let them medicate him anymore, but the surgeon said that would be a mistake."

Travis lifted his head, and in one motion he was out of the chair and walking gingerly toward the bed. He sniffed Armstrong's face, then rested his head on the pillow next to him.

Armstrong opened his eyes and reached for his dog.

Chapter 30

Mother

She rolled her chair over to Ramzi as Bassam Latif pulled another bone fragment from the wound with a pair of stainless steel forceps and dropped it in a ceramic soup bowl. Bassam had been one of her first students at the small schoolhouse in Al-Masafer, Iraq, but he was never one of the brightest. He had often sat staring out the windows while the other children were deep into their lessons.

"What do you see, Bassam?"

The failed medical student's face flushed, and Diwata wished she had another option, someone with more experience. Now twenty-six, Bassam was her only option, so she had him flown in from Elizabeth, New Jersey, while Ramzi was still in flight from California.

"That's the last one, Ms. Haddad. I think the radial nerve was severed. He will have little, if any, use of this arm. He lost so much blood in his other arm that gangrene is possible, even amputation may be necessary. As you know, I had only three years of medical school, so I can't tell you much more."

"Will he live?"

"Yes, I believe so. I will suture his wounds and treat him with antibiotics. That is all I can do. He will need physical therapy, of course, but the gunshot wound would raise the suspicions of the authorities."

"When will he wake up?"

"Once I close the wounds, whenever you decide. He's on propofol and morphine now. I can stop the propofol and he will come around soon after."

She was torn between two horrible options, take him to a hospital in Toronto and receive proper care, where he would surely be arrested, or let him recover here and inevitably be handicapped for life—if he lived at all.

"Keep him sedated until morning. We will wake him then and let him make the decision."

"Yes, ma'am. I'm sorry I cannot do more. Your husband and my father were close, and I remember the pain we all felt that day."

"Thank you, Bassam, your family's loyalty will not be forgotten. Danilo is my nephew, he will stay and help you. Chanda, take me back upstairs, I am fatigued."

As the old Otis elevator rose from the basement, she lit her first Gold Flake since Ramzi had arrived, the smoke burning what was left of her trachea. She coughed bloody mucus into her hand and wiped the mess across her dark skirt, where it mixed with similar crusty stains.

"Chanda, I worry about Bassam. He was always weak and stupid, but he is also an opportunist. He knows I will pay him well, but if he links Ramzi to the news in San Francisco, he may turn on us. Wake me if you see anything suspicious."

The girl lifted her out of the chair and into the Hill-Rom hospital bed, raising it twenty degrees so Diwata could breathe easier, then placed the controller on the nightstand.

"Yes, Diwata, I will watch him," Chanda said. "Sleep well."

Alone now, she stared at the ceiling and prayed Ramzi would live and be whole again. Whom do I pray to, she asked herself—Jesus?

She stared at the painting of Christ on the wall and asked, "God, are my sins so great they cannot be forgiven?"

Forgiveness, she said, and laughed, coughing up more mucus,

then took another long drag from the cigarette, watching the end glow fiery red.

Chanda and Danilo were Ramzi's cousins. They shared his blood, but with Madinah gone, the boy would need his true family, what was left of it. Surely once Leilah, and Araya, heard the news they would come home and help him. He was going to be a cripple, and that would ruin him.

She coughed up more blood and it arced across the bed, landing on the clean white comforter. Another cough shook her body. She reached for the call button and blacked out.

Chapter 31

Armstrong

Awake again, he expected to see something horrible. The armored personnel carrier on fire, acrid smoke filling the sky, or the specter of death lurking over him, dressed all in black and waiting to help him cross over the great divide between the living and the dead.

This time his dog was resting its wounded head on the white sheets. Travis looked different, not just his missing ear or the red rawness of the scars and sutures, but something in his eyes. There was profound sadness in those eyes.

Behind Travis, he saw the lieutenant standing in the doorway with a leash in his hand, *Marcus*. In the chair next to the lieutenant was his wife. Armstrong hadn't thought of Caitlin as his wife in years, and the word *wife* had lost its meaning. It felt different saying it now—*my wife*. He liked the sound of it, though, it felt right.

"You look horrible, Travis," he said, rubbing the dog's muzzle.

Caitlin sat in the chair wringing her hands, her eyes glistening as if she'd been crying, but there was a genuine smile on her face. "What day is it?"

"It's still Wednesday, you've only been asleep for three hours," she said.

"It seemed longer. My dreams seem to last for days."

He looked at Trufant, trying to read his emotions, trying to decide what to tell him first. There was so much to say and it would be easier to just close his eyes and sleep.

"Did I tell you the story yet?"

"No, you started to say something about Inspector Amato but didn't finish."

"Amato seemed like a good man, Lieutenant."

He tried to sit up, but the pain was too intense and so sharp he was afraid he would black out.

"Jesus Christ! The morphine isn't doing shit."

Catlin stood and raised the bed with the remote.

"The pain blocker has worn off," she said. "The morphine probably has too, but you said you didn't want anymore. You cried out once in your sleep, and the doctor gave you another dose. She's going to try and talk you into taking tramadol. She said there's too much damage in the joint to try and recover without any pain medication. She said it would also help you through the worst of your withdrawal."

"I know some of the guys at the VA are addicted to tramadol, they said it's just as bad as everything else out there."

"Yes, she said it can be addictive, but she wants you to try it for a few days, to get through the worst of the pain and then detox after it's healed some. David, I want you to try it."

He looked at the lieutenant and then at Travis. "What should I do, Travis?"

The dog shifted his weight from one leg to the other and stood with one paw on the bed.

"There's not enough room up here, boy."

He watched the dog's eyes droop and close, then open again as if he too was trying to stay awake. He finally curled up on the floor next to Armstrong and slept. The dog's hind leg began to twitch like he was running, and he wondered if Travis's dreams were as bad as his.

"You were telling us about Carlos," Trufant said.

"I'm sorry, let me try again. Inspector Amato wanted me to tell you something, I think it was important to him for you to know. But I want to tell you everything that happened from the beginning."

Trufant pulled a chair up next to Caitlin, and both of them listened.

"It was crazy. I saw him coming at us. He was looking at me, but his eyes were looking through me—like he was dead inside.

"Anyway, the man was mumbling something. I think it was in another language, then he swung that strange knife at me—at my throat, and I remembered your scar."

He was afraid he was drifting off again, his eyes felt like lead weights, and he moved his shoulder on purpose so the pain would help him focus. "Anyway, Travis grabbed his arm. Travis was locked on to him, shaking him and I could see it ripping into the flesh, but it was like the man couldn't feel a thing, and then the knife hit me. I looked at it, I saw it buried into my jacket and saw the blood soaking through the sleeve.

"I didn't feel it at first, I just remember watching Travis hanging onto that guy's arm. The guy was pulling on the knife, twisting it, trying to pull it free and I felt it snap. Then I fell and looked up in time to see him stab Amato with a piece of the knife. Then I heard the gunshot."

He looked at the sleeping dog, saw the stitches where his ear had been, and touched the bandages on his own shoulder, reassuring himself that what had happened was real.

"I was on the ground, and Travis's face was all bloody. I saw the blood in his teeth, and he was still snarling and moving toward the guy. I picked up Amato's gun. It was soaked in blood and hard to hold. I couldn't aim, but I fired at him anyway, twice, I think. It gets hazy after that, but I know I hit him once as he turned."

He stared out the window, at the redbrick building next door, not wanting to make eye contact with Trufant for the next part.

"Amato was dying. I knew it, and he knew it too. I've seen it enough times to know. The first time was in boot camp, sidearm training with our Berettas. The guy next to me shot himself in the thigh and died seconds later—DRT they call it, dead right there." He looked at Cait and back at Trufant.

"It was quick, Lieutenant, something you never get used to. I didn't know him that well, but he was alive one minute and dead the next. It makes you rethink your own mortality. Do you know what I mean?"

"I do. I think about it almost every day."

"Amato had a message for you, it was important to him. 'Tell him I didn't freeze,' were his exact words. That was it—and then he died. He died trying to help me, a junkie he barely knew. Why would a man do that, Lieutenant?"

"Why did you join the Marines? You were a sergeant, would you have done any different for another Marine?"

It seemed like a different lifetime, like he had become someone else since then, and he supposed he would have helped a stranger even now. He had probably helped many during those years in the Marines, but it had been so long ago.

There was a time all he ever wanted to do was to serve his country, even as a kid growing up, every time he saw the American flag, he promised himself he would be a soldier one day, to fight in some foreign land like Henry Fonda or Robert Mitchum in *The Longest Day*.

"It was so long ago I can't remember."

"Mrs. Armstrong," Trufant said, "I was going to talk to your husband alone, but I think we should all talk. You're in this now too and you deserve to know. This is not over, and I don't want you to think it is. The guy that killed Inspector Amato, the guy that almost killed your husband, is still out there, and he's not alone."

Trufant told her about the attack on his wife and the murders of the security guard and Dr. Williams.

"Right now, we don't know how bad he's hurt or how long it will take him to recover, but when he does, he will be coming for us. He and his family are on a mission of revenge, and we have no idea what they're doing right now. We don't even know how many people are involved. There could be cousins, aunts, and uncles, you get my point?"

"What should we do?" she asked. "David and I were talking about moving to Denver. There's a veteran's hospital right down the street from my condo and great rehab centers. I've done a lot of research, and I think it would be good for both of us."

"Denver sounds far away from here, I know, but in reality, it's an easy flight and may be a bad idea," Trufant said. "Ramzi Haddad and his sister had an excellent talent for tracking their victims. You haven't seen what they did to the Marshalls—a husband and wife just living their lives, never bothered anyone, never knew anything about this family, and now they're dead. They were hunted down and tortured. If they did all those things to a couple of strangers, how far do you think they would go to find the two of you? Until we know more, you can't be Cait and David Armstrong."

Armstrong looked at Caitlin and saw the fear in his wife's eyes. He felt it too, but he was also pissed—pissed off that some bastard freak was trying to kill him and probably his wife too.

It was almost as bad as fighting in Afghanistan, fighting an invisible enemy. Every waking moment he'd thought of the men, women, and even children wired with explosives, wanting to kill you and no uniforms to tell you which side they were on. Now he was living in the nightmare again. And this time, he wanted to be ready.

"What can we do, Lieutenant?"

"I've already spoken with the FBI Director. He's working out the details, and they know a lot more about witness protections than I do. But I worry about your families as well, they could go after your parents or your sisters."

"Shit!"

It was overwhelming. A few days ago this type of anxiety would have driven him straight to the tent city on Division Street, the best place for good dope. Somehow, though, his anger now actually calmed him. He found himself planning his defense like he had for his unit, prepping for battle, only this time it was for his family. It was a different type of rush—and it felt good.

"We can do it, how do we start, sir?"

"I'll call Director Merriweather. He's already done some of the work here. Two agents are on this floor and several more are roaming the entrances. Your names have already been scrubbed from the hospital records, but most of the staff on this floor know who you are, so the sooner we can transfer you the better."

"My mother, should I warn her?" Armstrong said.

"It's not a bad idea, anyone with a computer will be able to find her, it's public record now."

"Thank you, sir."

"I need to get back to the station," Trufant said, scratching Travis under the chin. "And I need to take this old dog outside. I'll stop in again tomorrow if I can. Meanwhile, you two have a lot to talk about, and I'll get things moving on our end. Be careful."

Once the door closed and he was alone with Cait, he felt the pain throb with each breath and knew it was going to get worse soon. What little pain killer remained was burning off fast. He didn't want Cait to see him suffering, but two people had died for him and the wife he'd abandoned sat three feet away from him. He *was* ready—or hoped he was.

"If he's not dead," Cait said, "he's going to try and kill us, isn't he?"

"He may try if he lives. Denver was starting to sound good, but as Trufant said, he may track us down there."

"I know he will find us here," she said.

"Cait, do you still have the gun I gave you, the little revolver?"

"No, it's in Denver, packed away in a box somewhere."

A sharp pain caused him to wince. "Cait, this is really bad. I was going to try the tramadol, but I should be alert if this guy comes back."

"Take the pain killer, David, let me watch over you for a change."

Take pain medication and put his wife in harm's way? It sounded wrong but he knew she was tenacious. "Okay, let's do it."

She leaned over him, kissed him, and pushed the call button.

As the tramadol kicked in and the pain began to dull, he knew he was more afraid of disappointing her than dying. It had always been easy to walk away. It was easier than seeing the pain in her eyes. But something was different now. She wasn't afraid, she was on a mission, and she was not going to fail.

CHAPTER 32

TRUFANT

The next day Travis was showing some signs of normalcy. The fentanyl patch was still doing its job, and although the wound still looked painful, the dog didn't seem to be bothered by it.

Trufant bought the largest K-9 crate he could fit through his apartment door, and Travis was content to stay in it while he was out. When he came home for lunch, the two of them took a long stroll around the neighborhood, but mostly through South Park.

It had been twenty-four hours now since that last glass of wine. He had been headache-free now for a day and a half, which was a good thing as he was out of the only pain killer that could touch those hangovers. If there was any side effect to sobriety, it was that he felt tense at times, and there was always that constant craving for the taste of merlot. But it was a trade-off he could live with.

"Right, Travis?"

The two of them walked through the manicured park, ignoring the stares of the young people as they passed, most of them at Travis, whose head looked lopsided, and a few at the huge .45 and gold badge clipped to his belt.

There was little for him to do now that he was detached and reporting to Merriweather. Lt. Gracia was finishing the details of Carlos's death, and he felt like he was just getting in their way.

The days were getting shorter, and driving through the early afternoon rush hour as the sun hovered over the horizon, he knew autumn wasn't far off. Soon he would be driving home in the dark.

He hated driving in San Francisco at night—the constant mist on the windshield, the wipers scraping across the glass, and the glare of oncoming headlights aggravated him, but he supposed all that wasn't as bad as the heat and the humidity of Pine Grove, Louisiana, and the bugs!

The blood-sucking mosquitos in Pine Grove were the size of small birds, and he and Adelaide had joked about them whenever they thought of home and how they were glad they made the move. That was thirty years ago now, and whenever the fog bothered him, he remembered the constant buzzing of the bugs.

Trufant watched Travis teeter, like a drunk, as he pissed in the same places every other dog had, hoping to mark his new territory.

"Travis, in five minutes some other dog is going to piss right there and ruin your day. That's life in the big city, my friend."

It was one of the good signs Dr. Sitahal had told him to look for. Travis was drinking plenty of water.

At the next lamppost, Travis almost fell over but caught himself. The vet thought the Lab was three or four years old and in good health for a dog living on the streets so long—other than the six-inch laceration across the top of his head—he had said, laughing.

Travis was always one foot in front of him, never pulling on the leash, never lagging, and when he stopped, Travis stopped. Maybe he feared pain if the leash tugged on the wound too hard, or someone had trained him—maybe even Armstrong.

"What's your story, Travis?" he asked the dog, not expecting any reply. Travis kept on walking until they reached another park bench and sat next to it, knowing his new human friend would want to sit too.

They sat close to each other, close enough that he could pet the dog's side and avoid touching the ugly wound, a wound made worse by the shaved, pale white skin starting just behind his shoulder and up across his muzzle near his eye. He could see how the vet had pulled the skin together where the left ear should have been. Hopefully, it wouldn't look as grotesque once the fur began to grow back in.

"Aren't we a pair?"

The green ornamental lamppost came to life, buzzing like the cicadas in the woods around his mother's home. He stood and buttoned his gray London Fog trench coat, feeling the dampness that had already soaked the outside layer. Still, it kept the cold out, and he wondered how the homeless dealt with the wind and the fog and the rain every day.

"C'mon, Travis, it's dinner time."

He found he enjoyed the walk and the dog's companionship. It surprised him. He had agreed to take the dog in out of respect for Armstrong and Amato, or maybe out of gratitude for Travis's own sacrifice trying to save the two men. Either way, he wasn't alone anymore, at least for now.

***

The Alpo can's ring tab popped as he cracked the seal, and the smell of fresh meat brought Travis into the kitchen, his nails tapping on the ceramic tile.

"Damn if it doesn't smell good to me too, Travis!"

He filled an old wooden salad bowl with the meaty chunks and put it on the floor, then went through his own collection of frozen dinners and started the microwave.

Travis ate what he wanted and left the bowl half-full, lapped water from the bowl next to it, then walked back into the living room and collapsed next to the big La-Z-Boy.

With his own plate of beef stroganoff, the two of them watched the news on the local NBC channel, and after a commercial, he saw a photo of Carlos in uniform. He turned the volume up and listened as the unseen narrator described his friend's death and the search for his killer.

"And if it wasn't for that dog," an eyewitness said, "the other man would be dead too. That dog is a hero."

"That dog," the reporter repeated, "was later treated for its injuries at a nearby animal hospital."

"That dog," Trufant said aloud, and Travis looked up.

The video cut away from the scene at The Dog Palace to another showing a uniformed police officer carrying Travis into Dr. Sitahal's clinic. Someone had put a leather muzzle on him and he could see Travis struggling in the officer's arms.

"There you are, hero."

Travis watched himself, panting lazily on the floor. If he knew what he was watching, Trufant couldn't tell.

"It was horrible," an elderly woman said. "We had just come out of the market, and I saw the dog attack the man. I thought it was a rabid stray at first, and I was afraid it would come at me too—then I saw the man's knife and . . . oh my God, what happened next was just so horrible, I can't describe it. It—" The woman began weeping, and the camera zoomed in, catching every detail of her face. This station had a reputation for "if it bleeds it leads," and tonight they were earning every word.

The woman shook her head and walked away, unable to finish her sentence. He had hoped there would have been more interviews, but it was already yesterday's news.

"Yes, you are a hero, Travis."

Travis looked up at the screen and rolled onto his side and closed his eyes.

"Had enough for one day? Me too," he said, changing channels. Then his phone rang.

"Trufant, it's Flórez, and I have some good news—the FBI has the guy's car. A Contra Costa sheriff's officer found it parked at a Starbucks, and the FBI towed it to their lab in Oakland. They're going to work on it all night. Do you have plans in the morning?"

"I guess I'm going to Oakland with you."

"Good, I'll pick you up for breakfast at seven."

Finally, the last of the puzzle pieces were falling into place. He stood and began pacing, imagining the car in front of him, some clue hidden inside that would lead to an arrest, maybe as early as tomorrow. He could feel his handcuffs snapping in to place around the bastard's wrists.

Without thinking, he poured half a glass of merlot and began running his fingers through the dog's silky coat.

"I've got to be sharp tomorrow, Travis, just this half-glass, okay? I know, I should pour it all into the sink and get some shut-eye, right?"

Travis was sound asleep though and didn't answer.

"But Travis," he said to the snoring dog, "my partner is dead, and it's only a glass of wine."

Sitting in his recliner, he thought back to his first few weeks with Carlos two years earlier. The kid had been eager, for sure, but he also had good instincts and a sense of humor.

As a lieutenant, Trufant had made it a practice to avoid learning about his inspectors' personal lives. Familiarity breeds contempt, he learned in a supervisory class. But he found himself close to Carlos that first year, and by the second, he thought of Carlos as family, maybe even as the son he had always hoped for.

The wine was hitting all the right spots, all the feels, as Carlos used to say.

By midnight he was on his third glass and still wide-awake. At two he was up and rummaging through the bathroom medicine cabinet, looking for something to help him sleep. The silence in the empty bed was almost painful, not that Adelaide's snore was loud, but no sound at all was like being in a vacuum. The last few nights he had stared at the ceiling until sleep came. The fog horns and traffic helped—but not tonight.

The small bottle of Xanax was still almost full. It was in front of a half-dozen other pill bottles Adelaide had left behind, most of which were expired. He swallowed two and went back to bed.

Travis followed him and put one paw on the mattress.

"You want help getting up there—the carpet not good enough for you now?"

He lifted the dog up and onto the bed—seventy pounds of dead weight, but at least he smelled better than the last time he had been in the room.

The room spun slowly in the dark, like he was on a carousel. Everything around the bed blurred, and he put his arms out wide, hoping to stop the spin as the taste of soured grapes rose in his throat.

***

In his nightmare, a police siren was wailing its sad song into the abyss. When he opened his eyes, it was still dark outside and it was colder in the room than it had been when he turned off the lights. The blaring alarm clock next to him was just a blur of red numbers and he switched it off. It was six o'clock.

He sat up and listened to another buzzing sound at the end of the bed and turned on the lamp.

"Jesus, Travis, you snore worse than Adelaide."

Leaving the snoring dog where he was, he got up and made coffee. Carlos and his funeral were consuming Trufant's every thought now. Once it was over, he hoped he would sleep again. His head ached and the acrid taste of wine was still in his throat, but at least he had slept for four hours.

He went back to the medicine cabinet looking for Advil or Tylenol, anything to ease the pain between his eyes, but there was nothing, not even an aspirin.

As the coffee brewed, he began to plan for the funeral tomorrow. His dress uniform was clean and pressed. He would take the dog with him and pick up Kira on the way to the church. Had Kira ever been to an officer's funeral? Probably not. The last funeral for a San Francisco officer was for Officer Tuvera, who was killed in 2006. She would have still been in school.

He poured the coffee into a Disney mug, his favorite, a gift from a coworker years ago. Grumpy's scowl stared back at him as he stirred the creamer, watching the whirlpool of shades of brown.

He heard Travis walk into the kitchen, his nails clicking across the tile, and found him sitting in the doorway, his one ear flopped backward.

"You're looking chipper this morning, my friend. I suppose you want to go for a walk?"

Travis walked over to the old leather leash, picked it up off the floor and dropped it at Trufant's feet.

"Yes, you are smarter than most people I know, but that's not saying much."

The two of them strolled out into the morning mist just after dawn. There was nothing but fog and gray clouds where the sun should have been, and people were already up and out, heading to whatever they did in San Francisco.

The woman walking in front of him left a trail of perfume like a ship leaving a wake on a calm sea. An old habit he enjoyed was guessing the careers of the people around him. Some were easy––the woman in front of him, dressed in sweats and comfortable running shoes and walking two matching white toy poodles, was probably a stay-at-home mom. The man to his left was young, in his early twenties, and carrying a new but cheap briefcase, probably working from a tiny cubicle in an office downtown.

If he passed the Haddad kid on the sidewalk, what would he see? Would he look like a psychopath? Or would he look like just another nameless man lost in a crowd of strangers?

One of the woman's dogs lifted its leg and peed on a lamppost, then looked back at Travis. The little dog hesitated, causing the woman to turn around. She stared for a second too long, turned, and picked up her pace, pulling on their leashes as the dogs' little legs struggled to keep up.

Travis peed on the same lamppost, darkening the green patina, his urine washing away the tiny spot the poodle had left behind. The shaved skin around his head and neck was still pale white, but stubbles of fur were beginning to show. And the bloodred wound and missing ear would cause anyone to run.

"That'll teach him, Travis."

Forty-five minutes later they were back in the apartment and he heard the knock on the door. It was exactly seven o'clock.

"Good morning, Major, come in."

"Christ," the man said, looking at Travis. "It looks worse in person. I saw a little of him on TV last night, how's he doing?"

"Great, he's sore, I'm sure, and he looks horrible, but he doesn't complain."

Flórez surveyed the kitchen and noticed the empty wine bottles and the single glass on the counter. "Rough night?"

"I can't sleep anymore . . . and wine helps. Where are we going?" he asked, trying to change the subject.

"I found a little artsy place yesterday near my hotel, mostly locals, so it must be good."

***

The Eight AM restaurant was off Columbus Avenue, and there were already people waiting for a seat. The ache between his eyes throbbed like a drum, but he was also hungry. Travis was ready too, pulling at the lead wanting to get inside where all the good smells were.

"Have you always had problems sleeping?" Flórez asked.

"Not really, it was bad right after my wife left, but eventually, I got through it. This is worse, though. It's a combination of things—my marriage, Carlos, of course, fears of my own death, and a little desire for revenge. Part of me wants to kill that guy. I stare at the ceiling and fantasize how I will do it. And when I do fall asleep, the nightmares start. I wake up in a sweat, scared shitless. That's when the wine helps."

"You should talk to somebody. I'm no good at it, but I've been through a few things myself recently. We'll grab a beer one night and talk."

"Beer," Trufant said laughing. "I'm not sure if that's a good idea."

Trufant wasn't sure he trusted the man enough to say anything more.

The young hostess looked at Travis as they went through the door. She started to say something, a word formed on her lips, but when she saw the badge and gun on Trufant's belt, she changed her mind.

The dining area was small, and they took the last seat in the back, giving them a good view of the front door.

The decor was minimal—white acoustic ceiling, brown wainscoting that appeared to be real wood, and plain but comfortable chairs. What the restaurant lacked in ambiance, it made up for in the rich aromas coming from the kitchen.

The big Lab hid from view, curling up between Trufant's legs and the wall like a trained service animal. He had never seen a dog so big blend into environments that most dogs couldn't. Like everything else, if the smell of food and two dozen strangers had any effect on him, it didn't show.

Everything on the menu looked good, and Trufant had trouble choosing which decadent breakfast entree he wanted to try.

"Excuse me," he said to the woman next to him, "is that French toast?"

"Yes, with blueberry compote. It's delicious," she said. "I have to ask, is this the dog I saw on the news? It must be. I heard about the attack, how terrible."

"Yes, it was, and his name is Travis."

"He's a very handsome dog, and very brave."

He smiled and thanked her, but as he said the words, a fleeting image of Carlos on the stainless steel table, cold, gray, and lifeless, ruined any thoughts of breakfast.

Even the smells were wrong now. The bacon smelled like putrid grease in a sink trap, the aroma of baking bread became cloying, and he was afraid he was going to puke. He looked for the men's room and fortunately it was only a few feet away. Hopefully it would not come to that.

The waitress asked them if they were ready to order.

"Just coffee for me, please."

Flórez ordered a bacon and egg sandwich and looked at Trufant with concern.

"I know what you're thinking, and I know what you're feeling. You've got to eat, though, it's going to be a long day."

"I know," he whispered. "I keep seeing a flash of Carlos in the ER, graphic, if you know what I mean, and the thought of eating nauseates me. It comes and goes, but I'll be okay."

He felt Travis move under the table and saw the woman had given him a piece of her toast. At least Travis's appetite was excellent.

Flórez' egg sandwich arrived, and Trufant felt his appetite creeping back, and the bloated feeling in his stomach eased.

"I've changed my mind, ma'am, I'll have what she's having," he said, pointing to the woman's French toast, "and a side of crispy bacon."

Flórez nodded in approval.

Neither of them spoke while they ate, and he stroked Travis under the table with one hand while he ate with the other. He broke a strip of bacon in half and put it under the table, feeling the dog take it from him gently. He would miss him when Armstrong was ready to take him back.

***

The FBI headquarters was a big, natural stone and glass building off Grand Avenue, and the suspect's car was in the lower level of the parking garage. Flórez maneuvered his vehicle around a series of temporary barricades and identified himself to two agents dressed in tactical gear and carrying MP-5 submachine guns.

"It's been a busy night here," Merriweather said, walking up to greet the two men.

"Glad to see you're not taking any chances with this guy coming back," Trufant said, nodding at the two agents.

"Not if we can help it," Merriweather said. "Let me show you what we've found. There are some large blood smears inside, but the car is spotless on the outside."

Merriweather handed him a clear evidence bag, marked with the case number and sealed with red tape, that contained a single blue strand of fiber two inches long.

"We found several of these on the exterior. This one was stuck in the headlight bezel."

Trufant was familiar with the strands. He'd found them on his own car. "It's from the brushes of a car wash."

"Yes, it is. The car was abandoned near a Starbucks. We located an automated carwash in the same shopping area and woke up the owner at midnight. He wasn't happy until he learned what we were looking for. He has two excellent security cameras, and we got great footage of a woman using her bank card for the transaction."

Trufant peered inside the Honda and saw the blood on the driver's seat and headrest. There was a lot of blood and seeing it was satisfying. Amato's bullet had done some major damage. Trufant had seen people lose less blood and die from their wounds. Some of the blood was probably from the dog bite, and Armstrong had seemed sure at least one of his rounds had hit the man too.

"We went through the interior once we got the warrant, and except for the blood, it's clean," Merriweather said. "All we found were the registration papers in the glove compartment. He had a FastTrack transponder on the visor, so we'll be able to track the toll roads he's been using."

"Do you have a name on the woman?" Trufant asked.

"We do, and better yet, we have her upstairs in an interview room. Care to see her?"

***

The elevator took them to the fourth floor, and Merriweather led them to an unmarked door. The room was dark inside and six seats faced a one-way mirror. Sitting on the other side of the mirror was a young woman wearing a blue floral bathrobe and slippers. She was probably woken up by a SWAT team and never given a chance to dress. Sitting next to her was another woman, probably in her forties, dressed in a dark green suit.

"That's Brienne Cosgrove on the left and her father's attorney on the right," Merriweather said. "We picked Cosgrove up just a few hours ago. She denied everything until we showed her a video of her face as she stuck her credit card into the machine at the car wash. Then she wanted a lawyer."

"Is she talking now?" Flórez asked.

"Yes. We offered her limited immunity, and she's agreed to testify whenever we need her. We're transcribing her statement now, and once she's signed it, she's free to leave."

"Anything good?" Trufant asked.

"Yes, she's a post-graduate student at Berkeley and was a classmate with our subject," Merriweather said. "Tuesday evening, the man she knew as Hector Bolivar knocked on her door with two gunshot wounds. She said they were in an anatomy class together two semesters ago. He thought she was a pre-med student and could help him.

"Was she," Flórez asked.

"Not really," Merriweather said. "She had a basic anatomy class but no real medical training. All she could do was clean and bandage the wounds. Then she drove him in his own car to Buchanan Field where two men were waiting for him."

"Who were they?" Trufant asked.

"She didn't know," Merriweather said. "She said they appeared to be EMTs but wore regular clothing. She watched them put him in a wheelchair, start an IV, and take him across the tarmac where a small jet was waiting. Minutes later, the jet took off and she hasn't heard from him since."

Fuck me. He's gone. Trufant's headache was better, but now he felt on edge and jittery, just the effects of adrenaline, he hoped.

"There should be an FAA record of the flight."

"That tower is unmanned after ten o'clock, and the FAA is searching now for any flight plans out of Buchanan Field,"

Merriweather said. "One thing, though, Cosgrove told us Ramzi made two phone calls, and she heard him say "mother" on both calls."

"Damn it, this whole fucking family is involved, and Christ, he could be in Europe by now." Trufant said. Knowing that Carlos's killer had been so close and now could be anywhere infuriated him.

He opened the door and stepped out into the hallway, taking Travis with him and hoping to cool off. This is not personal, he tried to tell himself. He stuck his hand in his pocket, hoping he had somehow left an oxycodone there, but all he found was a bit of lint. He should have brought a few of the Xanax.

So much for a quick end to this mess. The closer I get, the farther I am from this bastard.

The professional in him knew he was too close now, and if the situation were reversed, he would have removed anyone like himself from the investigation. A simple mistake could jeopardize a case this complex, and if Merriweather knew what was going on in his head, he would be politely removed and never know how it ended, and that would drive him mad.

He slowed his pace and his breathing in the empty hallway. The building was typical of all government offices. Void of decorations, it had cheap, cream-colored ceramic tile and matching walls. The color, psychiatrists said, had a calming effect on agitated persons. It was bullshit, of course, it was just less expensive.

The door opened, and Merriweather came out.

"We're getting close now, Trufant, it's just a matter of time and old-fashioned legwork."

He looked at the director, hoping he hadn't made a scene in the interrogation room.

"Can I talk to her?" he asked.

Merriweather didn't answer.

"I'm not going to make a mess in there, if that's what you're thinking."

"Okay, Marcus, but her attorney is sharp and she's cooperative at the moment. I want to keep it that way. Please don't ruffle her feathers."

"I won't, just hold this," he said, giving the director Travis's leash.

***

He was the third person in the room now. Both women stared at him, one scared shitless and the other smug and arrogant. Hopefully, he looked as confident.

The young woman did her best to look calm until he sat down and then she began to tremble. It started with her feet when she crossed her legs. One foot was in constant motion, up and down and side to side.

Good!

Usually, he would start with an introduction and simple questions. Like a lie detector, he would want to see and hear her answer questions he already knew. But it would seem redundant and if her attorney was any good, she would object and ask him to move on. First, he would let them sit, letting a moment of awkward silence work on their confidence.

The attorney leaned in as if to say something and he cut her off.

"Miss Cosgrove," he said. "I'm Lt. Trufant, can you tell me anything about the man who came to your apartment, anything strange you haven't already told the other detectives?"

She looked at the attorney for help.

"Lieutenant, Brienne has already told them all she can. She's cooperating, but until last night, she hasn't seen this man in over a year."

He ignored her, never even making eye contact and spoke directly to the young woman.

"You see this scar around my neck, Brienne? His sister did this, and of course, you now know he killed a police officer. He is a psychopath, and there has to be something odd about him. I want you to think back, what did you notice about him the first time you met? I want to hear it from you."

"I met him the first day of my anatomy class. He sat next to me, but we didn't speak for a few days. He was shy at times, but a little weird other times. I don't think he spoke to me at all until the third or fourth week."

"Weird? Tell me how."

"Okay, like one day I was early for class and sat on a bench just outside going over my notes and he sat next to me. We talked about different things. He said he wanted to major in forensic anthropology, you know—the study of the dead. I thought it was kind of creepy, but we became friends over the next few weeks.

"When you say friends, were you dating?"

"No, he came to my dorm a few times just before midterms, and we studied together. He was cute, and I remember hoping something might . . . you know, happen, between us but it never did. I asked him once if he was gay and he got angry. He didn't speak to me again for like a week."

Brienne was beginning to relax, her foot stopped and she put both feet on the floor and leaned forward. A sign she was remembering something she thought was important.

"I remember him interrupting the professor a few times, asking odd questions about death and mortal wounds. It wasn't so much the questions, but how he asked them—I think it excited him to talk about it."

"Why did you think he came to you?"

"I don't know. I never saw him speak to anyone else in the class, and I never saw him again after that one semester. He failed the class by the way, he never showed up for the final. I think he came to me thinking I was going to be a doctor, and I would know how to save him."

"How bad were his wounds?"

"They were pretty gross. He had a gunshot to the left shoulder, on the anterior part of the deltoid," she said and touched the front of her shoulder. "The bullet came out of his back through the scapula. It was really bad. The bone was probably shattered and I saw a lot of bone fragments. I think the bullet severed the big nerve too because he had no feeling below his shoulder."

Very good.

"Can you tell me anything more about his wounds," Trufant said.

"The inside of his right forearm was also shredded. There were lots of punctures, and about a four-inch-long rip in the flesh above his wrist. He said it was from a dog. I tried to clean it with peroxide, but it needed a lot deeper cleaning and maybe even surgery. I think some of the tendons were ripped away from the muscle."

The young woman looked up at the ceiling then down at her hands. She was recalling a memory, not trying to make one up.

"Oh, the index finger on his left hand was missing too, but he didn't know how it happened. He also had a bullet wound on his right thigh. It was simple, like a gouged-out a piece of flesh, but the pain was probably terrible."

"Did he say how any of this happened?"

"Like I told the other man, Hector said he'd found a credit card near campus and was trying to use it at an ATM when someone tried to rob him. He said he was afraid of being arrested, so he didn't go to the police. I knew he was lying, but I was afraid of him by then."

"Do you think he will live?"

"I'm not sure. The guys at the airport seemed like they knew what they were doing. They started an IV pretty quick, stuck him with a few syringes and wheeled him onto the plane."

"What is your major, Miss Cosgrove?"

"Child Psychology."

"You said he spoke to his mother. Do you know where she is?"

"No. I heard him say mother twice, but I got the impression she was far away and very wealthy."

"What made you think that?"

"Well . . . she sent a private jet to pick him up."

"I can see your point. Looking back now, did he seem capable of killing people?"

"He was a troubled kid, reclusive, an introvert for sure, but I know others much worse."

Trufant thought about it, the blank look on some kids' faces as they stared at video games on their cell phones all day, kids that would rather text friends than speak to the ones sitting right next to them.

"Thank you, Miss Cosgrove. Good luck to you."

***

"This guy is in my head now, Tristan, and I have to get him out," he said as they drove out and onto the freeway. Thankfully Flórez was driving because Trufant felt light-headed and flushed.

"Marcus, if he had to be flown out on a jet, and he's in as bad a shape as the girl said, he's not going to be a threat for a long time."

"I'm not just worried about him. He has two more sisters and a mother who's probably really pissed off right now."

They drove in silence on the way back across the Bay Bridge, and he noticed Flórez taking side glances at him occasionally.

Am I being paranoid or is he wondering if something is wrong with me?

Through Treasure Island and into San Francisco, Travis stood in the back seat, his head out the open window and his one ear flapping in the breeze. Trufant felt himself nod off, then his head jerked upright, and he realized they were already in his neighborhood.

"Ease up on yourself, Marcus, I'll see you soon."

"It's just the lack of sleep, Tristan. I'm okay."

The major nodded and drove away, leaving them in front of his building.

Instead of going in, he walked Travis back into the park, hoping the walk would clear his head. The headache was back and he felt dead tired.

Travis pulled on the lead, and he realized he had stopped just outside the park, and the dog wanted to reach the first lamppost.

"Sorry, boy, make it quick, okay? I want to get back upstairs."

He unhooked the leash and sat next to the sign that said All Pets Must Be On A Leash. Travis ran down the path toward the far end where he lifted his leg and re-marked the old lamppost. Trufant pictured Ramzi Haddad's face, the one from his driver's license, and imagined him with one of those crazy knives in his hand.

He's out there somewhere—alive and breathing.

His pulse began to race, his heart pounded, and he wondered if he was having a panic attack.

Ramzi would eventually kill him if he wasn't careful. He knew without a doubt that he would be the man's next victim, or maybe Armstrong. An obsessive-compulsive killer could not stop and it was just a matter of time. Every second that ticked by, the man was getting stronger. He would heal and finish what he had started.

Trufant had studied criminals like Ramzi his entire career, men and even a few women whose need to satisfy their compulsions meant hurting others, and in extreme cases, killing them. Ramzi would never rest until he satisfied that need.

"Your dog should be on a leash," a woman said as she jogged by. He looked at her and started to say something but called Travis over instead. The lamp clicked on, signaling the day's end and the beginning of night, and tonight he didn't want to be outside in the dark.

***

Travis waited patiently for him in the kitchen, licking the drool around his lips.

"Sorry, my friend, I'm hurrying," he said, opening a can of the wet, pink meat, as his hands shook.

Do I pour myself another glass of the goddamned wine or pop a few Xanax?

It had to be one or the other because he felt like he was coming apart at the seams.

Wine first.

He turned on the news and closed his eyes, listening to the drone of one reporter after another, sipping from the glass he held in his lap until it was empty. *No more wine,* he had said just yesterday. He fell asleep in the chair until Travis barked, startling him and knocking the fragile wine glass to the floor, where it shattered. Travis needed to go out or he was going to crap inside.

"Shit!" he said aloud, seeing four hours had passed. He had forgotten to eat and now it was near midnight and his stomach was cramping. Hopefully, the night's cold air would clear his head. Without bothering with Travis's leash, the two of them stepped out into the night.

The moon was full and the sky was oddly clear. Even the park was different, silent like the streets around him, foreboding, and even Travis seemed uneasy. He patted the bulk of the .45 under his coat but its size and weight did little to assure him. It's just late, he thought. Still the shadows created by the buzzing lamps were more than just shadows now, and each one seemed to be alive.

"Hurry, Travis, do what you have to do and let's get the hell out of here."

Travis did as he was told and they made their way back, Trufant looking over his shoulder every few feet as each new sound was surely someone sneaking up behind him, someone with a knife or a gun in the nearby alley.

They made it back to the apartment alive and he poured another glass of wine.

"One glass, Travis, and then it's off to bed, okay?"

Travis stared at him with eyes that seemed to know there would be more.

Chapter 33

Mother

"Where am I? Where is my son?" she asked the man staring down at her.

"You're in Mississauga hospital, Ms. Aquino. How are you feeling today?"

The balding, fat man had a lisp and a clipped foreign accent. She detested him instantly.

"Like shit! What is this?" she choked out the words as she tore at the plastic tubing wrapped around her face. "Who are you and why am I here?"

"I'm Dr. Paz," the frightened man said, backing away. "Your niece brought you in two days ago. You were unconscious. She is waiting outside. Would you like to see her?"

"Two days ago!" She tried to scream, but the words slurred and sounded meaningless.

What has happened to Ramzi—is he even alive?

"Yes, I would," she was able to whisper.

Chanda came in and the girl looked scared.

Ramzi is dead and she's afraid to tell me.

"Leave us, Doctor."

The man seemed relieved and rushed out of the room.

"What has happened, Chanda?"

"You fainted Aunt Diw . . . Ms. Aquino," the girl stammered. "Danilo and I brought you here. Doctor Latif was afraid you were dying."

Bassam Latif was an ignorant fool, a failure at every turn. "What has he done to Ramzi—does my only son still live, Chanda?"

"Yes, ma'am," the girl said. "He is awake now but in great pain. There is an infection Dr. Latif cannot stop. Ramzi needs better care, he said."

"He's no doctor, Chanda. Do you have my cigarettes? Light one, please."

"You cannot smoke in here. They are very strict."

"What will they do to me, Chanda—throw me out on the street? Light me a cigarette or get out."

She took a deep drag on the Gold Flake and choked out the blue-gray smoke, savoring the pain in her lungs. The pain was better than no feeling at all she reasoned, and it reminded her that she was still alive and that her time was precious.

Two days have been wasted!

"I need to get out of here, Chanda—send in that fat ass of a man."

Her niece looked at the half-smoked Gold Flake and started to say something, changed her mind, and went outside.

The doctor walked in, seeing the smoke drifting through the room.

"What are you doing? You cannot smoke in here. That's oxygen!" he said, pointing to the tube hissing on her chest.

"Discharge me at once, Doctor. I am dying of cancer—can you cure me if I stay? No? Then I am leaving at this very moment!"

She pulled the IV out of her forearm, leaving the bloody needle on the sheet next to the oxygen line.

"Chanda, a wheelchair, please!"

The doctor stepped back, as he realized the patient's departure was going to be a gift from God. He picked up the chart and began making notes as Chanda brought in a wheelchair.

"You must sign this release, Ms. Aquino!" the doctor said, chasing the two women down the hall.

***

Chanda maneuvered the van through southbound traffic on Highway 401 and pulled into the garage just as the sun set behind gray clouds.

"Chanda, I'm going to need my oxygen tank, can you prepare it for me?"

She rode up to the home's main level and found Ramzi awake in his old bedroom. She had left his pictures on the walls, his plastic dragons, the toy samurai warriors, and his trophies on his dresser, not for him, he could not have cared less about them, but in her worst moments of depression, she would often visit her children's rooms, reminiscing of better times.

Ramzi had been obsessed with those dragons and the warriors after moving to Manila, and his first trophy was from an FMA competition—and here they sat—collecting dust, but still able to soothe her.

She looked at her adult son lying in his old bed. He was pale and thinner than he had been just a few days before at Madinah's service, and there were more tattoos than she remembered on what she could see of his body.

Sitting in her wheelchair placed them at eye level. His eyes slowly focused on her, and he looked like the ten-year-old boy she knew in another lifetime.

"Mother," he said.

He was covered in a thin white sheet, concealing the wounds. There was a smell of old sweat mixed with urine and another scent she couldn't identify, like the smell of wet soil after a rainstorm. He was too weak and in too much pain to even use a bedpan, Latif had said.

"Ramzi, Latif has done all he can. He says you may die without proper care. Do you want to go to a hospital, knowing you may be arrested? The choice is yours."

"Mother, I *am* dying. What difference does it make?"

"If you live, you may spend the rest of your days in prison. If you live, there is hope, Ramzi. If you die in this bed, there is no hope."

She watched him thinking, then he closed his eyes and for a long time she thought he had fallen asleep.

His eyes opened and stared at her. That look of arrogance and the narcissism was back.

"But I'll be free."

"Free?" she said, laughing hard enough to trigger a torrent of coughing, then spit out a wad of brown mucus into the metal cup in her wheelchair. "What is your choice, Ramzi? You must decide quickly."

He lifted his right arm, studying the bandages, and saw that the redness now reached his fingertips. He brought them to his face, flexing them and making a fist. He could smell the infection, a smell like rotting flowers in a vase—but he could still hold a knife with this hand if he had to. His left arm refused to move at all. He pinched the skin of his wrist and felt nothing.

"Not a U.S. hospital, Mother."

CHAPTER 34

TRUFANT

Marcus Trufant wore his Class A uniform and drove his dark blue Chevrolet Impala into the lot and parked next to the chief's Lincoln Aviator. His head ached again, and he fished a Xanax out of his pocket and swallowed it with a sip of cold coffee. *Too much wine again.* Too much, he repeated aloud. *Once this funeral is over and Carlos is in the ground, I will put all that to rest, and I'll be fine.*

Kira Pinchon sat next to him, dressed in a somber, dark-gray dress. Her hazel eyes were already red and swollen from their conversation on the way to the church.

"Are you okay?" she asked.

"Just a headache, I couldn't sleep last night."

"I didn't sleep well, either."

Travis stood on all fours in the back seat, watching as two of the department's K-9 officers walked their Belgian Malinois along a sidewalk already full of people heading toward the church.

Trufant stepped out onto the damp asphalt, put his hat under his arm, and opened Kira's door. Travis trotted alongside him, sniffing here and there, and fortunately, the dog didn't feel the need to urinate this close to the church's front doors. The sight of him peeing on the nightly news wasn't something Trufant wanted to see.

It was a two-block walk down Fillmore Street. The street itself was barricaded for several blocks to allow the hearse and the procession of limousines to arrive and depart after the service.

The Calvary Presbyterian Church was a magnificent Edwardian building built in 1902. He knew this because the mayor had mentioned its history in his press briefing the night before. Trufant had passed by it often, never noticing the massive, ornate columns and the beautiful stained glass windows.

Carlos and his wife were married in this church, and now his new widow would sit in the front row near the casket. The image was a sight he was not looking forward to but one he would endure—for his sake and hers.

Low gray clouds mixed with patches of blue sky drifted eastward from the bay. The forecast mentioned a chance of light rain later in the day, and he hoped it would hold off until after his friend's burial.

"Are you ready, Kira?" he asked as they climbed the flight of steps leading to the entrance.

"As ready as I can be, Marcus."

Officers in Class A, or dress uniforms, stood at each of the four huge wooden doors, offering the funeral program. The three-page brochure included a picture of Carlos in his dress uniform and a brief history of his life and career. Trufant took two and gave one to Kira.

Kira held his arm at the elbow, and he held Travis's leather lead. He could feel her hand tremble as they entered the already half-full chamber.

"It's a beautiful church," she said.

There were three sections of pews, and the first four rows of each were reserved, cordoned off with purple velvet ropes. The first row in the center section was reserved for Carlos's wife and family, the rest would be for the politicians and VIPs, most of whom had never met Carlos. Carlos's friends and coworkers would fill the remaining pews, and the overflow would stand outside along the street, listening to the service through the portable loudspeakers he had seen on the way in.

If anyone objected to Travis being there, they didn't show it. Most of the attendees had heard or seen the news, and it only took one look at him to know this was the dog. Travis was oblivious to the attention and strutted down the aisle as if he owned it.

They took their seats in the ninth row as more of the department's employees filled in behind them, and twenty minutes later, every seat had been taken and several dozen men and women stood against the walls. He recognized many of them as coworkers, some were with the media, and Dr. Sitahal was standing next to a waitress from the café where he had met Carlos twice a week for coffee. She caught Trufant's eye and smiled.

Travis was sitting close to Kira, who was rubbing the dog's remaining ear between her thumb and forefinger.

Trufant looked up at the magnificent vaulted ceilings and the stained glass and noticed the deep brown oak pews in the balcony were filling up as well. How many people were inside— nine hundred—a thousand?

Surprisingly there wasn't much noise, only a low whispered murmur, then silence as Carlos's wife, Myra, entered, escorted by a man who appeared to be her father. Her two children followed behind. Trufant recognized them from the photos on Carlos's desk. His eyes began watering, and he blinked a few times, hoping it would help, but the first tear ran down his cheek unchecked.

A whole procession of people followed the children, the chief and the mayor leading the way. The chief gave him a look as he passed, similar to the one in the elevator a few weeks ago.

Then the pallbearers, all members of the department's honor guard, carried the casket down one of the middle aisles—the one closest to Kira, and she squeezed his arm as it went by.

It was quiet in the chamber now, so quiet he could hear the fabric of the honor guards' trousers brushing together in unison.

Trufant pretended to clear his throat but was choking back a sob as another tear ran down the same cheek. The tear embarrassed him, left him feeling weak, and he wiped it away.

The minister walked over and knelt next to the new widow, speaking words only she could hear, and she nodded. Then he stood and walked over to the casket, placed his hand on the blue field of stars, and said something to Carlos. Finally, he walked over to the pulpit and stood next to it so everyone could see him.

"Our Father . . . " he said, and Trufant couldn't listen to the rest. He covered his face and blotted out the remainder of the Lord's Prayer, grieving, seeing nothing but Carlos smiling as he sat across from him every day in the office.

One of Carlos's children was crying, and others around him began to sob. It was infectious, and he fought his own emotions, knowing that once it started, it would be hard to stop.

He missed some of what came after the prayer but listened as the minister recounted Carlos's life, a proud father who had watched his son and daughter being baptized in this church not long ago.

Then the chief spoke, and Trufant stopped listening and stared down at his hands and shoes waiting for the man to finish. Nothing he said was wrong or untrue, but the words sounded hollow. Fortunately, it was over quick. The chief had never liked speaking in public.

***

The mourners began filing out of the church with Carlos's wife and family staying behind. First were the dignitaries by rank, then it was his turn and the three of them walked down the aisle with Travis leading the way, his eyes straight ahead toward the door, occasionally glancing at someone as if acknowledging them. Trufant hoped he looked as dignified as the dog.

Outside, officers in dress uniforms and suits lined both sides of the street. Several hundred police motorcycles were lined up two abreast against the curb, each with an officer behind it. The first six were from Las Vegas, then Seattle, Los Angeles, and as far away as Laredo, Texas. There was a sea of naval officers and sailors in dress uniforms. Carlos had served in the Navy and spent time in San Diego and Pearl Harbor. Trufant wondered if they had been his shipmates.

They found a spot across from the church, and everyone lined up in even rows, four and five deep. They stood still, silently facing the church, then one of the big wooden doors opened again, and the honor guard's team leader brought everyone to attention.

Myra, the new widow, and her children, stepped out into the sunlight, followed by the flag-draped coffin. In the sun, the colors of the flag looked richer and brighter than normal, and he took a deep breath. *It's just the contrast of the somber colors around it.*

It was an emotionally challenging scene as the pallbearers came down the steps. Here was the end of a man—his last few hours of sunlight, and then an eternity of darkness in a grave below ground—Carlos deserved better. Trufant felt his knees weaken and he wished he hadn't taken the Xanax earlier. He worried about collapsing in the street, something he had seen another officer do at the last funeral.

He was a train wreck, and by sheer will, he stood at attention.

Was it patriotism, grief, or guilt he was feeling? Maybe all three.

"Present arms!" the leader said.

Kira jerked, startled by the command and a thousand men and women in uniform saluting. Those in civilian clothes quietly put their right hand over their hearts as Myra made her way to the black hearse. The big door closed, then with perfect timing, a flight of gray Navy F-18 fighter jets thundered overhead in the missing man formation.

The jets surprised him. Some Navy admiral must have heard the news and wanted to honor the former naval officer. Trufant wished he could thank him.

As the roar of the planes diminished, he heard the sobs of the officer standing next to him and someone else behind him and his own arm shook as he tried to hold the salute. Tears ran unchecked down his face and soon soaked the collar of his dress shirt. It seemed each tear created another and another until finally the hearse passed, then the honor guard marched by, holding the Stars and Stripes.

Once the hearse was out of view, the team leader shouted the order arms command and then at ease, and Trufant took a deep breath.

"Is it like this every time?" Kira asked.

"Pretty much, especially if the officer was killed on duty. It's been a while though, so this might be a bigger crowd than the last."

"It was so emotional. Two years ago, I was in Washington and saw the Tomb of the Unknown Soldier and the changing of the guard. This was similar."

"You never get used to it, but this one was hard because we knew Carlos and we know how he died."

They walked back to the car, and Trufant's thoughts turned from remorse to rage the farther he got from the church. *Was that going through Kira's mind too?*

"Trufant!" someone yelled.

It startled him, and the image of Ramzi running up behind flashed through his mind as he pulled at the gun in his holster. But it wasn't Ramzi, it was Major Flórez

"Mind if I join you two?"

"Of course not, Major. You remember Kira?"

"Yes, I do. Do you mind if I ride with you? I rode in with Merriweather, and he's not going to the cemetery."

***

For thirty minutes they sat in the Impala waiting for a gap in the motorcade. The procession of motorcycles creeping along at three miles per hour was followed by the first of the VIP's limousines. The mayor's big Lincoln was the first, probably rented for the day, and behind it was Chief Lozano in a matching Town Car driven by Captain Brown. Both men looked at him through their tinted glass, and Trufant wished he could read their minds.

Finally, he was able to ease out into a line of unmarked cars. These were the street cops like himself—the people who put their lives on the line every time they went to work.

People like Carlos.

He let the thought go. Carlos would want him to live in the moment, to savor the grace and dignity of the ceremony, not sink into the abyss where there is almost no escape. He had been in that abyss once too often, and recently, and it was hard to break free.

On the police radio, he heard that the hearse had already made it to the gravesite, and they hadn't even reached the Bay Bridge yet. At least the sun was out, and the mourners waiting in their suits and dress uniforms would remain dry until the last of the procession snaked through and around the city of Oakland.

***

The four of them parked and got as close as they could to the ceremony. They were too far to hear the minister's words, or even see the casket, but they heard the commands to bring everyone back to attention, and finally the twenty-one gun salute. Kira, like those around him, flinched as each of the three volleys were fired. Seven rifles firing in unison was deafening, and even Travis looked frightened.

"It's all right, Travis."

As the rifle fire echoed off the buildings, several officers turned their radios up loud enough for everyone to hear the city's dispatcher.

"Last call for Inspector Carlos Amato, ID 0534, you are clear to 10-7. Your watch has ended, may you rest in peace."

Trufant listened numbly to the end of watch transmission. It was tough to hear, and now Kira was crying. Flórez put an arm around her shoulder, and the four of them returned to the car, avoiding the bronze grave markers spaced evenly in the grass.

***

"Anyone up for an early dinner?" Flórez said as they came back into the city.

"I'm in," Kira said. "I missed lunch and I'm starving."

"Good. I want to try the Pier Market Seafood Restaurant, I know it's a touristy spot, but I've heard good things about it."

"It is good, and they have an outdoor section. I think it's pet friendly."

Trufant felt his phone vibrating and saw he had missed three calls from Adelaide. She hadn't called him three times in the last month, and he feared the worst. She answered before he heard it ring once.

"Marcus, where are you?"

"Adelaide, are you okay?"

"Yes. I tried to make it to the funeral, but the streets were all blocked off. I'm still stuck on Van Ness."

"We're on our way to Pier Market Seafood. Why don't you join us?"

"I will, and Marcus, I want to tell you something. I'll be there in a few minutes."

Whatever it was sounded important, and his first fear was that someone had tracked her to Louisiana. Hopefully it was just a snag in the divorce.

"Adelaide is going to meet us there."

No one spoke until he parked, and finally, Kira said, "How's that going? Should Tristan and I get our own table?"

"No, it's fine. She sounded worried, though, and it's not like her."

"How well did she know Carlos?"

"She met him a few times—lunch usually."

***

Adelaide was waiting outside at a table by the fire pit. Even with the sun out there was a chill in the air, and she'd wrapped her lace shawl tightly around her shoulders.

"Adelaide, this is Tristan Flórez and you know Kira."

"My pleasure, Tristan. Kira, nice to see you again. And this must be the dog I've heard so much about."

"Yes, this is Travis. He's become quite a sensation it seems. He looks a little better today. The fur is growing back, and the stitches will come out soon. That ear, though—it ain't coming back."

"The scar is not that much worse than yours, Marcus, and I'm glad you're wearing that tie." She gave him a look, and he knew what she was thinking. "He's very handsome. Can I pet him?"

"Sure, he loves the attention."

As if he knew what they were saying, Travis walked over and sat next to her, and she stroked his side and whispered something in his ear. His tail wagged, thumping the table like a metronome.

"I ordered a bottle of Sonoma-Cutrer Pinot Noir. I hope everybody likes red."

Trufant watched Flórez as he spoke to Kira. Something was starting there, and he was happy for her.

The wine arrived, and the server poured an ounce into Adelaide's glass. She held it beneath her nose, inhaled the aroma, and sipped. She loved that first sip and the formality of sampling good wine.

"Perfect!" she pronounced.

The server filled their wine glasses, and Flórez said, "To Carlos, no man should have to die so young."

Trufant took a small sip, just a taste at first, and wished he had the strength to leave the rest on the table. Adelaide was right, the first sip was always the best and he took another, longer, sip. He tasted blackberry fruit with a touch of vanilla, not the perfect wine for a seafood dinner, but Adelaide had ordered it and he was going to enjoy it.

With the flavors identified, he took a good swallow and felt the heat of the alcohol in his chest. It soothed him, even as he sat with his soon-to-be ex-wife. The wine was dulling the sharp loss of having just buried his friend and partner, and he immersed himself in the company around him. He was glad he was with them, both the old friends and the new.

"I flew in early this morning but I still missed the funeral. I couldn't even get close to it," Adelaide said. "Kira, was this your first police funeral?"

"Yes, and my last, I hope."

"I remember thinking those exact words years ago," Adelaide said. She looked at him, and her eyes sparkled, tears no doubt. She blinked them away and said, "But I went to a few more over the next thirty years."

They ordered, and soon a mesquite grilled salmon sat in front of him. For a few seconds he was afraid he wouldn't have an appetite, but just like breakfast a few days ago, the queasy sensation left him. The smoky mesquite flavor and the wine took over, and he asked for another glass.

"Tristan, where are you from?" Kira asked.

"I was born in Barcelona and moved to New Jersey when I was small. I live in Santa Fe now."

"Tristan doesn't sound Spanish," Adelaide said.

"No, it's Welsh—it means the loud one. My mother was part Scottish, the rest of me is all Spanish. Most of my friends just call me Flórez, though. I guess Tristan sounds too formal. When I was a kid I never understood why my mother named me Tristan—she called me Tris until I was old enough to make her stop."

"Well, I like Tristan," Kira said, and blushed.

They would indeed make a good couple.

It was a perfect finish for a rough day, and it was over too quickly. Trufant stabbed the last chunk of roasted potato and pushed his empty plate away.

"Adelaide, you said on the phone that you wanted to tell me something?"

"Yes! I had two strange phone calls last week. I forgot about them after Carlos was ki—" she caught herself as if the word stuck in her throat. "But now I'm worried. I was sitting with my sister on the porch, and I saw it was an unknown caller. I answered it anyway, expecting a recording, but a woman asked if she could speak to you. She hung up as soon as I said you weren't there and she called again the next morning. I called your office to tell you, but no one answered, then I heard the news and forgot about it."

"Did she give her name?"

"No, when I asked, she hung up. Something about her voice, though, was disturbing. It was deep, gravelly, but it wasn't just that, it sounded like she really didn't care if you were there or not, more like she was satisfied she had the right number."

He looked at Flórez, who was watching him, no doubt thinking the same thing.

"It's probably nothing to worry about, Adelaide, but remember he was seconds away from getting inside your apartment, so I want you to get another phone. Better yet, have your sister buy one for you and take the SIM card out of your old one and get rid of it. Pine Grove should be a safe place, and the guy we're looking for is probably in a hospital somewhere, or hopefully dead. The caller could have been a reporter trying to find me, but let's not take any chances. Another week or two and I hope this will all be over. How is your sister," he asked, trying to change the subject.

"She's fine, she's seeing someone now. I met him and he seems nice. Marcus, it's hot as hell down there, and I miss my gym."

She hadn't mentioned missing him.

"Dessert, anyone?" she asked.

He passed on dessert and wanted to pour another glass of wine, his third, but that would be too much, and he wanted this dinner to go smoothly with Adelaide.

And as if she knew what he was thinking, she said, "Are you driving, Marcus?"

"I am, but I've drank enough for one day."

Satisfied, she turned her attention back to the dessert menu.

He held back a sigh. Tomorrow was Sunday, and he was going to enjoy his day off.

Chapter 35

Armstrong

Travis was on the late news. The segment had been live on one of the local channels earlier, but Armstrong had slept through most of it. Today was his last day on tramadol, then the detoxing and physical therapy would begin, but for tonight, he was at ease. His demons were prowling in the periphery of his mind, biding their time—and he was ready for them.

Caitlin had finally agreed to sleep at a hotel across the street and would be in tomorrow morning. He was alone, and he felt warm, clean, and comfortable, better than he had felt in a long time, years maybe.

On the television, Travis was walking into the church with Trufant and a woman. The camera zoomed in on the dog and his missing ear. Travis looked happy, but Armstrong caught the grimace on Trufant's face as he disappeared into the church. Trufant was probably suffering from survivor's guilt. If he wasn't, he soon would be.

It had snuck up on Armstrong slowly, but once the shock of Travis's death wore away, guilt played on a loop in his head. *What if I had grabbed Travis and forced him to move? What if Travis had been standing just a little farther away, would I have taken the brunt of the blast? Would the shockwave have ripped me apart instead?*

He turned up the volume and heard the newswoman mention Carlos, then the scene at the church was replaced by the suspect's face.

It was his Berkeley ID photo taken last year. He was different then. His smile was forced, like he was mocking the camera or maybe the person behind the camera and his eyes looked normal. The yellow Berkeley sweatshirt was just visible, maybe the same one he'd worn the day of the attack. It would have a hole in it now, and the right sleeve would be torn and bloody. Travis had shredded that shirt, and Armstrong remembered all of it. It was a gratifying memory—the momentary shock on his face, the pain in those dead eyes.

"Police are looking for this man," the newswoman said. "Twenty-three-year-old Hector Bolivar, a.k.a. Ramzi Haddad, for the murder of Inspector Carlos Amato. Bolivar is also a suspect in the recent murders of homeless veterans in the San Francisco Bay area."

He turned the volume off as a different woman interviewed the city's mayor.

Travis!

How was he going to take care of Travis these next few days or even weeks? His detox and physical therapy would begin in earnest tomorrow, and the doctor told him it would be grueling.

He'd been with the dog for so long now and couldn't imagine living without him, but there was no place for Travis here, not until he beat the demons, and that worried him.

The doctor had said he would spend at least two more weeks in the hospital before he'd be transferred somewhere else for physical therapy. Now, with the threat to him and Cait, they wanted to move him to another part of the city.

Who would take care of Travis? Not Cait, she would be here. Trufant, maybe, Travis looked good with the lieutenant, and he had offered.

His nurse walked in with a small bottle and a syringe.

"This is it, Mr. Armstrong, your last dose. Are you sure?"

The pain of physical therapy, getting the muscles in his shoulder and arm to function again would be bad, but he could handle that. It should have been an easy question, yes or no. He was in no pain at the moment, free from all the side effects—the rushing high and crashing withdrawal—of heroin and its lethal sisters, like oxycodone, tramadol, and morphine.

He thought of Caitlin, who had never given up on him, even after all these years, and Dr. Williams, who died trying to save him, and Carlos Amato, who died trying to protect him.

"Yes, I'm ready, one last time."

There was no rush like that of heroin, no giant leap of euphoria, just a pleasant feeling and he slept.

And dreamed he was in a graveyard.

***

He was sitting in a cheap folding chair in a cemetery. Travis's mother, Dawn McClanahan, sat next to him and the two of them were alone among several acres of tombstones in Cypress Hills National Cemetery.

"He is my only son," she said. "I don't think any mother should have to bury her baby boy."

She was in her early forties, strong and proud, and shaded beneath a huge maple. The leaves had changed weeks ago and were falling everywhere. A cool breeze blew them off Travis's grave, exposing his full name and the date of his death.

"Did he tell you he was gay?" she asked, not waiting for an answer. "He told me when he was twelve years old. *Momma, I'm different.*"

"He had a busted lip that day. As big as he was at twelve, they still picked on him. I said, Travis, you don't even know what gay is! He said, *Momma, I know.*"

"It was hard on his father and me—you want the best for your children, you want them to be as healthy and as happy as the Lord will allow. But I know, Mr. Armstrong—being gay is not an easy thing, no sir, that busted lip was the proof."

"He told me."

"And what did you think? Did it change how you thought of him?"

"He was my friend—what does it matter to a friend or a parent? But we were Marines, and there is a stigma about what a Marine is, just like there is sometimes a stigma with being gay. He didn't want anyone to know, and I promised him I wouldn't say anything."

"Yes, sir, you are as right as rain. In my day they beat and killed gay men almost as often as they beat and killed Negroes when my parents were young. The world is changing, though, but not fast enough."

She leaned back in her chair and looked up at the blue sky. "Travis loved church when he was in grade school, and in middle school he went to every youth group meeting, always volunteering to help. But one day he stopped going. Just like that!

"I worried he had heard someone say homosexuals can't go to heaven, and they were doomed to spend all eternity in hell—the Bible says that, more or less. I even worried the pastor might have asked him not to come back if he knew. I asked Travis, but he would never say. What do you think, Mr. Armstrong?"

"I don't think God makes mistakes, Ms. McClanahan. He made men, and God loves them all. That's also in the Bible."

"Amen."

They sat in silence while dry leaves rustled against the marble headstones and a few crows cawed overhead in the big oaks and maples.

"You know, when his father passed away, he became the man of the house. He went to the gym every day, he wanted to be as big and look as mean as he could, but he was a softy. He would grocery shop for a few of the old people in our building every week until he joined the Marines. That was my son, Mr. Armstrong. I'm glad he had you as his friend, and I'm glad he didn't die alone."

***

In the darkness of the dream, someone was calling his name.

"Good morning, Mr. Armstrong."

A muscular young woman dressed in white scrubs peered down at him. She was in her late twenties or early thirties, thick but not heavy, and looked like she could crush a brick if she needed to.

"I'm Dr. Pissarro and I'm in charge of your recovery, I'm going to give you ketorolac," she said, sucking the fluid out of a small jar with a syringe. "It's an anti-inflammatory pain med. We'll use it for five days along with a Transderm-Scop patch for nausea. It will also help some with the pain from your wound and the withdrawal symptoms. I'll be honest with you—it's not going to be a joy ride."

The doctor and an LPN helped him into a wheelchair and rolled him out and into the hall for the first time that he could remember. Cait said they had taken him out for tests, but he had been so heavily sedated he couldn't recall any of it. Two uniformed officers followed them into an elevator and down another hall to the physical therapy unit.

With his arm in a sling, he walked a quarter mile on a treadmill and felt like he had just run ten miles carrying a twenty-pound rucksack and rifle.

"We'll take it slow, Mr. Armstrong," the doctor said. "This wasn't bad for the first day. It will get harder as you deal with the side effects of withdrawal and the lack of opioids for the pain you should already be feeling. You will feel anxiety and depression along with everything else. Just don't give up on us."

"My arm and shoulder hurt at the moment. I can deal with the rest."

"Good, I don't know if you remember speaking with me on Saturday—you were pretty doped up, but you told me quite a bit about your drug use."

"I don't remember much before Sunday. I saw some of Amato's funeral, and talking with my wife, but that's it. I've had some memory issues lately. I'm never sure if some of them are dreams or if they're real, and I was so fuck—oh, sorry."

"Sorry for cursing or sorry you can't remember? I've heard

worse, sir. I was in the Army for four years. I left Fort Sam Houston as an EMT and went overseas and helped patch up soldiers like you. I know what you went through. I've seen it firsthand—horrible wounds, morphine, more morphine, and then it's out on the street. The Army saw it too and they've made changes to correct it."

"Were you in Landstuhl?"

"Yes, sir, I was. I was part of a team transporting the wounded back to the States. Then the Army put me through med school and here I am—still patching up broken soldiers."

"So, you saw me, you saw what's under this robe—they couldn't patch that up."

"Yes, I did, and no, that's something you're going to learn to live with. Do you remember your drill sergeant from Paris Island?"

"McKnight?"

"Yes. He was here Friday afternoon. He wanted to see you, but you had just come out of another surgery."

"How did he find me, I thought no one knew I was here."

"He must have some good connection, because he knew who I was also," she said.

"McKnight rode Travis and me pretty hard. What did he want?"

"To see you, I guess, he said you were one of his brightest. He said he heard about you being injured, and your friend dying in Afghanistan. Another Marine killed that day was one of his recruits too. He wanted to see you in Landstuhl to pay his respects but couldn't get overseas, and he's regretted it ever since. He said to tell you Semper Fidelis and to remember what it means."

"Always loyal."

McKnight coming to see me! He had always thought the man disliked him. *One of the brightest!*

He never felt bright. Travis was the bright one.

"We're finished for today, Mr. Armstrong. Later tonight you can start walking around this floor, go visit the nurse's station if you want, sit in the lobby with the old folks, they love to chat, and your guards will probably enjoy the change of scenery too."

She rolled him back into his room, the two officers walking silently behind.

"The pain is going to get much worse as scar tissue forms, and we'll start therapy on that soon enough. In the meantime, we'll be focusing on your stamina and the addiction. Have a good day, sir."

***

Two days later, Caitlin stood by the window, dressed in her dark blue sweats and her hair tied back with a matching scrunchie. He smelled freshly baked pastries and saw the box on his bed.

"White chocolate macadamia nut cookies straight from Boudins. I went jogging this morning and saw them in the store window. Remember how I used to bake these for you years ago? I tried one, and I think theirs are better."

It was better than anything he had eaten in weeks, and from Boudin's' too, one of his regular stops along the wharf. Their day-old bread was still fresher than anything else in San Francisco.

"Yours were great," he said, taking another bite. "Did you see my dog on TV last night?"

"Yes, you and I watched it together yesterday. You said he looks good."

"We did? I don't remember. But he did look good. He likes the lieutenant, I can tell."

Cait's eyes were a crystal blue, like chips of a blue diamond sparkling in the sunshine streaming through the window. He looked at the spray of freckles on her cheeks, and her strawberry blonde hair looked like fire in the sun. She has always been beautiful. He had left her. He had walked away from her and it shamed him.

Guilt and anxiety. Those were the two reasons he had left her.

"I'm sorry, Cait."

"They're no good?"

"The cookies are great, Cait. I'm so sorry I left you. I look back now and I don't understand why I left. I remember thinking that leaving was the best thing I could do for you."

She helped him into the bed and rolled the IV stand back in the corner.

"It was a hard time for both of us, David. I don't blame you. I always knew how much you were suffering, and I couldn't find a way to help you through it. I blamed myself, sometimes. I still do."

He reached for her and held her as close as the pain in his shoulder allowed. Something was happening to the guilt and the anxiety that had pressed down on him for years. He still felt them, but they seemed less important. He could breathe without effort. It felt like a huge weight was off his shoulders, and somehow, even his fear of being dopesick was no longer all he thought of.

"I'm going to ask Trufant to take Travis," he said, changing the subject. "I think the lieutenant needs him now and Travis can't help me here."

He felt hot and cold at the same time. A bead of sweat dripped into his eye as the first physical symptoms of withdrawal began. Mentally he had a grip on his depression and anxiety, but the physical manifestations were another story. He picked up another cookie and his hands trembled. Brown crumbs began to cover his white sheet as the tremors found their way into the raw wound in his shoulder. Fever and chills would be next, and as if his thoughts triggered it, he felt nauseous and handed her the last few bites of the cookie.

"I think it's starting, Cait. This won't be easy. I love you."

Chapter 36

Trufant

Twenty-five hundred miles away, Professor Dean Chapman rolled his duffel bag up the ramp of the university's auditorium. He hated the first day of class after a long weekend. Students were at their worst. Twenty percent wouldn't even show, and those who did would still be suffering from three days' worth of drinking, and none of them would have studied Thursday's notes. He knew he would spend the entire day going over last week's lecture.

The plastic wheels on the duffel bag kept catching on the broken acorn shells that squirrels had dropped on the ramp, the wheels screeching like nails on a chalkboard. Truth be told, he was suffering from his own hangover, the result of one too many mojitos at the Alpha Lounge last night. The taste of mint, so refreshing a few hours ago, now gagged him.

The auditorium door clicked open as it recognized his New York University ID card, and he stepped into the lobby—and forgot about the mojitos and the mint. Something smelled rotten, and the janitors would pay if he had to endure this stench all day.

The two trash cans in the admission area were empty, and both had new plastic liners. The smell was not coming from the lobby, which meant it must be coming from inside. He opened the main doors to the three hundred seat auditorium and turned on the lights. The smell was worse now, and he covered his nose with the sleeve of his jacket.

Sitting in the center of the front row were three female students.

"Hey! You're not supposed to be in here!"

He rolled the now-quiet duffel bag crammed full of his notes, his laptop, and textbooks down the carpeted aisle to confront the three women.

He stared at the three bloated faces and screamed.

***

"Marcus, wake up! Jesus, he's out of it."

A man's voice was coming from somewhere close by.

I'm dreaming again.

A woman's voice said something he couldn't understand. He tried to open his eyes, to sit up, but slipped back into his nightmare.

Someone was chasing him down a dark, filthy street. He slipped and fell and his gun flew from his hand. He tried to reach out for it, but he was paralyzed, not even his fingers would move. He felt cold steel touch the base of his neck and waited for the bullet to end his life.

"Kira, grab his ankles and let's drag him to the shower."

Was Kira holding the gun?

He tried again to move, and it felt as if he were strapped to the asphalt pavement with Velcro. Shapes were moving around in the darkness now, and he smelled vomit. His fingers moved and he tried to reach his gun and kill the man behind him, but his gun was gone, replaced with ceramic tile and a toilet.

Water was running nearby and his vision began to clear, another bizarre dream, he thought, seeing himself in a mirror. He looked like a rag doll hanging limp in a man's arms. He closed his eyes again. The darkness was comforting, but the smell of vomit ruined the emotion.

"Cold water?" the woman asked.

"Warm will be better."

Like an electrical current running up his spine, he was instantly awake and jerked upright—and puked onto his black socks.

"Try and lie still, Lieutenant, I'll warm it up."

He looked at the voice and saw it was Major Flórez' face hovering above him. Behind him, Kira stared down at him, her face pale and her eyes wide in fear.

"Marcus," she said. "Are you okay?"

"I'm not sure."

Just speaking made his stomach turn and he wanted to puke again. He fought the urge, but his abs felt like Mike Tyson had punched him in the gut. Bits of vomit on his shirt caught in the stream of water and slid toward the drain near his feet.

I am my father.

"What time is it?"

"Three-thirty," the major said.

"Sunday?"

"No, Marcus, it's Monday," Kira said. "We both tried to call you this morning, but when you didn't answer we came by to check on you. The super let us in."

Monday? What happened to Sunday?

Trying to remember nauseated him and he let the thought go. "Travis?"

"He's fine, hungry, and nothing a long walk in the park won't cure," Kira said.

He heard the dog moving behind them in the hallway but couldn't see him without sitting up. The thought of moving made his stomach cramp again.

"Can you guys give me a few minutes. I want to take these clothes off and clean up."

Alone now and lying on the shower floor, he unbuttoned his shirt, seeing more chunks floating toward the whirlpool, then got his pants and shorts off. He sat up without triggering any new dry heaves and let the warm water splash on his head until he thought he could stand.

The bathroom began to rock back and forth, and he put both

hands on the wall to keep from falling. Once the vertigo eased, he put on his robe and made his way out into his living room.

Flórez and Kira sat on his couch, a little closer together than what seemed casual, and both of them wanting to check on him earlier now made sense.

"I'm so sorry and so embarrassed," he said.

"Don't be," Flórez said, looking sheepish. "We had our own hangover yesterday."

Kira smiled for a fraction of a second as her face flushed.

"This wasn't just a little too much, though, I'm drinking myself to sleep and taking all kinds of stuff to get me through the day, and it's getting worse." He directed the last part to the major and saw the acknowledgment on the man's face. The major was sharp, he knew what he meant.

"I had promised myself I would quit once Carlos was in the ground. I would throw the pills in the trash, drain the wine into the sink, and never touch them again. It sounded good, but when I actually held the bottle over the sink, I ended up drinking most of it. You know, I pride myself on my strength, but Kira, I don't think it's going to be that easy now."

"No, it won't be," she said, "not alone anyway. But I can help. Let me stay here tonight. I'll take care of you both," she said, glancing at Travis. "Tomorrow we'll start fresh."

"Thank you. I'm going to make some coffee. My throat feels like I've been swallowing ground glass all night. Anything new, Major?"

"I'm afraid so, Marcus. Three missing college students in New York were found dead in the university's auditorium this morning. They were staged like props and there was a note—a quote from Shakespeare."

"Oh shit, it can't be Ramzi, though, not his MO, and I don't think physically he would be able to carry something like this out, at least not alone."

"We know there are two more sisters out there. It could be one of them, or maybe both of them," Flórez said.

"Or a relative," Trufant said. "You said there was an uncle. The father's brother could be behind some of this."

"Marcus, you know they want you dead too," Kira said.

"Death would be an improvement right now. Just thinking of standing makes my stomach ache."

He let the silence hang as he tried to piece together the new puzzle part.

"So, three dead girls in New York, did he mention any time of death?"

"No, he didn't, but it was a long weekend. It could have been as early as Thursday night," Flórez said,

"Then she, or they, could be in San Francisco by now."

"Exactly," Flórez said.

"Tristen, I think you should take Kira home, I'll be okay. Remember they killed Dr. Williams just to send a message to us. Both of you are at risk now too, and right now the last thing I want to do is be anywhere near alcohol. Travis and I will be fine. Kira, if it eases your mind, why don't the two of you come back after dinner, that's when I seem to need the wine, but I promise, no alcohol or drugs until then. Deal?"

***

He watched them walk to the elevator holding hands, then he closed the door and looked at the dog.

"It's going to be another long night, Travis. I feel like shit so you're in charge, you understand?"

The dog chuffed, waiting at the door.

It was late in the afternoon and the park was already in deep shadows. An elderly couple walked along the gravel path away from him. A woman in sweatpants jogged toward him, young, fit, with wireless earbuds and a phone strapped to her arm. He eyed her, trying to find facial similarities, but she seemed too Caucasian and too tall.

He laughed. How many times had he ever used that term, too Caucasian?

Travis paid no attention to her, but he kept his eye on the woman until she ran past him, never making eye contact. Just someone trying to stay in shape, but still, she was new in the park. Without watching directly, he remained aware of her until she finished another lap and left through the main gate.

Alone now, he felt vulnerable and exposed. Travis wandered around in some random pattern, looking back at him once in a while, but was more interested in exploring the nooks and crannies now that he was off the leash.

Trufant took a deep breath and blew it out, watching the vapor in the cool damp air. Breathing felt good, like it was clearing out the cobwebs in his brain from the wine. He closed his eyes and listened to the sounds around him. Travis was behind him, trotting on the paved path, and a car horn honked on the street just north of the park.

The park was empty and dark now. Travis was spread out in the grass sleeping, and the first tendrils of fog were slipping in off the bay.

He shivered as the chill penetrated his coat, and suddenly, he was ready to leave and get behind his locked door. Someone wanted to kill him, and he or she could be as close as thirty feet or as far away as the East Coast.

Three dead students! How do these victims fit in with the Haddads?

"Let's go, Travis."

Travis marked a lamppost with a flood of urine one last time and seemed eager to leave as well.

***

His apartment was a mess. Wine bottles, dirty clothes, and dishes were everywhere. Standing at the sink, his knees buckled, and he almost collapsed on the floor, grabbing the countertop at the last second.

Travis walked over to him, sniffed him several times, and barked.

"What is it? I'm okay. I just feel like shit, boy. Do you know what that feels like? Probably not. Let's go sit in the living room, this mess will have to wait."

An hour later, Kira and Flórez were at the door. Brushing past him with two bags of Chinese food, the two of them began setting up plates on the dining table.

"Okay, Marcus," Flórez said, we have to talk. I mean *you* have to talk. Start by telling us all about the woman in Chicago, everything this time."

"Okay," he said, pawing through the fried rice looking for chunks of beef.

"It starts with my gun firing. I see the round hit her in the chest, just a red hole where there wasn't one before, and a spray of pink mist blowing out behind her, like paint from a spray can."

Two hours later, he sat back as if he had just finished running a marathon.

"Well," he said, "I killed a woman and it haunts me. Am I fucked up, Kira?"

"No, you're not, Marcus, but you need to get through this or it will destroy you. The drinking can ruin your job if you can't get it under control. My first advice would be to take a few weeks off and get out of town."

"Not happening, Kira," Trufant said.

"I didn't think so, but I'm telling you it would be the smart thing to do."

"Marcus," Flórez said. "I was in a firefight years ago, some small town in Iraq. I know I killed a few Iraqi soldiers, not up close like your woman in Chicago and we were at war, but the memory still pops up, usually when I least expect it. With the right people, I found it does help to talk about it."

Trufant thought about taking a week off, but the idea of being out of the loop while so much was happening was too much. This was his case, with or without the FBI's involvement.

"This will be over soon. I think the remaining family members have lost control and are making mistakes. Once it's done, I will take a few weeks off and relax."

"Let's hope you're right, Marcus.," Kira said.

He stabbed the last kernel of rice and analyzed it on the fork, turning it over and over and put it in his mouth, as if somehow doing so brought him closure.

The dishes clean, the dirty clothes in the hamper, and the trash emptied, the apartment looked a little fresher than it had in weeks.

"Thank you both for coming over, it has helped, but I'm going to turn in early. I don't need to tell you it's been a bad day."

***

Like last night and the nights before, sleep eluded him. He knew every pattern and every swirl in the plaster on the ceiling. He pictured his puzzle wall, and found it blank, then the pin map at the office, a nest of tiny red pins here and there across the country. He saw the two red dots across the border in Canada and thought something felt odd about them sitting there all alone. He let the thought go and tossed and turned until the sheets almost strangled him.

A day earlier, a glass of wine would have helped him sleep, but the thought of it made him sick to his stomach now. At two a.m. he broke his promise and swallowed two Xanax and minutes later he was out and in a deep sleep.

***

The smell of fresh-brewed coffee and six hours of sleep left him feeling refreshed. The hangover wasn't as bad as he had feared, having worked through most of it yesterday,

Travis sat in the kitchen with his leash in his mouth

Trotting alongside him, they made it into the park as the sun began burning through the fog. Shafts of sunlight transformed the park from what it had been the night before to a harmless patch of greenery in a city of gray concrete. Steam from his coffee mixed with a stray wisp of mist, highlighted in golden sunshine.

Pacing behind Travis, he thought again about New York. It had to be a killer driven by something different from Ramzi or his twin, maybe a copycat trying to cash in on the notoriety of the murders in San Francisco, or someone trying to throw the police off their track. He called Merriweather and left a voice mail asking to see an image of the actual quote.

A few minutes later he had his answer. The artistic note was written in cursive, with a smear of blood on the edges, blood probably left on purpose as a taunt. It was exactly like the letter sent after the murders on Mason Street, and the envelope was addressed using the same font, 14 point Calibri, odd but not rare. The killer wanted everyone to know the cases were related, for some unknown reason. Psychos always enjoyed the game as much as they enjoyed the killing.

"Time to go, Travis."

***

They rode in silence, Trufant fixating on the homicides in New York and moving puzzle pieces around in his head. Travis looking through the windshield, checking each car in the traffic around them.

Trufant pressed his thumb into his temple, trying to massage the new headache building in his skull. It wasn't as bad this morning, but it was still lingering just below the surface.

He took Travis up the stairs behind the station, wanting to avoid any questions about bringing a dog. K-9 dogs inside the station were a common sight, but Travis was not a common dog.

He spread a towel out on the carpet next to his desk. "This is your side, Travis."

His clerk-typist walked in and saw Travis curled up on the towel and stared at him. Travis lifted his head and stared back at the young man.

"Is he friendly?"

"It depends on who you are. He may have developed a taste for human flesh, and I'm going to take him up to the chief's office later and see. You want to come?"

"I'll pass," he said, laughing. "Inspector Connell is in interview room one with a man he says you will want to speak to."

His headache ratcheted up a notch. He opened his desk drawer, searching for the bottle of Advil, and remembered throwing the empty bottle away last week. He felt his pockets by habit and found them empty.

***

Inspector Connell was a short, Irish cop from Boston that had been in California for ten years but had never lost the accent.

"Morning Lieutenant, this man has an interesting story you will want to hear. Go ahead and tell the lieutenant what you just told me."

The man in the chair was well-dressed, not in business attire, but his button-down shirt and khaki pants looked new. He had a two-day-old beard, but his hair was neatly combed over a bald spot on the back of his head.

He seemed tense and uncomfortable sitting in the metal chair, but he was trying to appear relaxed, his left leg crossed over the right and his shoe twitching uncontrollably. Trufant eyed him, letting the man's own nervous system work against him. The man saw his twitching shoe and reached out and held it with one hand, while wiping the sweat off his brow with the other.

"Who are you?" Trufant finally asked him.

"Nathan Crisp. I'm a P.I.—I would have come in earlier, but I was in Las Vegas when I heard the news." The words flew out of his mouth as if he had been rehearsing them for hours.

"What news?"

"When the officer was killed—Amato. It was on the news in the casino, and I recognized the guy."

"You recognized the inspector?"

"No, the guy who killed him. I did some work for him off and on, electronic stuff, computer background information, and things like that."

"Tell him," Connell said. "Stop with the BS."

"I put trackers on people's cars. I sell a lot of them, and I do surveillance work sometimes. I put one on Inspector Amato's car. The guy said he had a beef with you and your partner, some type of lawsuit. When I saw the news and his picture, I knew it was Hector."

"Stop right there. Has he been Mirandized?"

"Yes, and he wants to talk."

"Okay then, Mr. Crisp, you said you installed a transponder on a police vehicle?"

"I did—and I put one on yours too. I know it's illegal, but I thought it was just some type of lawsuit against you, it's what he said. He was just some creepy college kid with a grudge, I never thought he could kill somebody, he was like a wimpy geek every time I saw him."

"There's one on my car right now? How long ago was this?"

"Three weeks now, you guys were at the Crepe Café one morning, I'm sorry, Lieutenant."

"Does Hector have a last name?"

"If he told me, I forgot it. It was something Spanish, but he paid cash, and I never asked again."

"What else have you done for this guy Hector?" Trufant said.

The man uncrossed his legs and now his knees were bouncing up and down.

"Background checks mostly. He would give me a name, and I would find everything I could about the person. I hired a few of the rats around the downtown area to follow some of them. I gave them cheap phones, you know, burner phones, and they would send me pictures and tell me where the mark would hang out and I would forward it all to Hector."

"Rats?"

"You know—vagrants. They'll do anything for twenty bucks."

"So all you know about him is his first name, what about a phone number or address?"

"No address. He mentioned once he lived near Berkeley, by the campus. I was starting to get suspicious. It seemed more than just a beef with you guys. We met face-to-face a few times, but usually he would call me from different numbers and sometimes the numbers were blocked. But he paid me a lot of money, you know."

"How long have you done work for this guy?"

"Two or three years."

"And that's all you know about him? His name is Hector, nothing more?"

"Like I said, we only met face-to face-two or three times a year. It was an easy job, an hour's work, and he paid me a thousand dollars cash. I gave him some pictures, some basic information off the internet, and I wouldn't hear from him for six months. Then in the last several months, he was calling several times a week, like things were heating up."

Trufant watched as sweat stains blossomed around the man's armpits and his eyes were darting all over the room.

"Go on Mr. Crisp," Trufant said. "Tell me the rest."

"He said he was getting close to screwing you guys. Again, I thought it was a lawsuit or something. That's the way a lot of my cases work—most of my clients are jealous husbands or wives wanting to know who their spouse is screwing. This guy wasn't any different."

"You understand he's killed most of those people, right?"

Crisp looked down at the floor, deflated and no longer trying to appear confident. He shook all over, like spasms were flowing from his chest to his feet.

"You're going to give Inspector Connell a complete sworn statement detailing everything you know. You're going to give him your phone and any other phone you may have used to contact this guy. If you're any good at your job, I know you have copies of everything. I'm going to get a search warrant for your home and your business, and you may still be charged as an accessory to a homicide, do you understand, Mr. Crisp?"

"Yes, I do."

Trufant held the door open for a stenographer and an ID tech carrying a video camera. He went back to his office where Travis and his clerk-typist were rolling around on the floor.

"No blood, I see."

"Not yet, sir."

"I need you to get Lt. Gracia to meet me in the parking lot. Tell him it involves Carlos."

***

Trufant found the transponder wedged between the gas tank and the left fender. On his hands and knees, with half his body under the car, his head felt like it was being crushed in a vise, a remnant of his hangover. *I'll never drink again,* he promised himself.

Travis sniffed at virgin landscaping and chased a lizard into the brush, ignoring everything else around him. Labradors were hunters, after all.

Gracia and one of his inspectors arrived, and soon both were under the car, examining the two-inch-square SpyTec GPS tracker.

"I've seen these before," Gracia said. "Our narcotic guys use them, it's an inexpensive, real-time GPS tracker. The battery is good for about a month. I just saw it blink, so it's still got some juice."

"Any way to backtrack its signal, see who's watching?"

"No, it's a send-only device. It would be nice to send the bastard a message, though—like fuck you! Hopefully, he's dead or dying as we speak. No luck with any of the hospitals?" Gracia asked.

"No, we're still assuming he flew out of Oakland and no luck yet tracking that jet. Someone sharp helped him get out of town. If I were him, I would go international, less chance of anyone seeing the story on the news, although it was on most of the big networks. My guess would be Canada or Mexico. Probably Canada, people don't go to Mexico if they need a hospital."

"Unless they know someone down there. Marcus, should we leave it there as bait if he comes back?"

"He would know the battery is about to die. I think it's safe to take it off. The guy upstairs says he just did the two cars but we should check the entire fleet. The guy who killed Carlos could have hired a dozen P.I.s if he wanted to. I don't want to underestimate him."

Back in his office he saw Carlos's now-vacant desk and the empty chair Carlos used to rock in while he was on the phone. It had been stripped of all his personal items, pictures of his family and the ceramic owl one of his children made in school.

Behind the desk was the pin map. It was old-school technology, but it helped when he could visualize patterns. Somehow computer images never worked as well.

There were red pins in Chicago, Florida, Georgia and California, but there were two pins stuck into the west side of Toronto. And he'd just mentioned Canada to Lt. Gracia. As he stared at the pins, he saw a familiar name, Mississauga. He had heard that name once before and it took a minute to remember where. The old abandoned house in Chicago had been owned by an investment company based in Mississauga, which led to New York City, where the trail had died.

Two cities with a role in his investigation. Madinah Haddad's passport had been used in Toronto, just miles from Mississauga, and the Shakespeare quotes had come from New York City. A coincidence? He didn't believe in coincidences. It was a long shot, but it was the only shot at the moment.

Pulling up a map of Mississauga, he searched for an airport, one that a small jet could get in and out of without attracting a lot of attention. There were several, too many, if you included all of

Toronto and its outlying suburbs. He called the Peel Regional Police Department and ended up speaking with the chief.

"It's a longshot, Chief, but I'm hoping for a break in this case. Mississauga is in your jurisdiction, and that city keeps coming up in our investigation here in San Francisco. Would you notify all the hospitals with a trauma unit capable of dealing with gunshot wounds to be looking out for our suspect. I don't think he would go to any of the major hospitals in Toronto. I'll bet he's going to try for something remote, hoping not to be linked to all the news coming out of San Francisco."

He ended the call and looked back at the map. "I know you're out there, Ramzi."

***

Six days passed and the wine bottles were piling up again. He fought the urge each night, but the shakes were causing more than just insomnia. The first glass always seemed to clear his head and the next few were an unconscious reflex.

He had just poured his first glass when his phone rang, and he stared at the Canadian number.

CHAPTER 37

RAMZI

Ramzi heard voices in the darkness. Not words—just murmurs, some were nearby, some up close near his face, others farther away, men and women, and no matter what he did or how hard he tried, he could not make sense of what they were saying.

Brief images of traveling through forested country were interrupted by long periods of darkness, how long those periods lasted he couldn't guess.

Similar to the voices were the sensations of pain. Some had been sharp, like a knife wound on a fingertip, others dull like a toothache that lasted for days. Time seemed fluid, and he tried to slow it down and make sense of what was happening to him.

The dog had ripped into his right arm but he felt no pain there. Maybe it had healed? He had been shot too. It had felt like a hot sledgehammer had hit him. The fire burned his flesh and bones, and the pain had lasted for days, but even that pain had eased. He was alive, though, of that much he was sure.

Ramzi Haddad? a woman asked, and words began making sense. The woman was close to him, and someone farther away answered, I think so.

His right arm itched. The sensation of beetles crawling on his flesh frightened him, and he wanted to brush them away, but he knew he couldn't move any part of his body.

Cold dark silence surrounded him again, a prison, and just like every nightmare he had ever had, he couldn't open his eyes. Suddenly the coldness vanished, replaced with soothing warmth, and the voices were back, far off now, drifting farther and farther and he was alone again.

The darkness he could deal with—he had always felt comfortable in the dark, but not being able to move, to open his eyes, or to hold a knife in his hand terrified him, he was trapped, like being bent over a chair, helpless, as men three times his size held him down.

Am I paralyzed?

"Ramzi Haddad?" A man's voice this time—and the man knew his name.

He was awake now, and the pain, fear, and words were sharp as razors.

Something touched his eyelid, and a sliver of the blackness turned red, dark red slowly brightening. Someone was forcing his eyes open, and he became aware of other colors moving in the redness.

"Can you hear me, Mr. Haddad?"

No one ever called him Mr. Haddad. Mr. Haddad had been his father's name, and his father had been dead for years.

The colors slowly became a man. A man dressed in a gray suit, peering down at him, so close he could smell the man's breath.

Instinctively he reached for his knife on the night table, or where the night table should have been, and felt a wave of pain. He sucked in a deep breath and closed his one open eye.

"That's better," the man said.

"You're in Hôpital de Hull Monsieur Haddad," the man said. I am Pierre Jean with the Canadian Security Intelligence Service. In the room with me is FBI Assistant Director Merriweather and I believe you know Lieutenant Trufant."

Ramzi looked around the room, and with both eyes open he could make out the shapes of the three men but nothing more. He felt like he was going to vomit. Was it anesthesia causing his stomach to cramp or the fact Trufant was in the room?

He stared at Trufant, trying to focus his blurred image. Trufant was smiling though, that much he was sure of.

"You and your two companions are in our custody. Do you understand everything I've said, Mr. Haddad?"

I've lost and I've shamed my family.

He closed his eyes, not wanting Trufant to see any sign of shame or fear. He cared less about the other men, but Trufant—Trufant was no doubt basking in his glory, untouched by his blade. Trufant had died in his dreams every night since his sister's death, and now the man stood over him, smirking. If it took him the rest of his life, he would kill this man.

"Mr. Haddad, I—"

Ramzi cut the Canadian off. "My father was Mr. Haddad. He was weak and now he is dead. You murdered him."

"I'm sorry you feel that way, Ramzi. We had nothing to do with what happened to your family. But as I was about to say, we have learned a lot about you and your sisters in the days since you came to us."

Days! How long have I been here?

"We hope to track down your sister, Leilah, soon." A different voice this time.

He looked at the other shapes. They were clearer now and it was Trufant who had said Leilah's name. He, too had an accent, was it Southern?

"I know what you're probably thinking, Ramzi," Trufant said. "You're probably wondering just how soon you can kill me. That might be more of a problem than you realize."

"You were near death when they brought you here," the French officer said. "Sepsis and gangrene almost killed you, and you still may die. I'm afraid the doctors here had to remove most of your right arm, and you may lose your left arm, not that you would be able to use it, of course. The bullet that your last victim fired destroyed the nerves and most of the blood vessels, and I'm afraid that arm is quite useless."

"Inspector Amato died quickly and probably felt very little

pain," Trufant said. "But you, Ramzi—you are going to live as a cripple in a United States prison for the rest of your life. I think you're going to envy Inspector Amato's death."

He lifted his head for the first time and tried to see himself. He was strapped to a hospital gurney, and thick, white canvas straps enveloped his ankles and knees, holding them to the bed. His right arm ended two or three inches from his shoulder, and the stump was concealed with white gauze, stained brown with what he hoped was betadine. A wide leather belt with a stainless steel buckle was strapped around his chest, so tight he couldn't take a full breath, and claustrophobia made him cry out.

"Where is your mother, Ramzi?" Trufant asked.

"Ask my cousin."

"Your cousin? One of the men who brought you here? That's more than we knew a few minutes ago," Trufant said.

"Why would I care, Lt. Trufant," Ramzi said.

"He has not been very cooperative . . . yet. But you have more to lose, I think, especially once we get you back into the States. Canada will prosecute your cousin and his friend. They will probably do time for harboring a fugitive and may eventually be deported. Canadian prisons aren't so bad, I understand, but you will be in San Quentin, probably in the adjustment center where they imprison the worst humanity has to offer. I'm afraid it will be hard to defend yourself in there, Ramzi."

He looked at his left hand and tried to make a fist, but his fingers never even twitched.

"Florida and Illinois are also interested in you once all the federal trials in California are over," Trufant said. "I'm guessing you will probably spend the next ten years just sitting through those tedious trials. Maybe, just maybe, you'll run into Leilah along the way. Like a little family reunion."

The lieutenant was enjoying himself. Ramzi, his vision sharper now, saw the thick scar Madinah had left on his neck. His twin had come so close to killing him. He closed his eyes in frustration, and ignored the three men until they gave up and left.

He would bide his time and survive whatever they did to him. He would, one day, hold a Balisong to Trufant's neck and relish the man's warm blood running through his fingers. It was inevitable.

***

They came for him the next day.

"No more morphine for you, Ramzi," Trufant said. "Too expensive and it's a long plane ride back to Sacramento. I want you to enjoy the ride—to feel it all."

Trufant pulled a canvas anti-spit mask over his face, leaving him nothing but a cream-colored view as the prison's medical van drove out of the hospital. Along the way the last of the pain medication burned through his system, leaving him raw and defenseless—and the pain exploded, like touching a high voltage wire.

Could Trufant see what he was feeling? Did it give him some satisfaction? If so, he was not going to let the man know it.

"Quebec is beautiful this time of year, Ramzi. I'm sorry you're missing it," Trufant said in his strange accent. *It wasn't southern.* He had been to Atlanta once, and it was different in the South. Trufant sounded like a French name, but the accent wasn't French. He let the thought go. The man was just trying to make him angry, to bait him into saying something incriminating, something he may regret later. Instead, he sat quietly, unmoving and listening to the sounds of traffic around him.

A train clattered alongside the highway for a few minutes, rattling as each car ran over the rough sections of steel rail. The blast from an air horn and clanging bells were close by.

The lieutenant must have tired of his bantering and was sitting close enough that Ramzi heard him breathing. Ramzi wished he could hear his thoughts. Soon, the noisy train faded away, and arriving and departing aircraft took its place.

The van stopped next to an idling jet. The engine's whine and the smell of kerosene told him his ride was about to begin.

"How is Adelaide, Lt. Trufant?"

CHAPTER 38

TRUFANT

The question stunned him. For weeks he had been praying for this moment, to feel the relief that seeing Ramzi in handcuffs would be enough to lift the blanket of anger and misery he had lived with for months now.

He was half out of the van and wanted to reach back inside and kill him, to reach under the canvas mask and choke him to death, to feel him struggle as he took his last breath. Instead, he squeezed the stump of the man's right arm and heard the satisfying hiss as Ramzi sucked in a deep breath. This man would never cry out in pain, he couldn't. Ramzi Haddad thought his mental strength made him superior to everyone around him. He was an egomaniac, and like most psychopaths, it was also his weakness.

"She's fine, Ramzi, and unlike you, she has full use of both arms." he said, trying to control his rage.

Someone grabbed his arm and pulled him out of the van, he turned, ready to drive his fist into whomever had spoiled his moment.

"Marcus, come with me," Merriweather said, leading him to the jet. "Don't let him get to you. I have agents in Pine Grove and she's safe."

He looked at the canvas bag on Ramzi's head and wasn't so sure.

***

The Gulfstream V lifted off from Jean Lesage International Airport just after noon, and as the plane reached its cruising altitude, Merriweather pulled off Ramzi's face mask and jammed foam earplugs into his ears. Satisfied he couldn't hear anything, he put the hood back on, depriving him of sight as well. Except for the rise and fall of his chest, he could have been a corpse.

The drone of the engines and weeks of fatigue made him drowsy, and he closed his eyes, but couldn't sleep. The earlier adrenaline rush and its crash were playing havoc with his nervous system.

Dead tired, frustrated, and still angry, he unbuckled the seat belt and began pacing the short aisle between the seats. Each time he passed Ramzi, he imagined different ways to inflict pain, jabbing a finger into one of the wounds, squeezing the stump of his arm again. Merriweather was watching him, concern on his face, and he let the idea pass.

"Would you like something to drink, sir?" one of the attendants asked.

"Water would be great, thank you"

He returned to his seat, facing the director.

"Marcus, I know what you're thinking. Let me tell you a story."

The flight attendant interrupted them, handing Trufant the water. As she left, the director continued. "When I was a new agent, maybe a year and a half out of Quantico, Pete, my supervisor, and I were knocking on doors, taking statements from a few bank robbery witnesses. 'Grunt work,' he called it.

"We were in Miami, a section known as Little Havana, when Pete knocked on the door. We heard somebody inside say, 'Just a minute.' Then the door exploded. Wood splinters and blood peppered my face, and Pete went down, convulsing on the front porch.

"I dragged him off to the side and radioed for help."

"To make a long story short, this witness had psychiatric issues. He heard the knock on the door and fired a 9 mm toward the sound. Pete died a week later, and at the man's trial I sat two rows behind him—and I felt what you're feeling now. Pete was a good man and a great agent, and he was my mentor.

"One of the other agents in my unit attacked the man at a recess, right in the courtroom, punched him in the face, blackening the guy's eye and breaking his nose. He did what I and most of the other agents in my unit wanted to do.

"The judge declared a mistrial and the agent was suspended and then fired. Three months later, he committed suicide. The perp was eventually retried and convicted, but my point is—let this go, don't become another one of this guy's victims."

Trufant had been holding his breath, trying to mitigate his anger with what the director was saying, but then exhaled and nodded. "You're right, of course, and I am trying. I keep seeing him at Adelaide's door, and I know it was just luck that I got there in time."

He closed his eyes, hoping to relax, wanted a glass of wine, but dismissed the urge. Instead, he concentrated on slowing his breath, slower but deeper, something Adelaide had taught him. It worked and for an hour he dozed, then somewhere over Lansing, Michigan, he sat upright with the feeling that Ramzi was awake and thinking about him.

Ramzi hadn't moved. He was still strapped down and looked like he was sleeping. Was he comfortable? Probably not, without any pain medication those wounds must be screaming. Still, the man lay there motionless, some martial arts skill maybe.

In all his years and all the deaths he had investigated, he had never felt anger like this. This was rage, and it had consumed him—every minute of every day for weeks, and even in his dreams, Ramzi and his family tormented him.

He was six feet away, just over an arm's length. He wanted to reach forward and grab the man's trachea between his fingers and crush it.

What would it feel like? I would want to see his face, though!

It would save years of trials and investigations, which would cost tens of millions of dollars—but it would also leave a trail of unanswered questions. He leaned back in his seat and flexed his fingers, noticing nail marks indented in his palms. Merriweather watched him until he closed his eyes.

Why am I so angry? The man is right there, he's crippled, handcuffed, and hog-tied like a pig—everything I've dreamed of for the last year—and it's not enough!

His hands trembled, his teeth chattered, and he needed a glass of wine. He was an alcoholic now, and it was this man that had driven him over the edge.

***

Hours later the jet touched down in San Francisco, and a team of agents took Ramzi to San Francisco General Hospital's detention center. The ambulance drove away and it felt like Ramzi was slipping through his fingers again.

He found his Impala in the long-term lot and sat behind the wheel, his pulse throbbing. His hand shook, and he couldn't get the key in the ignition. He pounded his fist into the padded dashboard until the pain forced him to stop, then sat behind the wheel sobbing.

Once the tears stopped, he held his fingers out and waited for the shakes to stop and called Kira.

"I should be home by seven. Can you bring Travis and meet me at South Park?"

"Only if you tell me all about Ramzi," she said.

***

Kira and Travis were waiting for him at the park's main gate. He had been gone three days and Travis looked happy to see him. The fur around his head and neck had grown in enough to cover most of the wound and all the shaved skin. Even the ragged flap of his missing ear looked better.

"Thanks for watching him."

Travis circled him, sniffing his trousers and probably smelling Ramzi's scent.

"Tell me about him," she said.

"Kira, there is so much to tell, and I'm exhausted," he said as they walked Travis around the paved path. "He's here now in the prison ward at San Francisco General. He's probably going to live, but they amputated the arm Travis tore up. Gangrene almost killed him, and his other arm will be useless. I don't think he will ever be a threat again. But he asked me how Adelaide was doing, can you believe it?"

They did another lap around the park's perimeter in silence until the dog had finished examining all the new scents and smells.

"I'll fill you in on the rest tomorrow, if you don't mind. I need to unpack and be alone for a bit."

"Sure, Marcus."

She bent down and hugged the dog, squeezing him gently. She hugged Trufant too, but with less passion.

"Tomorrow then," she said.

***

He tried sitting in the big recliner and sorting out his rage, regret, and frustration, and all of them were overwhelming. He walked to the window, drinking the last of the wine in the glass, and looked out at the bay and the twinkling lights aboard several big ships.

He was losing control, losing his focus on what needed to be done for the victims, all of them, including Carlos. Justice seemed to be the answer, but *justice* didn't feel right. Revenge felt right. *"Vengeance is mine saith the Lord."*

"I can't just sit here, Travis."

He grabbed his trench coat, and by nine he was sitting at the bar of the Grant & Green Saloon, brooding as Travis slept under an empty barstool. Maybe the dog liked the blues, if not, he wasn't complaining.

"Another shot of Jack Daniels?" the bartender asked.

"Sure, a double this time."

"That one's on me," a familiar voice said behind him. "And I'll have the same."

It was Chief Lozano. *What the fuck?*

"This is not a good time for us to talk, Chief."

"Is your new dog going to rip my throat out?"

He looked at the sleeping dog.

"Apparently not."

"Trufant, you've hated me for more than twenty years, don't bother denying it. But you were right, and I was wrong. I truly thought the kid committed the one burglary, and I thought he could have done the others. It seemed harmless at the time, and for all those years I've regretted it. I never had the courage to admit it, especially to you. I was never the officer you are, and I never felt comfortable on the street like you do. I wasn't a coward, I just never cared for it."

"Why the confession now, Chief?"

"Guilt, maybe. It feels good to get rid of it. During the funeral, I looked at my officers, and I was envious. I wanted the respect they have. All those years I climbed the ranks, getting farther and farther from the filth on the street, and I felt like a desk was my place. I thought it was where I belonged. But I always envied you being so comfortable around real crime."

The Chief looked older, he thought, maybe just bad lighting, but the gray in his hair was definitely whiter than it had been just months ago.

"I'm retiring next year. I'm not running for mayor despite the rumors going around. Truth is, I'm burned-out. I just want to wake up in the morning and *not* be the chief or the mayor or anything else. Do you know what I mean?"

"Maybe I do, Chief."

"When you wrap up all this Haddad stuff, come up and see me."

Trufant thought he was finished, then Lozano added, "Christ, the Haddad kid was living one floor below me. I think I was in the elevator with him a dozen times. A killer and I never knew it."

"No one did. Is he the reason you're retiring? Because you think you should have known?"

"No." He downed the double shot of whiskey and put two twenties on the bar. "Don't forget, come upstairs and see me one day next week."

On stage, a man a few years older than he and with a lot grayer hair sat on an old wooden stool. The man deftly lifted a Gibson Hummingbird off its stand and picked out the first few notes of Buddy Guy's "Five Long Years."

Come up and see me, the chief had said. He remembered his last visit to the man's office and ordered another double of Jack.

***

Something wet was pressing on his neck. A sharp throbbing ache pounded in his head and his stomach cramped as he heaved the last of the Jack Daniels onto his bathroom floor. Travis whined behind him, then pushed him again with his cold nose, causing another cramp in his belly.

Turning the light on was a mistake. In the bright glare, he saw he had slept in his own puke again and was still dressed in the clothes he had worn at the bar. He was stretched out on a rug in front of the toilet, and the smell was horrible. He stood and felt the room spin and reached out for the towel bar, missed, and fell into the shower.

Travis barked, and the sound hurt somewhere deep in his head.

Travis began whining, a fearful sound this time.

"I'm okay, Travis."

Turning on the shower he watched traces of blood mix with the water. He felt his temple and saw blood on his fingers.

"Just give me a few minutes, Travis."

Another drunken stupor. It was eight in the morning, and he

tried to remember how he had gotten home. He remembered talking to the chief, and he remembered walking out of the bar and nothing else.

Travis sat in the doorway of the bathroom still whining, his head tilted as if he was either concerned or distressed.

"I'll be okay."

Once he felt the cramping had run its course, he showered and dried off, stepping around the mess on the tile. The smell and the sight almost caused another heave, but he managed to get into the bedroom and dress.

The thought of making coffee came and went, he would never be able to keep it down. He brushed the horrible taste out of his mouth and took Travis to the park.

Sitting on his favorite bench, he let Travis explore while he closed his eyes, his pulse hammering. Any moment he was going to puke again.

I'm spiraling out of control. He had dealt with addicts and alcoholics his entire life, and now he was the one suffering. I'll never drink again.

He drifted off for what seemed like seconds and when he opened his eyes, a young woman was sitting next to him.

"You don't look so good," the woman said. She was blonde but shorter than the woman jogger he had seen the day before, and younger than the one with the poodles. This woman had an iPad on her lap and a pair of earbuds hanging from her neck.

"I've had a rough day," he said.

She looked at him, and he knew she was judging him the way he enjoyed judging others.

What does she see in me?

Deciding he didn't care, he closed his eyes again, not wanting to talk to her. When he opened them again, the woman was gone and two hours had passed. The alcohol was still messing with his judgment, he guessed.

Heading back down the path toward his building, he felt he *did* want to talk to someone, maybe keeping all this anger to himself was the problem. Merriweather must have seen some of it, and if he did, others probably did as well.

I'll sit down with Kira again and unload some more and see how it feels.

***

Cleaning the mess off the floor in the bathroom was the hardest part. He forced the stench and the image from his mind and focused on the real problem. He was wallowing in grief and anger and relying on alcohol to fight the symptoms.

His reflection in the mirror disgusted him. There was no denying it anymore, he needed serious help. No more promises to himself, he had seen enough of his friends and coworkers losing this battle to let it happen to him. In the next few days, his six open homicides of the veterans would be closed, Ramzi was no longer a threat, and if any of the other Haddads surfaced, he would deal with them then. It was time to focus on his issues.

The first thing he did was dump the last two Xanax in the toilet. He searched through the rest of the bottles and dumped them in too, adding their chemicals to all the other shit in the city's sewage system.

The wine was next. Only three bottles remained in the cabinet, and he poured each into the sink, watching the different shades swirling around as they made their way down the drain. The smell of wine nauseated him, which was a good thing he decided. He made another halfhearted promise to never drink again.

By two in the afternoon, he was feeling almost human and even hungry. The morning's dry heaves had left his abs aching, but he needed to eat something solid.

"Let's go out, Travis, I need some fresh air."

He grabbed his .45, checked the magazine, and walked Travis outside. The air did help some, but the glare off the windows across the street burned his eyes, eyes that felt like they'd been sandblasted. Fucking cheap whiskey! He knew the whiskey wasn't cheap and it wasn't the problem but blaming something was better than blaming himself.

He ate half a Cubano sandwich under the shade of an umbrella outside The American Grilled Cheese Café and dripped mayonnaise on his last clean shirt. Some days he couldn't get a break, and this was one of them. Travis ate the other half of the sandwich as he tried cleaning the mess off the shirt, making it worse. Tomorrow was Monday, and if he wanted a clean shirt, he would either have to buy a new one or do laundry tonight.

Even half a sandwich was pushing his stomach's limits, but he did feel better. At least the shit taste in his mouth was gone.

"I'll take another vacation day," he said to Travis. Why not? He and Adelaide had spent the holidays in Aspen each year learning to ski, and they loved the shops along Durant's. Then the homicides began, and there never seemed to be enough time. That's when their marriage went south.

***

Armstrong was alone in his room. The two uniformed troopers standing across the hall looked alert and Trufant hoped they were.

"How are you feeling today, Mr. Armstrong?" Trufant asked.

"I've had better days. Still a lot of pain anytime I move my arm, but I can move my fingers now. Are you okay, Lieutenant?"

"I had a rough morning," he said, looking at the drying mayonnaise stain on his shirt.

Armstrong didn't look convinced.

"I may have had a few too many drinks last night. How's your wife?" he asked, deflecting the conversation.

"She's good. She's out getting a few things. They're moving us next week—they wouldn't tell us where, just that it's temporary. I think the hospital is worried about their staff being in danger."

"I can't blame them."

"I see you and Travis are getting along," Armstrong said.

Travis was resting between them, looking back and forth as if he was following the conversation.

"We are. I enjoy his companionship. He's gotten me through a few rough spots recently."

Armstrong looked at the dog as if remembering a few of his own rough spots and nodded.

"He has a knack for it. I'm not sure where I would be if it weren't for him."

"Mr. Armstrong, what did you feel when you knew you were in trouble, when you knew you were an addict? Was it anything specific?"

"Why do you ask?"

"I woke up in a pile of my own vomit this morning. My father was an alcoholic. I watched him destroy his life a little each day. There was no rehab or treatment facilities back in the sixties. Addiction wasn't well-understood then."

"I knew it a week or so after I arrived at Ramstein," Armstrong said. "My first fully conscious day I knew. It was the morphine. The drug was more important than breathing. Part of you knows what's happening, but it's like you're just along for the ride, some other part of your brain is calling the shots, and I just knew."

Trufant moved a chair and sat next to the bed. "I used to sit and talk to my wife, Adelaide, after a bad day at work and talking to her got me through it. Then I needed a glass of wine every night, just something to take the edge off or so I told myself. Then the glass became an entire bottle. I think the wine subbed in for those conversations, then the painkillers helped me through the hangovers, and soon I was taking her anti-anxiety meds."

"I'm worried about you Lieutenant. I've seen you change in just these last few days. There was a look in your eyes, like steel. That's gone and now you have that hollow look and trust me, I know what it is."

"I thought I was stronger," Trufant said. "All these years I thought I was invincible, but here I am."

"Travis will help you get through it, Lieutenant, and I'm glad it's you taking care of him. Everyone needs companionship, someone to unload all the shit filling your head. If you can't vent some of it, your mind will explode."

"It feels like it's exploding right now," Trufant said.

"I know the feeling. You need to talk to someone though. Travis is a good listener and companion. But you need someone, someone you trust, that's one thing I remember Dr. Williams say. You can come by and talk to me anytime Lieutenant."

"I just might do that."

"Cait will be back soon. I couldn't talk to her before. I never really knew what to say, she would have listened, I know, but I couldn't find the words. My balls were blown off in the blast . . . and . . . well, even now I can't talk about it. How do you tell your wife how that feels? So back then, the drugs—and the absence of pain—were glorious. But I know I'm going to make it, this time will be different."

"I wish I had your confidence, Mr. Armstrong."

"Think of it as a fork in the road, one path is clean, it's smooth, and there are beautiful trees and nice things all along the way. But you can always see the other path, the dark path, lots of ruts and trash on it, but it looks beautiful too, it calls to you, and it's never far away."

Armstrong's eyes were focused somewhere else, and Trufant tried to picture that other fork, the nice one, but all he saw was turmoil, no sign of a golden path, nothing to help him define where he was going. Maybe it was just the death and misery Ramzi had left in his wake.

"I can still smell the vomit, so right now the choice seems easy, but tonight when I'm alone and trying to sleep in the dark, I fear I'll need something to help wipe the memories away."

"You won't be alone—you have Travis, just keep him close, he needs you just as much as you need him. Talk to him if you have to, he's a great listener."

"I hope it will be that easy."

Chapter 39

Mother

Two weeks and no word from Danilo or Bassam.

Danilo had called and said they were arriving, then silence. She had prepared herself for the worst. Ramzi had been detained or imprisoned, but at least he was being treated and he was alive. Or was he?

She tried Danilo's phone again and it went straight to voice mail.

"Damn it!"

Chanda knocked on the door. "Are you okay?"

"Leave me alone."

Then her phone buzzed.

"Danilo! What is happening?"

There was a hiss of static and a muted police radio and she quickly ended the call.

The phone was a cheap burner phone, one of a dozen Chanda had bought at Walmart weeks ago. She threw it against the wall and it shattered. Satisfied, she called Chanda back and had her niece light her cigarette.

"I feel the worst has happened, Chanda. I think the Canadian authorities have them all."

She took a deep drag, watching the glow illuminate the darkened room. Her eyes were sensitive to even the dimmest light now.

"I fear they will soon be at our door, Chanda."

She coughed, and the oxygen tube fell from her nose and under the cigarette. The embers brightened for a second as the oxygen fed the burning tobacco, and she wished the tank would explode.

Chanda was staring at her, open-mouthed, eyes wide, and the girl took a step backward.

Do I look that frightening to her?

She started to call Chanda's name, it was right there on the tip of her tongue, but the word stuck in her throat.

"What is it, girl? Why are you looking at me like that?"

Her voice slurred the words. The right side of her face was numb, and the cigarette fell to her breast, burning a small hole in her black polyester sweater.

Chanda picked it up and crushed the remains in the ashtray.

"Diwata, I think you're having a stroke!"

Chanda lifted the thin body from the bed and into the wheelchair, wheeled her outside and loaded her onto the hydraulic ramp of the old Ford Excursion.

Stroke? My son is dying. Why is this girl pushing me out of my own house?

Closing her eyes, she tried to make sense of what her niece had said, *you're having a stroke.*

"Ramzi!" she choked out. The girl was driving the old Ford too fast, hitting potholes and ruts on the country road that led to the highway. She slid on her chair, helpless. Her right hand was on her lap, the gnarled and bony fingers curled into a frozen fist. With her left arm, as weak as it was, she held on to the strap above her until they were on smooth asphalt.

Everything outside the window looked too familiar, as if she'd dreamed it last night. They were on the Queens Highway, the QEW, passing over a river she knew and she couldn't name the damn thing. She had been on this road a hundred times in the last ten years, and still, she felt lost.

The confusion was suffocating. Nothing she did helped clear her thoughts, those were trapped in fog.

I am losing my mind! She cried out, but even simple words

wouldn't come to her, only a sharp wailing sound croaked from her throat.

Somehow, the panic and paranoia began to ease, and she drifted off, never aware of being in the emergency room of the Mississauga Hospital or the short Life Flight to Mount Sinai Hospital in Toronto.

She had moments of intense clarity, but they were rare those first few days.

***

"Diwata, Ramzi is doing well and is in Quebec" Chanda told her. "The police are asking my brother questions, but he is refusing to speak to them. He will have an attorney soon, and everything will be okay."

"You lie to me, Chanda," is what she wanted to say but it sounded like something entirely different. The girl understood, though, her look of shame was clear enough.

"How long."

"I brought you here six days ago, don't you remember? We talk every day."

"Ramzi?"

"It's been three weeks, Diwata. He is in a hospital somewhere in California is all I know. Dr. Latif and Danilo have been arrested and are in Quebec. There hasn't been much in the news, but I spoke to my brother two days ago."

She tried to follow the girl's words but the more Chanda spoke, the less she understood. With her left hand she examined her face—her skin was so cold, and she felt the rough, dry fingers on her left cheek, but the right side was numb.

The girl stayed for a few more minutes, then left. Diwata was aware of several different doctors coming and going over what might have been days or even months, and even being pushed down a hallway as the overhead lights passed across her vision, one at a time.

She dreamed her husband was in the room, holding her hand, and Araya had finally come to see her, as beautiful as ever. They had a wonderful long conversation, as if the horrors of that day had never happened. Even her memories of that day escaped her, and the harder she tried to recall the screams of her dying daughter, the less significant they became.

Her firstborn was so beautiful. Despite a smile that still seemed forced, Araya had finally forgiven her, even after all she had done.

CHAPTER 40

TRUFANT

Another week had come and gone without any news of the deaths in New York. There was also no sign of Diwata Haddad. All Ramzi's homicides in San Francisco had been technically cleared now, but he knew the Haddads weren't finished, as long as one of them lived—they would come for him. It might be days or months, but they would come.

Diwata might still be the key, the family matriarch. Canadian law enforcement, with all their bluster, were just as hamstrung as those across the border—both Ramzi's cousin and the other man had requested attorneys and questioning them now was impossible.

One of the men, Bassam Latif, was a former student of Diwata's in Iraq. His fingerprints and immigration paperwork traced him back to Al-Masafer, but not much more.

Bassam had lived a quiet life in New Jersey since immigrating in 2013. He'd worked as a clerk for a realtor in Elizabeth, and now he was caught up in the investigation of several dozen homicides. He was probably the weaker of the two men, but there was no way to speak to him, two thousand miles and a room full of attorneys saw to that.

The other man, Danilo, was Ramzi's cousin, but trying to pry the information out of him had been fruitless and now impossible, he too, had lawyered up. How many others were there?

Ramzi, they said, loved to talk while sedated, threats mostly, and his attorney made sure he was not to be questioned by the FBI or anyone else—he was off limits, Merriweather had said pointedly. Ramzi was expected to live, although doctors were not optimistic about saving his other arm.

Trufant enjoyed picturing this adept killer spending the rest of his life in prison, never again able to hold a knife or even a plastic prison spork. It would drive the man insane.

"Travis, you awake?"

The big one-eared Lab perked up next to him. "Let's go see David."

The dog looked at him with no reaction.

"Armstrong!"

Still nothing, maybe he had never known Armstrong's name.

"Let's go for a ride." This got his attention, and the dog picked up his leash and stood at the door. "Do you miss Kira?"

Kira had watched Travis off and on over the last few weeks when he couldn't take him with him. Travis chuffed, which may have meant yes or let's go, he wasn't sure.

"We're going to see your old friend at the hospital, Travis, David Armstrong, you'll remember him."

He felt better this morning than he had in days. The craving for a glass of wine while sitting in the recliner at the end of the day was powerful, but the memory of lying in the shower was equally as powerful. He had stopped drinking coffee temporarily, hoping the lack of caffeine would ease the jitters he felt every morning and so far it was working.

***

He parked the Impala next to the curb at the ER and clipped his badge next to the Sig Sauer on his belt. As the automatic doors opened, he kept Travis on his right side so anyone looking at the dog would also see his badge and gun. Most people looked, some stared, and still others were oblivious to the dog and the gun as they made their way to the elevator. Somewhere above him on the seventh floor, Ramzi sat in an isolation cell.

Two women in pale green scrubs joined him and never looked down at Travis. As the doors on the sixth floor opened, Travis pulled on the lead, and Trufant followed. Travis knew where he was.

***

Armstrong sat alone in a chair next to the bed watching a football game. Travis went straight to him and put both front paws on the man's leg, his tail thumping the drywall. Armstrong pulled his head close, put his nose in the dog's fur and inhaled. "God, I love this dog!"

"Where's your wife?" Trufant asked.

"She stepped out for a minute. Today is our last day here. They're still not saying where we're headed. I guess it doesn't really matter, somewhere quiet, I hope."

"The FBI takes everything seriously. I'm sure you'll enjoy the change of scenery."

Armstrong looked different today, that animal in a cage look was gone, his skin was pinker, healthier, and his eyes were clearer.

"How are you, Mr. Armstrong? You look better."

"Two weeks clean now and I'm doing good, sir. I made it through the hardest part, the physical part anyway. They had to restrain me a few times, I heard. I was out of it. I'm not sure which was worse, the pain from withdrawal or the wounds and physical therapy. The mental part will be a struggle for the rest of my life, but I'm good. How are you doing?"

"Better, I think."

"Great, but don't get complacent. How are you and Travis getting along?"

"He's a good dog. I'm going to miss him."

"Travis isn't coming with me, Lieutenant. I've agonized over this for two weeks. He got me through terrible times, and he was there for me when I pushed everyone else away. He needed me as much as I needed him, but I think he needs you now and he's too recognizable to come with us. I can still see the two of you on television at the church, he likes you Lieutenant.

"I do like his company," Trufant said. "You've heard all the latest news?"

"I heard the officers outside talking about it. One of them went upstairs and saw them bring the guy in, and I think they're a little more on edge now, knowing he's so close."

"It's probably a good thing you're leaving today. I worry about one of his other sisters, the one they think killed those girls in New York. No one has heard from her since."

"Lieutenant, do you really think she may come here, for me?"

"No, but I'll breathe easier once you're out of here."

"Yeah, me too, I've had enough of San Francisco, I think. I've had nightmares these last few weeks, mostly about that day in the parking lot. But I've stopped dreaming about Travis and Afghanistan, at least the nightmare about his death. I've even had a few dreams about the good times we had. They sent a shrink by a few times to talk with me, but how do you tell someone about something you know they've never experienced?"

He laughed and said, "One of the first things the shrink offered was an antidepressant, but I told him I'm not taking any more pills. I've even stopped taking the Motrin and whatever they were giving me for nausea. I used to fear being dopesick more than death itself, but not anymore. Anything I feel now will remind me I'm alive."

His wife walked in carrying a take-out box from the Blue Bottle Coffee café.

"Lt. Trufant! I didn't know you were coming or I would have brought you something too."

Caitlin had changed too, the cold, all-business attitude he had seen in his office that day was gone. Her hair was loose, and she looked softer, more feminine, and for the first time, Trufant saw her smile. But there was also a fire in her eyes, like she was on a mission and everyone needed to stay out of her way. "Don't trifle with a woman when she has that look," his mother would always say.

"I'm fine, Caitlin, I grabbed a cup from the cafeteria downstairs."

"We're checking out sometime soon, whenever the doctor signs off on his chart. The day after tomorrow we start physical therapy somewhere."

Dr. Pissarro came in with the discharge instructions, shook Armstrong's good hand and hugged Caitlin and wished them well. "Come see me when you're in the city again," she said.

Armstrong gave Travis one final embrace. "Take care of this man, Travis. You understand? Take good care of him."

Trufant could see the sadness in Travis and the sorrow on Armstrong's face, but as they left the room, Travis looked up at him as if he knew he had a new mission, another human to look after now.

"Just you and me now, boy. You're going to have to listen to all my bullshit."

CHAPTER 41

RAMZI

He was awake, eyes closed but listening, learning, while they thought he slept. Knowledge is power.

Behind him were the familiar sounds of the monitors, some beeping softly, others clicking as circuits opened and closed, the rush of compressed air that filled the pressurized cuffs around his legs, and even the bed as it tilted back and forth in a feeble attempt to keep him from getting bedsores.

Somewhere to his left, probably sitting exactly where they were last night, were two armed state troopers. If he opened his eyes he'd see two more FBI agents through the glass window, a window embedded with a thick wire screen—not that escaping was on his mind. He was in no shape to even sit up, they could have left the door wide-open.

A newspaper rustled and the legs of one of the cheap chairs screeched across the tile floor. He opened his eyes and a new face stared at him, a tall, middle-aged woman in a brown uniform with sergeant's stripes. The woman dropped her crossword puzzle to the floor and stood over him, smiling.

Her uniform was pressed, sharp creases in her trousers, and her badge and the buckle on her gun belt reflected the bright ceiling light into his eyes. She checked the straps holding him on the bed, pulled each one, then tightened the one across his chest until it restricted his breathing.

"Lovely tattoos. They probably made you look fierce at one time, but I have to tell you, they look pretty pathetic right now."

He had analyzed people all his life, searching for their weaknesses, their flaws and how he would trap them. They were his prey. This was a hard woman—mentally and physically. Muscles curved a path over her forearms, and her uniform stretched tight across broad shoulders. Even if he were whole, she would have been a challenge.

But he was not whole. He had one useless arm and the stump of another. The roles had been reversed. Even if he could free himself from the confines of this horrible bed, she could kill him easily.

He had never trained to attack with his legs. The strength in his arms and legs had one purpose, to allow him to wield the Balisongs. His remaining hand and three fingers were gray, like old ground beef left in a refrigerator too long. Something stank, and he couldn't tell if he had shit himself or if it was his own rotting flesh.

The door opened and a doctor wearing gray surgical overalls entered. She examined his arm and scribbled on a chart. The sergeant stood next to her, and Ramzi saw the smile was now a sneer.

"Mr. Haddad," the doctor said, "I'm going to do another MRI, and if I don't see any improvement I'm going to remove your arm. There isn't enough blood flow, and it looks like the beginning of gangrene. I may be able to leave you with your upper arm, but from the elbow down, your arm is dead meat."

She looked at him as if she was waiting for a reaction— protest or approval.

"And if I say no?"

"You'll be dead in twenty-four hours—three days max, but I'm going to take it anyway. In my opinion, you're under duress and unable to make qualified decisions on your health. I want to make sure you live long enough to endure your upcoming legal nightmares, Mr. Haddad."

"Don't call me that."

The doctor leaned in close and whispered, "Brook Williams was my friend—why would I care what you want?"

She made a few more notes on his chart and walked out.

The sergeant was clearly smiling now.

***

An hour later a man and a woman wearing clear spit visors came in and wheeled him out of the room. Both uniformed officers and three agents in dark-gray suits followed them down the hall and into an open elevator.

Eight people crammed in an elevator and no one spoke. He listened to them breathe and the chimes announce each floor, sensing the car descending and the doors opening behind him.

The man pushing the heavy gurney toward the radiology department was tall and blond with a chiseled face. His brown eyes glanced down at him and quickly looked up.

The woman with him stayed just out of his range of vision. She was shorter than the blond man and insignificant. The sergeant, though, was right next to him, and her gold nameplate said HILL in capital letters. Her gun belt was inches away from his face, but the gun was on the opposite side. She carried an ASP baton in its own sheath, attached to her belt. One of his instructors had demonstrated the collapsible baton years ago. It was a lethal weapon meant to break bones, leaving her firearm as the last resort of deadly force.

The gurney stopped, and he saw the familiar tube-like device next to him. The lights were dimmer in this room but brighter in the smaller control room behind a glass divider.

Three men and the sergeant lifted him out of the hospital bed and onto the MRI table. They used different straps this time made from heavy canvas and Velcro, and once again he had just enough room to breathe.

Motors whined and the table moved him deep inside the tube, the hem of his hospital gown at the rim of the opening, and the surface of the tube inches from his face. Claustrophobia set in. Closing his eyes was his only recourse as he waited for the hammering sounds of the machine to begin.

People were speaking in another room nearby, and he tried to distract himself, matching voices to faces he knew, then doors closing, and finally the hammering that seemed to come from everywhere.

The hammering paused, and he heard Sergeant Hill speaking to someone and then a faint metallic tapping sound from the tube. More silence, then the hammering began again and lasted a full minute. When it stopped, there was a shrill pulsing sound that sounded like an alarm.

This was his third MRI in two weeks, and this sound was unfamiliar. Then there were new voices and doors closing and the machine stopped completely. Soft-soled shoes moved across the room and stopped behind him.

"I'm sorry, brother," a woman said behind him, and he felt a sharp sting on the side of his neck. "You know this is for the best."

It was Leilah's voice.

As he died, the door opened and closed again. His own warm blood collected in a pool under him. He wasn't supposed to die like this. He was supposed to die doing something heroic, some magnificent feat that would make his mother proud.

I'm going to die here, an invalid, alone, and killed by my own sister.

CHAPTER 42

TRUFANT

Travis had his head out the window as dogs love to do. Maybe it was a feeling of freedom or the sensation of flying they liked. Or maybe it was all the smells. He turned north on Potrero Avenue and passed the first of three red fire trucks racing south toward the hospital. He turned the volume up on his police radio and listened to the routine dispatching of officers around the city. Then the long alert tone sounded and as it did his phone rang.

"Trufant," he said, listening.

"Jesus Christ, I just left there!"

He ended the call and made a U-turn, listening to the blaring horns and screeching tires as drivers swerved out of his way.

Uniformed officers, plainclothes inspectors, and FBI agents were running everywhere.

"How did this happen?" he asked a patrol sergeant on Ramzi's floor.

"They were in the middle of an MRI. I was in the control room with the technicians when the fire alarm went off. We could smell the smoke, and I knew it was close, so they shut the machine down and we all went outside to see where it was coming from. I never got more than a few feet away from the door, and I could see the guy still in the tube."

"You saw no one enter the room?"

"No sir, the fire was in a laundry bin inside a maintenance

room, old linens and towels soaked in alcohol. The FBI agents were able to put it out with an extinguisher, but no one entered the room. I was right there."

"Damn it, look at him. Jesus Christ, five law enforcement officers assigned to him and his throat was cut right inside the machine. There's going to be a serious media frenzy here, Sergeant, and they are going to say we killed him."

Trufant looked up and down the hall and saw the two security cameras at each end.

"I need to see those recordings. Sergeant Hill, keep everyone out of this room until Merriweather and his team are here. No one in or out except them. I'm going to find security."

The FBI was technically in charge of this mess, but he was the one who was going to catch hell. They would blame him. He was the one with the sharpest ax to grind.

***

Trufant examined the color video feed as two people in scrubs pushed the gurney out of the elevator. Sergeant Hill and Officer Yin led the way, and three agents followed them down the hall. He recognized all three agents, and he had worked with both the sergeant and the officer on and off for years.

The only two he couldn't ID were the two people wearing the face masks, a tall man with blond hair and a shorter woman. With both cameras running he watched from opposite viewpoints as the gurney was pushed inside the room. How many people were already inside the room?

"There's no video inside?"

"No sir, there are usually two operators, the radiologist and the assistant."

"I need their names and the FBI is going to want their personnel files too. What about those two pushing the gurney, do you know them?"

"Not by name, but the guy looks familiar. He's an LPN that

subs in the prison ward. The other one I'm not so sure of—she could be a new nurse or an intern, it's pretty common to have new people working on 7D."

The seventh-floor detention known as 7D was the least desirable assignment for the hospital's employees, but a few actually preferred it. During his first few years in patrol, he had spent many hours guarding injured or wounded prisoners on the detention floor.

Ten minutes of watching nurses and doctors walking in and out of different rooms left his back aching. "It's tension, Marcus," he could hear Adelaide diagnosing him. "You need to make captain and let these young guys work the streets."

Smoke rolled from under a door near one of the cameras, and he could see but not hear the red fire alarm panel pulsing. Most of the people stopped and looked at the smoke, stunned, and some of them ran to the other side of the hall. Trufant ignored them, watching the door to the room where Ramzi was about to die.

The three agents reacted first. Two of them ran toward the smoke. It was odd watching them run from one camera toward the other. Then both Hill and Yin came out of the room, and Yin ran toward the smoke. Three more people in scrubs came out next, and two of them stood next to the sergeant, but the third, the short woman who had pushed the gurney earlier, walked all the way to the exit and out of the camera's view.

Sergeant Hill and the two employees walked back inside the room, and Hill came out again, shouting to the agents, who ran back inside. One of them, armed with an MP5 machine pistol, stood barring the door and scanning the hall. Some serious shit had happened inside the room and the FBI was ready for more.

In the last video, the short woman with blonde hair walked past the camera, out the doors and into the hospital lobby where another camera caught her walking outside. She stopped, took off her mask and a blonde wig, and looked straight at the camera mounted on the roof. She was a young woman with long, dark brown hair. The view wasn't the best, and it wasn't the perfect angle, but he had no doubt who the woman was.

You don't look so good, she'd told him, as they sat together on the park bench.

The woman lit a cigarette, blew the smoke toward the camera, and walked down Vermont Street and out of sight.

***

Merriweather arrived, and the proverbial shitstorm began. Twenty more FBI suits spread out on both sides of the hall and every doctor, nurse and clerk sat in chairs waiting to give statements.

"Merriweather, I want you to look at this," Trufant said, and restarted the recording.

"She's the last one out of the MRI station. It's Leilah, Ramzi's younger sister."

"Are you sure?"

"Not completely, but that woman sat next to me in the park last week, of that, I'm sure.

"Is this the best view of her?"

"It's the only time she doesn't have a mask on. Security can pull up every camera, and maybe we can catch her coming in, but that will take a day at least."

Chief Lozano walked in. Merriweather gave Trufant an awkward look and walked out, leaving him alone with his boss.

"Tell me what you have, Marcus."

It took ten minutes to describe what had happened. Lozano nodded now and then and wanted to see the body.

"Yes, that's definitely the guy that lived in my complex. I never saw any of those tattoos, though, he always had a long-sleeved sweatshirt on. You think those marks represent his victims?"

"I'm starting to think so, Chief. I believe we're just scratching the surface of what he and his family have done."

"I'm sure he looked a lot different when he killed Amato. He's so pitiful now I want to feel sorry for the bastard," the chief said.

"Yes sir, it will make you look twice at the next person you see in an elevator."

"Damn right. Good work, Marcus, let me know if you get any leads on the sister."

It was almost a pleasant conversation, one of the first he'd had with the man. Lozano had a different walk, he noticed, as the man strode down the corridor. He was standing a little taller and even looked younger. Like a man who had been carrying a heavy load for years and was finally rid of its weight. Maybe Adelaide was right, maybe he should get out too.

Soon.

***

Travis was waiting for him at the door, tail thumping. Trufant looked around his condo, but as usual, Travis had been on his best behavior. Trufant always left the door to the wooden kennel, or habitat, as the saleswoman had called it, open, and the blanket inside was still warm. Travis liked spending the day in the kennel, but at night he was in the bed. His snoring and the musical fog horns in the bay were better than the rainforest sounds CD Adelaide used to sleep to, and he had to admit the last few days he had slept better too.

"Let's go for a walk, Travis. I need some park time."

The dog jumped up and grabbed his leash, his tail pounding a steady beat against the kitchen wall.

Trufant locked the door, and Travis trotted down the hall, dragging the leash behind him all the way down Jack London Alley and into South Park. Travis stayed two feet in front of him, glanced back now and then, and stood tall. He was showing off to the other dogs—he was the one leading a human.

Just inside the gate, Trufant began his scan, profiling each person until he could rule them out, then peering into the shadows beneath the thicker underbrush. Leilah was out there somewhere, he could feel it. He touched his coat pocket and felt the comforting shape of the heavy .45, loaded with eight rounds in the magazine and one in the chamber. He would be ready this time. He hadn't had a drink or even an Advil in seven days.

"Bring it!" he said aloud.

Travis turned and looked at him. "No, not you, Travis, go ahead and do your business. Travis ran off and he sat on one of the cold, wrought iron benches. He stretched his legs and a knee popped, an old injury.

A drunk driver leaving Candlestick Park had T-boned him one night, destroying his patrol car. His knee got the worst of it, and each year the popping sound was a little louder. He'd been lucky through most of his career, others—like Carlos, had not.

It was a beautiful late afternoon, quite a contrast from the rest of the day. Tomorrow, another shitstorm would begin, but for now, he and Travis were going to enjoy the last of the daylight.

A small dog barked, a high-pitched yapping, and the woman with the two poodles walked toward him, then crossed to the other side of the park. Was she afraid of him or his dog?

He was wearing a four-hundred dollar London Fog trench coat and shoes that cost more than some people made in a week. Was it the gray stubble of his three-day beard or had she seen the scar around his neck on one of her earlier walks? Maybe it was Travis. If he'd wanted to, Travis could crush one of those tiny dogs and there was nothing he or she could do about it.

He looked over as Travis sniffed the same lamppost he sniffed every night. He tried to picture him tearing into the man's arm the way the witnesses described it, but he just couldn't imagine him attacking anyone.

His fur completely covered the scar now—it was almost hidden, but his ear was still missing, and that would never grow back. Travis looked over at him and wagged his tail once, and he sniffed another spot.

"Stay close, Travis."

The woman was now at the far end of the park making her way back down the sidewalk toward them. He watched her approach, wondering when she would turn away again and if he could read which of the two of them frightened her most, but she didn't turn and made eye contact first with Travis and then him.

"Hello," she said.

"Travis, come sit."

"What happened to him?" the woman asked as she got closer.

"He was attacked."

"Oh, how terrible! By another dog?"

"No," he said, not wanting to tell her more.

Travis sat close, leaned up against his leg, his tail wagging under the bench. He wouldn't hurt the two dogs. One of them, probably weighing only two pounds and wearing a pink collar, walked right up to Travis and sniffed him. It looked like a large white rat next to Travis. The other dog shivered behind the woman, wanting nothing to do with either of them.

"I think he's harmless, but I've only had him a few weeks. Do you want to sit?"

"No, I can't, I have to get back before it gets dark, maybe next time."

"Sure."

He watched her walk away, a divorcée, a widow, or maybe just a lonely woman who enjoyed walking her dogs. She and the dog with the pink collar looked back and he waved.

"It must have been you, Travis."

As night fell, Venus hovered above the horizon, the Roman goddess of love or the evening star, depending on how poetic one wanted to be. To him, it was just a planet, which seemed close but also very far away. Thinking about just how far away it was made him feel small. It was beautiful in clear skies, but dense fog was forecast for the morning and driving to the station would take an extra twenty minutes—if there were no wrecks along the 101. The constant construction on the highway was bad enough, but a wreck could add an hour to his daily commute.

"Time to head back, Travis."

It was dark, and he snapped the lead back on Travis and

walked along Third Street. Leilah Haddad knew where he lived, and knew his routine with Travis, so he decided to change his route once in a while, to be less predictable.

Third Street wasn't as well-lit and fewer people used it, still, every few minutes he checked behind him feeling like he was being watched.

Travis marked a few new spots along the way, then Trufant opened the rear door of his building and they rode the elevator up.

Travis sniffed around the elevator floors, scratching hard enough to leave marks, chuffed once, and started smelling the other side.

"What is it, Travis, you can't pee in here."

Then the dog's hackles bristled and he growled as he stared at the crack between the two closed doors. Shit, this is what Armstrong described. He felt his own hair rise on his arms and pulled his .45 waiting for the robotic voice to announce his floor.

As the doors slid open, Travis walked out into the hallway and froze, facing his apartment. One paw was raised, and he was crouched like a bird dog, ready to leap and attack something Trufant couldn't see.

"What the hell is it, Travis?"

With his gun out and ready, he looked down the empty hall and saw his door was ajar, and he knew he had closed and locked it using his key. He crept down the carpeted hallway and stood to the side of the door.

The big Sig Sauer was in his hand. Ever since Chicago, he had left the smaller .380 locked in his safe but now, even the .45 seemed too small.

His first field training officer had told him, if you have to think whether or not you should draw your weapon, you should probably leave it in the holster. Wise words from a wiser man.

Travis was right next to him now, silent but ready. With both hands on the gun, Trufant eased the door open with his foot, and it swung open into the darkened living room.

Oh, how I wish I had my Streamlight.

Travis brushed silently past his leg and disappeared into the darkness. If anyone was inside, Travis would find him first. In the hall next to the kitchen, he could just see the Lab staring ahead, his one ear tensed, waiting for him.

"Go on, boy, I'm right behind you."

Reaching around the doorjamb, he flicked on the light switch. From the threshold, everything looked untouched. No one had ransacked the place, still, he edged in so he could see the remaining section of the living room and kitchen and the doorways to the two bedrooms.

Travis, still on full alert, walked over to his recliner. A Balisong was on the end table. Trufant left Travis and opened both bedroom doors, then holstered his gun and without touching it, he examined the knife. It was an exact copy of the Balisong that had sliced through his throat several months ago. Stainless steel, with ornate engravings on each handle. An expensive and rare knife, Inspector Griggs had said, made by a master craftsman.

Trufant peered at the etched metal along the thin blade where tiny traces of dried blood mixed in with the oriental figures.

Underneath the knife was a note, a simple sheet of printer paper folded in half with indentations left by a ballpoint pen.

Do I read it or do I call a unit and have a technician process my whole apartment?

He thought of Merriweather and a team of forensic technicians spending all night going through his apartment and pushed the knife off the note.

Using a pair of latex gloves, he unfolded the note and read.

The beautiful handwriting was in cursive, resembling calligraphy without the flaring brush marks.

> *You have questions, and I have the answers, Lieutenant. You can come alone and get them and end this madness personally, or you can alert your coworkers and you will never know. Either way, it is almost over. Don't delay, Lieutenant, time is precious.*
>
> *–A*

Araya, the missing daughter, the one who had been in school during the attack. Underneath the signature, in bold block letters, was an address in Canada.

He reread the note twice, refolded it, and put it in a sealed freezer bag along with the knife, then put both of them in his safe and called United Airlines. Next, he called Flórez and left a message on his phone. *I'll be in Canada for two days.*

Finally, he called Kira and made arrangements for her to watch Travis.

***

Walking through the international terminal he thought he saw Leilah wearing a red jacket in a crowd at the check-in counter. Ever since Ramzi's death, he had seen her everywhere, paranoia no doubt . . . but this time he wasn't so sure. Was it Araya who had left the note or was it Leilah? And who or what would be waiting for him in Toronto?

He was early. His flight wouldn't begin boarding for forty-five minutes, so he backtracked all the way to the arrivals gate, scanning everyone, looking for a young woman with long brown hair and a red jacket. But the more he looked for her, the more every woman looked like her.

Jesus, I'm out of my mind!

Frustrated and not sure if he could even pick her out of a lineup, he walked back to his gate and sat facing away from the window, watching the crowd of passengers until they began boarding. His section boarded last, and he looked up and down each row of the Boeing 777, part of him wanting to see her and part of him glad that he didn't.

He was in the second to last row near the lavatories, and fresh coffee was brewing in the galley. The plane was at capacity and his fellow passengers were cramming their carry-ons into the overhead bins.

He should call Merriweather, or the chief, or at the very least his fellow lieutenant. Gracia was handling his cases, but everything else including Ramzi's death was under the FBI's umbrella now. Not making the call could end his career . . . but was that such a bad thing?

He looked out his window at the blackness and all the blinking red and white lights. He needed the answers, he needed to see it through, and if it was Araya who wrote the note, she was right—it had to be him.

And he could always call them once he was there. It would be hard to explain, but it was too late to worry about it now.

He put his phone in airplane mode and listened as the engines began to spool up for the long flight into Canada.

Chapter 43

Armstrong

The government jet touched down at Miami International Airport as the sun was setting over the Everglades. Cait's face reflected the red and orange glow coming through the tiny windows, and her hair looked like spun gold.

He had been clean now for six weeks, and the mental and physical anguish of withdrawal was fading, although the mental craving for heroin would always be with him. He thought of Lt. Trufant and Travis. He hoped they were okay and one day he hoped to see them again.

With Leilah Haddad still at large, the FBI had kept them on the witness protection program. Ramzi Haddad had been identified as Amato's killer and the FBI estimated he and the rest of his family may have been involved in several dozen deaths.

Caitlin had picked a rehab facility in Miami Beach, and the thought of lying in the sun with her was appealing. He was not going to miss the cold fog in San Francisco, but he would miss Travis.

He looked at his fingers and moved them, one day soon he would have full use in that hand, the doctor had promised.

He remembered that day when he and Cait talked about having children.

I want three, but at least one has to be a girl, she'd said.

It was that sentence that had caused him to leave, and he'd

spent eight years running from it. How foolish he'd been. The fact remained that he would never father biological children, but he had never thought of adoption, until now.

The adoption service said his history of addiction would be an obstacle, but his service and disability would be mitigating factors. "David," the attorney had said, "it will be challenging, but I believe once you tell your story, the board will find you would be an excellent father."

In any case, he was ready, and he was finally free.

CHAPTER 44

TRUFANT

Dvora Aquino was written with a red Sharpie on the closed door of room 427, the same last name Leilah Haddad used at NYU and another puzzle piece clicked into place. He opened the door and stepped into the dark room, only the soft red glow of the monitors allowed him to see the woman's face.

She looked like every other dead woman he had seen over the years. Her cheekbones and forehead were covered by paper-thin skin, deep grooves lining her face and her closed eyes sunk into her skull like a Halloween mask. Long gray hair, dulled and brittle with age, spilled across the white pillowcase beneath her and more than a few loose strands lay on the sheets.

It was hard to compare the woman in the photograph to the face in front of him. Something other than age was eating this woman alive, but it was Diwata Haddad, he was sure of it.

He moved closer, listening to the ventilator inflate her lungs and the beeping of the heart monitor tracking her steady pulse. The breathing machine was plugged into a red electrical socket above the bed along with several other machines, all he had to do was reach across and unplug it. The urge to end this woman's life both terrified and thrilled him.

Then her left eye opened.

The woman stared at the ceiling with that one single eye until it moved and focused on him. There was no sign she recognized him, no movement at all except the steady rise and fall of her chest.

"You're almost too late," a woman's voice said from behind him.

He spun around and reached for his Sig Sauer, which was locked in his car a thousand miles away.

Sitting in the dark corner was the shape of a tall woman, too tall to be Leilah.

"You've come a long way to kill my mother, Lt. Trufant. I wanted you here, you see, I couldn't do it myself. I couldn't take someone's life, not even hers. But I don't want to leave here knowing she's still alive. Somehow, I know she would want to keep killing people, somehow, she would try. I just know it. Would you be able to walk out knowing that, Lieutenant?"

"I'm not sure."

"She could die tonight, if not, maybe tomorrow," the woman said.

She moved and a lamp next to her came on. She was a beautiful woman, and in her, he saw the old photo of Diwata Haddad, she was the final piece of his puzzle—Araya.

"Sit down, Lieutenant, we have much to talk about."

"You sent Leilah to my apartment to bring me here. I would have thought she would have wanted me dead."

"Leilah is a disturbed woman. In all these years since we left Al-Masafer, I've tried to help her, but she is beyond help. I've often wondered if insanity is genetic. Does my family carry a gene that causes people like her to exist, and will I one day be like my brother or my sisters? Or is it what happened to them, was it enough to make them want to kill so many innocent people?"

"I can't imagine what they experienced."

"Leilah is worse than Ramzi and Madinah in a way. They started out wanting revenge, my mother pushed them in that direction, and they went willingly. But Leilah is different—she kills without motive. She couldn't care less about revenge, in fact, I don't think I've ever heard her talk about the attack. She kills on impulse. Say the wrong thing, do something she doesn't like and you're a dead man."

Diwata turned her head toward Araya. The left side of her mouth twitched as if she was trying to speak, but the ventilator wouldn't allow it.

"I knew after we moved to Manila that Ramzi had killed a man. Ramzi was only twelve or thirteen, and my mother hugged him, and she said she was proud of him. 'Thank you, Ramzi,' she said."

"He had killed an innocent man, and she thanked him. Then there was the fire, and I thought they were all dead. Part of me was relieved, and part of me died with them. But a year later Leilah called me from Singapore. My family was alive and well, well, maybe not so well," she said, looking her mother in the eye.

"Madinah was next, Leilah said. Madinah was literally a mirror image of Ramzi, and I knew she was going to kill someone too. I remember them practicing with those damn knives, knives she gave them," she said, nodding toward her mother.

"I lived for another year at my church in Manila, and when I was eighteen, I moved away. With the money from the lawsuit, I moved to the United States and bought that house in Chicago, the house where you killed Madinah."

"She tried to kill me."

"I know, and I'm glad she didn't. Ramzi wanted to kill you too, and Madinah was on her way to San Francisco to help him. God intervened and they're both dead now," she said.

"You moved again. I tried to track you down, along with the rest of your family."

"I did move. I felt good in that house for a while. I joined a Baptist church I could walk to—you probably saw the steeple when you were there. I had a job at an attorney's office, and I was making plans to go back to school, then Ramzi and Madinah showed up. I saw what they had become and I fled. I was so afraid of them. They were good kids before, Lieutenant, I want you to know that. Just good kids."

She was quiet for a full minute, looking at her mother, and

Trufant could hear her breathing, slow and deep. Then she looked at him and he saw the chips of blue diamonds locked onto his own.

"I moved back to Manila. I changed my name and I met my husband. I'm no longer Araya Haddad, Lt. Trufant. That woman is dead."

It was awkward talking with her as her mother's one-eyed stare followed their conversation.

"For years I heard nothing from them. Only Leilah had my current phone number. She often called to let me know how she was doing. I was proud of her when she said she was at NYU studying fine arts.

"Then I realized what she was. She was the one who told me Ramzi and Madinah had been killing men every year on my dead sister's birthday and on the anniversary of her death. Leilah said our mother was behind it all, and Leilah, had been sending out cryptic notes to the police—to mock them. It was all a sick, twisted obsession to my brother and sisters—to everyone but her," she said, pointing at her mother.

"My mother fed on the deaths of those men. Leilah said they would send her pictures and videos of the dead. She was too old and sick to do anything herself, but she still wanted her pound of flesh."

"You never called the police."

"No, they terrified me Lieutenant, and I will carry that guilt to my grave."

Araya stood and walked over to her mother.

"She was a good woman once. She taught everyone in my neighborhood to speak English, and most of them became Christians. Everyone loved her and my father. But there was a great civil war going on between the Sunni and the Shia and both sides hated the Christians. Al Qaeda and ISIS were also beginning to enter the city and the only people protecting us were US soldiers. Dozens of brave Americans died so we could live, how cruelly ironic is that?"

The two women stared at each other and Trufant tried to imagine what each was thinking

"After the attack, I tried to tell her it was the soldiers keeping us alive, but she was too blinded with rage. How do you tell a mother who watched such a thing not to hate?"

Trufant watched the old woman's pulse jump from sixty-five beats per minute to eighty-five.

"She's dying a slow, painful death now. Cancer and a stroke are God's answers to what she's done."

"She understands what we're saying," he said as the woman's pulse reached ninety-five.

"Good. I told her last night I forgave her. After all those years I think it's what she wanted, my forgiveness, so maybe now she knows. When I talked to Leilah yesterday, she told me what she had done, how she had killed Ramzi with his own knife. Like a Greek tragedy, he was killed by his little sister and with one of his own precious Balisongs.

"I think Leilah wanted my approval. She pitied him in the end, maybe she thought it was mercy, to spare him from his own future. It was my idea to tell you, leaving the knife was hers. I'm glad you're here, Lieutenant."

"Where is she now?"

"She seldom tells me where she is, only where she's been, or what she's done."

"Will she come after me?"

"Who knows? My guess is she's already where she wants to be. She thinks differently than Ramzi. She said she spoke to you weeks ago and let you live so I doubt you will see her again."

"What about her," he asked, looking at her mother.

"What do you want to do? You could call the police, and they would be here in ten minutes. They will probably find her in another day or two anyway—if she lives that long. Is that how you want it to end, some Canadian official making all the decisions?"

"I came here wondering the same thing."

He stood and walked back over and looked down into

Diwata's single cloudy eye. It had been light blue once, and she had been a beautiful woman, just like the woman standing next to him.

He reached over to the plug and held it, feeling the warmth in his fingers as it fed the machine that kept her alive. He thought of Carlos and pictured him at his desk, smiling, and at the hospital so many weeks ago. He thought of the old Marine with the black and yellow patched coat, a man who had fought honorably for his country and was forced to sleep in the rain on Mason Street, pumped full of Xanax.

He remembered the conversation he had with Deputy Director Merriweather at 30,000 feet over Michigan, and the image of Ramzi wearing the spit mask.

And finally, seeing Ramzi at Adelaide's door, knowing this woman was somehow behind Ramzi's desire to kill her.

CHAPTER 45

MOTHER

Trufant!

She wanted to scream once his face came into focus. The man stood right next to her, peering down at her face, inches away, and it might as well have been a hundred miles, here he was in person, and she was paralyzed.

My God, let me speak! Let me at least curse him!

She listened to Araya at the far side of the dark room, somewhere nearby but she couldn't see her. The stroke had muddled her ability to understand exactly what they were saying, but she caught enough to know what they were talking about.

If only Ramzi were here! He would kill this bastard right in front of me, and I would welcome his blood as it rained down on my face.

But where was her only son? Was he alive? Did she hear her daughter mention him?

Trufant walked farther away, and now all she saw was the white ceiling bathed in the red lights of the machines around her.

She understands what we're saying, the man said. She tried to raise her head, to face him and see Araya but her field of vision never changed, just the dull red ceiling. God, she needed a cigarette.

One last drag is all I need, and then I'll stick the embers in his eye!

What cruelty, so much rage and I can't even lift my finger to accuse him.

Trufant's voice was moving around the room, she could hear him but what was he saying? Then he was right over her again, his brown eyes focused on hers. She could see a few inches of the fading scar on his neck, the stubble of his beard, and she could even smell him, and yet all she could do is glare at him. She hoped he saw the hatred in her eyes.

"What about her," he asked as Araya came into view.

My beautiful daughter!

The steady beat of the monitors and the sucking sound of the ventilator drowned out whatever Araya said, but his eyes never left hers. There was anger in those eyes, a little hatred of his own, which was gratifying.

He reached behind her and said, "Diwata, I can end your life right now. I want you to know that."

In these last few months, she had assumed it would be the cancer that killed her, but no, it was going to be Trufant.

Oh, Jesus, are you going to allow this final injustice?

Chapter 46

Trufant

Her one opened eye blinked once and stared at him. He wanted to yank the plug and watch this evil woman die, so he could sit at Carlos's graveside and tell him he had avenged his death.

But it was the image of Carlos he saw now, and Carlos would disapprove. Don't let it change you, he had told him. Trufant let go of the plug and there was a quick look of recognition on her distorted face.

"No, I can't do it, Diwata. You're going to have to suffer a little more, I'm afraid."

He sat on the sofa next to Araya and wept.

This was the end of his nightmare and it was time to put his life in order.

"I thought I could do it. I thought I would enjoy ending it this way," he said, once the crying was over. "Too many good people died, and the men who destroyed your family are paying for their crimes. That has to be all the justice I need."

"Justice," she said. "I hope it is enough. I let the Lord deal with it long ago,"

"Araya, I'm sorry for all your family has suffered, and everything you've been through. I do understand how that kind of horrible experience can break someone."

"Thank you, Lieutenant, you're a good man. I'll sit with her until it's over. It won't be long now."

He turned toward Diwata. Her heart rate was up another ten beats per minute and still climbing.

"Goodbye, Diwata. I don't think we will meet again."

"Take care of yourself, Araya," he said, "and if you see your sister . . . "

"I don't plan on seeing her again, Lieutenant, and I don't think she needs to see you either."

His footsteps echoed as he walked down the hall and passed the nurse's station. As he waited for the elevator, he heard an alarm go off and two nurses ran toward the door where Diwata Haddad had taken her last breath.

As the doors closed behind him, he felt her pass, and with her passing, he was going to be okay.

***

Travis ran through the yard chasing crickets as Trufant watched from the rocker on his mother's weathered porch. Cicadas sang their familiar song in the old pine trees lining the hardscrabble road in front of the house, and a fresh batch of sweet tea was brewing in the kitchen.

He hadn't had a drink or needed the relief any pill could offer in weeks. Whatever was stoking that anxiety had died with Diwata Haddad and he had slept soundly that first night back from Toronto.

He was a captain now, Chief Lozano promoted him in his last week before the man retired. The mayor appointed Brown as the acting chief until a permanent replacement was made. Chief Brown—from bad to worse. Lozano hadn't done him any favors by retiring. Still, he was now a captain in the criminal investigation division. No more pounding the streets tracking psychopaths, no more disinfecting the soles of his shoes at night, or worrying what he was stepping in. His lieutenants, sergeants, and inspectors would be doing the dirty work now.

The old oak rocker he sat in squealed each time he leaned back, the sound marking the cadence was comforting. It was rustic and primitive, and it reminded him of his youth when all he worried about was having a date for the prom.

He found himself gazing west between two yellow pines toward San Francisco. It was hard to put into words the grief and anxiety he had left there, and more of it was waiting for him, some new case with some new victim.

To the north, several thousand miles away, the ashes of a dead woman sat unclaimed, according to Toronto's medical examiner's office. The woman's pitiful death comforted him and eased some of the dread he still felt as he rocked in the humid breeze.

The screened door opened and the porch's pine boards protested and at that moment he could have been thirteen again, and his mother telling him supper was on the table. Now almost ninety, she handed him a fresh glass of iced tea and sat in the rocker next to him.

"Is it like this in San Francisco, Marcus?"

"No, it's not, Mom."

"You sure you want to go back there?"

No, he wasn't sure. Going back would mean he would be back in the thick of things, and there was still the Haddad girl.

"I'm not sure, I have two more weeks of vacation time to burn. I don't want to decide until I've used every minute of it."

"Do you hear from Adelaide?"

"I do. We're still talking and maybe one day we'll work it out."

"I don't like you working over there, Marcus, I read the papers and I can still read you."

"And what do you see, Mom?"

"I see a tired and lonely man. A man who still has many good years left in him. I saw that in your father in those last years. I wish you knew him before the war, he was a good man."

Inside the house, he heard his phone chirp, the generic sound of someone the phone didn't recognize leaving a text message.

"You want me to get it for you?"

"No, it's not important."

He was relaxed, in the zone, void of tension, surrounded by bliss, and whatever the message was—it was threatening his zone.

Their two chairs creaked to a slightly different cadence, and he thought about the text waiting for him. He looked back through the two trees, toward San Francisco and wondered if Leilah was back, or was it Araya this time?

Merriweather had eventually rounded up all his agents and returned to Washington one week after December 1st came and went without another homicide. There had been no new entries in ViCAP mentioning any of the signature MO's the Haddad family had left in their wake, and life around the station had returned to normal. So, who was texting him?

"I have to see the text," he said, standing up and fearing the worst.

He opened the text and read the short message.

Trufant, I need to run something by you. Look me up when you get back in town, Lozano.

He'd had lunch with his old chief on the day of his promotion. Lozano had looked rejuvenated, younger, and the conversation had actually been pleasant.

He and the chief would never be friends and each of them knew it, but they wouldn't be adversaries either. That chapter had been written and the page had been turned.

He looked back at the phone trying to interpret the man's message.

He typed in *Will do* and hit the send button, delivering his reply two thousand, one hundred and eighty-three miles away.

"Who was it?"

"No one you know, someone from work."

He eased himself back into the rocker and soon the two rockers creaked in unison.

He had come to Louisiana to put as many miles as he could between himself and the last year in San Francisco. The case died with Diwata Haddad, and with her death, he'd found sobriety. He hoped his new friends David and Caitlin Armstrong were at peace as well.

His next step was to restart his marriage, and Adelaide was back in San Francisco.

"I'm going back tomorrow, Mom."

Nothing killed time faster than being on the job, getting things done and making a difference in someone's life.

Besides, he was born to be an investigator, and nothing was going to stop him from doing what he loved.

www.ingramcontent.com/pod-product-compliance
Lightning Source LLC
Chambersburg PA
CBHW030537310726
48979CB00010B/1947/J
9781665303149